Frances Gordon is the daughter of an Irish actor and after a convent education worked in newspapers and the legal profession. She now lives and writes in Staffordshire. She is the author of four acclaimed fantasy novels, written under the name of Bridget Wood, and two previous horror novels, BLOOD RITUAL and THE DEVIL'S PIPER, which are both available from Headline Feature:

'A superior example of the vampire genre ... a pleasure from start to finish' *Time Out*

'A chilling, blood-curdling novel' *Peterborough Evening Telegraph*

D1262271

Also by Frances Gordon

Blood Ritual
The Devil's Piper

Writing as Bridget Wood

Wolfking
The Lost Prince
Rebel Angel
Sorceress

The Burning Altar

Frances Gordon

Copyright © 1996 Frances Gordon

The right of Frances Gordon to be identified as the Author of
the Work has been asserted by her in accordance with the
Copyright, Designs and Patents Act 1988.

First published in 1996
by HEADLINE BOOK PUBLISHING

First published in paperback in 1996
by HEADLINE BOOK PUBLISHING

A HEADLINE FEATURE paperback

10 9 8 7 6 5 4 3 2 1

All rights reserved. No part of this publication may be
reproduced, stored in a retrieval system, or transmitted,
in any form or by any means without the prior written
permission of the publisher, nor be otherwise circulated
in any form of binding or cover other than that in which
it is published and without a similar condition being
imposed on the subsequent purchaser.

All characters in this publication are fictitious
and any resemblance to real persons, living or dead,
is purely coincidental.

ISBN 0 7472 5238 6

Typeset at The Spartan Press Ltd,
Lymington, Hants
Printed and bound in Great Britain by
Cox & Wyman Ltd,
Reading, Berks

HEADLINE BOOK PUBLISHING
A division of Hodder Headline PLC
338 Euston Road
London NW1 3BH

We travel not for trafficking alone;
By hotter winds our fiery hearts are fanned;
For lust of knowing what should not be known,
We take the Golden Road to Samarkand.

We are the Pilgrims, master; we shall go
Always a little further: it may be
Beyond that last blue mountain barred with snow,
Across that angry or that glimmering sea.

James Elroy Flecker, *Hassan*, V. ii.

Chapter One

Extract from The Times, *2 January 199–*

Lewis Chance, the descendant of the notorious Victorian traveller Patrick Chance, is to be created a baronet in the New Year's Honours' List for his charity work over the last 15 years. The announcement has caused renewed interest in a family which has seldom been out of the news for long.

Sir Lewis, 50, has twice been in the 'Ten Most Eligible Batchelors' list, and although he has had a number of close female companions, he has never married.

His early life was eventful: following his father, Charles's, conviction in 1970 for misappropriation of funds from the famous House of Chance – one of the last remaining private banks in England – he spent some months in Tibet, reportedly retracing the footsteps of Patrick Chance whose autobiographical book, *A Lecher Abroad*, was published in unexpurgated version shortly after *Lady Chatterley's Lover*, which it outsold. The sensation it created became a legend in publishing circles, and the Lord Chamberlain's famous remark, 'It appears that women would rather take a Chance than have a Game (keeper)' [*sic*] now appears in many contemporary books of quotations.

Patrick Chance left England in the 1880s, according to rumour because of his close friendship with one

1

of Edward VII's female companions, but his later life was surrounded by mystery. However, despite a number of approaches, Sir Lewis has always declined to be interviewed on the subject of his great-uncle – a determined silence that stimulated the public's interest in him.

Sir Lewis has recently acquired a derelict property in St Stephen's Road, in London's East End, which he intends to restore and use as a centre for helping the homeless and despairing, and also as a headquarters for the Chance Charitable Trust.

Readers will recall that St Stephen's Road has lately been the focus of a number of unsolved disappearances, almost all of them known prostitutes. Sir Lewis, when asked briefly about this, said he could not see that it would affect his centre's aims.

Extract from the Daily Banner, *10 January 199–*

BARONET TO TAKE A CHANCE IN JACK THE RIPPER LAND?
VICTORIAN RAKE'S DESCENDANT TO DESCEND TO CANNING TOWN

Lewis Chance, last week honoured for his charity work, was yesterday spotted on a tour of inspection of the tumbledown property in St Stephen's Road, which he intends to turn into a charity centre. With the tally of vanished rent boys in Canning Town already at five, it appears that the noble Sir Lewis is going intrepidly into a part of the East End where a twentieth-century Ripper in gay mood might very well stalk . . .

The property itself was a music hall in the 1880s when it was frequently patronised by the Prince of Wales, later Edward VII, and the Duke of Clarence who came to watch their actress ladyfriends on the stage. Today, it's doubtful if Dirty Bertie would recognise his old stamping ground.

Certainly the elegant baronet would have been wiser not to make his tour wearing Italian leather shoes and a Savile Row overcoat. What's *de rigueur* in Chelsea is disastrous in Canning Town, Sir Lewis!

The newspapers had not missed much – the tabloids had not missed a thing – but Lewis thought that on the whole he had been treated more sympathetically than he had dared hope, although he could have done without *The Times*'s thinly veiled insinuations that he had made mysteries in order to make money, and he could certainly have done without the *Banner*'s jibes about Savile Row and Chelsea.

Inevitably most of the papers had dug up Patrick's book – and equally inevitably there had been a fresh wave of speculation about his own marriage intentions, one of the women's page journalists going so far as to cull his circle of friends, and come up with a kind of shopping list of possible wives. Most were plain and some were downright ugly and all were dull, and Lewis was damned if he was going to marry anyone purely to satisfy the gutter press.

The *Banner*'s crack about Jack the Ripper in gay mood would bring down the wrath of every homosexual organisation in the country, and the editor would probably be hauled up before the Press Complaints Committee, but if rent boys were vanishing from the area, it was probably fair game for the journalists.

Only the *Banner* had bothered to come up with anything about the house itself, which Lewis found surprising. The place was one of the many sad lost music halls that had fallen into disuse, though this one had suffered a fire and had not even survived until the twilight that fell across the Edwardian theatre after the First World War. Others had rallied, and enjoyed brief renaissances as picture palaces and dance halls in the twenties and thirties, but St Stephen's Road hall had prematurely rotted quietly into

3

dereliction behind its peeling plasterwork and flaking stucco. It would be an act of madness to buy it, but it would be an act of chivalry as well. The notion of making a chivalrous gesture to coincide with the newly bestowed title rather pleased Lewis.

According to his solicitor, tutting over the haphazard title deeds and frowning at surveyors' reports, the place had been the home of a recluse from around the turn of the century, until the First World War. Since the Allies signed the Armistice, it had been the home of tramps. The solicitor had taken one look at the structural surveys, and groaned and reached for the phone.

'I see you're on one of your mad altruism trips again, Lewis,' he said. 'Don't come to me to bail you out on this one because I shan't do it. If you buy this rotting hulk, you do so against my advice. It's got fifty kinds of dry rot, and every one's listed in Latin.'

Lewis said temperately, '*Merulius lacrymans* and *Xestobium rufovillosum*,' and heard through the phone a half-strangled curse. 'Dry rot and deathwatch beetle.'

'I might have known it was no good advising you,' said his solicitor, crossly. 'I dare say you'll buy the place no matter what I say – yes, I thought you would. Well, it's your decision, but it sounds to *me* as if the place is tumbling into the Thames brick by brick. Listen, for the love of all the gnomes in Zurich make sure you get those grisly sounding cellars looked at.'

'Bodies and smugglers?'

'Rats and rising damp,' said the solicitor caustically. 'Although come to think of it, bodies wouldn't surprise me.'

'You've been reading the tabloids,' said Lewis, and rang off.

He would buy the property, even if the cellars turned out to be flooded by the Thames twice a day, and even if bodies floated in the debris. The ground and first floors would provide the kind of hybrid centre he had wanted to

4

build for a year or more: part soup kitchen and canteen for derelicts and runaways, and part counselling centre for the newly divorced or bereaved or redundant. The helpless, the homeless and the despairing, *The Times* had called them.

The recluse had evidently gone some way towards turning the place into an ordinary house, but traces of the original music hall lingered. Lewis, prowling through dusty, high-ceilinged rooms, saw that the dividing walls were flimsy affairs, easily torn down. In some of the rooms the partitioning had been done so sketchily that the plaster mouldings near the ceilings had been chopped up so you got a leering cherub's head in one room and his feet in the other.

But Lewis could see where the stage would have been and the dressing rooms, with supper and smoking rooms on the first floor. Once an elaborate curving staircase would have led to the upper floors: a wide sweeping affair of polished mahogany the colour of molasses and treacle, framed in crimson velvet and gilt, and cream walls. But the original stairs had long since gone, the banister had been torn out by enterprising vandals and the walls were cheesy with damp and defaced with graffiti. It was remarkable how most of today's wall-writers seemed unable to spell even the most basic of Anglo-Saxon epithets. Piles of distasteful rubbish lay in corners: greasy papers that had enclosed hamburgers or foil trays of curry, and smashed beer bottles and sodden newspapers and used condoms. You could make out a very convincing argument for the things the human race regarded as necessary to survival just by studying the rubbish in derelict buildings. Shelter, food, drink and sex.

Lewis went up to the first floor, keeping a wary eye out for rotting boards and slumbering tramps. Would it be possible to make a set of apartments out of the very top floor, always assuming the very top floor was sound? The penthouse suite? The attic suite would be nearer the mark. To live here would be the maddest thing he had done yet; this was London's Dockland but it was not the smart overdeveloped docks of the eighties; this was the older, vaguely sinister wharfland beloved of thriller writers before the last war. Nayland Smith stalking Limehouse after the evil mandarin, Fu Manchu. Sherlock Holmes prowling Chinatown on the trail of Moriarty. Patrick Chance making assignations with actresses . . . ? Yes, Patrick might easily have come out here; he might well have been in the audience when the place was a music hall. Had he been one of the Prince of Wales's set? There was no mention of it in the insouciant travel journal which had been published after his death by a cousin, but at this distance it was impossible to know what had been expurgated beyond recall by his scandalised relatives and what had not. Lewis thought it served them right that Patrick's diary had finally emerged to that blaze of shocked delight fifty years later, although much of the credit had to go to the enterprising editor at the publishing house who had turned up the original manuscript by sheer chance, scrapped Patrick's modest title of *Travels in Tashkara*, substituted the tag *A Lecher Abroad*, and so precipitated one of the biggest bestsellers of the decade.

He looked through the grimed window panes into St Stephen's Road. Whatever it had been in Patrick's day it was a slum now, even without the press's coverage of the vanishing rent boys. If you were foolish enough or reckless enough to walk down the street by yourself after dark, you could count on being accosted by prostitutes of both sexes at least half a dozen times. If he lived out here he would go in permanent fear of muggers and the house would probably end up being burned to the ground by meths drinkers and drug addicts – and all anyone would say was that it served him right, poor Lewis, he was always a bit eccentric.

But the idea of abandoning the elegant comfortable Chelsea house and living out here attracted him. How practical was it? Supposing the attic floor was beyond rescue?

But the long light attics were spacious and had a tranquillity that Lewis had not expected. He had no idea how to test for the safety of the floors, but although they creaked ominously as he walked across them, they felt firm enough. If *Merulius lacrymans* and *Xestobium rufovillosum* had ventured inquisitively up here they had not inflicted very much damage.

Last of all he descended to the cellars, the sounds of traffic and the street noises from St Stephen's Road dying away. The cellars were a small subterranean labyrinth, a secret world: at the foot of the rickety wooden stairs was a narrow tunnel like a culvert, the walls rippling greenly with waterlight from the nearby river. Several small doors opened off the tunnel, and from somewhere up ahead was the faint drip of water, echoing softly in the enclosed space. There was a smell of wet brick and decay.

Lewis looked about him. Someone had brought not only the old gas lighting down here – several rusting brackets hung from the walls – but electricity. He tried the old-fashioned switch, and incredibly was rewarded by a faint glow from the single bulb hanging on a long cord from the roof. So far so good.

As he went cautiously along the tunnel, he began to have the feeling that he had slipped through a chink in the house's history. I'm going back, he thought. I'm going back and back, maybe as far as the recluse's day. Was this his hiding place?

The room was at the far end of the cellar tunnels: a large cavernous chamber with stone walls and a groyned ceiling. There was no light, but the faint overspill from the passage cast a glimmer. At some time someone had furnished the room, and a sad air of decayed Edwardian grandeur still remained. Tattered hangings adorned the walls, and there was a small desk, once beautiful but now scarred and worm-eaten beyond repair, and an old day bed, the fabric so mildewed that it was impossible to know what its original colour had been. There was a stench of damp and mould, but damp and mould could be dealt with. Electricity should be properly laid, on the very credible basis that the wiring in the passages was so old that it was probably dangerous.

His lips curved into a smile. If he had hired a team of architects to design this it could not have been better. It did not matter if this rotting crumbling place had been a music hall or a recluse's hideaway or a brothel; he was going to buy it.

The cellars that his solicitor had so deprecated were exactly what he had been looking for.

What he had not bargained for was the curiously persistent legends, not of the old theatre, but of the recluse himself.

The workmen – most of whom were local – related the faintly grisly tale with relish, smacking their lips over mugs of strong tea and chomping down bacon sandwiches. No one knew the recluse's name, which added to the mystery – it might be that nobody ever had known it – but until quite recently you could find very old people who remembered seeing him: tall thin bloke he'd been, and a bit of a posh plum by all accounts. They glanced at one another as they said this, because Sir Lewis was a posh plum himself, not that he didn't speak very polite when he set you to do a job, and not that he wasn't being very pleasant now, perching on the window ledge and accepting a mug of tea – a good strong brew he'd find it as well – and asking about the legend.

The workmen, quick to spot and resent patronage, were very happy to tell what they knew, it being their tea-break and all, and always supposing he had the time to listen, him being a sir and everything. They dared say you didn't get ghosts in Chelsea?

'I'm afraid not,' said Lewis. 'This is very good tea, by

the way. I'm not interrupting your break, am I? Do go on about the ghost.'

So they settled in for a bit of a gossip, and told how the recluse had seldom been known to emerge from his dark seclusion, but how now and then he'd come creeping out, when the streets were deserted or maybe thick with one of the old fogs – real pea-soupers in those days there'd been, said the workmen. London Particulars they'd called them, and there was nothing like a London Particular for hiding them as didn't want to be seen – yes, *and* for having a bit of the old how's-your-father up against the wall— But here they recollected their company, and came abruptly back to the subject of how the recluse would prowl the streets, wound up in a long dark overcoat, with a wide-brimmed hat pulled well down to hide his face, and how people would tell children not to go near the house, and say things like, If you aren't good the Fog Man will get you. Like you might say, The Bogeyman will get you. There was some as maintained he'd been horribly mutilated in the First World War, and daren't show his face for fear of people running screaming from him, but there was others as said, No, he was a bastard of old Edward VII's, and so like him in appearance that he'd been paid to keep his face forever masked, for fear that anti-Royalists might use him in a plot against the Throne. Not everyone had supported the Crown in those days – well, not everyone did today.

'That's very interesting,' said Lewis, entertained by this sudden plunge into Dumas territory, and the workmen, pleased, said it was very interesting indeed. Ah, people talked about the Phantom of the Opera, but they'd had their own Phantom here in St Stephen's Road, *and* there was people as maintained he still walked, although nobody knew what he walked *for*. Still, it was the kind of thing that would make a good plot for a book if you was inclined that way, or better still, a film. People liked being frightened; they liked to feel their flesh creep, said the workmen cheerfully, switching unwittingly to Dickens, and borrowing the sentiment of the Fat Boy who had expressed much the same opinion and in almost exactly the same words.

They went amicably back to their work – relaying the entire ground floor it was, and a proper job Sir Lewis was making of it too, not wanting you to cut corners and skimp on timbers, not that he couldn't afford it. Lewis smiled, tipped the foreman a ten-pound note to buy everyone a drink, and left them to it.

It was fashionable to complain about poor workmanship and unwilling workers, of course, but he thought the men were doing a good job of the flooring. The ten-pound tip had pleased them, and it had been diplomatic to spend a few minutes talking and drinking a cup of tea with them. In fact he had found the story about the recluse rather entertaining, and the idea of his house having a ghost amused him.

Extract from Patrick Chance's Diary

Cheyne Walk, London, November 1887

Am due to accompany Alicia to Drury Lane this evening, which am not looking forward to since secretly find opera rather dull and would far rather go to St Stephen's Road Music Hall and be vulgar.

However, opera is *La Traviata*, which may be significant, since the story centres about a lady of easy virtue and might persuade my own lady of easy virtue to succumb. According to rumour she's succumbed to half of London already.

Father v. boring at breakfast: droning on about tradition and honour, and, Since you came down from Oxford, Patrick, you've done nothing but waste your time chasing women, and if that brazen hussy Alicia whatever-her-name-is is any better than she should be, I'll be *extremely* surprised ... He must have guessed what I'm plotting.

Wonder how private the Drury Lane boxes are?

Chapter Two

Extract from Patrick Chance's Diary

Cheyne Walk, November 1887

Do not entirely recommend seduction on the floor of a Drury Lane box during *Traviata*. As the Italian soprano reached her climax, I reached mine – and there is nothing *in the least* romantic about coming to a violent ejaculation to the strains of a coloratura aria. At least I missed the velvet curtains.

Alicia to accompany me to St Stephen's Road Music Hall next week, and will introduce me to Lillie Langtry. Thinks we shall 'enjoy one another'.

God help the Prince of Wales.

Elinor Craven, paying off the taxi outside Lewis Chance's Chelsea house, thought that this was going to be rather like meeting a legend. It was a bit eccentric of Lewis Chance to be leaving here to live in St Stephen's Wharf, but if he was as rich as people said, he was entitled to a few eccentricities.

And you wanted something different, said Elinor's inner voice, in the sort of tone people use when they are saying: We knew you wouldn't go through with it! You wanted something different and now you're within sight of it you're ducking out, you fraud!

And this was certainly different. It would not be like anything Elinor had ever done, and it would be light years away from stifling Kensington, where Father's law friends came to argue with self-conscious wit and to name-drop, and where Mother's sycophantic admirers gushed over her newest over-sugared romance novel.

Lewis Chance – *Sir* Lewis Chance – had no particular reputation for wit that Elinor had ever heard about and he would not need to name-drop because he was a name himself. And whatever else he might turn out to be, Elinor was pretty sure he would not be gushing.

He received her with understated courtesy in a small study at the back of the house, and seated himself behind a large, leather-topped desk. He wore an ordinary dark suit and a plain shirt, which pleased Elinor, who found male mutton dressed as lamb repulsive and had been fearing medallions and designer jeans. *The Times* had given Sir Lewis's age as fifty, and he looked as if he did not in the least mind appearing fifty. He was thin-faced, with dark hair, just greying, and cool grey eyes, and although he was not dazzlingly good-looking, he could probably be called distinguished. Elinor's mother had said, with one of her irritatingly knowing laughs, that he had had *rather* a lot of women in his thirties and forties. As if she wants us to think she was one of them, thought Elinor crossly – but her father had said that Chance was rumoured to possess a bit of a gambling streak. 'Appropriately named,' he had said, and had gone on to produce a few witticisms, none of which Elinor could remember.

Sir Lewis – yes, he *was* rather distinguished – was offering her a cup of tea or coffee, and Elinor, accepting tea, managed to look covertly about her. The small room was conventionally furnished with leather armchairs and rows of books that looked as if they had been bought by the yard by Sir Lewis's banking ancestors. It was probably unfair to equate financial acumen with dullness. In an alcove at one side of the chimney breast hung a small portrait of a young man dressed in the correct formality of the 1890s, with glossy hair the colour of honey with the sun shining in it and the same appraising eyes as Lewis Chance. Whoever he was, he had certainly been neither dull nor financial.

Sir Lewis was explaining the details of the post at the newly created Chance Centre.

'And you understand that the position is something of a hybrid, Miss Craven?'

'Secretary, PA, housekeeper.' Put like that it sounded horribly dull and domestic, so that it was nice of him to call it a position. Within the family it was already being referred to as 'Elinor's new job', midway between deprecatory laughter and despairing shrugs. It did not matter, because she would not be offered it; Sir Lewis would have already made up his mind that she was awkward and stupid. It was infuriating how being made to feel awkward ended in *making* you awkward. Elinor would probably fall over her feet when she stood up and drop the teacup, or open the broom cupboard in mistake for the way out.

Lewis Chance was not thinking that Elinor was awkward, although he did think she was brusque. What the Scots called dour. But she had a very beautiful voice to be brusque in. People tended to overlook the voice as a source of attraction. She was no beauty – too stern with those black-bar eyebrows and brooding eyes and square chin, but he was not looking for beauty, in fact it would be safer to steer clear of female attractions for this post. She appeared intelligent and perceptive, and as far as he could tell she had no irritating mannerisms.

He said, 'It's a peculiar mixture for a job, isn't it? But it's a peculiar setup. As well as dealing with ordinary administration, I need someone who doesn't mind mingling a bit with the people who'll be coming to the centre, because that'll be unavoidable. You do know we'll be getting what some people term the dregs of society, do you?'

'Meths drinkers and drug addicts and suicides,' said Elinor. 'Yes, I understand all of that. I can cope with it, I think.' After Mother's 'nerve storms', which generally took

14

place when she could not think up her next plot (it would be unkind to say rehash the last one), wrung-out drunkards in honest need of help would seem almost straightforward. Elinor, who had come prepared to think scathing thoughts about bloated capitalists and slick tax evasion schemes, found herself rearranging some of her ideas. Lewis Chance was not in the least what she had been expecting. The well-mannered philanthropist who provided such good copy for the press was certainly in evidence, and also the eccentric, because only an eccentric would be making plans to live in Canning Town. So far there was no sign of the gambler.

She said, 'I've worked in a few different types of places.' It would not be the time to list all of the jobs she had held, but at least she had acquired passable shorthand, and rough but workable organisational skills. She could drive competently and operate a computer after a fashion. The family had sighed over her lack of university background but Lewis Chance did not want an Oxford double first to help him run his centre and minister to the raff and scaff who would come to the door.

'I wouldn't mind helping with the canteen side a bit as well, if you wanted,' said Elinor, hoping this did not sound ungracious. She was hardly *haute cuisine* level, but she could whip up a pot of soup or ladle out stew with the best. It was beginning to be a pity that she would not be offered this post, because she was getting quite interested in it.

And then without the least warning, Lewis Chance said, 'I think we might give it a try, Miss Craven. When could you start?'

Elinor stared at him. This, then, was the gambler. He could not possibly have made enquiries about her and he had certainly not asked for any references. She said, 'Any time. Straightaway if you like.'

'I have explained, haven't I,' said Lewis, 'that it'll be a way of life, rather than a job? And that it can't really be nine to five? I've turned the upper floors into a couple of apartments – nothing hugely grand, but quite comfortable.

I'll be living there myself for a good bit of the time.' He smiled suddenly, and Elinor blinked and remembered the rumours about all the women he was supposed to have had. Dozens had Mother said? If he smiled like that at them, it was no wonder.

'My idea is that you have the other flat.' said Lewis. 'You would be absolutely private, of course. No questions asked about what you get up to.'

Earlier on had not been the time to list all Elinor's previous jobs, and now was not the time to say it was unlikely that she would be getting up to anything, because no one had ever been interested in getting up to anything with her.

'Well, Miss Craven?' said Sir Lewis, and now the smile unquestionably held the gambler's glint. 'Would you object to living in wharfland?'

Living with a gambler and a womaniser. Quite private with no questions asked, but living in the same house with him. Smack in the middle of one of London's roughest dockland districts, with tramps and drug addicts and alcoholics queuing up for food and succour every day. Yes, and where a sinister killer was said to walk. Something about Jack the Ripper reborn, the papers were saying, and warning people not to walk the streets alone after dark. You're mad, said Elinor's inner voice. You're asking for fifty different kinds of trouble. Yes, but if I'm mad, so is he.

'Well, Miss Craven?'

Elinor said, 'When can I move in?'

It was not until she announced – half defiant, half brusque – that she was moving out of Kensington and into St Stephen's Road, that the family woke up to the fact that this was a bit more than just another of poor old Elinor's dreary make-do jobs.

Elinor's father made a few discreet enquiries, because they could not have Elinor, trusting unworldly oddity, getting mixed up in anything at all off colour; frankly none of them could afford it. Elinor's father certainly could not afford it. He could still remember that very shocking business with Sir Lewis's father – hundreds of thousands of pounds salted away and probably even now languishing in a Swiss bank somewhere – and everyone knew about the dissolute Patrick and the scandalous account of his travels. There'd been a rumour of some kind of quarrel with Royalty as well – Edward VII they said, though he'd been the Prince of Wales then, not that it made any difference. Elinor's father had no opinion of people who fell out with Royalty and even less opinion of bankers who got caught with their hands in the till (metaphorically speaking) and then hanged themselves from the light cord in their prison cells, rather than face the consequences. And he was not having any of the family getting drawn into anything that looked all right on the surface but might later blossom into something unsavoury. He reminded his family that his chambers were a touch old-fashioned and that people had been disbarred for lesser offences than innocent associations with fraudulent bankers. More to the point, solicitors were inclined to be fussy where they sent briefs.

But no breath of scandal seemed to have brushed Sir Lewis's name, in fact quite the reverse. He appeared to have spent the last fifteen years setting up the blameless and rather prestigious CCT, and if he had dabbled in anything fraudulent or obscene along the way, nobody had ever heard about it.

In fact it began to look as if Elinor, so far from getting mixed up in anything questionable, was allying herself with a rather admirable organisation, to say nothing of an apparently wealthy knight of the realm. Her father had frequently had occasion to deplore what he had called Elinor's stubborn streak, but this might be the one time when it worked to their advantage. He substituted 'single-minded' for 'stubborn' and began to name-drop in Chambers (discreetly, of course). Elinor's mother, her mind running on similar lines, issued several dinner invitations. It was a shame that Sir Lewis was so busy that he could not accept any of them.

There was no official opening of the new Chance Centre in St Stephen's Road, but the old building, restored and renovated, came alive very quickly. The mysterious network that linked the waifs and strays and the gentlemen of the road (more and more frequently ladies of the road as well) had its own methods of communication. Like dropping a stone into a pool and seeing the ripples go out and out, thought Lewis. Like casting a net.

He began covertly to study the miscellany of people who came to Chance House. He had found Elinor Craven in a conventional fashion: Elinor herself was conventional, although once or twice Lewis had received the impression that beneath the surface she might be very unconventional indeed, which rather intrigued him. He caught himself wondering how she would deal with a difficult or dangerous, or even downright bizarre situation, and thought she would deal with it very well. She was small-boned and not tall – slender ankles and wrists as well, thought Lewis, who approved of fragile looks in females – but there was an impression of inner strength. But what he needed now was someone so utterly different as to be a one-off. A specimen of the type sometimes called *sui generis*. A creature apart.

The helpers and counsellors and probation officers were beginning to frequent the place now; most of them would only be around for a couple of hours at a time, giving advice about marriage problems or homosexuality difficulties, and they would probably overlap with one another a bit. The centre would become a little like a small town. Lewis passed them under mental review and discarded them almost at once. All worthy and hardworking and sincere. But all too conventional. All too law-abiding.

18

But the midday soup queue yielded a different species. It was already a focal point of the day, and it was presided over by local women who came in to cook vast pots of soup or stew and brew steaming urns of tea. They skimped the scouring of saucepans but they were cheerful and willing, which counted for a good deal. They sang the latest pop songs or TV commercials as they worked, and bandied bawdy remarks with the down-and-outs who entered zestfully into the spirit of it all, because if you could not enjoy a bit of sauce while you queued for your dinner, you might as well curl up your boots and die.

Lewis took to mingling unobtrusively with this assortment of transients. A good many were recognisable old lags and chronic layabouts or modern-day professional beggars, which was inevitable, but an astonishing number were gently spoken and obviously scholarly: men and women who had found themselves unable to cope with today's loud practical world and ended up as part of a drifting semi-homeless populace. There were two or three university dons and several teachers, and a handful of what looked to be foreign language students from the nearby hostels and bedsits.

And there was a thin man with a face like a Reformation martyr who wore an aged herringbone tweed coat that brushed his ankles, and hummed Chopin and ate beef stew with industrious but fastidious pleasure. Lewis studied him covertly, and the gambler's smile curved his lips.

Sui generis.

The thin man sat facing the desk, the trailing skirts of his coat disposed negligently about him, his expression unreadable.

Lewis, his mind working on several levels, thought he was taking one of the hugest risks he had ever taken, but he said, quite calmly, 'You understand what I'm asking you to do?'

'Certainly.' The man's voice was as unexpected as the

19

rest of him. 'We are meeting each other's needs. You require a – guardian for what is in the cellars of this house. I am in need of a job. That's why you approached me. Although what you are offering is not quite what I was expecting.'

You're not quite what I was expecting either, thought Lewis, studying the man, thinking it was absurd to trust someone so fully on such a slender acquaintance. I know nothing about him, other than that he looks like the Holbein portrait of Sir Thomas More, or a grave austere Fra Angelico saint. More had been a humanist and a scholar – but he had also been a fanatic, and fanatics could be uncomfortable people. I'm going purely on instinct, thought Lewis. Aloud he said, 'I don't know your name.'

There was a pause, as if the man were considering how to reply. Then he said, 'I am sometimes known as Raff.'

'Raff? Ralph?' It was a preposterous name for someone who looked like Sir Thomas More. Lewis said cautiously, 'Raphael?'

An unexpected smile showed. 'How perceptive of you, Sir Lewis. Actually I was baptised Raffael – my mother was an admirer of Renaissance art – but it is not a name that goes down well in Canning Town. Here I am known as Raff.'

'Nothing more?'

'I don't think so.'

'And – will you take the task on?'

Raffael made a quick gesture. His hands were thin but they were clean, and he had the long sensitive fingers of an artist. Painter? Musician? There was an unmistakable foreign air about him. He did not quite speak with an accent, but there was a certain formality about the way he put sentences together. 'You could command whoever and whatever you wanted, Sir Lewis,' he said. 'You seem to be trusting me very fully very early on. Why?'

'Because,' said Lewis, unable to help himself, 'you have the face of someone of extreme integrity, but also of a rebel.'

The man smiled fleetingly. 'It has been of great use to me, that,' he said. 'You think I would go to the stake for my beliefs, perhaps? Yes, it is what others have thought.'

He paused, and Lewis felt a twinge of disquiet at having his thoughts read so easily.

'I might risk the stake for my beliefs,' said Raffael thoughtfully. 'But you do not ask what my beliefs are, Sir Lewis, and you should remember that a man can as courageously face death for the wrong beliefs as for the right ones.' He sat back, his eyes in shadow, but the light from the desk lamp falling across the lower part of his face. Lewis realised for the first time that Raffael was considerably younger than himself. Forty? Even thirty-five?

Raffael said, 'I will take your proposition, Sir Lewis. I understand the dangers and I will do it.'

'I'm sometimes away for a night or two. It's unavoidable—'

'Because since you received a title you are so much in demand,' said Raffael. 'Yes, I understand. You are something of a public figure, after all.' His tone was perfectly courteous, but Lewis caught an edge of faint irony. But then Raffael said, 'And are you prepared to trust me, even though you don't know who I am?'

'Who are you?'

The unreadable eyes met Lewis's. 'Someone at odds with the world,' said Raffael. 'As you have sometimes been at odds with the world.'

We're two of a kind, thought Lewis, staring. That's why I'm trusting him. But he only said, 'Shall we have a month's trial – for both of us, to see if it works? I can give you no clear idea of how to go about the task, or what hours you should work. You would have to find your own way.'

'A very good idea,' said Raffael gravely. 'I shall come and go between Chance House and my rooms, and I think I shall continue to form part of your derelicts' queue at noon. You have a rather unusual set of people there, did you know that?'

'In what way?'

Lewis felt a prickle of apprehension, but Raffael only said, 'There are a few people I should not have expected to find here. But it is more likely that the world has changed, and I have not kept up with the changes,' and he smiled. 'Ostensibly I think I should perhaps be known as a security watchman. That will give me a reason for being about the premises at odd times without making anyone curious, and also—'

'Yes?'

'The beef stew you serve here is very good.'

Chapter Three

Cheyne Walk, December 1887

St Stephen's Road Music Hall with Alicia, who introduced me to L. Langtry, as promised. HRH present, along with Prince Eddy, so introductions necessarily formal and decorous. HRH stouter at close quarters than I had realised; Prince Eddy a bit vacant. Alicia says he's called Dawdly Eddy within the Royal family. I don't wonder.

Left Alicia in dutiful attendance and went on to supper at Kettners – scandalous prices but excellent food – with two of the female performers, who turned out to have appetites like wolves. Persuaded them both into private room with me for an hour (one carries her wolfish appetites into the bedroom: have never felt *teeth* in such extraordinary – and *vulnerable* – place before!), and finally got home at 5 a.m.

Father choleric over breakfast; demanded to know what I meant by staying out until such hours and keeping such low company – assume he means music-hall performers, and not the Prince of Wales and Duke of Clarence. Says he has had bad reports of East India Company and thinks country going to the dogs.

Later. Have gone more thoroughly into matter of anti-conception, since coitus interruptus always inconvenient from several points of view, and turns out to be embarrassing when two ladies involved at the same time. Not something I experienced at Oxford, since cannot really count that time in Hilary Term which was *three* men and *one* girl, and Flowerdew and Pontefract turned out to be more interested in each other anyway.

Scoured shops around St Stephen's Road (since area boasts large population of merchant seamen), finally discovering boxes of rubber items, labelling discreet but purpose unmistakable. Shop owned by greasy Whitechapel Jewess, who does side trade in secondhand clothes (v. smelly) and leered at me.

Amused to find that manufacturers trying to give air of solid respectability by decorating boxes with illustrations of Queen Victoria and Mr Gladstone.

St Stephen's Road was seedier than I remembered, and the stage door in the side alley was filled with creeping shadows. In late afternoon, whole place has vaguely sinister appearance, but probably this is only due to presence of river fog and sparse street lighting.

Raffael smiled quietly as he walked away from Chance House. It was all being so very easy. So easy to attract the attention of Lewis Chance, and from there to make diffident enquiries about work within the centre.

The nature of the job offered had been unexpected, but it might have been made for his purpose. And the circumstances under which Lewis Chance was employing him meant that there were going to be no awkward questions about previous employment, or references, or even National Insurance cards.

'A cash payment once a week,' Sir Lewis had said. 'You will not, of course, appear on any salary records, in fact officially you won't exist as a member of staff. Income tax and so on is your own affair. It's the only way it can be done, and if it doesn't suit you, say so now.'

'It suits me very well indeed, Sir Lewis.'

'Good.' He had reached into a desk drawer for a small leather address book. 'But I think I had better know where you live.'

'I have two rooms described as a studio flat in a converted house nearby,' said Raffael, and gave the street number. 'My immediate neighbours are two young men who ply their trade by night and sleep or play regrettable music by day. They are either rent boys or small-time burglars, or possibly both. In the basement is a gentleman of dubious nationality who almost certainly peddles drugs. Yes, it is a little difficult to imagine me in such a setting.'

But when he left Chance House it was not to the split-up house in Canning Town he went. He made his way across the river, and from there by Tube and bus in the direction of Bloomsbury. It was tedious to take such a circuitous route, and it was probably not necessary. But several times lately he had been aware of soft footsteps following him out of the centre, and although he had turned sharply to see who was behind him, each time there had been only a glimpse of an anonymous figure whisking out of sight. Someone tailing him? Or only his imagination playing tricks?

Chance House was the kind of place that did play tricks with you, of course; Raffael had been aware of this from the outset. There were pockets of darkness: sudden deep wells of desolation into which you stepped without realising. Like passing out of sunlight into deep shadow. Like falling neck-deep into black freezing water. Was it the shade of the unknown recluse who cast his shadow and left these imprints? He remembered the dank dripping tunnel that wound beneath the old house. Shadows did not need to come from the past; they could come from the present and the future.

Halfway along the narrow side street, he paused and looked about him. The hum of traffic from the main thoroughfares was muted here and the street was deserted.

If he had been followed he had shaken off whoever it was. Good. He went quickly up the steps of the anonymous white-fronted building and rang the bell.

He was shown immediately into a second-floor room, with books in several different languages lining two walls, and a large inlaid desk between two of the long flat sash windows. There was a glimpse of the British Museum through one of these and Raffael felt an inner twinge of amusement that even in these circumstances the people employing him should surround themselves with so much scholarship.

The two men behind the desk welcomed him with wary courtesy and indicated to him to be seated.

'And we have to ask how you prefer to be addressed?'

'I am known as Raffael now.'

The younger of the two men smiled rather disparagingly. 'Something of a misnomer, surely,' he said drily.

'I considered changing it to Lucifer but I thought it might attract too much attention,' rejoined Raffael, meeting the man's regard unblinkingly. 'And if we have disposed of the polite formalities, I will now tell you that I have done what you asked.'

'You have got into Chance House? Already?' This was the older man, leaning forward, his eyes alight.

'I have. As a kind of night watchman, and . . .'

'Yes? And?'

Raffael appeared to hesitate and then said, 'Nothing.'

The older man's eyes flickered but he only said, 'How did you manage it?'

'Lewis Chance thought he sought me out. In fact I sought him out. As you asked.'

'And offered you the watchman job?'

'Yes.'

'Does he trust you?'

'Not completely. Not yet. But he has an assistant, Elinor Craven, who might be brought to trust me,' said Raffael. A sudden smile curved his lips. 'With a little

26

judicious persuasion,' he added, and the two men exchanged glances.

The elder one said sardonically, 'There would, of course, be a lady involved.'

'We expected that of you, Father,' put in the other one.

'I'm sure you did. By the way, I should prefer not to be addressed as Father. You will recall that I am no longer entitled to it.'

'I do recall.' The thin-faced man picked up a pen from the desk and turned it over between his hands. The square ring on his left hand caught the light. 'Do you never regret, Raffael?' he said.

'Never, Eminence.'

The man wearing the cardinal's ring smiled unexpectedly. 'So you are aware of my recent elevation.'

'Of course. Are you going to tell me what I'm supposed to be doing in Chance House, or are de Migli and I to exchange a few more veiled insults?' Raffael glanced at the younger man. 'Because if so I may as well leave now.'

'Always the defiance just under the surface, Raffael,' said de Migli. 'You do not change.'

'I do not. Nor,' said Raffael politely, 'do you.' He looked back at the older man. 'Well, Eminence?'

There was a pause, as if Cardinal Fleury was assembling his thoughts. Then he said, 'Something extremely disturbing has happened, Raffael, and we believe that it is linked to Lewis Chance. That is why we wanted you – or someone like you – in his house.'

'Yes?' Raffael waited, and after a moment Fleury leaned forward, his old eyes shrewd.

'Have you ever heard of the League of Tamerlane?' he said.

'No. What is it?'

'Very broadly, it's a group of dissidents belonging to a primitive tribe in a remote part of Tibet,' said Fleury, 'a splinter group who have become discontented – or perhaps impatient – with their people's archaic way of life.

Parts of Tibet, you know, are still almost biblical – worse than Third World countries in some ways. No electricity, scarcely any sanitation—' He broke off and spread his hands. 'They plough the fields by walking oxen and the good seed is scattered on the land by the hands of women and children following the furrow wheels. But they have the Buddhist contentment and that lack of materialism that is so enviable—'

He frowned, and Raffael said gently, 'But the League of Tamerlane has rebelled against that vaunted contentment? How do you know all this? Or don't I ask?'

'We have our spies,' said Fleury shortly.

'Ah. A stupid question.'

'And,' said the cardinal, 'our spies tell us that the League is about to draw attention to its people and their primitive ways in a manner that would be very damaging to Rome.' He leaned forward, the hard light showing in his eyes again. 'We have every sympathy with backward peoples, Raffael,' he said. 'We would gladly send what aid we could – missionary parties, medical parties, the creation of centres for educating the people, and preliminary surveys to see if better roads could be provided, or even electricity taken in.'

'You've offered that?'

'Well, we've let it be known that it might be available under certain circumstances,' said the cardinal cagily.

'Yes, I understand.' The Vatican was a political creature in its own understated way, and its offer of help would have been filtered across discreetly. If a quid pro quo had been involved, it would have been a very subtle one. 'Was the response favourable?'

'No,' said Fleury. 'This League of Tamerlane is headed by some very power-hungry people and it begins to look as if they intend to take their place on the stage of world events and in world politics. Greed, Raffael, is a wicked thing, and power-greed is a great evil.'

Raffael said absently, 'It always was. But, Eminence, to

make these threats – is *threats* too strong a word?'

'I'm afraid not.'

'To make threats with any kind of confidence this League must be very sure of itself. What possible hold has a small primitive tribe got over the Catholic Church?'

There was an abrupt silence. Then Fleury said, 'We believe that the League of Tamerlane is about to make public something the existence of which the Vatican has kept secret for almost two thousand years. Something that would certainly deal a hugely damaging blow to us – perhaps destroy us altogether.' He lowered his voice. 'Something which you – and a small handful of others – know about.'

The silence came down again. Raffael stared at the cardinal, his thoughts in tumult. At last he said. 'The Tashkara Decalogue. The Ten Satanic Commandments. That's what you mean, isn't it? This League of Tamerlane is about to blow the whistle on it after—' He stopped, appalled.

'After nearly two thousand years of secrecy,' said Fleury softly. 'Yes. We dare not let it happen, Raffael.'

'And that,' said de Migli, 'is where you come in. It's why you're inside Chance House.' Raffael waited, and de Migli said impatiently, 'Lewis Chance's ancestor, Patrick, travelled to Tibet in the late 1880s.'

'So?'

'We think Patrick found the Decalogue.' said Fleury. 'The infamous journal published after his death refers to it.'

'Only very briefly, however,' put in de Migli.

'We believe that although on the surface Patrick was very frank about his travels—'

'*Extremely* frank,' said de Migli sourly.

'– he withheld something,' finished Fleury smoothly. 'We don't know what it was, but something happened to him in Tashkara, something that changed him in a very fundamental way. It was almost as if the real Patrick had been vanquished by a demon, or as if he had made a journey into hell and had only been allowed to return to the world on some kind of devil's pledge. I'm quoting, you understand, from the notes made by my predecessor.'

'It had not occurred to me that the words were your own,' said Raffael politely. 'Patrick Chance talked to your predecessor?'

'He requested an audience,' said Fleury, looking up. 'Why?'

'I've never read *A Lecher Abroad*,' said Raffael. 'I was a dutiful young ordinand in Milan when it was published in the sixties, but I remember the outcry. And if he was even half as promiscuous as he was made out to be, the thought of him hobnobbing with His Holiness – even one of the lesser minions – is pretty staggering.'

'There's a brief case history on him, and a hand-written memorandum dated November 1890 that says he was courteous and sensitive and receptive and surprisingly widely read,' said Fleury repressively. 'Also that he had a strongly developed sense of duty. What today would be termed a social conscience.'

'I'm sorry, Eminence. Please go on.'

Fleury said, 'Patrick made his journey to Tashkara at the end of the 1880s. About eighty years later, Lewis Chance made the same journey.'

'He was after the Decalogue,' said Raffael thoughtfully. 'Yes, that's possible.'

'Is it? You've met him, Raffael; how acquisitive is he under the urbane philanthropic exterior?'

'As much as most men, I should think. He's quite difficult to read – I'd guess the publicity surrounding his father's scandal caused him to grow armour. I wouldn't put it past him to have gone hellbent after the Decalogue when he was a young man – there'd have been the double reason of escaping the media limelight as well as the lure of the thing itself.'

'It's also possible that he knew something that wasn't in

the journals,' said Fleury. 'He might have had access to other papers – letters, private diaries.'

'And that's why I'm in Chance House? To find out how much Lewis Chance knows about the Decalogue? Or even if he's involved in the League of Tamerlane?'

Fleury said carefully, 'When Lewis came back from Tashkara he brought a child with him – a boy. We don't know who the boy's mother was, but we think Lewis himself was the father. He placed the boy in an institution – a very private, very discreet house near Highgate, and – yes? You were about to speak?'

'Only to ask how you know that.'

'Anything relating to the Decalogue has always been very carefully watched,' said Fleury. 'The publication of Patrick Chance's journal in the sixties might have stirred up curiosity in dangerous quarters, and so when Lewis Chance left England it was thought prudent to keep a discreet tail on him.'

'I am sure the Vatican's spies would be immensely discreet and hugely prudent, Eminence,' murmured Raffael, and de Migli frowned.

'Our people lost him for a time – it's a very remote area, of course,' said Fleury, 'but when they picked the trail up again, the child was with him.'

'And placed in the very private house in Highgate.'

'Yes.' Fleury leaned forward. 'But a month ago we learned that the child – now a young man of twenty-three or -four – is no longer there. We don't know much about him but we think it possible that the League kidnapped him.'

'Why?'

'That we don't yet know. But his background's a bit of a mystery. They might want him as some kind of hostage.'

Raffael sat back in his chair, his eyes on Fleury. 'The boy wasn't kidnapped,' he said. 'But you're right about the rest. He's twenty-three, and he's been in one institution after another since he was very small. The Highgate

31

house was actually the last of a longish line of similar places. And his background, as you say, is very mysterious indeed.' He paused, and then said deliberately, 'The boy was removed last month – the fifteenth, to be exact. Lewis Chance took him.' For the first time he smiled properly. 'He is at the moment locked away in the cellars of Chance House.'

'In the – *cellars*?'

'Yes. He's an exophagist,' said Raffael, and then, as they looked up, he smiled again. 'I thought the word might catch you off balance,' he said softly. 'It's a word used by anthropologists, and loosely speaking it means a particular kind of cannibal.' He saw the shocked surprise leap into the two men's eyes. 'Frazer uses the expression in *The Golden Bough* several times,' he said smoothly. 'So there's quite a scholarly precedent for it.'

'The boy is a—' Fleury stared at Raffael.

'He's a ghoul,' said Raffael. 'I don't mean a horror story creation. I mean a real one. At some point in his very early life he appears to have been introduced to the ritualistic practice of eating human flesh – that's why I used Frazer's word *exophagist* – and it's an appetite that has never left him. Between the spells of what Sir Lewis terms the *hunger* he's lucid and quite intelligent. Under the mania there's a logical, even sensitive mind, but the mania is such that—' He stopped. 'You would not wish me to become graphic, I think.'

'Dear goodness, no. But that,' said Fleury, 'is why you were employed? To – look after him?'

'To act as his keeper,' said Raffael.

Chapter Four

Cardinal Fleury had been merely Bishop Fleury when the young Raffael, newly ordained and still slightly dizzy from the prestige attached to his secondment to the Vatican, stood before him. Fleury's apartments were the most astonishing blend of the austere and the sybaritic that Raffael had ever seen, and the thought that Fleury had probably had to struggle against the sensuality of the mind rather than of the flesh occurred to him.

'The post is little more than a minor librarianship,' His Lordship said, eyeing the young man before him. 'But your scholastic achievements are very good indeed, and I have been thinking how best we can make use of your particular gifts.' He paused and then said, 'After you were ordained, you spent a year working in the Ambrosian Library in Milan, I think?'

'Yes. I was one of Cardinal Rustichi's secretaries.'

'I'm aware of it. In fact I have written to His Eminence about you,' said Fleury. 'It's your work with him that makes you highly suitable for what I have in mind now.' He paused and then said, 'Tell me, Father, how familiar are you with the Apocrypha?'

'The secret writings of the Church?' This was not quite what Raffael had been expecting. 'I know of their existence, of course,' he said cautiously.

'Of course. How would you define them?'

'They're mostly prophecies and prognostications the Church doesn't dare to make public.' Raffael made a quick gesture almost of repudiation. 'The date of the ending of the world or of a holocaust war, or the coming of the Antichrist.' And then, because he had the impression that this was some kind of minor test, he said, 'I imagine you don't expect me to dissimulate?'

'Heaven forfend,' murmured Fleury.

'Then I should tell you that I've always thought most of them attributable to hysterical visions by the Early Saints after prolonged fasting or torture,' said Raffael. He eyed Fleury levelly. 'Also, I didn't think many people believed in them any longer.'

'Cardinal Rustichi said you were a mixture of pragmatism and mysticism,' said Fleury thoughtfully. 'It's an odd mixture to find in a religious these days.' He gave the word its Gallic slant and Raffael remembered that the bishop was supposed to hail from French nobility of the *ancien régime*. When he had been reading Theology in Milan he had believed such things did not matter. Facing Fleury in a private wing of the Vatican Libraries he was not so sure.

Fleury said, 'You would perhaps not know that within the Apocrypha is a section referred to as the Codex Vaticanus Maleficarum?'

'No. What is it?'

'Well, there are various documents that come into that section – undisclosed portions of the Book of Tobit, of course; and some of Arnobius's writings from the fourth century which are very explicit, also St Ecgbert in the eighth. Those two were inclined to be rather colourfully descriptive about—'

'Fornication with demons, and bestiality,' said Raffael, expressionlessly.

'Quite. I see you profited from your lectures on theological history, Father. Or do Ecgbert and Arnobius still rank next to soft pornography for ordinands?'

'I think it's possible to get pornography easily enough these days without resorting to Arnobius,' said Raffael politely, and Fleury shot him a sharp look.

34

'I was told you were also something of a rebel, Father,' he said frostily. 'But I understood that it had been curbed.'

'I think I have some way to go yet, Your Lordship.'

'I think so as well.' Fleury frowned and then said, 'The Codex Vaticanus Maleficarum is a very small section of the Apocrypha, but it contains some very ancient and very interesting documents.' He paused. 'It is this section that is to be your especial province.'

'I see.' It would not do to say that it sounded enormously intriguing, and Raffael waited obediently.

'Within the section,' said Fleury, 'is a document that has been given the designation Maleficarum Decalogue. That roughly translates as—'

'The Ten Malevolent Commandments.'

'Yes. The few of us who know of the document's existence believe its contents to be half legend, half folklore. It might even be a gigantic hoax. But hoax or not, it's one of the most dangerous of all the Apocrypha writings. In fact,' said His Lordship, descending into sudden, slightly disconcerting modernity, 'the wretched thing is a virtual time bomb.' He reached into a drawer of his desk and brought out a key. 'All of the Codex Vaticanus Maleficarum are closely guarded,' he said. 'But the Maleficarum Decalogue is so potentially damaging that we keep it locked in the vaults.' He paused, and then said, 'Beneath the Borgia apartments.'

'How eerie.'

Fleury stood up. 'Come and judge for yourself,' he said.

Descending to the ancient secret vaults in company with Fleury was one of the most sinister experiences the young Raffael had ever encountered.

This was where the infamous Borgia Pope, Alexander, was murdered; this was where the legendary Pinturicchio frescoes, commissioned by the Borgias, had been covered up by the family's disgusted successors and left to fall into

35

neglect until the end of the nineteenth century. Raffael, following his preceptor obediently through the maze of frescoed corridors and ornate gilded galleries and down twisting staircases, felt the heavy elaborate richness of the place fall about him like Dante's leaden cloak. Had the Nazarene Carpenter envisaged this sumptuous dark grandeur when he had issued that edict to build His Church on a rock? Some Church, thought Raffael sardonically. Some rock.

'The Maleficarum Decalogue is actually quite a brief document but it's so fragile we've never dared submit it to any dating tests,' said Fleury, leading Raffael to a low pointed door at the end of a narrow stone corridor and unlocking it. The scent of old leather and crumbling parchment and foxed paper breathed gently outwards, and Raffael stood for a moment letting it soak into his mind, feeling it lay a caressing hand across his senses. Marvellous. There was nothing quite so evocative as this miasma of ancient scholarship and long-ago wisdom.

Fleury flicked a switch and dim light bathed the small room. 'The very lowest of lights always,' he said. 'Most of the documents are too fragile for anything brighter. But you will know that.'

Raffael nodded. 'Also a cool dry temperature,' he said.

'The Vatican Libraries are never exactly greenhouses,' said Fleury caustically. He unlocked a lead-lined bookcase set against one wall and drew out a vellum-covered folio, approximately three feet by two, the front and back laced together at the spine by thin leather strips, the whole wrapped in oiled silk. As Fleury folded back the covering, his hands moving with great care, he said, 'You see the extreme age, Father?'

The words 'culpable negligence' could not be uttered, but – 'Oughtn't the inner parchment to be between glass?' said Raffael, appalled.

'Yes, perhaps. That would be a decision you might make when you're more acquainted with the contents.

But secrecy must be the paramount concern.'

'You think glaziers might talk?'

'I think anyone might talk,' said Fleury coldly.

He set the folio on the leather-topped table at the room's centre, and Raffael bent over it in fascination. Dozens of centuries ago someone sat at a table and wrote this. The aura of age, of some long-dead scribe or calligrapher, brushed his senses, and he was glad that he could look down at the table, veiling his eyes so that his emotions should not show. Even the Ambrosian Library had not possessed anything so immensely ancient as this.

'Is there a provenance?' he asked, after a moment.

'All we have ever been able to say is that the folio came into our keeping around the first or second century after Christ,' said Fleury. 'We think it was during the reign of Pope Linus, who as you know—'

'Succeeded St Peter himself.'

Raffael was trying to decipher the thick pale hieroglyphs, and as if understanding, Fleury said, 'Unless you read hieroglyphics you will need to see the translation which I will show you presently, although even that is so old that we have not been able to make it all out. But in essence the Codex seems to set down the story of an exiled tribe of the Bubasti who left Egypt under a cloud in the reign of the Pharaoh Amenemhat III.'

He stopped, and Raffael looked up in astonishment. 'But that would be – at least two thousand years ago.'

'Nearer three.' Fleury indicated the dry curling parchment. 'This calls them either the damned tribe of Egypt or the lost tribe – it's impossible to be more precise – and it relates how, as a final gesture of defiance, the tribe stole Ten Stone Tablets which Amenemhat's High Priests called the Stones of Vengeance. Each Stone is said to be carved with the name of a different sin or an offence – again the translation can only be approximate – and it seems that the tribe carried the Stones deep into Tibet. They settled in a place called Tashkara – it's supposed to be one of the loneliest, most remote valleys, even today – and practised a worship that seems to have been a mixture of the cat-goddess Bastet and the goddess of fertility and childbirth, Touaris. They used the Stones as a kind of law and order system: if anyone committed any of the carven sins – especially if by doing so they damaged or offended against the tribe or against Touaris herself – then he was punished by the method engraved on the Stone. The punishments varied,' said Fleury, 'but they all appear to have been extremely unpleasant.'

'The Ancient Egyptians were no more merciful than the Romans or the Spanish Inquisition,' remarked Raffael. 'Is that the reason for the double locks and the cloaks and daggers surrounding this?'

'No.' Fleury looked back down at the hieroglyphs. 'Towards the end of the document – I think on the third and final page – is set out the belief of Amenemhat's rebels regarding the real origin of the Ten Stones.'

'Yes?' Raffael found that his heart was suddenly beating uncomfortably fast. I'm about to be told something remarkable, he thought. Something that the Vatican has kept locked in a dark almost-forgotten corner for nearly two thousand years.

Fleury, speaking as if he was selecting each word with extreme care, said, 'The legend handed down by the Tribe of Touaris is that when Moses received God's Holy Commandments on Mount Sinai, the devil, not to be outdone, created ten commandments of his own.' He looked down at the thick ancient parchment sheets. 'These describe how Satan's Decalogue was forged in the deepest fire-drenched cavern of hell, and then cooled in the snow-capped mountains of the world,' he said, and with a gesture of distaste drew the oiled silk back over the vellum sheets as if to veil something disturbing.

Raffael said softly, 'So the denizens of hell had their Commandments as well as the Children of the Light, did they?'

'They did. And,' said Fleury, 'although it's no more than a legend, you see the need for the extreme secrecy, Father?'

'Oh yes. If it was ever to be known that the Roman Catholic Church had guarded for two thousand years a document purporting to describe Ten Commandments that came from Satan, every tenet in the Bible would come under question. There would be a huge public outcry. And sadly,' said Raffael, 'the Church is no longer so strong that she could withstand such a blow. It would be the severest test of credibility since—'

'Go on.'

'I was going to say since Alexander Borgia's day,' said Raffael, and grinned suddenly. 'But the Borgias didn't have to contend with twentieth-century media. The press would make a feast out of this, wouldn't they?' He looked down at the shrouded folio.

'Exactly,' said Fleury. 'Which is why, Father Raffael, knowledge of the existence of the Maleficarum Decalogue and Satan's Ten Commandments must never get out.'

'And so,' said Raffael, sitting back in his chair in the book-lined room of the Bloomsbury house, 'the knowledge is about to get out.'

'We are afraid so. When Patrick Chance went into Tibet and entered the valley of Tashkara he disturbed something that had been shrouded in immense secrecy for dozens of centuries,' said Fleury.

Below them the home-going Bloomsbury traffic was a muted roar. It sounded very far away and the long-ago world of Patrick Chance seemed much closer. Raffael could feel it reaching out to him, and beyond it, like a sticky spider's web, he could feel the beckoning strands of a much older world. The renegade Bubasti, the damned tribe of the legend, living on in a remote valley in Tibet, once itself known as the Forbidden Realm ... Guarding the time-drenched Stone Tablets of the Satanic Decalogue ...

'We intend to destroy the Codex ourselves,' said Fleury. 'It's regrettable but it's unavoidable, and it will spike this League of Tamerlane's guns in one direction at least. But—'

'But there remains the Decalogue itself. Could it possibly still exist inside Tashkara?'

'Assuming,' put in de Migli drily, 'it ever existed in the first place.'

'You are one of the doubters?' Raffael thought he should have expected this.

'I am. It's nothing more than a fable,' said de Migli. 'A fairy story for the credulous. But,' he added, fairly, 'even a fable can cause damage.'

Raffael said, 'I should enjoy challenging you on that sometime, de Migli. It's a pity this isn't the time or the place.' He looked back at Fleury. 'Eminence, if these people have threatened to make the Decalogue's existence public they must be very sure of themselves.'

'My sentiments exactly.'

'They've got the real McCoy, haven't they? The Satanic Decalogue?'

'I am afraid so.'

'And – you want me to find it and destroy it,' said Raffael, and felt Fleury's relief at his comprehension.

'Yes. Will you? Perhaps I should say, Can you?'

'It sounds,' said Raffael slowly, 'as if I must. But it's a – an awesome task you're handing me.' He frowned, and then with a return to his customary flippancy, said, 'And even if it takes seven men with seven axes seven years – But I expect I can smash the things to eggshells, if all else fails. But *can* is different to *will*. I'm quite happy to take on these jobs of dirty work for the Catholic Church from time to time, but I am quite expensive.' He caught de Migli's flicker of distaste, and smiled. 'I was brought up to believe that it was ill-bred to discuss money,' he said. 'But circumstances alter cases and these days I am extremely ill-bred.'

'Also extremely ruthless, we hear,' said Fleury.

'That also. But the Vatican still trusts me, it seems. What am I – a special envoy or a maverick trouble-shooter?'

'A little of both,' Fleury said coolly. 'You may have broken half the commandments and trailed the Church's reputation in the dust, Raffael, but you should recall that His Holiness gave you absolution and that you are still a son of the Catholic Church.'

'I am silenced,' said Raffael solemnly.

'And,' said Fleury levelly, 'you are one of the most trustworthy men I have ever met.'

Raffael stared at him. Now I'm really silenced, he thought.

'Also,' said Fleury, 'there's the advantage that you already know about the Decalogue. At this stage, the fewer people we have to bring in the better.'

Raffael sat back and regarded the two men. 'Before we go any farther,' he said, 'there's something you had better know.'

'Well?'

'There's something odd going on in Chance House. I can't explain it, and I'm not sure that it's any more than my imagination. But several times I've definitely been followed, and several times I've certainly come across some unexpected people there.'

'What kind of unexpected?'

'Odd nationalities,' said Raffael. He paused, wondering if he was deliberately delaying the moment when he must grapple with the appalling task of finding and destroying the Decalogue. Am I simply chasing irrelevancies? No. He looked back at his auditors. 'People from the East,' he said. 'It might be that someone – perhaps several some-ones – from your League of Tamerlane is already inside Chance House. Are any of them in England?'

'Yes, we believe so.'

Raffael sat back in his chair and eyed the two churchmen

with sudden mischief. Chasing irrelevancies or not, there was a beautiful irony about this situation. He said, 'You know, there's a certain wry humour in all this.'

'I don't see—'

'Oh yes. Think about it, de Migli. After nearly three thousand years of secrecy somebody's apparently about to blow the whistle on one of the Vatican's darkest secrets,' said Raffael. 'And you're calling me in to prevent it. You're asking an ex-priest to help you prevent the Roman Catholic Church from being made to look a fool in the eyes of the whole world.'

Chapter Five

Extract from Patrick Chance's Diary

Cheyne Walk, January 1888

Father even crustier than usual this morning due to report in *Morning Post* that German Emperor's health failing. Prophesies darkly that the eldest boy, Wilhelm, too keen on German Imperialism for comfort. Mark his words, we're heading for another war.

Has invited several people to dinner and bridge, since says, with double chins solemnly tucked into neck, that this is suitably restrained entertainment for Sunday evening. (Truth is that he has his eye on well-endowed – in every sense – widow who has come to live on other side of Park, and can enjoy patting her shoulder while he is dummy.)

Will have to think of excuse to leave these bacchanalian revels early, since have rendezvous at St S.'s Road with Chloe Cambridge (she of the wolfish appetite at board and bed). Not real name, of course, but probably much more euphonious than baptismal one, so why not?

Midnight, Arrived at St S.'s – Hall virtually deserted since no performance on Sundays – and entered by stage door as instructed. Chloe or someone had at least left a couple of the gas jets burning so that I could see my way up the iron staircase. Dear God, those iron treads! They echo like the crack of doom when you climb them and the sound reverberates alarmingly around the stairwell. Tried to imagine performers scampering up and down a dozen times a night and failed. No wonder the females have those strong lean thighs . . .

Every corner of the stair is littered with bits of discarded stage properties and with people's cast-off wigs and cloaks and mustachios, and this is the other side of the make-believe world in earnest – the place where the baseless fabric melts and the gorgeous palaces and cloud-capp'd towers dissolve. This is where you climb through the tear in the shimmering insubstantial pageantry and see the pinchbeck and paste for what it really is.

On consideration, would have preferred to preserve the illusion. Few enough illusions left these days.

The attics stretch the entire length of the building and have intriguingly slanted ceilings. They were probably servants' dormitories in the bad old days, but old man Barnabas has had them divided to make 'rest rooms' for the performers and their friends, nasty old lecher. Would not put it past him to be in cahoots with Whitechapel Jewess who sells unmentionable rubber items down in street.

'Do come straight up, Patrick,' Chloe had said, in dulcet tones. (A touch *refained* in her vowels, our Chloe, in fact Cheapside with Pont Street grafted on, but there are worse things than that. And she possesses an hour-glass figure and her bosom is the consistency of cream with honey beaten into it; also those slightly protuberant front teeth that have that astonishing facility to scrape your skin so that you lie shivering, poised on the very cusp between shooting a sky-high ejaculation without warning (v. shaming), and panic that a miscalculation by the exploratory teeth might bring about quite a different conclusion. Circumcision by biting and *without* an anaesthetic – *very* nasty.)

'The door will be on the latch,' the lady had purred. 'And I shall be waiting for you.'

The door was on the latch. I tapped, and then receiving no answer went in. It took several confused seconds to assimilate what I was seeing.

The attic room was lit by more of the gas flares, and the jets flickered in the draught made by the opening of the door. Thin curtains shut out the night, but we were so high up there would probably be a stunning view towards the river by daylight. I took in a jumble of discarded clothes and sprawling satin cushions and stubs of make-up and odds and ends of discarded stage properties. There were some half-unrolled bolts of velvet and thin gauzy cheesecloth, as well as a pile of the lime cones used for stage lighting. More fragments of the splintered make-believe and a lot grubbier than the pieces on the stairs.

She was not waiting for me, the bitch. She was so far from waiting for me that she was consoling herself with someone who was puffing and pumping and heaving away between her thighs – the two-backed beast's extraordinarily ugly unless you're directly involved in making it. They were tangled sweatily on a green satin chaise longue, their heads nearest me, and as I stared, the man lifted his head and looked straight at me.

The sofa was directly beneath one of the gas jets, and the flickering light fell across his features. Appalled horror slammed into me. Impossible not to recognise the slightly bulging eyes, slumberous-lidded as if with too much sleep, and the heavy Hanoverian chin and jaw inherited from his Guelph ancestors.

The son going where the father liked to tread. Particularly this son, who was reputed to be so pliable and so easily led that he had more than once been led into male brothels.

The gentleman lit to such embarrassing clarity, the gentleman who had been disporting himself between Chloe Cambridge's legs until I gate-crashed the party, was the heir apparent to the Throne of England. Dawdly Eddy. Prince Albert Victor, the Duke of Clarence.

It was one of those situations where almost anything you say is going to be disastrous. I'm frightfully sorry to have interrupted, sir . . . Shall I wait outside until you've finished, and if so how long do you think you'll take . . . ? Or maybe you've finished already – oh no, I see you haven't . . .

By rights he ought to be given his Royal title, of course, but I defy anyone to achieve a court bow and say 'Your Highness' under such circumstances.

The best thing to hope for was that he was drunk enough to be amiable, but that he was not so drunk, poor old easily led Eddy, that it would occur to him as a good idea to invite me to join them. I yield to none in my loyalty to the Crown, but I do draw the line at sodomy with the Duke of Clarence.

He sprang up at once, fumbling at his gaping trousers, his face suffused with crimson. The situation hovered between melodrama and outright farce and might have tipped over on either side, if Eddy, shoeless and virtually trouserless had not tripped over his feet and gone crashing helplessly backwards into the jumble of cheesecloth and discarded stage properties. He clutched wildly at the air, vainly trying to keep his balance, and as he went down the bales of cheesecloth overturned and went down with him. The thin light stuff billowed upwards like a pale cloud and brushed against the gas jet.

A sheet of flame blazed up at once: fierce greedy

orange and scarlet tongues that gobbled up the flimsy material. Eddy stumbled to his feet, upsetting several more bales and overturning the careful stack of lime cones. They skittered down, cascading about his head, catching the heat shimmer as they came, and Chloe, clutching a handful of anonymous draperies to her bosom, lunged towards Eddy. She reached him seconds before I did, and grabbed at him, pulling him clear. He was gape-mouthed and bulgy-eyed with panic, and although he was gasping and mouthing, since he was clearly unhurt I pushed him out of the way (he would probably consign me to the Tower for it afterwards, but there was no time to worry) and turned back to where Chloe was trying to stamp out the flames.

The tumbling lime cones were already half melting and incandescent from the sudden fierce heat, and they toppled straight on to her. There was a sickening hiss: like droplets of water being flung into a fire.

Chloe cried out and fell back, clawing at her face, but it was too late. The side of her face had taken the full brunt and the lime had seared into it. Her left eye and the flesh of her cheek were already a bubbling mass, and as her mouth stretched in agonised screams, the white-hot lime trickled inside.

It took almost half an hour to get a physician to her. She stopped screaming long before then because her vocal chords had been burned away.

Elinor loved her attic flat from the start.

St Stephen's Wharf was one of the odd little pockets of London's Docklands that had not been tarted up in the seventies and eighties, and the Chance Centre, which was already being called Chance House, was surrounded by crumbling Victorian mansions, most of which had been sloppily split into bedsits, and with sinister warehouses that probably housed terrorist guns and heroin caches, and seedy smoky pubs and eating houses and pawn shops. It had not previously occurred to Elinor that pawn shops – real pawn shops run by greedy-fingered greasy-haired Whitechapel Jews, and smelling of stale second-hand clothes – still existed in London.

There were tiny crammed-full general stores as well, catering for every creed and every human need: gefilte fish and curry, hamburgers and pastrami. The food shops were mostly owned by Indians of multifarious religious persuasion but canny business sense. It was interesting to Elinor to think she would probably become familiar with them all.

Her flat was at the very top of the house and it was considerably larger than she had been expecting – Lewis Chance's idea of what was 'not hugely grand' might have meant anything – and although the ceilings sloped because of being directly under the eaves and the floors were a bit uneven, there was a view of rooftops and chimneys and glimpses of the Thames. Whoever had chosen the fittings had picked out a brown haircord carpet which covered the entire apartment, and whitewashed the old walls the colour of Cornish cream. There were flame-orange curtains at the windows, and deep squashy chairs in mole-coloured velvet with glowing bronze and orange cushions. When the sun was setting over the roofs outside, the long low-ceilinged living room would look as if it were on fire. An oak gate-leg table stood under one window, so that you could sit and eat your evening meal watching the sun sinking into the Thames. The bedroom had splashy yellow sunflowers on the covers and cushions, and a deep wicker basket chair and white-painted shelves for books. Elinor would hang her prints of Georgian London in the sitting room, and the framed Arthur Rackham drawings which her godmother had given her.

Lewis was committed to attending a Charity Commission dinner on her first night in the centre – 'Boring but necessary,' he said.

'Noblesse oblige,' rejoined Elinor, but with such a complete lack of expression that Lewis glanced sharply at her.

'Well, hardly that. But it does mean you'll be on your own here until—'

'The small hours?'

A smile narrowed his eyes. 'It's men only,' said the womaniser unexpectedly.

'I know. Speeches with the brandy, and rude stories while the port goes round,' said Elinor. 'But of course I'll be all right on my own.' He must not think she was a child who could not be left by herself.

'The house probably won't often be empty again at night once we're up and running and properly staffed,' said Lewis. 'I've taken on a security watchman, but his hours are a bit flexible, and I don't think he'll be around tonight. You've got keys though, haven't you? I mean you've got a key to the street door as well as the one to your rooms up here?'

'Yes.' Elinor had been given the key not to the main wide doors that opened directly on to St Stephen's Road, but to the small side entrance which had been the stage door of the old music hall, and which gave on to a rather narrow dark alley with cobblestones. When the grime had been sand-blasted away, the words 'Stage Door' had been still legible. They were trying to decide whether this ought to be preserved or whether it would look a bit twee. You did not want to destroy fragments of London's history but on the other hand you did not want to appear twee when you were dealing with people who swigged meths each morning.

'Make sure you lock the street door after I've gone, won't you?' said Lewis.

'Yes, of course. I'll come down with you now and do it.'

He appeared to hesitate. 'Come and go in here as you want,' he said. 'Of course you must do that. Only—'

'Yes?'

49

'You hadn't better go down to the cellars, Elinor. In fact I'd better stress that you never do.' He looked at her and for a moment the suave smile of the laid-back philanthropist vanished and in its place was a cold hard stare. It was like seeing a blade suddenly unsheathed and the honed edge glinting, and it was unexpectedly unnerving. And then the image disappeared and Lewis said in an ordinary voice, 'They're a bit unsafe, those cellars, and I think the river sometimes overflows. At least we'll say it's the river, it might as easily be the sewers.' The smile was the ordinary one. 'Rather nasty if it is.'

'Oh I see.'

'So if you could make sure to avoid them—' There it was again, the glimpse of razor-edged steel. And beneath it a trickle of something darker. Like one of the grislier fairy stories, thought Elinor. Go anywhere you like, my dear, only don't open the door to the seventh chamber. Aloud she said, 'Of course I'll keep clear of the cellars. There's no reason for me to go down there anyway.'

She stood at the door for a moment watching Lewis walk down St Stephen's Road. He would probably pick up a taxi from the rank near London Bridge.

In the damp misty evening he might have been the ghost of one of the elegant gentlemen who would have frequented the old music hall a hundred years earlier. He had shrugged a long dark overcoat negligently over his evening clothes, and the cold vaporous air clung to him as he walked along. One of the carpenters, finishing some cupboards in the centre's communal kitchen downstairs, had told her the story of the long-ago recluse, and Elinor shivered suddenly. It was a disturbingly evocative tale even while you were discounting most of it as blatant exaggeration. A tall muffled-up man, prowling fog-bound London streets . . .

Elinor frowned to chase away the images, and locked the stage door, leaving the bolts free so that Sir Lewis could get in later. And now I'm safe, she thought, not pausing to question her use of the word. I'm locked inside and I'm perfectly safe from long-dead reclusive gentlemen who affect ridiculous forms of dress and prowl the streets long after their deaths . . . More to the point, I'm safe from street gangs and tramps looking for somewhere to spend the night. Or from modern-day Jack the Rippers, creeping through the dark streets.

She went back up to her flat, using the iron spiral stairs which the performers would once have used on their way to the dressing rooms. Her footsteps rang out on the open treads and echoed a bit eerily and she was glad that she had left lights on at the half-landings. The rest of the building was in darkness, but she would leave these on for Lewis's return. It was probably good security to leave lights burning more or less permanently, in fact. She had better start thinking like a proper householder.

It took less time than she had expected to unpack her suitcases and arrange the few things she had brought with her. The prints and the Rackham sketches looked very good indeed, and she had brought several bunches of bronze and yellow chrysanthemums from a flower barrow on the way. She arranged them in beaten copper jugs and set them about, and then walked slowly through her small domain with delight – it did not take long but she did it anyway – occasionally touching a wall or a door. Mine. My own place where no one can come in. I can get up to whatever I want in here. Lewis said so. He would probably draw the line at drunken orgies, but he would clearly not question the presence of a lover for the night. If only, thought Elinor, half bitter, half ironic. Her niece, Ginevra, pursuing what sounded like a pretty riotous career at Durham University, undoubtedly knew more about spending nights with a lover than Elinor did. It was shameful to have reached twenty-eight and never have been to bed with anyone: it would not have been so shameful if anyone had even asked.

She found a concert of Viennese music more or less by

luck on the radio, and listened to it while she scrambled eggs in the minuscule kitchen that opened off the long sitting room. Should she have a bath and curl up in her dressing gown with a book and a mug of coffee? Yes, why not? Sir Lewis would not return for ages, but he would certainly not disturb her when he did return. This was not going to be the classic seduction scene: the brandy-and-cigar-scented roué, dressed in a crimson smoking jacket and making fumblingly lecherous suggestions. Do have some more Madeira, m'dear. And then come into the bedroom to see my very curious etchings... Not that Lewis Chance would ever fumble.

It felt odd to be in a huge old building like this on her own, but she was perfectly safe – that word again. The main doors were bolted and barred, and the old stage door was locked. She had locked it herself. As the evening wore on, she kept reminding herself of this. The Viennese concert finished, and Elinor, half listening to the play that followed, half reading, occasionally paused to lift her head. Old houses had their own sounds at night; anyone knew that. Rafters creaked as timbers cooled and settled. Plumbing made peculiar noises. Stairs creaked loudest of all. If you were unduly fanciful, you might almost imagine that someone was creeping up them now. If Elinor listened, she could hear it quite plainly. Cre-e-ak. And then a pause. And then another creak. Exactly the sound the iron stairway would make if someone were coming up it very slowly, pausing every third or fourth tread. And there was a kind of faint swishing sound. Like skirts brushing against the floor. Or a long dark overcoat...

Elinor reached out to switch off the radio, and put down her book. The ticking of the tiny mantel clock was suddenly very loud. Ten o'clock. Much too early for Sir Lewis to be returning. His all-male dinner had probably reached the port and bawdy jokes stage. His own apartment was up here, of course, across the landing, but he would not creep furtively up the stairs, not as early as ten o'clock. He might if it were two or three o'clock, for fear of waking her.

The stairs creaked again, and something brushed against the wall on the landing outside. Elinor shrank back in the chair, gripping the sides with her hands. I locked the door! cried her mind silently.

And back came the response: Yes, but supposing there was an intruder already inside? Hiding somewhere. Waiting until everything was silent and still? Supposing you locked the someone in with you?

There was no conventional hall in the flat; the main door led straight into the sitting room, with the bedroom, bathroom and kitchen leading off it. If Elinor turned her head she could see the door that was really her front door. It locked and bolted. She was going to have a tiny card printed with her name on it. And a knocker or a bell so that people could knock properly. At the moment there was only a brass handle, a round old-fashioned knob.

She stayed where she was, her eyes fixed on the door. If the phone had been connected she could ring the police. She might sound like an hysterical woman, but she would rather be written down as hysterical than written off as murdered. But so far, her phone was only connected to the small switchboard in the office downstairs and there was certainly no one manning it tonight. Or was there? There was a sudden surge of hope as she remembered the night watchman, followed by a plunge back into despair because he was not on duty tonight – Lewis had said so quite definitely.

If she stayed very quiet, perhaps whatever was out there would go away. She had not switched on overhead lights; she had been reading by the single light of a table lamp, which had cast a cosy circle of light, but the rest of the apartment was in shadow. If it was an ordinary intruder out there, he could not possibly know that anyone was here.

An ordinary intruder would know quite well that some-one was here, because of the stair lights being on. Elinor looked involuntarily down to where a sliver of light spilled under the door from outside. Her heart came up in her mouth.

The door fitted snugly enough, but the old floors were uneven and there was a gap between the floor and the bottom of the door of perhaps an inch. The light shone through and it was sufficient to show the furtive movements on the other side of the door.

Someone was standing on the landing.

Ghosts did not stand outside your door. The sinister gentleman who walked the streets hereabouts did nothing more than make his slow way through foggy night streets.

Then it's an intruder, thought Elinor. And that means there's nothing for it but to remain absolutely silent and absolutely still and hope he goes away. But if he tries the door – if the doorknob turns – I'll certainly scream. Her neck muscles were beginning to ache with tension and with keeping her head twisted round to stare at the door, and the palms of her hands were dented where she had been gripping the chair arms.

And then there was another of the shadowy movements, followed by the creaking of the stairs again. He's going away. Is he? Yes, I can hear the stairs creaking down. She sat up, discovering that she had been holding her breath and exhaling it in a huge grateful rush. She pulled her chaotic thoughts into order and put up a shaking hand to her face, discovering that her forehead was sticky with sweat.

She was safe for the moment, but there was someone in here who clearly had no right to be here. Someone who had crept up the stairs to see what he could find and who was even now prowling around the rest of the building. Incredibly it was only twenty past ten. Sir Lewis would not be back before midnight at the very earliest. I can't sit here for two hours knowing that someone's out there, thought Elinor. I know it isn't a ghost, that's one good thing – at least, I'll say it's a good thing. It'll probably turn out to be a tramp but I can't count on that. Supposing it's someone lying in wait for Lewis? This was suddenly entirely possible. People who were in the public eye – however modestly – were targets for all kinds of things: kidnapping and death threats.

She forced her mind to visualise the layout of the building. To go down the stairs to the canteen and the offices on the ground floor where a small switchboard had been installed was out of the question. But what about Lewis's own flat on the other side of the landing? He had insisted that they each have a key to the other's flat. 'For emergencies,' he had said. 'I'll respect your privacy utterly, I promise, and you'll do the same for me. But one of us might be taken ill, or a fire might break out – a dozen things.'

If this was not an emergency, Elinor did not know what was. She stood up, pulling the robe of her gown more tightly about her. It was extraordinary how vulnerable you felt in a dressing gown and pyjamas and bare feet but getting day clothes from the wardrobe would take too long and might make a noise.

She slid her feet into slippers and padded across the floor, reaching for the key which she had hung just inside her own door, and stood listening for a moment. Nothing. I'll have to do it, thought Elinor. It's only a few feet anyway. I can be through the door and across the landing and into Lewis's flat, and I'll have slammed the door and locked it within seconds. I'll be as safe in there as I am in here. And his phone extension's bound to be working. The police could be here in minutes.

She paused with her hand on the door, and then taking a huge breath, turned the lock and stepped outside.

Chapter Six

The attic landing was brightly lit, which ought to have been reassuring, but gave the old building a vaguely sinister appearance. Elinor looked towards the iron staircase which spiralled round and down so that it was impossible to see beyond the curve. Was anything moving there, crouching just out of sight around the curve? She thought there was not. Across the landing was the door leading into Lewis's apartment: it was perhaps twenty or twenty-five feet away. The brown cord carpet covered it; she could be across it soundlessly and through the door within seconds.

Elinor took another deep breath and pulling her own door shut so that the Yale lock clicked home and carefully pocketing her own key, sped across the floor.

The lock to Lewis's flat turned like oiled silk and she was inside. She closed the door with barely a whisper of sound and turned the key. Nobody could possibly have heard the soft click. So far so good.

The flat was larger than Elinor's, and although it was shrouded in darkness, the curtains at the window overlooking St Stephen's Alley had not been drawn. Silvery moonlight slid across the room, lighting the portrait of Sir Lewis's ancestor which he had brought from Chelsea. It was the kind of portrait where the eyes followed you, which could be a bit shivery, but it was also the kind of portrait in which you wished you could have known the subject.

The phone was on the desk and Elinor snatched it up

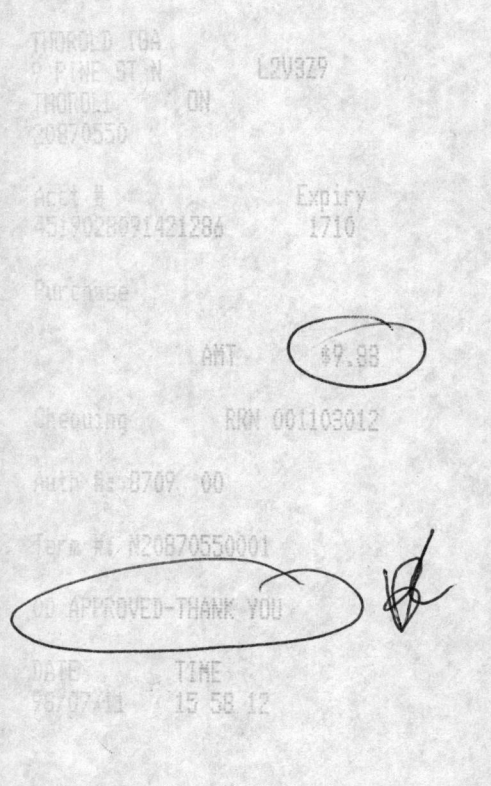

TRANSACTION RECORD

THOROLD TOA
9 PINE ST N   L2V3Z9
THOROLD   ON
20870550

Acct #   Expiry
4512020091421286   1710

Purchase

              AMT $9.98

Chequing   RRN 001103012

Auth #: 0709 00

Term #: N20870550001

00 APPROVED-THANK YOU

DATE   TIME
16/07/11   15 58 12

Top copy-customer Bottom copy-merchant
Retain this copy for your record

and tapped out the magical 999, her mind framing the brisk sentences that would bring help in a blaze of flashing blue lights and blaring sirens.

She had not expected the call to be answered quite so swiftly; in fact there was not even time for the ringing-out tone to sound at the other end and the sudden whispery voice in her ear sent a queer shiver through her. But of course the emergency service would be on its toes. She should thank heaven that it was.

The close-sounding voice said, 'Night service.'

This was unexpected but it was no time to start wondering how emergency calls were answered. Elinor said, 'Please will you come at once—' Her voice sounded shaky as if she might start crying at any minute, which would not do. She tried again. 'I'm speaking from St Stephen's Wharf – the Chance Centre in St Stephen's Road.'

'What's wrong, my dear?'

It was absurd to feel a cold wave of fear scudding across her skin. It was ridiculous in the extreme to think that the voice was exactly the kind of sinister breathy voice that might make a frightening anonymous phone call in the middle of the night. It's the 'my dear' bit, thought Elinor. That's all it is. He means it reassuringly only it sounds a bit sinister. She said, very determinedly, 'You are the police, aren't you? I am through to the emergency service?'

There was a pause. Elinor thought that when novelists wrote about the hairs lifting on the nape of your neck they got it dead right. 'Who are you?' she said, and heard how her voice came out tinny and a bit shrill.

'I'm the night watchman,' said the voice, and Elinor felt a flood of relief, because of course that was who it was; he must be around after all. Perhaps it was an extra shift or something.

'Did you come up to the top floor a short while ago? Was it you outside my door?' Her hands were gripping the phone so tightly that the knuckles showed white. Please say it was you. Please say something ordinary and reassuring.

'Well, of course that was me,' said the voice and this time it sounded more normal. Elinor thought it was probably only the odd closeness and the faint whispery echo on the line that was disconcerting her.

'I'm glad to hear it,' she said. 'You frightened me to death!'

'And who are you?'

'Elinor Craven. I'm Lewis's – I'm Sir Lewis Chance's assistant.' For some reason, saying this gave Elinor un-looked-for confidence, like touching a talisman. Nothing dreadful could happen to someone who was Sir Lewis Chance's assistant.

'Where are you?' said the voice. 'Are you inside the house?'

'Yes, of course. I'm on the top floor. I'm in—' She paused and then said, 'I'm in my own flat.'

'All by yourself?'

'Well – yes.' This, of course, was the one thing you should never do: you absolutely never admitted to an unknown man that you were in the house on your own. Elinor said, 'Sir Lewis is due back very shortly, however.'

'Oh, you're quite safe, my dear.' This ought to have been the reassurance she had been waiting for, but instead there was an impression that the owner of the voice had drawn in his breath with wet gloating.

'I'll make another check of the building, just to be sure,' he said. 'And what you must do is stay safely in your flat. You did say the top floor, didn't you?'

'I – yes.'

'Yes,' said the voice. 'That's what I thought you said.'

'You – where are you?' said Elinor sharply.

There was the ghost of a chuckle from the other end. 'I'm in the house with you,' said the voice.

Going out on to the brightly lit landing again was like going on to a lighted stage. Elinor felt horribly vulnerable and exposed, but the stair lights were on and she had only to step across the short stretch of floor.

As she pulled Lewis Chance's door to and turned to cross the landing the scents of freshly sawn timber and new paint lay on the air. But underneath was a darker older scent: something musty and ancient and cruel. Damp and dry rot still lingering, said Elinor to herself firmly. But she could almost feel the old building listening and watching. As if there were eyes everywhere. *I'm in the house with you* ... Would a night watchman really say that? But if it wasn't the watchman, who was it? Someone who's in the house with me ... Someone who knows I'm up here on my own ... Her heart began to pound and her palms were slippery with sweat. But all she had to do was get back into her flat and lock the door.

As she thrust her hand into her dressing-gown pocket for her own key there was a click and the stair lights went out.

Elinor froze at once. The suddenness of the darkness was like a blow and the lack of windows on the landing or the iron stairs made the blackness absolute.

It was ridiculous to think it was anything other than a power failure. It was entering the realms of fantasy to imagine that the click had been the sound of someone pulling the main switch. Yes, but the switches were at the foot of the stairs, just by the cellar door. *You hadn't better go down to the cellars, Elinor* ...

This was absurd. No one had pulled the main switch. Power failures were always happening and with appalling timing as well. This one could not have been timed much worse if the electricity company had planned it a fortnight in advance.

She began to inch her way across the landing. If she kept her back to the wall she could not possibly go wrong. Lewis's flat was behind her and her own was dead ahead. You can't go wrong, Elinor.

It was remarkable how much more clearly you could

hear in the dark: that was the absence of sight heightening the other senses, of course. Blind people developed hearing to a superhuman degree. To all intents and purposes Elinor was blind for the moment and she could hear the creakings and the stirrings of the old house very vividly indeed. She could hear timbers in the roof contracting as they cooled and she could hear the old iron stairs swaying a bit. Exactly as if someone were creeping up it very quietly and furtively. She stopped dead, trying to penetrate the blackness. Surely her eyes should have adjusted by now? Wasn't that a glimmer of light in front? Overspill on to the stairs from the floor below? There were offices and three or four small interview rooms on the next floor down, and a telephone room where they were setting up the Lifeline service. The large communal refectory-cum-kitchen was on the ground floor and the cellars were beneath, with the entrance at the very bottom of the iron stairs.

The light was stronger now and it was *moving*. Elinor shrank against the wall. A moving light. Someone coming up the stairs carrying a pencil torch or even a small candle. Yes, it was a candle, it was flickering and dancing and throwing eerie shadows on the wall . . . And whoever was carrying it was coming stealthily and secretly, not cheerfully and openly like a night watchman would come, calling out as he approached so that you would know who it was.

Because it wasn't a night watchman you spoke to earlier, you know quite well it wasn't . . .

Her own flat was only feet away – she could see the faint outline of the door now. She would be inside within about eight seconds and she would drop the latch and shoot home the bolts, and then drag the furniture across the door. And if anything tried to get to her she would break open the windows and yell down to the street for help. The light was coming closer, but it was coming very slowly. He's taking his time, thought Elinor. He doesn't

want me to hear him. But I won't panic. Here's the door –
at least I can see better now.

It was important not to fumble with the key. Elinor's
hand closed over the familiar comforting outline in her
dressing-gown pocket, and she felt for the lock halfway up
the door. At least four of those seconds had ticked past.
She risked a glance towards the stairs. Oh God, he was
coming closer. I must be quick, and above all, I mustn't
drop the key in the dark.

The key slid into the lock, and Elinor drew in a shaking
breath of relief. Almost there. It was then that she felt the
resistance to the key, and the sickening truth dawned on
her. She had taken both keys with her into Lewis's flat,
but she had brought only one out.

She had picked up Lewis's instead of her own.

It spoke volumes for the frayed state of her nerves that at
least ten appalled seconds ticked away before she realised
that all she had to do was return to Lewis's flat.

As she fumbled for his lock again a movement on the
stairs made her turn. The wavering light was on the curve,
spilling on to the landing, casting shadows. Elinor could
see her own shadow; she could see the bundly outline of
her dressing gown and the trailing cord.

The second shadow fell across the wall of the stairwell,
fuzzy at the edges and slightly blurred, and horror flooded
Elinor's mind.

A figure the size and breadth of a man, the body that of
a man, normal, legs and arms and feet. Except for— The
head, thought Elinor. There's something wrong with the
head. It's too big, it's twice the size of a human head . . .

There was the scrape of a footstep on the stair, and as
the figure came nearer, Elinor's mind spun in sick terror.

The head was huge, a monstrous grotesque shape. The
names of ancient, virtually extinct illnesses raced across
her panicking mind: encephalitis – water on the brain,
hadn't they called it? And some of those poor things with

Down's syndrome had a lumpish distorted look. The shadow was hunched slightly over, as if the swollen head were too heavy for it to carry. As it came into sharper relief, it turned, so that she saw the silhouette more clearly, and disbelief warred with fear for a second, because the thing, whatever it was, had pointed, pricked ears and a snout-like muzzle. The frozen panic broke then, and Elinor pushed the key home with trembling hands, and felt the lock turn. She half fell into Lewis's sitting room and sobbing with panic, slammed the door and dragged the bolt home.

Lewis had left the Savoy Hotel rather earlier than he had indicated to Elinor: the dinner had been mildly enjoyable but the company had been dully predictable. He had talked to a few people who might contribute to the centre and who might further one or two projects, and he had listened to the speeches and the smoking-room stories. On balance the speeches had been more entertaining than the blue jokes. A reluctant grin lifted his lips as he remembered Elinor's dry observation earlier.

It had caused him immense inner amusement to be welcomed as a valued guest tonight, and it had afforded him sardonic pleasure to find his company sought and his opinions listened to as if they were Holy Writ. No one had mentioned his father; Lewis sometimes even thought people had forgotten. But he had not forgotten and he never would forget. It had been dubbed the most complex pension fraud ever to be uncovered, and when twenty years afterwards the Maxwell scandal broke, some newspapers had dragged up the Chance trial and drawn parallels. But Charles Chance's brilliant criminal juggling had made Robert Maxwell look like a street pickpocket.

Lewis picked up a taxi in the Strand and noted the reaction to the St Stephen's Road address. It was only when you were older that you could appreciate real irony, and there was irony in what he was doing now: leaving the lavish hotel, replete with an excellent dinner (the Savoy do a very good partridge aux choux in season), mellow with good claret, but directing the taxi to a run-down area of London's wharfland. Probably the taxi driver thought he was cruising for a prostitute.

The prostitutes of both sexes were out in force; mostly walking in twos and threes, which Lewis supposed was because of the murder scare. The subterranean demi-world closing ranks as it so often did. Looking after each other.

They seemed, to Lewis, incredibly young and the boys appeared younger than the girls. Was it the thick make-up and the clothes the girls affected that made them look older? He glanced at a group of them: cracked leather mini-skirts and high heels and impossible hairstyles. They were more aggressive than the boys as well, but under it they were as young. There was the old joke about knowing you were ageing when the policemen started to look younger, but Lewis thought you could as easily say you were ageing when street women began to look like schoolchildren. Two of the girls called a raucous good night as he paid off the taxi outside Chance House and one of the boys gave a shrill wolf whistle. Lewis grinned and sketched a half-wave, half-salute. None of them would bother to approach him because they knew him by now, but some of them would come to the centre. They would get beaten up, or they would get into debt, or their boyfriends would leave them. The girls might get pregnant, the boys might contract Aids or syphilis. They would all panic as they got older and some would turn to drugs or drink.

Chance House was quiet, and the stairs and landing lights were all switched off. Lewis reached automatically for the switch, and glanced routinely towards the cellar door – closed, of course; all's well – and went quickly up to his flat.

Elinor had switched on every light in Lewis Chance's flat – so much for power failures – and then had curled into a chair facing the door and stayed there. Her mind was swinging between panic and disbelief, because surely, *surely*, nightmare creatures with monstrous beast heads only existed in books and horror films? The Thing from the Black Lagoon. The Beast in the Cellar.

She was listening with fierce intensity for the smallest sound from the stair but there was nothing. Whatever had come creeping up the iron stair had gone away. Because it heard the lock turn and the bolts draw? The building had fallen back into its brooding silence and Elinor thought nothing moved beyond the door. It was not a matter of hearing, it was a question of feeling. I'd *know* if the thing was out there. But no matter how much I know, I'm not going to open that door until Lewis is back.

Incredibly it was only eleven o'clock, which meant that barely three-quarters of an hour had passed since she heard the soft step outside. Could she sit it out until Sir Lewis returned? The phone was plainly not connected – it took a good deal of resolve to pick up the phone and make sure about this, but she forced herself to do it. Dead. Then I'm on my own. What about a weapon in case the thing tries to get in? She looked around: lamps, books, radio. No, something heavier. She made her way into the kitchen, keeping her eyes on the door, and found an empty wine bottle. If anything tried to get in she would smash it to pulp.

She had thought fear would keep her alert and wide awake but she had not realised how draining fear was. It had not occurred to Elinor that she might actually have to fight sleep off, but the quieter the house grew, the heavier her eyelids became. Several times her head fell forward and she felt herself spinning downwards into a dark shadowland where sinister creatures who wore long dark overcoats and deep-brimmed hats to hide their unnatural heads, crept up on her. Each time this happened she managed to drag herself awake and each time there was only the calm quiet sitting room and the curious comfort of Lewis's belongings about her. Elinor sank back into a half-doze and it was only when the scrape of the alley door being quietly opened below roused her, that she realised she had after all slid into real sleep.

She sat bolt upright at once, her eyes going to the hands of the wall clock. One a.m. The smallest of the small hours.

The light quick footsteps coming up the iron staircase were unmistakably Lewis's. He had just that way of going up and down the stairs; not running but not walking either. I'll have some explaining to do, thought Elinor, suddenly aware that she was wearing a dressing gown and that it was one o'clock in the morning. Supposing he's brought someone back with him? This embarrassing possibility had not until now occurred to her.

But the footsteps were plainly solitary, and huge thankfulness flooded Elinor's mind.

'Brandy,' said Lewis, holding out the glass. 'Very good for shock.'

In a minute he might even say, 'Drink this,' thought Elinor, who was annoyed to find that now it seemed to be all over she was shivering violently from nervous reaction. They always said, 'Drink this' in books. And you drank it and then, depending on which book you had fallen into, any number of things happened. If it was a country house whodunit you went bowling round the room, heels to head, in a loop of strychnine death-agony, which served you right for not spotting the murderer's identity. Or if it was science fiction you turned into a soulless bone-crunching robot. If it was Lewis Carroll's *Alice*, of course, you either became tiny enough to slide under the door or too big for anything, and if it was Robert Louis Stevenson you metamorphosed into the slavering half-human Mr Hyde prowling the fog-bound streets of Victorian London— Elinor shut off the rest of this hysterical fantasy and pulled herself together sufficiently to take the glass.

They had gone back into Elinor's flat, and Lewis had switched on all the lights and checked every room.

'I've switched your heating up as well,' he said. 'Is that all right? Extreme cold always follows an unpleasant experience.' At the sound of his voice – at the *ordinariness* of his voice – Elinor began to feel very much better. And the brandy was setting up a glowing core of warmth.

'Can you tell me what happened? I mean properly tell me.'

Elinor had stopped shivering sufficiently to think about what she was going to say. It was very important not to let him think she was apt to be hysterical and it was even more important that he did not think she was a person who saw monsters creeping up stairs.

Selecting her words with care, she said, 'There was someone in the house – an intruder – a burglar. Footsteps on the stairs.'

'Yes?' He was watching her from over the rim of his own brandy glass. The upper part of his face was in shadow and although pinpoints of light flickered in his eyes they were silvery lights – cold – and the eyes themselves were unreadable. He had discarded his dark overcoat and the silk evening scarf but he was still wearing his dinner jacket. If men realised how devastating they looked in well-cut evening clothes they would never protest about putting them on. Lewis Chance's evening things were extremely well cut and he looked very devastating indeed.

Elinor sipped the brandy, drawing her brows down in a scowl. 'I went across the landing to use your phone extension. Mine isn't connected yet and I'd heard the – burglar go downstairs, so I thought it was safe.' It was probably imagination to think he looked up at the hesitation or that he had paused in the act of lifting his own brandy glass. Elinor said defensively, 'You insisted we each had a key to both flats. For emergencies. And I thought—'

'That if this wasn't an emergency nothing was. Of course. Go on.'

'I was going to ring 999 – I didn't realise your phone wasn't on yet either. But then the – the night watchman answered and said it wasn't an intruder at all, it had only been him checking all the floors.' She thought this sounded reasonably believable. It was pretty ironic that the first time a man should ply her with brandy when she was in her night clothes it had to be her employer, and he was only here because of a suspected burglar.

'And then?' said Lewis. 'What happened then?'

'Nothing,' said Elinor shortly. 'I virtually locked myself out, heard what I thought was the intruder again and dashed back into your flat. I bolted the door and grabbed an empty wine bottle.'

'An—'

'As a weapon in case the man broke in. It's probably still on the floor in your sitting room.'

'At least you spared my Nuits St Georges,' observed Lewis, drily.

'It isn't meant to be funny.'

'I wasn't thinking it was.'

'Well you looked it.'

'I was thinking how resourceful you were.' And I'm thinking how right I was to suspect you'd react well to an unconventional situation, said his mind. How many females would have thought of the wine bottle – or any weapon at all?

Lewis sipped his brandy, and smiled at Elinor over the rim of the glass. He had been very quick in bringing the brandy but he had still brought the correct glasses: crystal goblets. That's style, thought Elinor with irritated admiration. I'd have sloshed it into a mug.

Lewis regarded her thoughtfully. His eyes were the sort that mother often bestowed on the revolting heroes of her books, and unfailingly described as 'luminous'. It was annoying to find that luminous grey eyes actually existed.

Elinor, staring at Lewis Chance, saw for the first time how closely he resembled the portrait over his desk. His hair was darker and he was about twenty years older, of course, but in the rather low light neither of these things was noticeable. His hair had been tousled by the night air, and the brandy – or maybe the lavish dinner earlier – seemed to have melted the barriers a bit. If he smiles he'll almost be the Victorian portrait come to life, thought Elinor. If I start thinking that portraits are stepping out of their frames to sit drinking brandy with me, I'm nearer hysteria than I thought!

She said firmly, 'I have to say I didn't much like the sound of the night watchman,' and Lewis frowned into the dregs of his brandy. In a minute he would say something about the watchman being a bit eccentric, or foreign, and not to worry. He might even produce the famous line about trying to get some rest. And if he says that, thought Elinor, the spell will break and just as well, too!

Lewis did not say any of it. In an expressionless tone, he said, 'Elinor, I'd rather not tell you this, but I think you'd find out for yourself.'

'What?' Elinor felt as if someone had tipped a bucket of ice into her stomach. I know what he's going to say. And I don't want him to say it.

'It couldn't have been the night watchman,' said Lewis. 'He's a bit unusual but I'd stake a couple of fortunes that he wouldn't have spoken to you in the way you've described.' He paused, and then said, 'And also, Elinor, I'm still waiting for the locksmiths to bring spare keys. Raffael hasn't got a key to the building: he won't have one until the end of the week.'

After what seemed to be a very long time, Elinor said, in a horrified whisper, 'Then – who was I speaking to? Oh God, who was I speaking to?'

Chapter Seven

Private memorandum from Sir Gervase Withering, aide to the Prince of Wales, to Rt. Hon. Frederick Inchcape

30 January 1888

Sorry to land this one on you, old man, but HRH is in a great dither about this business with Prince Eddy and the little music hall gel. I must say that to have to listen to Bertie holding forth about morality was one of the more edifying experiences of the century, because we all know he's had more women than is countable. Still, the point is that he does it more or less discreetly (and with females who know the form), and that Eddy doesn't.

I believe you know the Chance family – is there any possibility that they would agree to ship this young ruffian out to the colonies for a year or two before he can spread the story all over London?

Private memorandum from Rt. Hon. Frederick Inchcape to Sir Gervase Withering

2 February 1888

Well, a nice pup you are handing me this time, Gerry! I suppose HRH never takes into account the fact that the 'young ruffian' is the heir to the Chance Banking Company or that half the Marlborough House set have investments there! But I'll speak to George Chance, and see what I can do. As you say, it would be better if the boy were sent out of harm's way for a time.

By the by, is it true that Prince Eddy has been seen once more in the vicinity of Cleveland Street? I ask purely from the security angle, because if he's at it with boys again we need to be aware. I personally do not give a tuppenny *hoot* what pickle Eddy dips his rod into, and as *you* know it's unlikely that he'll ever succeed to the Throne. But it'll be a bit awkward if he does and somebody ups and blackmails him! The pox we can hush up (it wouldn't be the first time), but extortion for buggery would be a bit more difficult!

Extract from Patrick Chance's Diary

Cheyne Walk, February 1888

Frightful rows with Father who has verged on apoplexy ever since visit from Freddie Inchcape, who presented himself more in sorrow than in anger, wily old tortoise, bearing with him a version of events at St S.'s so distorted I hardly recognised them. Never realised Prince of Wales's aides so devious!

Father listened, frog-eyed, to Inchcape (who made Eddy out to be suitable candidate for canonisation and me a priapic Satan incarnate), and then flew into towering rage. Passed from there to head-shaking sorrow, and pontificated about shame being brought on House of Chance – Never hold my head up again, and, Only thankful your poor mother not spared to see the disgrace, etc., etc. It's a bit much of him to drag in Mamma, who ran off with a penniless Italian portrait painter and died in Siena when I was six, only they hushed it up on account of the scandal and the fear of a run on the Bank.

However, at least poor Chloe apparently 'being dealt with generously' which is main concern, and I

70

am truly relieved, even though 'generous' might only mean buying her silence by giving her a house somewhere out of the way. The Outer Hebrides, I shouldn't wonder. Managed to get address of private nursing home in Surrey where she has been taken pro tem, and have sent flowers, fruit, etc. Will try to sort out some kind of annuity, since am suspicious as to what constitutes Inchcape's notions of generosity. I suppose in time I'll forget the sight of her clawing at her face in an attempt to wipe away the lime as it burned into her ... The nursing home say the scarring should fade a bit in time, and although vocal chords irretrievably burned, at least one eye unharmed, which is a mercy. Cannot see this being much of a consolation to Chloe.

Lewis stood in the empty cellar room beneath Chance House and felt black bitter despair slice into him.

Empty. The strange tormented creature he had guarded so closely and so carefully, that he had removed from the private and discreet Highgate institution only three weeks earlier, and charged Raffael to guard, had escaped. Inevitable, of course. Face it, Lewis, you always knew this might one day happen. You knew it had happened the minute Elinor Craven began to speak. He sat down in the rocking chair with the patchwork cushion and looked about him.

The underground room that had once housed discarded fragments of the former music hall was now very comfortable indeed. The decaying remnants of Edwardian grandeur had been removed, and in their place had been put bright modern furnishings from Habitat and Heal's. Lewis, furnishing the place in secrecy, had remembered the boy's pleasure in vivid colours and also his enjoyment of music, and there was a good-quality CD player and a radio. The bed was covered with a scarlet spread and there were bright green and sapphire cushions and a scarlet and blue square of carpet. On the wall were two paintings: a Sisley and an early Monet. Lewis could still remember standing in the small gallery just off Bond Street, writing a cheque for the Monet, and how the absurdity of it had struck him, because no one bought original French Impressionists for a creature who could descend into ravening madness between one heartbeat and the next. But he had not bought it for the mad slavering thing that the boy could become: he had bought it for the gentle bewildered creature who took pleasure from colour and form and light and who, given paper and a child's paintbox, could produce a wash of vividly beautiful colour instantly recognisable as an autumn sunset or a buttercup meadow.

The paintings had softened the walls of that first nursing home at Hampstead, and then the small private manor house at Gerrards Cross, and finally the Highgate institution with its discreet reputation for helping such *hopeless* cases – 'Drink and drugs and *sex* problems, and we have had some wonderful successes, Mr Chance.'

In the end, of course, Highgate had been the same as all the others. Lewis had learned to read the warning signs by then; he could almost have written the dialogue word for word. Some unexpected traits: an unpleasant incident last week and a real tragedy only just avoided . . . No longer sure if we are the right place . . .

The end would be that the boy would be sectioned and taken to an asylum where they would sedate him heavily and persistently, until finally he slid down and down into darkness, the patches of bright intelligence buried for ever.

Standing in the deserted cellar Lewis beat down the memories – painful, black memories – but they crowded helplessly in, as sharp and as hurting as they had been all those years ago. The innocent-eyed toddler smiling with guileless lips, the mutilated rabbit or the bird at his feet and his baby hands smeary with blood . . . And then the terrible night shortly after the boy's third birthday when he had known, once and for all, that the child's sinister ancestry was surfacing.

In those days Grendel had a nurse – what was called a nanny nowadays. Odd how the Victorian term had returned. But when Grendel was three, with the scandal of Charles Chance beginning to fade and Lewis himself beginning to reverse the House of Chance's fortunes at last, there had been a young and rather pretty nurse. He could not recall her name – he thought the horror had wiped it from his memory – but he did recall that he had eyed her speculatively and that there had been the beginnings of attraction. 'Perhaps you would join me for a drink when your charge is asleep...?' Thinking: and perhaps you might like to join me in bed, as well.

Until he saw what Grendel had done to her.

The child had the large room at the top of the house; there was an old-fashioned sash window with a padded window seat under it and a view of the park. The nurse liked to sit on it because the light of the low night-bulb fell directly across it, and she could see to read to Grendel from one of the brightly illustrated books that he liked: *Winnie-the-Pooh* and *Rupert Bear* and *Thomas the Tank Engine*.

He heard the single terrible scream and then the abrupt silence that had followed it, and he had frowned, unsure whether the sound had actually come from inside the house at all. Someone outside? The screech of machinery even? Better go up to make sure nothing's wrong.

She was seated on the window seat, just as she so often was, and for a moment Lewis stood in the doorway, not understanding, because there was something wrong about all this, there was something dreadfully wrong. Was she wearing a mask over the lower part of her face? A new game? If so, it was rather a frightening game; it would terrify a child. The lower half of her mouth was wet and glossy as if it were covered with blood.

73

A nose bleed. A fall where she had cut her face? But there was a very great deal of blood; it had spattered her chest and front and there were red finger-streaks on the window pane and the curtains, as if she might have clawed at them in a struggle.

She stumbled towards him, her hands held out in entreaty, and there was a moment when he still did not understand, when his mind was still running on conventional lines: ice from the fridge for the bleeding, brandy for shock, a phone call to the nearest GP, or even a rapid drive to the casualty department of the local hospital . . .

It was only when she fell at his feet that he saw with horror the white glint of bone and teeth through the blood. Her mouth and part of her face had been torn away. *Bitten* away. Something that was still in the room, seated in a corner, its eyes innocent but its lips smeary and crimson, had bitten away her face. Something that wore Grendel's skin and had Grendel's eyes and mouth. Something that still cradled a fragment of bloodied flesh in its hands, and squealed like a scalded cat when Lewis tried to take it from him . . .

A nightmare. I have fathered a monster.

But within the surge of appalled knowledge had been that other emotion: protect Grendel. Shield him from what he cannot help. The emotion had been so strong that it had almost choked him but he had thought: if he can be kept away from the world – and kept *comfortably* – I'll do it! No pitiful communal asylums, no soulless institutions.

Somehow he had managed it. He had paid for medical care for the nurse and later for plastic surgery. After a year he had bought an annuity which would bring her a moderate income. She had gone to live in the north somewhere and she had remained loyally silent.

It had been then that the struggle to keep Grendel safe had started. The nursing homes, the subterfuge. Each year a little more difficult, each year the pretence a little harder. He had spared no expense, because by then, by

74

dint of throwing himself into work, he was already dragging the House of Chance back from bankruptcy, first into what the accountants called break-even, then into profit, finally into prosperity. And although Grendel must be shut away from the world, he could be shut away *lovingly*. Humanely.

But all the time had been the fear, because the ancient darkness that had attended Grendel's birth was a darkness that could cast very long shadows.

Dawn was silvering the sky when Lewis finally shut the door on the dreadful, memory-drenched cellar and returned to his own flat at the top of Chance House.

He had tapped at Elinor's door, and spun a story about an ordinary intruder and the discovery of a broken window near the cellars with a disposable hypodermic thrown down. It told its own story, he said.

There was an unnerving moment when Elinor looked at him very directly and said, 'So it was an intruder, high on something.'

'Probably roaring drunk in addition. There was an empty whisky bottle as well.' Don't overdo it, Lewis.

'Yes,' said Elinor thoughtfully. 'I see.' She did not quite say: So that's the story we're selling ourselves, is it? But the words had hung on the air.

There had been that other moment as well, when he had felt what the poets called the thin batsqueak of sexuality between them. He had repressed it instantly because to succumb to even such a tenuous shiver of attraction would be very unwise, and Elinor Craven was not the sort of girl he would want to get involved with. She was brusque and awkward and although she was far from being ugly, she was no raving beauty, and Lewis had always carelessly and arrogantly demanded a high level of physical and mental charm. She had unusual eyes and good skin and that intriguing voice, but that was all. Even in the right clothes – dark exotic crimsons and mulberry colours or glowing jade greens, with slightly bizarre jewellery, garnets and chunks of amber – even if she stopped scowling at the world—

Lewis switched on the lights in his own flat and poured a large whisky, discarding his dinner jacket and the stiff uncomfortable evening tie as he did so. He pushed aside the suddenly vivid image of Elinor as she might look if something or someone could give her some self-confidence, and threw himself down in the chair facing Patrick's portrait. There were lines of exhaustion about his mouth and at the corners of his eyes, but the resemblance to his ancestor was strongly marked. If I had any sense I would burn you, he said silently to the enigmatic regard. I should have made a huge symbolic bonfire of you years ago and ensured that nothing was left.

If any blame was being dealt out Patrick had to shoulder a good deal. Patrick had been feckless and reckless, and he had travelled beyond the last blue mountain and across the angry glimmering sea, sought by and beloved of all the legendary pilgrims in all the myth-laden cultures of the world. Patrick had not cared about Homer's wine-dark seas or Flecker's snow-barred mountains: he had taken the Golden Road to Samarkand for lust of knowing what should not be known – and if only half the stories about him were true, lust had probably been the driving factor behind most of it. Lewis refilled his brandy glass and thought that he was dredging up a fine ravelled richness of poets tonight.

But I had my own lusts, he thought. And for lust of wanting to know what Patrick really found, I took the same road. Tashkara.

The road was probably still there, even today: winding its secret way into the lost city; dry and dusty and desolate, and so far removed from the modern world that it was like stepping back in time. Not golden – the road to Tashkara was never golden, just as the road to Samarkand was only golden in the poem, just as the streets of London were only paved with gold in the visions of the ambitious and the gullible. In both cases it was fool's gold, only you did not find that out until it was too late.

Lewis met Patrick's stare again. We both took that golden dusty road, Patrick, and for you it ended in some appalling destiny that you never revealed and that I can only guess at, and for me it has not ended at all.

But the road had its vein of gold for all that, said a sly little voice in his mind. Remember? Remember how it enabled you to restore the House of Chance?

But at what cost? Because the ancient, blood-drenched legend – the dark revenge that I've spent the last twenty-odd years running from and guarding Grendel from – is reaching across the years again.

Chapter Eight

London, March 1888

I'm writing this surrounded by cabin trunks and Thos. Cook itineraries and a general atmosphere of upheaval.

It's been decided to send me abroad, which is a way of keeping me quiet about the Duke of Clarence/Chloe Cambridge scandal, of course. Expect they think another scandal in the Royal Family would be untenable at present, what with poor old Eddy reportedly prowling the streets around Cleveland Street on the lookout for young boys again. Still, if they never say any worse of him than that, he'll have cause to be grateful.

I thought of protesting, but after listening to Father ranting about shame and ruination for the last three days will happily take the road to hell to get out of earshot – it's said to be an easy road to travel anyway, quite apart from the gate being permanently open and broad the way that leadeth. Father and Freddie Inchcape seem to think I'm halfway there as it is.

'And you'll take a travelling companion,' shouted my father, by way of Parthian shot as he stormed off to the City, empurpled as to complexion and choleric as to humour. 'You're not rampaging and womanising across Europe unchecked, Patrick, so don't think it!'

It would serve them all right if I *did* rampage and womanise across Europe and then write my memoirs afterwards.

Am afraid that by companion he means keeper, which will be a dreadful bore, unless it turns out to be Theodore Chance, who's some kind of second cousin and hasn't a bean, but is reasonably good company, although a touch prim. But if I have to go abroad I don't see why I shouldn't have some fun while I'm travelling, and it might be amusing to corrupt the virtuous Theodore.

We've settled on the very Far East although Thomas Cook's people are sepulchral about the choice – Can't guarantee safety, sir ... Extremely hazardous routes, to say nothing of lack of sanitation and uncomfortable travelling conditions. And then there's the language problem ... Dear me, sir, wouldn't you prefer Kitzbühel – very nice at this time of year – or perhaps Venice?

But I have stuck out for Tibet from sheer contrariness, because if they're sending me into exile I'll damn well make it a dramatic exile and as much trouble to everyone as possible. Freddie Inchcape and the Withering idiot can sort out visas and permits and whatnot; it'll serve them right for stirring up scandal-broth.

Dare say the actual journey will be unbearably tedious, even so.

Lewis had found the journey into Tibet almost unbearably tedious.

If this was the road that Patrick had taken it was a very long and arduous road indeed: in fact it was more like the road to hell than Flecker's visionary Golden Road to Samarkand.

Even in the high-tech 1970s, reaching the East was an exhausting affair of long hours in the air, of swapping planes at half-staffed airports, and of uncomfortable

Eastern hotels with nonexistent air-conditioning and a plenitude of insect life, some of it nocturnal, most of it apparently on permanent cannibal duty.

But he had been twenty-five and his name had become synonymous with greed and deceit on that huge scale, and the thought of running away – of donning Patrick's mantle – had been immensely tempting. The thing had had to be done on a shoestring, of course, because there had been hardly any money left by that time. What had not gone in dividends to creditors (shamefully small), had gone to pay the costs of the public examination and the later court costs for the fraud hearing.

But even without the money, he had done it with panache. He had donned the arrogance he was already learning to assume – Patrick's arrogance although no one had ever guessed – and although Tibet was still wrapped in its deliberate isolation in those days, he had bullied visas and permits out of government departments. In the end he had actually gone directly to the airport from his father's funeral, the smooth black limousine speeding effortlessly through sheeting November rain, its boot loaded with suitcases. I'm leaving it all behind, thought Lewis. I'm stepping out of one world into another – through that falling curtain of rain, and out the other side. There was delight in the knowledge but there was a trickle of unease as well. Because of what might lie beyond the beaded rain-curtain? But at least I'm going beyond the reach of the accusing whispers and the curious stares, and out of range of the swarming newsmen.

But the newsmen had tracked him down; they were waiting at the airport like buzzing flies, firing machine-bullet questions and flashing cameras as he loaded a trolley with luggage.

Why should he not leave England? he had said angrily. What was there to stay for? The Belgravia apartment and the Wiltshire property had been sold along with the rest of the disposable assets. The Banking House was in the hands of its trustees and Lewis himself had no money and no job.

'And,' he had said coldly, 'I certainly don't intend to live in furnished rooms in Watford or Hackney.'

Hackney had been an unfortunate choice of word because half the subeditors in Fleet Street had seized on it with glee, and the next day's headlines had read: 'Disgraced banker's son refuses to live in Hackney-ed squalor.' Lewis, scowling at this gem at a stopover halfway across the Northern Hemisphere, thought you could always trust the gutter press to dredge up the *mot juste*.

I'm an exile, he thought, folding the newspaper and waiting for the continuation flight to be called. I'm an exile, just as Patrick was an exile.

Patrick would not have had swift hire cars at his disposal, nor, of course, air travel, although it was astonishing to count the inconveniences that Patrick would not have had to endure and that Lewis did. Inconveniences such as discovering that two pieces of luggage had not found their way to Delhi Airport, and queuing for two hours with a cosmopolitan assortment of travellers in similar plights.

Patrick would simply have directed a few porters to load a cabin trunk on to a steamer, paid a few more to reload it on to a ponderous but probably not uncomfortable railcar, and sat back and enjoyed the journey in between. That he had enjoyed it was evidenced by his book, in which he devoted an entire chapter to describing two separate encounters with two different ladies en route in the railcar, which must have enlivened the journey very considerably. Trying to recapture his belongings, struggling with unfamiliar languages and incomprehensible dialects, Lewis began to think that by comparison, Patrick's journey must have been almost luxurious, particularly if you took into account the railcar.

But Tibet, the remote rooftop world, the ancient realm of the Dalai Lama, certainly would not have changed much since Patrick's time. It was for ever drenched in its pre-Christian beliefs and its deep tranquil religion, and Lewis, hurtling through the streets of Lhasa in a ramshackle cab, stared out at the tumbling raucous market stalls and the baked-clay houses, and the beggars and vendors and scavenging dogs, and thought this must be almost exactly how it had looked to his ancestor.

Beneath the rattle-trap cars and the modern cool hotel and the unexpectedly efficient English-speaking desk clerk, he was aware of an undertow; of beliefs and rituals and cults that had been old before Man had learned to speak and walk upright. The machines and the urbanity were grafted on, and although there was a thin veneer of civilisation it was so thin that the slightest tap would shatter it and you would be through to the real Tibet. The ancient realm where magic sometimes walked; the place ruled by the priest-king in the glowing crimson pavilion that dominated Lhasa. Lewis glanced up at the glittering tiered palace of the Dalai Lama, and a tremendous sense of excitement began to unfold. I'm nearly through the curtain, he thought. I'm almost there.

It turned out to be unexpectedly easy to engage a guide who would drive him into the remoter parts of Tibet's interior. This was a thing many travelling gentlemen requested, explained the hotel clerk, all smiling urbanity, all modern civilisation. And there was a very good route that could be taken, very nice, very full of interest, although perhaps – the now-familiar spreading of hands – perhaps a little arduous for those of advancing years.

'I'm not of advancing years and I don't mind an arduous journey,' said Lewis, and asked how the journey would be made.

It appeared that a Jeep would be used for part of the journey. 'As much as possible,' said the desk clerk, avoiding Lewis's eyes. 'Then by walking. The Jeep is of American manufacture,' he added. 'Very good, very strong.'

He eyed Lewis optimistically, and Lewis said, 'American. How unexpected. Will it take me to Tashkara?'

The thin shell of civilisation splintered. I've hit a nerve, thought Lewis. He leaned on the desk and waited, and presently the clerk said uneasily that Tashkara was a very difficult journey, very long, very hazardous . . .

'Very expensive?' said Lewis sardonically.

'Oh, very. It is not,' said the hotel clerk, 'a journey many make.' In another minute he would say in a sepulchral voice, Many go there, but few return.

Before he could say it, Lewis said, 'Never mind. I'll thrash it out with the guide.'

'Thrash? What is thrash, please?'

'Outmanoeuvre,' said Lewis, and booked the guide for the following day.

The Jeep turned out to be a relic from the Second World War, and looked as if it might have been abandoned by Roosevelt's troops when the suspension gave out. Lewis eyed it doubtfully, remembering the hotel clerk's explanation about making some of the journey on foot. He had been prepared for that but it looked as if the on-foot part would come sooner than he had expected.

Patrick, in his diary, had not given much detail about the practicalities of this part of his journey: probably he had thought it too tedious to record. 'Looked out of the window of the railcar for four hours this morning. Played chess with companion for two hours this afternoon. And so to bed.' He had usually recorded the bed part.

Thomas Cook's seemed to have provided a guide for most of the journey, and Patrick had referred to two or three Sherpas who had taken him and his cousin into Tibet's interior, and whom he seemed to have found companionable. Good for you, Patrick. Gregarious all along the line. You probably fared a whole lot better with your Sherpas than I shall with this rusting heap, thought Lewis. It'll break down before we've gone five miles.

It did break down. It misfired like a shying horse at the sight of the treacherous rocky gorges and the desolate mountain passes, emitting furious clouds of steam from the leaking radiator like an angry dragon, and refusing to budge. The guide, whose exact name and precise calling Lewis never managed to elicit, but who answered amiably to Cal and spoke English with a cheerful blend of accents acquired from other travellers, said they would be on foot now, this was all right?

Lewis turned to look up at the towering mountain peaks and gorges, and the glinting threads of fast-flowing streams and rivers. The curtain parting . . . These mountains were the guardians to Tibet's remote mysterious interior. They were awesome, but then mountains were always awesome. They were like mirrors and cats, they had a secret inner life of their own.

For the first time since they had left Lhasa, he said, 'And Tashkara? Can we reach Tashkara?'

There it was again, the flinching, the quickly averted eyes, exactly as in the hotel.

'You wish to go to Tashkara?' said Cal at length.

'I do.'

'It is not possible.'

'Why? Doesn't it exist?' Lewis was almost prepared by now to find that Tashkara was nothing more than a figment of someone's imagination, a dark Shangri-la. He would not have put it past Patrick to have amused himself by adding a few touches of fiction to his travel account.

Then Cal said, 'There is an ancient stone palace which is called Tashkara's Gateway. I know it – everyone knows it.'

'A palace?' This was not quite what Lewis had been expecting.

'Once it was the home of a royal people who ruled – many hundreds of years back,' said Cal. 'My grandfather knew of it. There were rituals and feastings, all held in great secrecy, and if anyone witnessed them, he was given a terrible death. The people had their own laws and to offend against them brought down the punishments of their gods.'

'Really?' said Lewis, but his heart had begun to race. Rituals . . . And the punishments of their gods . . . Is this it? Is this what you found, Patrick? He said, 'What happened to the tribe?'

'They were driven out, and they went deeper into the valley, taking their strange customs with them. Perhaps they are all dead.'

'Or perhaps they're not. Tell me some more.'

'For a time the palace was a *gompa* – your word is monastery – with a shrine to the Buddha, and *thankas*, which you would call wall paintings.'

'I see. Do you know where it is, this palace?'

'I know,' said Cal. 'All know. But it is a place of great danger now. Bad evil. Not to be visited.' He turned determinedly back to the Jeep. 'We should take off the luggage. We have to walk some part, but this is a trade route and we shall meet other people as we go – hill folk, traders – all very interesting. There is a hill station where we shall sleep tonight. Very comfortable, very clean: market stalls and a small village. There are cups of *tchai* to drink, and then a very excellent supper, perhaps lamb with apricots and rice or—'

'What kind of bad evil?' Lewis was damned if he was going to be fobbed off. 'And what kind of danger? Cal, tell me.'

'It is a very bad story,' said Cal apologetically. 'Told about the people who live inside the palace now.'

'The monks? You said it was a monastery—'

'No, once there were monks but no longer.'

'But – people live there? Cal, if you don't tell me, I'll tip you into the nearest gorge.'

Cal said, 'There are people living there.' He sent Lewis a sudden fearful look from the corners of his eyes, and Lewis felt his skin prickle. Something here that Patrick either did not find, or did not record. Or perhaps something that was not here in his day.

He said, 'What people?'

There was an abrupt silence. Lewis was uneasily aware of the brooding mountains and the vast listening silence.

Then Cal said, 'They are known as the Flesh-Eaters of Tashkara.' And, as Lewis stared, 'You understand me?' he said. 'The flesh they eat is human flesh.'

Eighty years is only a drop in the glimmering seas of Tibet's timelessness, and the palace Patrick had found and described would certainly not have altered. Lewis, staring across the deep gorge with the foaming fast-flowing river at the bottom, had the feeling of time fusing. Patrick, you had the gift of painting word-pictures in addition to everything else, he thought. This is your palace. This is the Gateway to the secret city of Tashkara.

Patrick had described the ancient palace as a huge awe-inspiring edifice, stark and grim and built like a medieval fortress into the side of an immense crag so that it was impossible to tell where the man-made structure ended and the rockface began. It clung to the sheer mountainside, overhanging the gorge, and it was unbelievably remote. Clear pure light spilled over the stark rockface, ravens wheeled overhead and in the distance was the violet and grey smudge of the Himalayas, drenched in magical eastern twilight. I will lift up mine eyes to the hills from whence cometh my help. But what else might come stalking out of those purple shadowy summits? Lewis thought: this is one of the eeriest places I have ever come across, and when he spoke, his voice was just slightly too down-to-earth.

'It looks virtually inaccessible, although I don't suppose it is.' He looked at Cal. 'How do people get across the gorge?'

There was another of the nervous pauses, then Cal said, 'There is a rope bridge. Woven ropes and cables and wires, nothing more. If you fall, you are smashed against the rocks below. It is said that it is put there for the Tashkara people to catch victims.'

'Like snaring a rabbit for supper?' said Lewis, with a lightness he was not feeling. He looked down into the gorge. The river hurtled along its channel, dashing against the crags and the boulders, white spume rising up.

'I do not go beyond here,' said Cal. 'Never at all. If you pay me the wealth of all my ancestors together and double it tenfold, I still do not.'

'Then,' said Lewis, hoisting the larger of the haversacks on to his back, 'I shall have to go without you.'

Into the ancient Palace of the Flesh-Eaters.

Chapter Nine

Extract from Patrick Chance's Diary

Tibet, June 1888

Promised ourselves we will cross the gorge at first light and request admittance to the ancient stone palace. Theodore worried about etiquette of this, but have pointed out that behaviour suitable for Kensington probably inappropriate out here and it'll be perfectly in order to ask for a night's lodging and a bite of food before going on across the valley.

According to Sherpa guides (English virtually nonexistent but we communicate by sign language), the palace was once some kind of gateway to a forbidden realm in the valley beyond. They point and use the word *gompa*, which means a monastery, and I have pointed out to Theo that all monks, no matter their religious persuasion, are honour bound to provide rest and food to travellers; in fact it's a basic Buddhist tenet. Theo promptly said, Not all monks, what about Trappists? and looked disapproving, exactly as he did when I locked him out of our railcar in order to while away afternoon with little Eurasian car attendant.

(On subject of which am rather pleased to record that I managed to time rhythms to coincide with vibration of wheels, although just as I was congratulating myself, the engine hit a fast downhill stretch and I nearly succumbed to premature ejaculation, which is a bêtise in any country and would have been embarrassing with a total stranger. These Eastern females appear more concerned with *giving* pleasure than with receiving it, and their ideas on massage are v. erotic, although fear may suffer irritation in awkward place from too-liberal application of scented oil . . .)

Later. I'm not sure I like this place much. We are facing the gorge and have made camp, setting up a tent and lighting a fire on which we cooked our supper. (Rice and dried strips of an anonymous meat – think it was lamb, which I don't much like, but beef impossible out here, of course.) The Sherpas stayed to eat and then unaccountably took to their heels and, as one man, left. This was extremely disconcerting, although Theo says he never trusted them in the first place, what can you expect from foreigners, and we should never have come. No spirit of adventure, Theo. All the same I'm beginning to think he may have a point . . .

Later still. Darkness creeping over the mountains now, and it's getting colder by the minute. That's the altitude, of course. We're on the roof of the world, and on balance I'd prefer to be in the cellar – at least it would be warmer. We have each had a good pull at the brandy flask, in fact we have had several, and it's helped the cold, never mind letting down a few barriers because Theo suddenly apologised for chronic disapproval, which he said was because he envied me. I said, Why? Nothing about me to envy, dear boy.

Whereupon he replied, with owlish insobriety, 'I envy your success with women, Patrick. M'father said that you've only got to look at them and they—'

'That's nonsense,' I said, quickly, half from embarrassment (cannot cope with displays of naked sentiment) and half because of proximity of religious establishment across gorge.

''S true. Money an' looks an' panache. Got everything. Unfair distribution.' Upon which he fell abruptly asleep.

This is too astonishing a revelation to digest when half-drunk, and I will have to re-examine it in sober daylight.

Unfortunately daylight is many hours off and by night the mountains are brooding and sinister as if they have taken on a different persona. It's the creeping murmur and the pouring dark filling up the vessel of the universe, and God alone knows what's out there watching us.

The fire is burning well and has warded off some of the cold. But the flames cast odd shadows and I keep thinking about the teachings of one of the old philosophers (Plato?), who handed down that vivid eerie picture of Man crouching in the dark, studying the shadows cast by the fire flickering on his cave wall, but never daring to look out at the reality of what cast those shadows . . .

What in God's name am I doing huddled on the side of a Tibetan mountain, freezing cold, swigging brandy and quoting philosophy?

Elinor was trying to be philosophical about the strange creature she had glimpsed on the iron stairs, because Lewis's explanation had to be the true one. An intruder, some poor confused soul high on drugs or drink or both. It was the only logical conclusion. The creature she thought she had seen could not exist outside of the mind of some mad surreal artist or some way-out film-maker.

And the image was fading, exactly as all nightmares faded, although it did not quite vanish. One day, thought

Elinor, one day when Lewis is away, I'll prove that that wretched ghost doesn't exist. When he's attending one of his conferences or his dinners, I'll go down into the cellars, and I'll prove there's nothing there: recluse or subhuman or anything!

She was trying to be philosophical about the way he had sat with her in her flat as well, and she was certainly keeping at bay the memory of how he had given her brandy for shock and talked to her in his velvet voice and smiled with his silver eyes. It was important to keep it in proper proportion and Elinor thought she was just about managing it. Her niece, Ginevra, would have said: Why keep it at bay? And: I hope at least you had your Janet Reger nightgown on, Nell. And Elinor would not dare admit that she had been wearing the pale blue candlewick dressing gown that she had donned to eat her solitary supper and that made her look bundly. Lewis would not find bundliness attractive; he would be used to satin and lace and to sexy slithers of perfumed silk on his women. All those dozens of them.

Ginevra was due home from Durham this weekend, and in the half-guilty hope that she might find Kensington stifling, Elinor had written a hesitant invitation for Ginevra to stay at Chance House. It had been very gratifying to receive Ginevra's enthusiastic acceptance – 'Because the thing is, I've been tangled with somebody I shouldn't have been tangled with, Nell, and I've been dreading Kensington on account of being preached at.' Elinor had been touched to be regarded as preferable to Kensington and preaching, although she had misgivings about the tangle.

She might even be able to tell Ginevra about Lewis, because although Ginevra was likely to say something flippant such as, 'Jesus God, Nell, trust you to fall for the boss!' she would be whole-heartedly on Elinor's side. She would instantly want to drag Elinor off to a ruinously expensive hairdresser and through half a dozen outlandish

91

boutiques with the idea of Elinor's outshining the slitherers – 'Because all you need is *confidence*!' – and she would come up with a bagful of outrageous seduction plots, none of which would be practical but all of which would seem perfectly possible and even rather fun when Ginevra outlined them.

Elinor was going to find her a great comfort.

Raffael's reaction to Lewis's carefully worded story of Grendel's disappearance was unexpected.

He said, 'You are satisfied, are you, that Grendel was taken against his will?'

Lewis, who had been half expecting protestations of self-exoneration, stared. 'Of course he was taken against his will,' he said. 'It's a classic case of kidnapping. Why?'

'Just a thought. You haven't called in the police?'

It was the obvious question and this time Lewis was prepared. He said coldly, 'I have not. And I must ask you not to do so either. Not yet, at least. Grendel was always a prime target for a kidnapping and I was always a prime target for blackmail.'

He held Raffael's eyes, and after a moment Raffael said softly, '"*Wealthy philanthropist keeps maniac son hidden away for twenty years* . . . Pay what we ask or that's the headline we'll give to the press . . ."?'

'Precisely.'

'But,' said Raffael softly, 'your instant response to that would be, "Publish and be damned!" Wouldn't it?'

'Certainly.' Lewis was not going to be tipped off balance a second time. He said, 'You know that, but a blackmailer wouldn't.'

'What are you going to do?'

'What all victims of kidnap do. Wait for them to make their next move.'

'Yes, I see.' Raffael studied the man in front of him. 'What about Miss Craven?' he said suddenly. 'You said she heard something—'

'I told her it was an ordinary burglar, although I don't think she entirely swallowed it. She's a very perceptive lady.'

'Could she have guessed? Because if so, it might be better to trust her with the whole.'

'No. The fewer people who know the safer. I don't know what Elinor thinks really happened, but I'd stake any sum you like to name that she doesn't know about Grendel.'

'Ah yes, I recall that you have been spoken of as a gambler,' murmured Raffael.

'It is possible that Grendel's genuinely been kidnapped,' said Raffael, seated opposite to Cardinal Fleury in the book-lined room in Bloomsbury. 'And his mental condition would make him very suitable for a blackmail plot – Lewis Chance is quite right about that. To have it made public that he had been hiding the boy for twenty-three years would ruin him. For the second time,' said Raffael. 'And that's something else that rings an odd note,' he added thoughtfully.

'What?'

'How did he get back to prosperity so soon after he returned from Tashkara?' said Raffael. 'His father's debts were described as monumental. I could bear to know a great deal more about what happened in Tashkara twenty-five years ago, because whatever it was, the noble baronet came out of it with a sum of money so substantial he not only paid his father's creditors in full, he also set the House of Chance on its feet again.'

'Do you think this is an ordinary kidnapping?' said Fleury

'I don't know. There's been no demand for money yet – or if there has, Lewis Chance isn't saying. But he's certainly wealthy enough to make the boy a prime target.' Raffael broke off and frowned. 'No, it's too coincidental. I think we should assume that the League of Tamerlane have taken Grendel. And I think Lewis Chance knows it – or at least guesses it.'

'Why?'

Raffael said, 'Think about what we know, Eminence.' He ticked the points off on his fingers. 'Grendel was almost certainly born while Lewis Chance was inside Tashkara. Somehow he got the child to England in what seems to have been immense secrecy, and from then on he *kept* him in immense secrecy – one nursing home after another, always moving him, never leaving him in one place for too long. Why?'

'Because a moving target is seldom hit.'

'Exactly. And with the emergence of the League of Tamerlane out of Tashkara, what's Chance's first reaction?'

'He buys an old house with exactly the right accommodation to hide the boy once again,' said Fleury, 'and removes him from the Highgate nursing home.' He considered this, and then said, 'You are sure that the boy couldn't have got out by himself?'

'I couldn't be surer. The door to his room was double-locked, and so was the outer cellar door. They were both good stout doors and there was no sign that they'd been forced. Grendel himself was always chained and the chain had been cut through with steel pliers—' Fleury made an involuntary gesture of distaste and Raffael looked up. He said gently, 'A thin strong steel linkage about one ankle, but the chain long enough for him to move about his small realm with complete freedom. I dare say he hardly noticed it. And it was far more humane than gradually destroying his intelligence by huge doses of sedatives.'

'I have to accept your judgement,' said the cardinal, 'although I question the reasoning. What is your conclusion?'

Raffael smiled inwardly at the switch to theological polemics. What is your point? Keep to the argument. Reason with logic and precision and brevity, and present your case with a *quod erat demonstrandum*. He said, 'You told me that the League of Tamerlane were dissidents: a rebel group trying to overturn the ways of their people.'

'Yes?'

'What do dissidents do when they're trying to topple an existing rule?' Raffael leaned forward, his eyes alight. 'They set up a figurehead, someone to rally their followers. A lodestar.'

'But no resistance group would use a madman as a figurehead,' said Fleury, staring at him.

'They might,' said Raffael. 'And Grendel has considerable charm when he's sane. It's a possibility.'

'It's a very remote possibility,' said Fleury. 'But I agree it should be borne in mind. What are you going to do next?'

'Lewis Chance is due to speak at a conference in Bath this weekend,' said Raffael. 'He's going ahead with that and I think he's expecting some kind of demand by the time he returns – or at the very least something that will give us a clue. His instructions are that the police are not to be called in until he gets back. And of course,' he added wryly, 'it's unlikely that the police would send out the might of the Metropolitan Forces just because a young man of twenty-three had been missing for twenty-four hours.'

'If they knew about the – flaw – they would,' said Fleury.

'Oh yes. But I'd rather trust Lewis Chance's judgement,' said Raffael. 'Because if he does know anything about the League of Tamerlane he might lead me to them.'

'And from them to the Decalogue?'

'Of course. I haven't lost sight of the original mission, Eminence.'

'You should be careful, Raffael,' said Fleury. 'If they – if anyone – should suspect what you're doing . . .' He made an abrupt gesture with one hand, and Raffael felt an icy finger of fear trace a path down his spine. Fleury said, 'The League of Tamerlane will certainly kill anyone trying to reach the Decalogue. You do realise that?'

'I do realise it,' said Raffael, and then, summoning up the flippancy that fooled most people but probably did not fool Fleury for a second, he said, 'But I shan't be in any danger, Eminence. You're forgetting the old adage about the devil looking after his own.'

Chance House always felt empty when Lewis was away, but this time Ginevra was arriving for the weekend so Elinor would not notice it so much.

He had left after lunch on Friday to attend a charities conference in Bath, where he would be one of the after-dinner speakers. His speech would touch on the particular problems of the homeless in London's East End and he would speak well and everyone would be enrapt. The women would be very enrapt indeed.

It was a good speech – Elinor had done quite a lot of the research for it, finding some interesting anecdotes both about the early days of Dr Barnardo's Stepney Mission in the 1860s, and also about the less well-known Father Hudson's Homes of the Catholic Church in the 1940s and 1950s. It was astonishing how long ago this all seemed.

She had rather diffidently suggested that Lewis might consider using these examples as a springboard, drawing parallels with the Chance Centre, and Lewis had liked the idea and asked her to draft something, which had been totally unexpected. It was very gratifying that he was going to use her draft almost word for word: he had even commented that the slight touch of wry humour she had unconsciously allowed to get in made it human and entertaining. Elinor had stored these words away to gloat over, although she would only allow herself ten minutes' gloating per night. She had asked the typist to print three copies of the speech, one to be retained for faxing to the hotel in case of mishap, and two to be bound into a folder to place in Sir Lewis's briefcase.

The conference would mostly be organisers and helpers from various charity organisations, but there would be bound to be a few silk and lace slitherers present, and it was entirely possible that Lewis would find himself sharing a drink or a late supper with one. Elinor dwelled with vicious masochism on this image, deliberately exploring it so that it would hurt even more. At what point did you signal that you were willing to be propositioned? And how did you do it? Did you go to his room or yours, and did you undress and get into bed and wait, or did you wait for him to undress you? And what did you do about contraception?

Elinor went down to lock the doors at half-past six. She liked the early evening when the centre settled into quietness, and when it almost felt as if Chance House was hers. And although Lewis had never once intruded into her flat – not even to borrow the farcical cup of sugar – Elinor liked the feeling that he might. Sometimes she played out little scenarios in her mind: I'm awfully sorry to disturb you, Elinor, but I've run out of . . . Oh that's all right, come in and have a glass of wine . . . No, I don't want to intrude – oh, how cosy your room is . . . Perhaps I'll just have one drink, then . . . This is very good wine . . . No, don't switch your music off – Schubert, isn't it? I'm particularly fond of Schubert.

Quite of lot of these scenarios ended with him staying to supper, with Elinor off-handedly whipping up an *haute cuisine* meal out of absolutely nothing, and almost all of them ended in him still being there for breakfast. The in-between bit varied from the merely romantic to the downright explicit. It was as well that none of it would ever happen because the reality would be a crashing disappointment.

She wished everyone good night and stood for a moment at the old stage door, watching them all go off into the gathering dusk. The two typists were giggling about their plans to go to a wine bar later, and a probation officer, who had called in earlier and got caught up in a discussion with a couple of the Lifeline phone people, was going to have a drink with them on the way home.

After everyone had left – especially with Lewis away – a subtle darkness seemed to steal over the house. As if something that had had to lie low during daylight crept out? Don't be ridiculous, Elinor. But the feeling remained, even after she had shut the door and locked it firmly. As if someone were watching. As if the house were filled with people peering out of the shadows.

She would not think about it; she would go up to the flat and have a quick shower, and then she would cook herself a dish of pasta and mushrooms with smoked ham, and pour a glass of sharp dry Chablis. Being able to do all this was still one of the delights of having left Kensington; there was no one to ask why she was spending her evening at home *again*, or why she was stewing in an armchair with a book instead of going out and having fun. Elinor hated her mother for not realising that the world had changed since the frenetic sixties of her own youth, and for not understanding that when you were plain and awkward and, more to the point, excruciatingly shy, you ran away from all opportunities anyway.

Except Lewis. She would never run away from Lewis. He would be donning his immaculate dinner jacket about now, preparatory to going in to pre-dinner drinks with a roomful of slitherers. How would it feel to be at his side, smirking complacently at them? It would feel appalling, thought Elinor crossly. You'd be clumsy and you'd look like a sack of potatoes even in a designer dress, because you always do look like a sack of potatoes. You don't have any conversation. You might as well leave him to the slitherers.

She turned to go up the ringing iron stairs. After she had eaten, she would make up the bed in the tiny slit of a room which would be Ginevra's for two nights. Ginevra

98

had not known what time she would be arriving: it all depended, she had said vaguely on the phone. She might get a lift if someone was driving down, or she might hop on an overnight bus and go from town to town, which would be a bit long-winded but quite good fun. If she got stranded somewhere she would wait for another bus or find a railway station. Anyway, Nell was not to sit around waiting for her: she would get there when she got there.

Elinor started up the stair, wondering whether Ginevra would arrive in time for lunch, and whether she might like to eat at the Prospect of Whitby or the Anchor if so, when she heard a scrape of sound that turned the blood in her veins to ice water.

There was someone in the cellar.

Elinor had no idea how long she stood motionless, staring at the cellar entrance.

She could see the door clearly: it was tucked under the iron stairs, and although the workmen had ripped out most of the old worm-eaten doors and replaced them, this one had been left intact. It was low and damp-looking and somehow imbued with a sinister aura. Elinor, who disliked cellars and basements and underground places, had always avoided looking at it when she went up the stairs, and was thankful that it was always closed.

It was not closed now. It was partly open; she could see the band of black all around it and her heart leaped.

There was someone in the cellar. There was someone on the other side of the forbidden door where there would probably be rats and mouldering piles of nameless debris, and where the Thames occasionally overflowed... At least, that was what Lewis had said.

She took a deep breath. You said you'd investigate, but you might have known you'd duck out when it came to the crunch. You're a fink and a coward.

There was probably not anything to be finkish about, because the chances were that whoever was in there was

99

simply someone who came to the centre – somebody a bit confused or distressed who had got lost, or was looking for the loo. If that was so it was Elinor's clear duty to haul him out politely but firmly. It was a pity that everyone had gone home because it was not really a brilliant idea to go into a dark cellar on your own to rout out an intruder. On the other hand you could hardly ring the police at quarter to seven in the evening, just because somebody had got lost on the way out of a large building.

Elinor took another deep breath and reached out a hand to the door. It swung easily back and a faint dank breath of air gusted out to meet her.

Chapter Ten

It was dark beyond the door, but not as dark as Elinor had feared. It was shadowy and dim and there was a fetid clammy stench, but a faint green waterlight rippled on the walls and it was possible to see quite well.

She had pushed the door back almost to the wall and light spilled in from the hall. Wooden steps led down and Elinor tested them cautiously: they were a bit rickety but they seemed fairly secure. With her heart thumping erratically she began to descend. This is the place Lewis forbade me to enter, insofar as Lewis would ever forbid anyone anything. Unsafe, he had said, and unhygienic. Occasionally flooded by the Thames. *So whatever you do, my dear, don't open the seventh chamber* ... Of course not, M'sieur Bluebeard.

It would probably be sensible to go up to her flat to get a jacket and even a torch, except that if she did that she might not have the courage to come down again. And she was only going to turn out whoever had got in here by mistake. Either that or she was going to lay the ghost. It was a ridiculous expression: you could imagine a crowd of men in a pub saying it raucously. Hey, I'm laying a ghost tonight, fellas.

At the foot of the rickety steps – at least they had not splintered and deposited her in a broken-bone heap at the foot – was a long dim tunnel with the sides and the roof rounded, rather like a giant brick culvert. It was about eight feet from roof to floor at its centre, and the green light rippled over the dank bricks. It was rather horridly cavernous and the tiniest sound reverberated against the walls. From somewhere up ahead was a faint drip of water and the echo caught that as well and bounced it back over and over. Drip-drip. Drip-drip. It was the kind of dank hollow sound that would grate against your nerves if you were shut in with it for long. Not that Elinor was shut in. She glanced back at the wooden steps. The cellar door was wide open; she could go back at any time she wanted. Like all those wide-eyed heroines in fairy tales, who went trippingly and trustingly into the dark gusty castle of the ogre, gaily saying that it was quite all right because they could go back . . .? Yes, but I'm not in a fairy tale. Not unless it's Bluebeard, of course. Not unless it's a nightmare version of Jekyll and Hyde, with the house as the main character. *I am changing, my dear, I am fearfully changing . . . Once I was an ordinary house, sheltering ordinary people, but now I am turning into a gobbling monster . . . regressing to the days when this was the lair of a recluse who dared not go abroad in daylight because he was so repulsive that people would run screaming from him . . .*

Elinor gasped and put out a hand to the wall to steady herself. A touch of claustrophobia. Making me imagine all kinds of weird things. I don't suffer from claustrophobia. I wish I hadn't lit on the word *lair*. I wish I hadn't thought about the recluse, either.

Apart from the echoes it was very quiet; she could no longer hear the drone of traffic in St Stephen's Road, which added to the sense of isolation. And the tunnel seemed to be deserted: the echoes would have betrayed the presence of a mouse. There was nothing and there was no one, but she would just go a little farther along and then she could go back to the flat with a clear conscience and enjoy the pasta and the glass of wine. She would probably have a couple of glasses after this, in fact she might very well finish the bottle.

I'll just go a little farther, thought Elinor firmly. I'll

make absolutely sure there's nothing here, and when I know that there isn't – because of course, there won't be – I'll feel a whole lot better. Like looking under the bed before you got into it. Like checking that the noise you heard at two o'clock in the morning really was the cat coming in through the kitchen window and not a burglar.

She went past a smallish door set deep into the brickwork, and paused. It would be sensible to try it, but in fact it resisted Elinor's tentative push. Locked. It was probably only an old storeroom anyway. The entire place was probably only storerooms.

There was the impression of immense age down here, and Elinor reminded herself that Chance House was very old and that very old houses were often built on the sites of houses even older. But the aura down here had nothing to do with Victorian grafted on to Regency, or even Regency grafted on to something much earlier. It was an aura of creeping darknesses and ancient evils, as if something tainted and malign had lived down here and as if the malignancy had soaked into the stones and the bricks. The recluse again? Or something else? Something that lived down here in dark secrecy, and came prowling up out of the cellars when everyone was asleep . . .?

The rippling light was getting stronger and the echoing drip of water was more distinct. Then I'm going towards the river. Or am I? Well, if not the Thames, maybe a tributary.

And then she rounded a curve and came up against a flat stone wall, with brackish water oozing down it and oily puddles on the ground. Dead end. Then I've done what I set out to do; I've checked the boundaries. I've looked under the bed, and there's nothing there.

It was then that a blurred movement caught the edge of her vision and she looked down. Near to the ground was an oblong opening, a kind of half-window half-ventilator, rather like the ones you saw in the basements of large Victorian town houses. It was about seven feet across and probably four feet deep at the highest point; there was no glass but there was a barred grille. Sluggish light poured through, casting the outline of the grille across the ground. Had something moved on the other side? Elinor bent down to look, her heart almost in her mouth with terror. Beyond the grille were stone steps leading down to a lower tunnel. There were the same dark wet brick walls and floor, and as Elinor pressed closer a stench of decay breathed into her face.

Padding down the tunnel, going away from her, was a creature with a slender, black-clad body and a monstrous nightmare head. A cat's head, with snarling lips and a blunt snout and gleaming teeth that protruded upwards like fangs. The terrible head turned slightly from side to side as it went as if scanning the shadows, and the eyes, yellow and feral, caught the light. In the thing's arms was the limp body of a young man, his head falling back, a rim of white showing under his eyes. The hands holding the boy were paws, massive and claw-tipped, with coarse bristly fur along the backs.

For ten hideous seconds Elinor almost lost her hold on sanity altogether – that's the creature I saw on the stair! – and then understanding washed over her mind. It's a false head! Of course it is! It's like a Mardi Gras head or an elaborate mask! And the hands are gloves! She was about to draw in a shaky breath of relief when a different fear came scudding in. What kind of person deliberately donned a nightmare mask and claw-gloves, and prowled through dark houses and dank dripping tunnels? And carried prone bodies to some unguessed-at lair . . .?

She crouched closer to the grille, trying to see more, and it was then that she realised that the grille was in fact a hinged gate. To lift it and go down into the lower tunnels with the stench of dank dripping decay and the nightmare creature padding ahead would be complete and utter insanity. But to let the thing take its victim to some impenetrable hideout was also unthinkable. If I can just see where it goes, thought Elinor, I can go back up to the house and get help and I'll have clear evidence. But if I've only got the evidence of my own eyes I don't think anyone's going to believe me. 'You saw something with a man's body and a cat's head in the sewers, did you, madam? Dear me, very upsetting. And how long have you been seeing things like this?' You could very nearly write the dialogue.

And as long as she was very quiet and very stealthy, and as long as she kept so far behind the creature that it did not know she was there, it would not really be very dangerous. She reached for the grille which lifted easily and noiselessly in her hands, as if somebody kept it well oiled.

Elinor glanced back down the tunnel, and then bent to climb through.

The lower tunnel was larger and at intervals it was reinforced with brick pillars and arched groynes under the roof. It was dark but not completely so, and it felt rather like walking along an abandoned section of the Under-ground – Mornington Crescent, or one of those 1940s British films about ghost trains that came out of nowhere and thundered along closed tracks.

At intervals were smaller tunnels, snaking away into complete blackness, and in the floor, every few yards, were huge old-fashioned iron drains. Elinor caught the stench of wet decay again, and the glint of dark stagnant water. An old sewer tunnel? Dear God, I'm in the sewers following a madman who thinks he's a cat!

Whatever he was, he knew the way through the tunnels. He went forward, his arms holding his victim easily, stepping between the gaping drains, his footsteps echoing hollowly. Once he stopped and looked back and Elinor's heart jumped and she froze in the shadow of one of the brick pillars. But after a second the man continued, turning off into one of the intersections and going up another flight of steps. There was the sound of a door being pushed up – a trap door? – and then being closed. Elinor, keeping well back, tried to think what to do. The intersection was marked with a faint chalk cross on the wall and it would be easy to find again. But supposing the creature was only depositing its victim and was coming back down the tunnel almost immediately? If that was so he would certainly catch her. But to go forward after him was clearly out of the question. I've painted myself into a corner. No, I haven't, he's coming back – I was right to stay put then! She pressed back into the lee of a brick pillar again, thankful that she was wearing a dark sweater and skirt which would make her fairly unnoticeable. But her heart was pounding so loudly she thought the echoes would pick it up.

However, the cat-headed man seemed unaware of her presence. He was no longer carrying the boy and he came down the steps, walking quickly and lightly and went into the green darkness of the tunnels. Elinor heard him lift the hinged grille and go along the upper tunnel. There was the sound of the cellar door closing.

She came thankfully out of her makeshift hiding place. Almost safe now. But I'll hurry: through the half-window, fold the grille back into place – yes, good, cover your tracks, Elinor – and now along the tunnel and up to the cellar door. She was nearly but not quite running and her mind was racing ahead, to getting back to her own flat, to ringing the police – this time there would be no sinister whispery voice on the other end – and unbolting the old stage door to let them in.

In a very few minutes she would be doing all that . . .

As she turned the cellar door handle she felt the resistance at once. She frowned and tried again, twisting the handle up and down. Jammed? She moved the handle from side to side, but panic was beginning to slick the palms of her hands with sweat, and cold fear was welling up. It was perfectly clear what had happened.

The man, whoever he was, whatever he was, had a key to the main cellar door. And as he went out he had locked it.

He had locked her in the cellars. And on the other side of the cellar door, Chance House was deserted. Everyone had left for the weekend.

It was important to remain calm. It was very important indeed to work out what time it was and to think when people would be coming to the centre.

It was half-past seven – barely an hour since she had come down to lock the side door. No one would be coming to the centre tonight – they had had one or two open evenings and talks by people from organisations like Relate and Shelter, but there was nothing on tonight. The Lifeline phone had been switched through to whoever was on night duty. No one would be coming back.

Lewis would certainly not be returning because the conference would not end until Sunday afternoon, when there was a service at Wells Cathedral, and then a buffet lunch. He would not return before Sunday afternoon, or even Sunday evening.

What about the security man – the real one: what was his name – Raffael? Would he return to Chance House tonight? But even if he did, he would simply see that the cellar door was locked as normal. If she banged and shouted would he hear? More to the point, would she hear him come in and know when to bang and shout?

There remained Ginevra's weekend visit. Once Ginevra got here she would almost certainly institute a search; Elinor could easily visualise her telephoning Lewis at the Bath hotel, demanding that he come home, even summoning the police. But the trouble was that between trains and buses and lifts that might not have materialised, Ginevra would perhaps not get here until tomorrow morning. Elinor glanced uneasily into the tunnels again. Supposing the cat-headed creature returned? And what about the boy? He might be lying helpless somewhere; it would be dreadful to find that he had died all alone because Elinor was too spineless to do anything other than crouch up here shivering, waiting for someone to come and find her.

She stood up and began to retrace her steps along the tunnel.

It was important to keep to the main tunnel and to go to the intersection with the chalk cross. She absolutely must not get lost down here where she might easily wander about in the dark for hours, going round in circles without knowing. Mad ideas of marking the turn-offs by scratching the brick like ramblers or gypsies, or unrolling a ball of twine like Ariadne tracking the Minotaur to its grisly lair through the labyrinth, scuttered across her mind but she dismissed them. This was not the time to start exploring, and nor was it the time to begin hunting about for pencils or reels of cotton. She reminded herself that the Minotaur with its human body and bull's head was only a legend. The business about seven maidens and seven youths being fed to it each year was a legend as well. Anyway, the cat-headed thing had only been carrying one boy. Yes, but he couldn't carry seven altogether, he'd have to bring them down one at a time . . . Stop it, Elinor!

The sensible thing would be to go to the marked tunnel and find out if there was another exit there. Probably there was. Probably there were any number. She would get out without any difficulty and she would go to the nearest police station or a phone box, and in a very short time she would be back in her flat and explaining all this to some nice sympathetic police officer.

She reached the top of the stone steps. The trap door was above her head, as if it might be sunk into the floor of a room directly above. It was easily reachable, and Elinor levered it up a cautious inch so that she had a thin line of vision without making her presence too apparent. There would not be any bull-headed (or cat-headed) things on the other side, and there would not be seven maidens and seven men queuing for ritual slaughter. But it was better to be wary.

Beyond the trap door was a long wide room with what looked like corrugated-sheet walls and a vaulted roof, criss-crossed with girders. And there's gas lighting, she thought, disbelievingly. Is it? Yes, those are the brackets. I can hear it spitting and I can see it flickering. Does that mean there's someone there? Dare I go up? Well, I've got to do something. She pushed back the trap door and stepped up into the huge room.

The gas jets flickered in the current of air from the opening of the hatch, and shadows leaped across the walls, making Elinor's heart miss several more beats. She looked about her. An old warehouse? Packing cases and boxes were stacked at one end, and in the middle was an untidy heap of discarded furniture: old wardrobes and ancient desks with scarred surfaces; chaise longues with the fabric torn and dirty; a couple of oval cheval mirrors, the glass dim and spotted. Thrust against one wall were a dozen or so elaborate straight-backed chairs.

It was a warehouse or it might even be a disused wharf. How near to the river was it? There was a stench of something too sweet and pulpy somewhere that made you think of over-ripe fruit leaking decay through its skin, but she might still have the smell of those appalling tunnels in her nostrils.

She moved towards the jumble of old furniture, scanning the shadowy corners, trying to see if the cat-head man's victim was lying helplessly in one of the corners. There was a bad moment when her face swam into eerie reflection in the dim drowned depths of one of the mirrors, the eyes huge and terrified, so that for a moment she thought someone was peering at her through the thick smeary gloom.

Elinor gasped involuntarily and stepped back, and it was then that she heard the whispering.

Chapter Eleven

Her heart came up into her throat and she whipped round at once, scanning the room frenziedly. Someone in here with me.

The whispering came again, echoing about her head, glancing off the walls and shivering through the far-off roof girders.

'A pretty little one for the sacrifice ... A plump juicy one, fair-skinned and wide-eyed ...'

It was the most terrifyingly menacing thing Elinor had ever heard but she summoned up her last shred of courage and said loudly, 'Who's there? Who is that?' Her voice came out shrill with fear, and for answer there was a slurry chuckle, the kind of chuckle that made you think of repulsive words like phlegm and mucus.

'I smell the blood of an English girl ... Come into my parlour, little English girl ... Come inside and let me stroke you ... Let me part your white thighs and stand between them while I peel back your skin.'

'Who are you?' shouted Elinor, and the echoes came back at her: *ARE YOU ... are you ... are you ...* She began to retreat to the trap door again. A quick dive down and back through the tunnels. But the tunnels were a dead end; the cellar door was locked. And supposing the owner of the voice followed her? She had a brief vivid image of herself running frantically through the darkness, becoming hopelessly lost, with something pursuing her greedily all the time.

'I'm not alone, you know!' she cried defiantly. 'There

are people waiting for me upstairs!' This sounded, even to her own ears, so much like defiant whistling in the dark that for good measure she added, 'They'll be here any minute!'

For answer there was a volley of laughter. 'We're alone, my dear,' said the voice. 'We're all alone – you and me and the dead men—' It lingered on the word *dead*, and Elinor shuddered.

'I don't believe you!' she shouted. 'I don't believe any of what you're saying!'

'We're down among the dead men,' said the dreadful voice. 'And you're shut in with me, my dear – isn't that a beautiful thought? Tamerlane's people brought you for me, just as they've brought all the others.' It paused, and Elinor thought: oh dear heaven, I was *right*! It really is the Minotaur at the centre of the labyrinth, being fed sacrifices. And I'm its next sacrifice . . .

The voice said, 'I'm going to stalk you through the darkness. And no matter how fast you run I shall catch you, and no matter how you try to hide I shall find you.' There was a sudden gloating inhalation of breath. 'And the longer it takes to catch you,' said the voice, 'the *hungrier* I shall be.'

It was the cat-headed man. It absolutely had to be. There was some kind of vent somewhere – an old-fashioned speaking tube, the kind once used in Victorian houses for the master to summon the servants from below . . . Who on earth would fit a speaking tube from sewers into a storehouse?

Elinor said, 'Only cowards hide and shout threats in the dark! Why don't you come out into the open!' And thought: I don't believe I've actually said that. What do I do if he does come out in the open? Is it better to see the enemy, even if it proves to be a slavering maniac or a half-human Greek fable?

She scanned the room again and then began to advance cautiously to the jumble of furniture at the centre because if she could arm herself with a weapon she might have a

111

fighting chance. The brass candlestick? Yes, good enough. Her hand closed about it; it felt comfortingly heavy and strong.

The voice had stopped, and the only sound now was the soft hissing of the gaslights. But he's waiting, thought Elinor. He's listening and maybe even watching – I can feel him watching! – and he's rubbing his hands together in anticipation because he can smell the blood of an English girl . . .

'Shall we play hide and seek in the tunnels?' whispered the voice, and Elinor jumped. 'Would you play that with me, little white-skinned, soft-fleshed one?'

'You're mad!' shouted Elinor. 'Whoever you are, you're mad!' The echoes came back at her. *You're MAD . . . mad . . . mad . . .*

There was the sound of movement from behind the cartons and packing cases – someone climbing down from the stacked-up boxes – and a figure walked towards her.

In the moment when it was still in the deep shadow cast by the packing cases, Elinor's heart lurched. She took a firmer grip on the brass candlestick. She had no idea what she was going to see, but she was prepared for anything by this time. The cat-headed man again; one of the centre's down-and-outs, roaringly high on meths or drugs; the Minotaur growling for its yearly sacrifice – even the ghost of the recluse.

But as the figure came into one of the blurred circles of light, her senses spun in disbelief. A ghost after all, but a ghost from the future. I'm either looking at a splinter of the past or something yet to come, thought Elinor in confusion.

Her first shocked response, that this was Lewis Chance, vanished as quickly as it had come. This was not Lewis: this was a boy of twenty-three or -four, darker-haired and lighter-skinned. But apart from that the resemblance was astonishing; this was Lewis as he might have looked nearly

112

thirty years ago, in the days before the whiplash created by his father's scandal had made him don that courteous impenetrable armour. The same silver eyes and thin fastidious lips and narrow sensitive hands. The unmistakable damn-your-eyes arrogance of the portrait that hung over the desk and that occasionally showed in Lewis. Lewis's son? Was that possible?

The young man smiled and said in a perfectly ordinary voice, 'How do you do? Did I frighten you just now?'

'I – well, yes.' Elinor's voice came out tinny with fear.

'I wasn't sure who you were. And I know all the things that frighten people. I save them up and use them.'

'To – frighten people?'

'Yes.' He smiled, and for a second his eyes glinted redly. Elinor braced herself for a sudden attack, but then he said, 'You weren't brought by Tamerlane's people, were you.' He said this also in a perfectly ordinary voice, and not as a question but as someone suddenly making a discovery.

Elinor stared at him. 'No. No, I wasn't. I'm Elinor Craven. But I – don't know who you are.'

'My name is Grendel.' There was no trace of the thick evil whispering now: he spoke with careful politeness, like a child remembering its manners. Elinor, feeling reality spinning away again, said, 'Who is Tamerlane?'

'His people serve Touaris,' said Grendel. 'I serve Touaris as well. They bring me the sacrifices. They've done so for a long time now – lots and lots of sacrifices.' He nodded to himself like a child hugging a secret, and suddenly beckoned to Elinor. 'Come here and I'll show you.'

The classic line. Come over here, my dear, and let me show you something . . . I could run back into the tunnels, but he'd surely come after me. And I've got the candlestick: if he springs I'll smash it down on his head. Only I hadn't bargained for his looking so like Lewis.

Grendel had walked back to the corner where he had

first appeared, and was pointing. Elinor followed the line of his finger and said, 'I can't see—'

'There!' There was a sudden imperiousness in his tone and Elinor's stomach lurched with panic. 'All in there!' cried Grendel, and bent down, crouching over the floor. Elinor, keeping a tight hold of the candlestick and resolving to use it if she had to, took a step nearer and for the first time saw round the corner of the stacked boxes. Horror reared up and slammed into her mind.

The old storeroom was not completely underground but it was plainly a little below ground level, more or less level with parts of the disused sewer culverts like the one she had come through earlier. Directly behind Grendel, near to the floor and barely eight feet long, was another of the grilled half-windows with the same black vertical bars and the same dank green waterlight seeping through. But beyond the grille—

It was one of those moments when your brain does not immediately make sense of the images conveyed by your eyes. Elinor's brain received a confused impression of meaty carcases pressing against the grille: butchered animals that had been forced into the tunnel and heaped against the bars in a macabre bonfire pile of bloodied torsos and gaping wounds livid with dried blood, and chewed-off hands and legs... *Chewed-off*... Elinor gasped and took an involuntary step backwards and the monstrous jigsaw kaleidoscoped into an understandable shape.

Human bodies. They were human bodies. Corpses. Because we're down among the dead men, Elinor. Yes, that's what he meant. Dead men, at least six or eight of them, all flung into a messy heap, flopping over one another like Bonfire Night guys. I can see the eyes and they're glazed and open like dead fish, but they're unmistakably human eyes. Whoever they were, they died screaming, because I can see their mouths as well, and they're stretched wide. They died in screaming agony,

114

thought Elinor, appalled. Or they died pleading for mercy, perhaps. And then rigor mortis set in and they stayed screaming and pleading . . .

The boy brought here by the cat-headed man lay against the wall, his head lolling back, his eyes rolled upwards. Elinor noted with detached irrelevance that he was wearing a velvet jacket of the kind that very young people without much money bought, and that looked good for about two weeks before the thin cheapness showed. He looked as if he were dead.

Grendel was reaching down to the grille as if he were going to open it, and Elinor cried, 'No, don't! Leave them! Please leave them there!'

The thick bubbling chuckle welled up from Grendel's throat and Elinor felt the sudden fearsome *otherness*, the dark persona of the creature who had whispered through the darkness, surfacing again.

She fought for calm because there must be a perfectly sane solution to all this. The bodies might not be human after all: the warehouse might be the outlet to a slaughterhouse or a butchery. Or, conceivably, she might be going mad. This seemed the likeliest solution of all, because outside of the grimmer stories of Grimm nobody stored chewed-up human beings in a drain and crouched crooningly over them, caressing the dead flesh through iron bars.

Nobody but a madman. Understanding broke then. He is a madman, maybe schizophrenic. Split personality. Whatever medical label you give it he's that creature the papers have been writing about – the Canning Town Butcher or the Ripper reincarnation or something. Gay Jack – yes, they called him that as well, because most of the disappearances were male prostitutes. Was the boy in the fake velvet jacket a male prostitute? And all those poor things in the culvert as well? And there are people feeding his madness – Tamerlane's people he called them. It's some kind of cult, involving sacrifice and murder and he's at the head of it.

Grendel stood up in a single fluid movement and turned to look at her. Madness, glaring and unmistakable, blazed from his eyes and Elinor took a firmer grip on the candlestick.

'You see what I've done,' said Grendel, his voice thick and slurry. This was the whispering voice again – funny, I never thought a maniac killer would have an attractive voice, but he has. 'I've done everything,' said Grendel softly. 'All the sacrifices – and I *enjoyed* the sacrifices.' To Elinor's horror he began to salivate, slavering mouth fluids spilling out and running down his jaw. His tongue came out to lick the running wetness and his lips drew back from his teeth in a snarl. His hands were opening and closing hungrily, and there was a moment when the planes of his face seemed almost to shift and become leaner, the upper lip lengthening, the nose flattening, Dr Jekyll becoming Mr Hyde . . . No, more like the metamorphosis of the poor cursed werewolf.

'I'm not supposed to take girls,' said Grendel. 'Touaris wouldn't want girls. And you aren't pretty. But you're nice. You have a face people like to look at. You have a face I'd like to paint. I'd paint you against a thunderstorm or a sun sinking into an ocean.' He came closer, slowly, like a stalking cat, and for ten dreadful seconds Elinor was caught in mesmerised terror. At any moment he'll leap forward. He's going to kill me. He'd like to paint me, but he's still going to kill me. He isn't sane, of course. He's scarcely even human. I didn't really see his features blur like that, did I? And that lovely voice – that *cultured* voice – it's treacly with madness and blood lust. He sounds educated – I don't know why that should be odd, because you can as easily be torn to bits by an educated maniac as by an illiterate one. One hand on a Shakespeare sonnet, the other on a dripping axe. I think I'm becoming hysterical. Can I stun him with the candlestick, I wonder? I could run, but there isn't anywhere to run to. I don't think I can even move.

Grendel leaped and Elinor fell back, lifting the candlestick ready to strike.

There was the cold slither of iron on the floor and Grendel was jerked back. He's chained! thought Elinor incredulously. He's chained to the wall!

Only the cold scrape of the chains on the concrete floor stopped Elinor from descending into complete hysteria. She fell back against the wall, Grendel's screams of rage ringing about her head.

He had rounded on the chains, dragging at them in fury, and Elinor sank in a shivering huddle on the ground, wrapping her arms about her body in fear.

The chains were holding and he could not reach her. This was instantly apparent. He spent several minutes fighting the restraints, his lips drawn back in a snarl and his hands pulling against the links so ferociously that Elinor began to fear he might actually snap them. Keeping her eyes on him she reached for the heavy candlestick again.

But wherever the chains were anchored they were held firmly and after what seemed an age, Grendel gave up. The madness in his face and his eyes dimmed and he lifted his head and looked about him in a bewildered manner. Elinor felt an unexpected tug of pity because quite suddenly he was like a puzzled child. The resemblance to Lewis was so strong that her heart twisted.

He looked across at her and she thought he was about to speak. But then he turned his head, listening. At the same instant Elinor heard the sounds of footsteps below the trap door. Someone was coming along the tunnels.

Hope warred with panic – someone coming to rescue me? or someone coming to catch me! – and the trap door began to lift. The monstrous cat-head was grotesquely silhouetted against the sick rippling twilight of the tunnels.

He came up into the warehouse, bounding forward with terrifying swiftness, and sprang on Elinor at once, knocking the candlestick from her hand with a sharp blow across her wrist bone, and twisting her arms painfully behind her. Elinor fought, struggling and kicking, trying to bring one leg sharply up in the time-honoured ruse of a knee in the groin, but he overpowered her easily and pulled her across to the wall. There was the cold scrape of steel and Elinor felt with horrified disbelief a chain circle her waist. There was the click of a padlock snapping home.

He threw her to the ground and although she scrambled to her feet at once, he was already out of her reach, crossing to the gas jets and reaching up to adjust them. Stronger light leaped up, sending the shadows scurrying back into the corners, and the man finally turned to survey Grendel.

Grendel said, 'Timur. Have you come to prepare for the feast?'

Timur. The pronouncing of the name reduced the man's sinister aura a little. Elinor waited, and presently the cat-headed man spoke for the first time. The mask muffled his voice only a little.

'The feast will be on Sunday night,' he said. 'That is the day after tomorrow, and also the ancient Feast of Sekhet, the lioness-headed goddess of war.'

'War,' said Grendel softly.

'Yes. War between our people and the people of Tashkara. That is why the day has been chosen,' said Timur. 'The League of Tamerlane will assemble here and you will be given homage.' He spoke in English, but there was a foreign intonation that Elinor could not place.

Grendel drew in a quick breath of delight and Elinor saw that the faintly bewildered look had vanished and the mad alter ego was surfacing. Mr Hyde sliding into carnivorous mode; nice Dr Jekyll sloughing his skin again. And this time I'm chained and if he reaches me I won't be able to run away.

'The day after tomorrow,' said Grendel, his eyes on Timur. 'Sekhet's Feast.'

'Yes. Our feast also.'

The masked face turned to regard Elinor and when Grendel said greedily, 'It must be a worthy feast – a great feast,' Elinor almost believed that the cruel cat-mouth smiled.

Timur said, 'It will be a very worthy feast. It will herald the start of our plan to overturn the old tired regime of our people and bring Tashkara to the world's notice.

'At midnight on Sunday we will chant the time-worn ritual that was once used inside the stone palace of Tashkara; we will pay homage to Touaris, and we will fire the Burning Altar of our ancestors.' And then, turning back to where Elinor crouched against the wall, he said, softly, 'And you will have all the victims you wish.'

Chapter Twelve

Extract from Patrick Chance's Diary

Tibet, June 1888

If the gorge leading to the ancient stone palace is awe-inspiring at night, it's breathtaking by day. Have never seen such towering splendour, although even with the early morning sun pouring over the crags – a rose and gold river of pure light and impossibly beautiful – I'm aware of a dark menacing undercurrent.

Theodore has decided to paint watercolour of scene before we set off – 'As a record,' he says solemnly, as guileless as if he thinks I don't guess he's trying to delay our arrival at the mysterious palace, if not avoid it altogether.

Pointed out we had not come four thousand miles to paint mountain vistas, and in any case secretly doubt Theo's ability to capture scene, since his forays into the world of art so far have been solely botanical. Making anatomically correct studies of snowdrops and *Calendula officinalis* (pot marigold to the rest of us), hardly ideal training for doing justice to the sweeping grandeur of the Himalayas or the dark romance of a Tibetan mountain palace, several centuries old and probably drenched in pagan religion. Also, he left his paintbox in Lhasa.

Left him furrowing his brow over precise little

charcoal sketch, and went off to inspect rope bridge which seems to be only way across gorge. Even from a distance it looks extremely perilous and I have an uneasy suspicion that walking on it will be very nasty indeed.

Later. I was right. The bridge is suspended across the gorge, and a ramshackle affair of cables and ropes and bits of brushwood it is. The least breath of wind sends it swinging creakily back and forth, and if you missed your footing or a rope snapped you would be smashed to pieces below. The river hurls itself along the bottom of the gorge directly beneath, crashing against the rocks and sending up spume and misty vapour so that the swaying bridge is constantly enveloped in clouds of fine spray.

Am beginning to regret very much indeed that last grandiloquent gesture that drove me across two continents, when probably a couple of months in Kitzbühel or Monte would have satisfied Father and old Inchcape, to say nothing of Thos. Cook's man. The thing is, I had not really visualised quite such massive desolation. I would feel a whole lot better if the Sherpas had not run away last night: all very well for Theo to say they were probably frightened by some local superstition. Sherpas not given to excess of sensibility, or not that I ever heard about.

Am writing this in stone chamber with stub of candle made from yak fat (or something equally repulsive) as only means of light. We're inside the stone palace at last, and I think the setting down of what has happened may be a calming exercise. God knows I need something to calm me.

Must do Theo the justice to admit he has not once said, 'I told you so.' What he has said is that it might be sensible to record everything in the diary in hope that someday someone will find it – clutched in our blackened skeletal fingers, presumably.

But if I'm writing a diary at all, I'm writing it so that my descendants (whoever they might be) will be able to have some fun out of it.

Between Theo's reluctance (he managed to make his sketching last until noon), and my reconnaissance, we set out across the gorge much later than we – that is, I, – had intended. Theo had never intended to set out at all if he could help it.

The setting sun was unfurling thousands of oriflammes that blazed across the skies: banners of crimson and burning gold that streamed over the entire horizon, so that the sky itself seemed close enough to touch and we both remembered about being on the roof of the world. Directly in front of us the mountain fortress was drenched in pouring fire, and for a moment I could have believed we were looking on the rose-red city half as old as time, except that Petra could never have been nearly so beautiful. Far below us the swirling river was a torrent of molten bronze so that as we crossed the bridge we might have been fording Kubla Khan's ancient sacred Alph, or travelling through the fire-streaked skies of Aegia. (Refuse to apologise for outbreak of rhetoric, since have never seen anything to equal unearthly beauty of Tashkara on that sunset evening.)

'The river turns that colour because of the copper salts in the rocks,' said Theo unnecessarily.

Two-thirds of the way across the rope bridge began to shudder and creak ominously (the rope floor was all of two feet at the *widest* part), and Theo became convinced it was about to snap and deposit us in the river, so we abandoned poetical rhapsodies and dived for the far end. It was certainly remarkably eerie that the sun sank behind the peaks at that precise instant, plunging the entire crag into shadow as we stepped on to it, and it was unfortunate that a section of the bridge did indeed fall away.

'Impassable.' said Theo, surveying it. 'We can't go back.'

'We don't want to go back, we want to go forward.'

'It's an omen, Patrick, mark my words.'

'Oh, balls.'

At the centre of the ancient palace we made out huge stone pillars with iron gates, approached by a roughish path with the cliffs rising steeply on each side, shutting out the last slivers of daylight. I summoned up a few rallying calls as we went, to cheer Theo along, but only got as far as, 'Cry God for Harry, England and St George' (I left out 'Into the Valley of Death/Rode the six hundred' on grounds that it was a bit too close to home for comfort), when Theo suddenly said, 'Patrick. There's someone watching us.'

Have to say this was the most chilling thing yet. The watcher was standing above us on a narrow shelf of rock, and with the sheer cliff-face behind him and the shadows enshrouding him like a ghostly mantle he was an extraordinarily sinister sight. He was clad in a long grey cloak with a deep hood hiding his face and wide full sleeves, which added to his air of mystery.

'Is he one of the lama monks, do you suppose?' whispered Theo. 'I thought they all wore yellow robes and carried prayer wheels.'

'They do.'

The figure had turned away from us and was touching a glowing taper to bronze – or maybe even gold – wall sconces that seemed to have been hammered into the rockface. Light flared up, flickering wildly in the night wind that was scurrying in from the mountains, and the flames cast fantastical silhouettes.

Could not forbear thinking of all those unpleasant legends where sinister anonymous beings lure unsuspecting humans into mountain fastnesses for any number of grisly reasons.

But the bridge was down and the bitter Tibetan night was already stealing over the mountains, and there was nothing for it but to go forward. In any case I was curious by this time; I wanted to know who these people were who hid themselves away in their desolate mountain citadel, because whatever else they were they were certainly not lama monks. We had met several of these on our journey: some had been small travelling parties of twos and threes, others had been hermits eking out a sparse existence in caves, living partly on charity, partly on scavenging and partly on nothing at all. We had shared our food with them – Buddhist monks are forbidden meat and alcohol but nuts and fruit seemed always welcome – and communicated by means of signs and the odd word of each other's language picked up along the way, and by goodwill. They are an interesting people, these monks, gentle and philosophic and remarkably happy. I had said to Theo that there seemed to be a good deal in favour of a contemplative life, to which he had replied uncompromisingly, 'What about the celibacy?' Think he may have formed an exaggerated idea of my sexual requirements, although suppose he can't be blamed.

But whatever this grey-robed figure above us was, he was clearly not a monk.

It was at this stage that I began to have the uneasy feeling that we might have disturbed something better left alone, but it was too late now and we followed the cloaked figure along the narrow path until we came to the palace entrance.

The gates might have been built for some ancient race of giants: the stone columns flanking them were

124

easily fifteen feet high and, as we approached, night shadows were already wreathing them in violet and indigo. I had the impression of stone gargoyle faces looking down on us but in the gathering twilight it was impossible to be sure. On each side were more of the elaborate bronze torch-holders, each with a flaring cresset of wood. The hooded figure stood framed in the gates, watching us, and when he spoke Theo and I both jumped because he spoke English.

'You wish to enter, travellers?'

We looked at one another. Then I said, 'We do. We saw you lighting the path and in our world that would indicate that travellers are welcome.'

'The path is always lit,' said the cloaked figure.

'By you?'

'Tonight it was my task. The lighting of the boundaries,' said the figure, 'is a very old custom out here.'

Whoever he was he spoke and understood English well. But I was aware of the prickle of fear again, because his voice was harsh and blurred and there was something wrong about it. It was like listening to the notes of a musical instrument, once beautiful and precise in tone, but shut away and forgotten for centuries. The word *tarnished* formed on my mind.

Theodore said, 'You are part of a community? You live in the palace?'

'The palace is a frontier. A gateway.'

'To where?'

'The city of Tashkara,' said the man. 'But that is a place forbidden to all travellers. No man is ever permitted to enter Tashkara.'

'Why not?'

'Because of the ancient secrets,' said the man, which, as I pointed out to Theo later, was the kind of vague sinister remark that sounded as if it meant a good deal but actually said absolutely nothing at all.

125

The man said in his spoiled voice, 'You would do better to return to wherever you come from.'

'We can't,' I said. 'We can't get back across the gorge. The bridge has collapsed.' I looked at him, trying to penetrate the deep hood, but there was only the faint glint of eyes within. 'If you could give us shelter tonight we would be very grateful.'

'And in the morning? You would leave in the morning?'

Theo and I exchanged glances again. 'Yes,' I said. 'By daylight we will probably be able to mend the bridge and return the way we came.'

This, of course, was a monumental untruth, because I had absolutely no intention of going back the way we had come, even if the bridge was repairable. I wanted to see the inside of the ancient palace, but more than that I wanted to see the city of Tashkara with its ancient secrets, whatever they turned out to be. Forbidden cities and ancient secrets probably litter the whole of Tibet, but they aren't something you come across in Chelsea very often. So I trod on Theo's foot just as he was drawing breath to say that the bridge was certainly beyond repair, and said, 'We would be no trouble to you or your people. We have food with us which we will gladly share, and we could pay—'

The man said at once, 'There is no question of accepting payment,' and for the first time his beautiful distorted voice held a note of arrogance. Whoever he was, he was accustomed to commanding. 'But it is better that you are not in company with us at all. Even for a single night.'

'Why?'

'There is danger,' said the man and although he did not quite shrug, by now he had clearly accepted the inevitable. He stepped back and indicated to us to enter.

As we passed through the stone pillars flanking the gates a little breath of wind caused the wall torches to flare up, illuminating the leering gargoyles above. It was as well that Theo did not see it, because he would have been sure to think it another evil portent. As things turned out he would have been quite right.

Directly inside the gates was a large courtyard paved with stone and set here and there with carven idols in niches and alcoves. I made out several portrayals of Buddha, the face expressing that remarkable serenity and wisdom that no other religion ever quite achieves, and there were the squat shapes of stone chortens which are a bit like elaborate cairns, but often house the ashes of dead holy men. These were shoulder-high and in the gathering dusk they looked like crouching monsters waiting to pounce. It was absurd to think they were creeping up behind us as we crossed the courtyard. I remembered about keeping them on our right: the Thos. Cook man had been very explicit about that. 'Walk clockwise around the halls of all monasteries, and keep shrines and prayer banks and chortens on your right shoulder,' he had said firmly. 'It's important to show respect at all times in Tibet.' If any of my descendants ever do read these diaries, at least they'll know that whatever else I was, I was never discourteous.

It was very quiet and very still inside the palace, with an eerie silence that made me want to keep glancing behind me because nothing, not even a Tibetan monastery, could possibly be this silent. Not that this turned out to be a Tibetan monastery. If only it had.

Our companion stayed some little distance from us and pointed to the far side of the courtyard, to what looked like a small stone outbuilding with narrow windows. 'There you may rest until light,' he said. 'Then you can leave.'

Now I admit that neither of us had been expecting deferential servants or a Kettners or Café Royal supper hastily prepared in our honour – 'Dear me, sirs, *of course* it's no trouble, and we always get the theatre crowds in about this time anyway' – or cans of hot water brought in by acquiescent chambermaids (this last a pity). But it had not occurred to either of us – at least, it had not occurred to me – that we would not even be shown to a room and provided with the means to wash. Theo said later this was natural arrogance and due to my having been spoiled from birth, but this is unfair. Arrogant or not, this off-hand dismissal, to say nothing of banishing us to what looked like the Tibetan equivalent of the cow-shed (yak-shed?), set my teeth on edge. Whatever else people might say about the British no one can say they take kindly to being dismissed to yak-sheds.

So I said sharply, 'What is this place? And who are your people?'

'This is the gateway to the city of Tashkara.'

'You said that before. But we still don't know who you are.' I waited, and the cloaked figure seemed to flinch for a moment as if an immense weight had been placed across his shoulders and as if he were summoning strength to bear it. Then he seemed to stand up straighter, and turning so that the moonlight fell across him, he pushed back the hood and stood with the cool silver moonlight shining on his face.

At first I thought it was a huge dog who stood there and wild ideas of some kind of freakish mating ritual skittered across my mind. This was something not wholly human: it was a giant hound that had learned human speech and ways and put on human clothes.

And then the blurred voice said, 'The leonine appearance is characteristic of some stages of the disease. The nose flattens as the bone dissolves and the cheeks become pendulous.' His tone was so dispassionate, yet so edged with defiant bravery, that the grisly visions splintered and formed in a different pattern.

But neither Theo nor I spoke, and after a moment the man said, 'I am sorry to subject you to it, but only by seeing would you have believed and understood. And in other circumstances, gentlemen, I should take your hand in the ancient courteous gesture of welcome and I should invite you to join me and my people at our evening meal. But you understand that to touch me is very unsafe for you.'

Theo made an abrupt movement and then was still. I was staring at the man – I'm ashamed to admit it, but I could not look away – and the dreadful pattern was locking into place, and pity and fear and dawning comprehension were all tumbling chaotically through my mind. Fragments of barely known, half-forgotten knowledge jostled for recognition, and with them memories of terrible superstitions surrounding an old, old disease, disfiguring beyond imagination and fiercely contagious, and progressing relentlessly to an early and agonising death.

Leprosy. We were about to spend the night inside a leper colony.

Lewis had taken a train to Bath, partly because he wanted to avoid the M4 commuters, but mostly because he enjoyed railway journeys.

It was not something you were supposed to do these days. You were supposed to complain bitterly about the rail services, and make jokes about the food and the lateness of the trains. Much better – much more convenient – to go to and fro by road, said people.

But Lewis, who disliked driving and found motorways tedious, liked trains. He enjoyed the atmosphere of railway stations with all the transience of travellers and the anticipation of dozens of different journeys. He rarely spoke to fellow travellers but he liked the brief propinquity as much as the anonymity. You got the same kind of thing at airport lounges, of course, and ferry terminals.

He bought a newspaper at Paddington and unfolded it when he reached his seat. All kinds of awfulness in the headlines as usual: wars and famines and plunging economies and recessions. There was another of the half-sensationalist, half-prurient articles about the disappearances of male prostitutes in London's East End. Lewis read it with only half of his mind. It was the kind of thing the press hyped up these days, and if the disappearances had not taken place close to Jack the Ripper's old hunting ground, and if most of them had not been rent boys, the national press would never have bothered with the story.

He folded the paper and sipped his cooling coffee, staring unseeingly through the window. The press would make an even greater hype over Grendel if they knew about him: Raffael had seen that at once. He had not believed Lewis's story about a kidnapping; Lewis had not expected him to. Because, of course, Grendel had not been kidnapped.

Grendel.

Through the modern sounds of the swaying train and of other passengers talking and a faint distorted hum from somebody's Walkman across the aisle, Lewis felt his mind loop back, and the dark ancient evil that he had fought to bury, begin to uncoil once more.

He had been thinking of the journalists as he crossed the perilous rope bridge to the ancient stone palace all those years ago. The son of the disgraced Charles Chance had still been strong news in those days, and Lewis had thought with cynical amusement how livid the press would have been at missing such a piece of copy as this and how they would have had a field day with the headlines.

'Dishonoured banker's son enters cannibal lair...
Charles Chance went into the money-lenders' den and lost
his head: now his son goes intrepidly into that of the
carnivores...'

Cal, the guide, had not viewed it as intrepid; in fact he
had viewed it as suicide. He had fled, shaking his head in
horror at the madness of the Englishman who went out in
the midday sun to meet the Flesh-Eaters, but before he
fled Lewis had persuaded him to return in two days' time
at noon for the journey back to Lhasa.

'Because I shan't pay you until we're both safely back.'

'Sir, I would give up all the wealth of my ancestors,
ten-fold, not to face the Flesh-Eaters.'

Lewis was inclined to be extremely sceptical about
flesh-eating tribes in the twentieth century – unless you
were going to count beefy-jowled gentlemen who dined
richly in London clubs – and he was exasperated rather
than anything else by Cal's behaviour. But he let him go
with a cursory nod and, without looking to see in which
direction Cal went, turned to face the awe-inspiring
mountain palace across the gorge.

Negotiating the rope bridge was awkward and his
balance tilted dangerously for the first few feet, but it was
not as bad as he had feared. He looked once at the
foaming hurling river below and did not look again.

When he finally reached the other side he was light-
headed and dazzled by the pure clear light, but he was
safe. He rested for an hour – he was fairly well adjusted to
the altitude by this time, but it still took its toll – sipped
some Evian water from the bottle in his haversack, and
then set off along the narrow cliff path that wound up to
the stone gates. Giants' gates, Patrick had called them:
the gates to hell. Why had Patrick seen them as that?
Because of the Decalogue? Even the silent acknowledgement of the word sent shivers of apprehension through his
mind. But you might as well face it, thought Lewis, this is
what this is all about: the ancient Stone Tablets of the lost

Tribe of the Bubasti. The Taskhara Decalogue. It's got a seductively evocative ring to it – I don't blame Patrick for trying to find them. I don't suppose he'd blame me either. I shan't find them, of course, because I don't believe they exist. But I shan't be able to forget about them until I've disproved Patrick's story.

Patrick had called the Stone Tablets Satan's Decalogue, but it was probably better not to trust entirely a young man who had left that astonishing account of dark romance and ancient allure but who, in modern parlance, had ducked out in the end. He told a good deal, thought Lewis between exasperation and admiration, but he kept a good deal back as well. From a spirit of mischief, or from fear? For all Lewis knew, Patrick could have been on the payroll of Thomas Cook and the whole legend of the Tashkara Decalogue a nineteenth-century publicity stunt. I don't know what I'm going into, he thought a bit grimly. But here I go anyway.

It was faintly disconcerting to find that despite the thin translucent daylight, the twisted bronze wall brackets did indeed hold burning torches. Lewis paused, eyeing them. Lights always left burning for the traveller... But how many travellers would come this way in the course of a year? His sense of unreality increased. But I wish Patrick hadn't written that about the gates of hell. Or, if he had to write it, I wish I hadn't remembered it.

The dark-clad figure standing silent and motionless inside the gates sent his heart racing with sudden fear, and he stopped abruptly. The light from the burning torches fell across the figure, and for a disconcerting moment Lewis thought his eyes showed red. And then the man stepped forward, smiling and holding out his hand and after all he was quite ordinary, dressed in unremarkable trousers and cotton shirt, and if he was not European, he was clearly not Eastern either. He had the black silky hair and the soaring cheekbones that Lewis associated with Eurasians, and his hair was worn rather long, although not in the lank Western fashion of the time. His skin was the colour of light clear honey and his eyes were not red but a hard clear green. There was absolutely no reason to be afraid of him.

The man said, in heavily accented but recognisable English, 'Welcome, traveller, to the palace of Tashkara.'

Chapter Thirteen

If he was a Flesh-Eater, he had very good manners. He took Lewis through the palace into a small cool room with a breathtaking view of the mountain, and slanting light falling in pure luminous swathes across the polished wooden floor. There was a narrow bed and a chair and a tiny deal table with an old-fashioned copper ewer filled with water. A tranquil-faced Buddha figure with a tiny brass burner beneath it looked down from a small alcove, and there was a drifting scent of something that in a Western church Lewis would have identified as incense.

'When you have washed and rested you will join us for supper? We shall eat in a little more than one hour from now. Someone will come to show you the way.'

'I really only intended to ask if I could rest here before going on,' said Lewis.

'But tonight we hold one of our feasts,' said the man, and a smile lifted his lips. 'You will be very welcome to join us.'

'Then thank you very much,' said Lewis. 'You speak very good English, by the way.'

'I learned it as a child from an English missionary worker.'

'Whoever he was he did a good job. I'm sorry, I don't know your name—'

'I am known as Kaspar,' said the man.

'Then thank you, Kaspar.' Lewis waited until the man turned to leave, and taking a deep breath, said, 'Tell me, do you know anything about Touaris?'

Touaris . . . It was as if he had dropped a stone into a quiet forest pool, or scratched a jagged fingernail across thin silk. The name rasped on the air with jarring dissonance. Kaspar stopped abruptly in the act of opening the door and looked back at Lewis. I've rattled him, thought Lewis. I don't think I'll mention the Decalogue yet; I'll see how he copes with this first.

Kaspar was regarding Lewis unblinkingly and for an instant it was as if a veil had lifted, and there was a brief vivid glimpse of something alien and cruel. Lewis felt an icy finger trace a path down his spine, but he met the man's regard levelly and at last Kaspar said, 'Where did you hear of Touaris?' He pronounced it almost as Lewis had done, but there was a noticeably different emphasis.

'I don't recall,' said Lewis untruthfully. 'Perhaps it was mentioned in Lhasa. What is Touaris?'

There was another of the pauses, this time as if Kaspar was considering how to answer. Then he said, 'Touaris was a tribal queen who ruled over her people in the valley beyond this palace for many centuries. Once the palace was one of the gateways to her realm. You have a word – fortress? Meaning a guarding place.'

'Bastion, perhaps. But – the same lady ruling for hundreds of years?' said Lewis disbelievingly.

'It is a very old legend,' said Kaspar. 'But it is possible that as each queen died a selected one took her place.'

'Like a female Dalai Lama?' Lewis had said it half flippantly, but Kaspar appeared to take it straight.

'Yes, that is a good way to explain it,' he said. 'The legend tells how she and her ancient religion were very closely guarded and that a terrible punishment was dealt to those who dared enter her realm.'

'The Forbidden City?' said Lewis lightly.

'There are many forbidden cities in Tibet,' said Kaspar dismissively. 'But the Tribe of Touaris has long since died out. You will join us for our feast?'

'I will.' Lewis did not say that he did not seem to have much choice.

'I shall send for you in an hour's time.'

'I shall be here.'

'Oh yes,' said Kaspar. 'You will be here.' He paused and added very softly, 'We shall enjoy having you at our table.'

He went out and Lewis sat down on the bed. Only someone monumentally thick-skinned would have missed the menace in Kaspar's voice, and only an absolute fool would fail to pick up the dark undercurrents. The fact that the setting had most of the elements of the classic horror story could be disregarded: the lone traveller requesting shelter in the remote mountain fortress: the hints of grisly practices from the frightened guide. And that Parthian shot: *We shall enjoy having you at our table.* It was all so obvious – it seemed so *contrived* – that you could say it was stagy, in fact you could very nearly say it was farcical. Look chaps, here comes another sucker, set up the atmospheric lighting and slap on the weird make-up. And then let's just run through the low-pitched *I-am-a-sinister-character* voice again, shall we . . .?

Thinking all this made Lewis feel very much better, although none of it altered the fact that there were any number of unpleasant fates that could befall lone travellers: you did not have to enter the fantastical realms of cannibalism or ritual slaughter to visualise them, either. 'Accidents' could happen very easily out here where there were no police or embassies or post mortems. A stumble on the hillside, a footing missed crossing the gorge . . . The Englishman has fallen to his death – how very unfortunate. Still, there are a good many valuable things in his knapsack, and there is a large sum of money as well.

Lewis frowned and got up to rinse away the grime of his travels. The water was soft and pure and it refreshed him physically and mentally. He dried his face and hands and moved to the window.

Under his room, some thirty or forty feet below, was a large courtyard enclosed on all sides by the palace walls. The smoky eastern twilight was already veiling the vast palace, but more burning torches had been thrust into the wall brackets and in the flickering light Lewis could see forty or fifty people apparently preparing for a banquet. They all bore a strong resemblance to Kaspar himself and to one another, although Lewis, watching unseen, thought this was to be expected in such a remote district where there would be inbreeding. The men all had straight black hair like watered silk, growing low on the forehead. Widow's peak? Vampire's brow? No, you can't have cannibals and vampires both together, that would be really overdoing it. The women were as tall as the men and well-muscled, and there did not seem to be any of the subservience that Lewis, recently come from the bra-burning women's libbers in England, had found so noticeable in Lhasa and Delhi.

They were arranging platters of fruit and bread near to what looked like a low stone table, roughly ten feet square, and several of the men were carrying out stone flagons which Lewis supposed contained wine. There was an air of festivity and they were all calling to one another and laughing, and although Lewis had no knowledge of their language he could hear the spiralling excitement. A growing fear tugged at his mind again. I think this is the time to beat a retreat. If I go now, while they're absorbed in their preparations, I might be able to creep through the palace unseen and out into the night. He remembered the dangers of the Tibetan night – wild animals, parties of marauding robbers, never mind hypothermia from the bitter cold – but he would rather face any of them or all of them than Kaspar's people.

In the courtyard one of the men began to tap against the sides of a deep-throated skin-drum, producing a steady rhythmic thrumming, so filled with dark throbbing anticipation that Lewis felt his scalp prickle. A death roll: a

137

dirge. Yes, but filled with such potency. It was at this point that the whole thing suddenly ceased to seem stagy and faintly absurd, and became menacing.

Kaspar's people were assembling on the edges of the courtyard, several of them holding burning torches aloft. Several more had joined the wine- and fruit-carriers, and it was impossible to avoid the impression of an audience gathering to witness some kind of spectacle. The flickering light poured over the scene, showering the watchers with twisting crimson and orange. Most of them wore only a narrow loin cloth made of some dark soft stuff, and the women had a twist of the same material over their breasts. The feeling that something was about to happen mounted, and Lewis's heart began to pound with fear and anticipation.

And then the women who had been setting up the stone table moved back to take their places, and for the first time Lewis had a clear view. A wave of cold sick horror lashed against his mind, and for a moment the small bare room spun around him.

The stone table was not a table at all; it was a huge open clay oven, fired from below: crude, but effective. Its surface was already throwing out fierce heat, and thick meaty-smelling smoke was beginning to drift across the courtyard. Lying along the centre of the oven was a long narrow terracotta pan, lipped and rimmed and slightly concave, fitting into a shallow depression scooped out of the oven. Even from here Lewis could see that the pan was exactly the shape and size of a human.

Cal had been right all the time. These people were Flesh-Eaters: they were cannibals and down there was their roasting oven. Dear God, I must get out of here before they come for me ... *I shall send for you in an hour's time* ... Lewis looked at the door. Supposing it was locked? Supposing there was no escape?

There was a flurry of commotion at the courtyard's far side and a door was flung open. Lewis turned back to see, and through the door came four of the black-haired men, half carrying, half dragging a struggling prisoner. He was naked and his hands were bound in front of him, but he was holding them cupped protectively over his groin in a piteous attempt to preserve a final shred of dignity. A rope halter was about his neck so that if he tried to escape he would be throttled.

Lewis recognised the prisoner at once, even though his features were distorted with terror, the eyes starting from the head with panic. Cal, the guide who had brought him here and then fled into the night. They had caught him. Did they have scouts out for lone travellers? Panic gripped him more fully and he was across the room and turning the door handle. It stuck and resisted at once. Locked. But you knew it would be. He walked slowly back to his post at the window.

Two of the men lifted Cal bodily and carried him shoulder-high towards the terrible oven. Lewis, gripping the sides of the small window so tightly that the stones cut into his skin, felt a violent surge of anticipation from the watchers. This was what they had been waiting for; this was their feast. The drum-beat increased: it built to a pulsating vibrancy, filled with sensual greed and swollen with crude sexual anticipation. Lewis was starting to feel very sick, but also dreadfully compelled by curiosity.

Cal knew what was going to happen to him. He was being carried towards the oven in horizontal native-bearer fashion, his head pointing towards it, and he had twisted round to stare at the glowing clay pan. As they bore him forward, he began to scream: terrible trapped-hare screams, pleading for mercy, fighting his gaolers and bringing up his bound hands in an attempt to claw his way free. But he won't do it, thought Lewis, in horror. They've got him in a grip of iron. Can I get through the window and somehow down the wall to him? But the courtyard was a sheer drop and the wall all around and beneath the window was smooth bland stone.

The watchers were swaying and Lewis caught a low chanting from them, a hypnotic measured resonance that reverberated all around the courtyard. The scene shimmered and blurred in the spiralling heat from the clay oven and the flaring torches, like an ancient portrayal of hell, and Lewis remembered Patrick's description of the giant gates of hell. I've passed through them, and I've descended into the fiery caverns. And there at the centre is the burning furnace . . .

The four men reached the oven and hoisted Cal above it, and Lewis saw his skin turn instantly scarlet from the fierce heat. There was a moment when they held him aloft, and when his body began to scorch, blistering and cracking and running with thick colourless fluid: human fat – the subcutaneous fat melting and oozing to the surface. As the smeary fluids dripped down over Cal's body and on to the hot clay, there was a furious spitting. A low murmur went through the watchers, and despite the belching heat from the Altar, Lewis felt cold sick terror fasten about his vitals.

The men had started to lower Cal: in ten seconds – five – he would be in that grisly clay pan and there was nothing Lewis could do to stop it. Cal was screaming, but his cries were almost drowned by the fierce heat-sizzle and the crowd were pressing forward, swaying with excitement, the chanting louder.

With a final smooth movement the four men dropped Cal straight into the waiting heat of the terracotta pan and a sigh swept the courtyard. The oven spat frenziedly, almost drowning the anguish of the creature already roasting to his death, and a greasy pall of smoke rose up.

Behind Lewis, a key scraped in the lock and as the door of his room opened he turned. Kaspar, with four of the black-haired men, stood there surveying him.

'Well, Englishman,' said Kaspar, the cruel curving smile lifting his lips, 'you have seen a little of our ways.'

'The Burning Altar,' said Lewis, still staring down into the courtyard. 'That's what that is, isn't it?'

'Yes. One of the most ancient rituals in the world.'

'And,' said Lewis, turning to regard Kaspar, 'one of the punishments of the Tashkara Decalogue?'

Kaspar became very still. At last he said, 'You know the legend of the Decalogue?'

'I do.' But please don't let him ask me how much I do know, thought Lewis in silent entreaty. Because what I know could be written on a postage stamp! Patrick, you bastard, why didn't you bequeath a bit more about that side of your journey instead of listing all the women you screwed?

But he held Kaspar's stare, and after a moment Kaspar said, 'The Burning Altar is the punishment for what we call jackals. Those who guide spies into a forbidden place.'

'It's also an echo of the ancient cult of hunting the gods and feasting on their cooked limbs,' said Lewis. 'And the roots of that religion are somewhere deep in ancient Egypt. Am I right?'

'Yes. How do you know that?'

'How do you?' countered Lewis.

'We are descended from a very ancient people. We follow customs that are older than Osiris himself.'

'How convenient,' said Lewis politely, 'that this particular custom fits so neatly with your inclinations.'

Kaspar smiled. 'All religions can be adapted,' he said. 'And we are sworn to guard the secret city of Touaris from intruders. Our reputation is known in Lhasa and only the very inquisitive or the simple-minded ever approach the palace.' The insult was implicit but it was clear. 'You preserve your Christian religion,' said Kaspar. 'Why should we not do the same with our religion?'

'Then,' said Lewis, 'Touaris still lives.'

'Oh yes, she still lives.'

Lewis glanced down at the courtyard. Cal was not quite dead; his body was the colour of half-cooked meat but he was still struggling feebly. His legs had curled up helplessly, drawn in by the heat like an insect's, and his hands were scarlet shrivelled claws.

Lewis turned back to Kaspar, the fragile outline of a plan beginning to form. It would probably be the biggest gamble he would ever take and it would depend on how superstitious these people were. But it was worth a try. He said, 'How can you be sure that you won't incur Touaris's wrath if you sacrifice me on the Burning Altar?'

'Why should we?'

'Have you never heard,' said Lewis, 'of the prophecy of the Traveller from the West? The One who will come to Tashkara and save it from a great catastrophe?' I'm very nearly in biblical country now, he thought. Dare I start in about plagues and scourges and seven-year curses? No, you fool, you'll ruin the whole thing! His heart was racing and his palms were wet with sweat but he met Kaspar's eyes levelly.

Kaspar said, 'There is no such prophecy,' but Lewis caught the note of doubt, and hope sprang up. I've rattled him! He doesn't really think I'm anything other than an ordinary traveller but he isn't sure. Oh God, I'm walking on ice so thin it'll probably crack at any minute and then they'll fling me into that grisly thing and I'll die in slow screaming agony. But if I keep my head I might just get away with it.

He said, 'You can't be sure. How many travellers would know of Touaris and the Decalogue? Remember I mentioned them both before you did.'

'Prove what you claim!' said Kaspar challengingly.

'That my coming here was foretold?' And *now* I'm descending into outright blasphemy!

'Yes,' said Kaspar. 'Prove it!'

'How?'

'Join our banquet.'

'As a victim?' said Lewis sarcastically.

'As a participant.'

The silence closed down again, and now there was something extraordinarily intimate about it. He knows exactly what I'm thinking, thought Lewis, staring at Kaspar. He knows what I'm thinking and I believe he knows what I'm feeling as well. What the hell do I do?

Several lifetimes ticked away and then he heard his own voice saying, 'Very well.'

'You are willing to eat from the table of the Burning Altar? To eat the flesh you have seen cooked tonight?'

Lewis said, 'I am willing.'

Chapter Fourteen

Extract from Patrick Chance's Diary

Tashkara, June 1888

This is an eerie place, quite aside from its being a colony of lepers.

The leper who met us (have not yet established his nationality but his name is Fenris and his English is excellent), says the palace has been used many times by nomad tribes: they live here for a few years, or a few generations, and then move on. It's fallen into strange hands during its long history, he says; evil hands. This I can believe, because I've never encountered a place so filled with brooding menace.

'But it is not the evil from the past that overshadows us, Patrick,' says Fenris. 'It is the evil that stalks us from the future, that waits for us in the shadows of our unfolded life, that we have most to fear.'

On reflection, do not think I have ever heard quite such a macabre pronouncement.

Later. Fierce argument with Theo who thinks we should stay safely shut away in our stone hut and set off at first light without seeing or speaking to any of the lepers.

'Because it's a sinister, hungry thing, leprosy,' he says, as if he visualises some kind of ravaged-faced Middle Ages Death symbol prowling the night in search of prey, rattling its crumbling bones and huffing its diseased breath through the cracks in the windows. 'A few hours here is as much as we dare risk, Patrick.'

But I'm curious about these people, and – although I haven't admitted this to Theo – I would like to feel more comfortable about them. To ignore them tonight and walk away in the morning would only make me feel even worse.

(Wonder if this is the feeling that really charitable people experience. Like giving your last coin to a starving beggar, because it's less agonising to feel hungry yourself than to imagine someone else doing so.)

Anyway, when I saw a small fire being lit in the courtyard and a huge black cooking pot slung gypsy-fashion over it, I stumped off, leaving Theo to please himself what he did, and approached the group of people. (Did not do so without a qualm of apprehension, but this is an admission I make only in these pages.)

They appeared to be preparing their evening meal. Several of them were building the fire, and two were stirring the contents of the cooking pot. It smelled savoury and good.

They looked around as I approached and fell silent, and it was left to Fenris to say in his mocking blurred voice, 'You are either very brave or very unusual, Patrick. Most people would barricade themselves in the stone building and scuttle off at first light.' (He's either a mind-reader or was listening through the keyhole when I was arguing with Theo.)

I said, 'I can't see that an hour or so spent talking with you is any extra risk. And it might be that we could arrange for help to be sent out to you – medicines, clothing. Perhaps we could talk about that. Is this your supper time? Am I intruding?'

145

'Yes, it is our supper hour and no, you are not intruding,' said Fenris. 'Unless in extreme pain, or suffering from physical sickness, we all gather to eat the evening repast together, usually in this courtyard, but occasionally in the stone hall in the east wing. The palace is big enough for us to live a little apart from one another, but we all meet each evening.'

'We like to do so,' put in another of them, a bit hesitantly. 'It means we can bring to the supper table the details of our day, and hear how the day has been for others.'

'A time for sharing,' said a third. 'Little pieces of news about our work, or perhaps an amusing or an interesting occurrence.'

'You save it all up for the evening,' said one of the women. 'You know the others will be doing the same.' She was ravaged and thin, but it was possible to see that she must have been very good-looking once. I glanced at her with interest, and she smiled. There was a fleeting impression of dark slumberous eyes and of an immense inner tranquillity.

Two other women sat with her and I saw that although they were helping with spooning out the food, the men were joining in with the task. The dark-eyed woman studied me and I had the feeling that she had heard my thoughts. When she said, 'You see that all are truly equal here,' I knew I had been right.

'You all help with the work?'

'Yes, for as long as possible. Those who can no longer walk are carried here. Those who no longer have the use of their hands are fed. We do not shut ourselves away to suffer and die alone.'

I remained silent, and Fenris said, 'Sridevi is right, Patrick. It is important to preserve normality for as long as possible.'

It was pitiful. It was brave and admirable but it was so pitiful I wasn't sure I could bear it. But they had to bear it. I said, 'There is – forgive me – there is pain and sickness at times?'

'Yes. As the disease progresses. But it is not,' said Fenris firmly, 'a discussion to have whilst eating. If you are determined to stay, Patrick, will you sit here? There will be a portion of stew ladled for you.'

It was an extraordinary experience to sit there with night stealing across the mountains, and to watch these poor spoiled, cursed human beings crawl out of their doorways and across the courtyard. Several had to be helped to the fire, some leaned heavily on sticks, and three or four could not walk at all. These last were brought on a kind of litter which the others carried. I had to repress the urge to jump up and help them all, because I guessed this would be wrong. They clung to independence for as long as they could. In the end, they had all congregated around the fire, some half lying, some propped up, and food was ladled into small wooden bowls and passed around. It was mostly rice – what's called *tsampa* out here – but it was flavoured with apricots and nuts and some kind of local vegetable. There was a wedge of coarse-grained bread to go with it, and it was all surprisingly palatable. Theodore was probably skulking supper-less in the stone room. Serve him right.

'Are you self-sufficient here? What happens about food?'

'Some of us are still able to work the land a little,' said Fenris. 'We can grow much of our food. And there is milk from our goats and sometimes we can make cheese.' His voice was so full of patient accept-ance that I wanted to cry or throw things about. In his place I would probably have hurled the cooking pot across the courtyard and smashed things to pieces out of sheer frustration. But probably he had gone beyond that point. 'There is no cure for this curse, you know,' he said.

147

Curse . . . So he saw it like that as well.

I said, 'Is there nothing that could be done to make life easier for you?'

'No. No cures, no medicines. We shall die early,' said Sridevi. 'We shall not suffer easy deaths, because this is not an easy disease.'

'There is the corroding of bones, the eating away of flesh and muscle,' said Fenris. 'A gradual loss of sensation. Perhaps blindness or deafness—' From the deep hood, his eyes caught the firelight.

'But we have accepted it,' said Sridevi. 'And we are more comfortable than you would think.' She made a quick gesture with one impossibly thin, but still beautiful hand, taking in the people seated in the circle of firelight. 'We are amongst our own people: creatures who will not shrink from us in disgust. No one makes us walk the land with a bell about our necks to proclaim our filth so that people can scurry away. We tend our own, and that is more of a comfort than you can imagine.'

'We exchange whatever skills we have brought from the outside world,' said Fenris. 'That is why some of us know a little English. And there are evenings when we celebrate birthdays or other events we remember from our earlier lives. Sometimes we have a story-telling evening, sometimes music.' He studied me, the hooded head on one side. 'Occasionally,' he said, with a sudden glint of amusement, 'there is even the pleasure of sharing a bed.'

'Ah. Indeed?'

'Not all the senses vanish, Patrick,' said Fenris, and the wry humour was there again. I saw him exchange a sudden smile with Sridevi and I wanted to sit down and cry again.

One of the lepers who had not spoken until now, leaned forward and said in careful hesitant English, 'Will you try a little of our wine? We keep it for special occasions.' He held out a small stone jug.

'And to have a guest with us for supper is a very special occasion indeed,' said another.

There was such pride in their voices that I felt the twist of pity all over again, not in the heart this time, but in the gut. Pity is an emotion that ought to stay in the region of the heart; it oughtn't to gouge unromantically into your bowels like a twisting white-hot knife.

The wine was absolutely terrible. I sipped it and then downed it in one go, hoping they would take this for eagerness rather than the wish not to let the taste linger on my palate any longer than necessary. When I had stopped being cross-eyed, one of them was saying something about the palace being a gateway to the real Tashkara.

'The Forbidden City?' I said.

'Yes. We are permitted to live on the boundaries, because we form a natural barrier.'

'We are therefore treated generously,' said Fenris expressionlessly.

'By who?'

The lepers glanced uneasily at one another, and then the one who had proffered the wine said, in a whisper, 'By Touaris.'

I set down my dish. 'Who,' I said, 'is Touaris?'

'A *what*?' said Theodore, sitting up crossly and glaring at me across the dim stone room. 'You are proposing to search for the temple of *what*?'

'I know it sounds far-fetched, but her name is Touaris and—'

'*How* old did you say she is?'

'Well, Fenris and the others said nearly three thousand years, but of course that can't be right—'

'You said a cat goddess,' said Theo, bristling with hostility. 'You said a three-thousand-year-old cat

149

goddess who lets the lepers live here and occasionally sends them the scraps from her ceremonial feasts.'

'Yes, the crumbs that fall from the rich man's table, or rather the woman's—'

'With a temple deep inside a forbidden city.'

'Well, yes, there's supposed to be a temple. Actually it all sounds very interesting. According to Fenris and Sridevi the cult started in ancient Egypt with the Bubasti tribes. A group of them were exiled sometime during the eleventh dynasty, when the princes of Thebes were beginning to spread their power under one of the pharaohs – I forget which one. Anyway, a small group travelled east until they reached a remote part of Tibet.'

'Why were they exiled?' demanded Theo suspiciously.

'Religious persecution. The Egyptians worshipped the cat goddess Bastet, you see—'

'Yes, I do know that, Patrick.'

'And the original Touaris was the divinity of childbirth and horribly ugly, but the rebels held that that was a distortion, and that the real Touaris was dazzlingly beautiful.'

Theo muttered something that sounded like, 'Trust you to come across the legend of a beautiful woman even out here.'

'According to Fenris, some of the tribe had begun to practise a forbidden mixture of the two worships,' I said, repressively. 'The cat goddess and the fertility goddess. But it was frowned on by Pharaoh, and if Pharaoh frowned on you in those days, you were destined for a very nasty end indeed. So the Bubasti rebels brought Touaris – their Touaris – and the cult to Tibet.'

'And Touaris is still living – how many years on did you say?'

'Well, three thousand was mentioned, but obviously

it isn't the *same* Touaris, and if you'd only listen—'

'I don't want to listen,' said Theo irritably, punching his thin pillow and hunching the blanket crossly about his shoulders. 'I don't want to know about any of it, because if anyone is going to commit the supreme folly of going into the ancient temple of some pseudo-immortal cat goddess it isn't going to be me!'

It's a pity about Theo. Wonder if I had told him that Touaris is believed to be guarded by four score female attendants of outstanding beauty he would have changed his mind? Apparently there's a ceremonial mating ritual as well, which Fenris, suddenly and surprisingly prim, says is licentious, depraved, orgiastic, and, what's worse, performed in public.

'Not,' he says firmly, 'anything that English gentlemen would care to witness.'

To hell with witnessing it. If we can find it we'll take part in it.

Later. The gut-wrenching pity I felt earlier turns out to be not so much due to what the Bible terms shutting up the 'bowels of compassion' as to bowels scoured by unripe wine. I only wish mine *had* shut up, because I've just crawled back from an exceedingly unpleasant half-hour in the rudimentary but mercifully serviceable wooden hut on the edge of the palace compound. To start with I feared the lepers simply dig holes like soldiers in battlefields, but they have a couple of earth closets discreetly situated, and I staggered into the nearest and prayed not to die. Squalid and sordid to die crouching over a wooden box with a hole in the top, retching your guts up at the same time.

On the second trip I discovered with horror what I had been too far *in extremis* to notice the first time: namely that the hut and its contraption are wedged precariously on a couple of planks suspended over part of the swirling river. Everything simply drops through! Remembered with fresh nausea all the times Theo and I had drunk from mountain streams (tributaries of this very river, of course), and then had to dash inside again for another bout of vomiting and purging.

'Serve you right for drinking too-young wine,' said Theo disapprovingly, but at least he put a basin by my bed, and brought me a glass of milk.

'The sanitation here is appalling,' I said plaintively.

'There isn't any sanitation. I don't know about leprosy, we'll both be lucky if we don't end up with cholera.'

At this rate I'll never get within leering distance of the four score females of outstanding beauty, never mind what somebody once called prick-ing distance. Perhaps it's as well. After three trips in as many hours to that noisome wooden hut I couldn't prick so much as a flea.

The pulsating drumbeats had ceased when Lewis and Kaspar reached the courtyard, and the Flesh-Eaters were clustering around the terrible Altar, eager greed in every curve of them. Their half-naked bodies gleamed in the flaring torchlight and their lips curled back, showing the pronounced canine teeth. The air was rich with the aroma of roasting meat and laden with voracious hungers, and Lewis had the extraordinary sensation that if he reached out he could plunge his hands wrist-deep into the atmosphere and scoop up handfuls of it.

Kaspar moved to the head of the Burning Altar. He's their leader, thought Lewis: I ought to have seen it straightaway. I wonder if it was only by chance that he was the one who met me at the palace entrance?

The burned mound of flesh that had once been Cal was no longer moving, but it was still recognisable as a human being. The hair had gone and the fingers and toes had blurred and melted into twisted lumps. A scatter of small hard chippings lay beneath the hands and feet where toenails and fingernails had fallen out. The face was shrivelled and almost burned away; scorched bones protruded through the cheeks and the jaw had fallen apart, showing cracked teeth. Around the eye sockets was a thin crispness where the eyes had burst and leaked. But the body – the trunk and the upper legs and arms and shoulders – was a huge meaty carcase, juicy and succulent, ready for the carving.

As Lewis stood silently at the Altar's foot, Kaspar's people looked up, but no one moved and they were all plainly waiting for their leader's signal. But anticipation shivered and thrummed on the air, thick and strong and powerful.

Lewis said in a voice devoid of all emotion, 'So that is how a human looks after he has been roasted on the Burning Altar.' He met Kaspar's gaze coolly. 'And now?'

'Now,' said Kaspar, 'we eat him.'

At once the Flesh-Eaters surged forward, and the low groan of anticipation that Lewis had heard earlier on broke from them. The drumming began again, faster and filled with throbbing urgency. Kaspar regarded his people with a thin smile, almost as if he felt faint contempt for them, and then reached for the long glinting knife lying on the Altar's edge.

As the knife-blade was driven through the breast of Cal, thick fat spurted, and the watchers moved at once, holding out their hands to catch it and instantly smearing it sensuously into their bodies, their heads thrown back, their eyes half closed. Several more pressed forward eagerly, and Kaspar cut again. The flesh parted and Kaspar began systematically to slice portions away from the trunk and thighs, handing the steaming cooked flesh to his people. They took it avidly, the fat running over their hands and dripping from their fingers. As they crammed it into their mouths, grease ran down over their lips and chins, and several who had not yet been served leaned forward, salivating like animals.

After the first few mouthfuls, the Flesh-Eaters began to dance at the courtyard's centre, whirling in a frenzied leaping rhythm, holding up the remains of their food, their fingers running with grease, their lips and chins shiny. Three or four of the older ones sat cross-legged on the ground, holding thin rib bones horizontally to their lips, nibbling at the shreds of meat and then sucking on the bones.

'The heart and entrails and stomach we burn,' said Kaspar, glancing at Lewis. 'But almost everything else is consumed. You are ready?'

'Yes.'

The dancers were growing more frenzied with every minute, and the men were seizing the females, flinging them down on the ground and thrusting between their legs. Hands that were slicked with human grease and human fat slid between thighs and across breasts, leaving sticky trails. The burning torches flickered wildy, casting their reddish glow everywhere, and throwing the shadows of the dancers across the palace's walls, grotesquely enlarged and distorted until they were scarcely human at all. The night sky was suffused with the crimson radiance, and Lewis, looking about him, thought: I was right about being in hell. These are the fire-drenched caverns that Dante wrote about and Milton.

Kaspar waited with a kind of impersonal courtesy until the jerking coupling was over and the men and women sat up, and then handed Lewis a portion of the cooked flesh. It was warm and unexpectedly smooth to the touch, and as the scent reached Lewis's nostrils, his mouth flooded with hunger-juice. A great waiting silence had fallen on the courtyard, and then without warning, the drummer began to tap against the skin-drum, not with the pounding sexual rhythm he had used earlier, but lightly and insidiously. At once the Flesh-Eaters began their chant again, and although the words were still unfamiliar, the meaning was unmistakable.

'*Eat . . . Eat . . . EAT . . .*'

Lewis wiped his mouth with the back of his hand, and breaking off a piece of the flesh, put it in his mouth and swallowed it.

There was a low groan of triumph from the Flesh-Eaters. Lewis looked at them and then, meeting Kaspar's stare across the Altar, held out his hand for more.

Chapter Fifteen

Ginevra Craven, arriving in a tumble of untidily packed weekend bags and flying hair at King's Cross early on Saturday morning, thought she had done rather well to get out of a boring family weekend.

It had been nice of Elinor to ask her to the peculiar charity centre where she worked, and it was even better that poor old Aunt Nell had finally got some kind of life going for herself. Ginevra, diving into the Underground, which was already filling up with Saturday shoppers, thought it was exactly like her aunt to land herself some dreary charity job in the East End, although Lewis Chance sounded anything but dreary. She had seen a newspaper photograph of him and he had the slightly aloof good looks that you associated with front-bench politicians or captains of industry. He had an unmistakable air of authority as well, and authority was always tremendously sexy.

Sexy authority was the reason why Ginevra was ducking out of Kensington this weekend. She would probably have to present herself for the family's disapproval on one of the days, and if the family found out what she had been up to there would be a row the scale of the Hiroshima bomb, which would be ridiculous because screwing your English tutor was not a Hiroshima-level matter; it was only breaking the rules a very little bit. Anyway, Grandmother, with her stable of toy boys, had no room to talk. Grandfather, with his procession of bimbo secretaries had even less.

Elinor was a different matter, though. She would listen

with absorption to the details of Ginevra's entanglement, and she would be round-eyed with astonishment over the good bits ('Did he *really* say that to you, Ginevra? How marvellous!'), and comfortingly furious about the bad bits: 'How dare the bastard leave you to pay the bill . . . borrow money . . . let you go home alone at 3 a.m. . . .'

Ginevra had so far managed to don a flippant two-fingers-to-the-world face, but confronted with Elinor's sympathy it might be difficult to maintain. She might very well find herself confessing that actually it had all been too devasting for words. In fact, if she were honest it had felt as if a knife were gouging her guts out when it ended, and it still sent her dashing into the loo to wail like a banshee at the least provocation. She had so far managed to keep the gut-agony and the banshee-wailing private, because when you were looked on as a bit of a heart-breaker yourself it was humiliating if people found out you had been taken in by the biggest screwer-around on the campus. It was mortifying to find you had been lured into bed with velvet-voiced quotations from John Donne and Shelley and Elizabeth Barrett Browning. Twenty years ago he would have been called a wolf and a rat, that tutor. He was a rat anyway. He was not even a very good English tutor and he had probably looked up the Shelley and Donne lines in a dictionary of quotations.

Chance House, when Ginevra reached it, impressed her. It looked as if there was still a good deal of work to be done, but whoever had controlled the renovation – Lewis Chance himself? – had done so tastefully; there did not seem to have been any self-conscious attempts to recreate the original Victorian floridity or to force jarring modernity into the old façade. The Prince of Wales had, in fact, mentioned the centre with approval in a speech to some Worshipful Order of something-or-others, and had called it an honest preservation of the old, blending harmoniously with the functional new. Ginevra, studying the building critically, saw what he meant. This was simply a place where people came to work, or be fed or helped, and where the most important things were not tarting up bulgy-cheeked cherubs or reproducing fleur-de-lis wall-coverings, but providing warmth and food and practical sympathy. She was not in an anti-Royal mood just now, so it was all right to acknowledge that she and the heir to the Throne had similar outlooks on architecture.

It was a bit disconcerting not to be met by Elinor, but to be approached by a thin shabbily dressed man who came up to her in the large canteen-ish room beyond the main doors. 'Miss Craven? Ginevra Craven?'

'Yes?' This was certainly not Lewis Chance, in fact it was more likely one of his down-and-outs. It might be someone they were rehabilitating because he looked a bit like a Pre-Raphaelite painter or writer ploughed under by drink, or a consumptive poet from the days when romance had a capital R. Oh God, not Keats again. Probably if you got to know him, rough trade would be nearer the mark.

The man said, 'This is a little difficult, Miss Craven, but I think you should come into Sir Lewis's office and sit down.'

He was not, after all, your usual run-of-the-mill down-and-out, in fact now that Ginevra came to study him more closely, he was not a down-and-out at all. There was not the pervasive unwashed-skin, greasy-hair smell. He had a slight unEnglish accent and although his clothes were shabby, he wore them with careless arrogance.

'I am afraid,' said the man, seating himself behind what was clearly Lewis Chance's own desk, and looking entirely at home there, 'that there is some awkward news to explain.'

'What kind of awkward news?' Wild notions of Elinor kidnapped, Elinor dead or raped, or locked up raving mad in an attic tumbled through Ginevra's mind. *My aunt...? Oh, we never talk about her... She's kept chained and handcuffed in the garret...* Concentrate, girl, this is important and serious. 'What's wrong with my aunt?' said Ginevra.

'I am afraid, Miss Craven, that she has vanished,' said Raffael. And, as Ginevra stared at him, he added, 'And up to now I have been unable to reach Sir Lewis Chance.'

'Why not? Elinor said something about a conference in Bath—'

'I have telephoned the hotel,' said Raffael softly. 'Lewis Chance was expected on Friday afternoon – yesterday. He had a room reserved and he was to address a seminar later today as well as being one of the after-dinner speakers this evening. But he did not arrive, and no one knows where he is.'

As Lewis got off the train at Bath and made his way to the exit, he was trying to put the corroding fear for Grendel to the back of his mind.

He had considered and discounted the possibility that Grendel might have escaped of his own accord and was somewhere at large in London. Mad as Grendel was, he could not have sawn through steel chains and got through two locked doors by himself. The chains had been strong: Lewis had made sure of it, even while his mind was shuddering from what he was doing. I'm chaining my son up in a cellar. It's a silk-lined cellar and it's very comfortable, because I've made it so, and he'll barely be aware of the chains. But it's still a cellar, and these are still chains.

The only way the chains could have been removed was if someone had taken a blowtorch to them, or hammered free the lock. And the only way the doors could have been opened was if someone had opened them either with a duplicate key or by force. He frowned. It was beginning to look as if somebody had been very anxious indeed to get hold of Grendel. His mind considered the likelihood of Raffael being implicated, but this was something else that could be instantly discounted. I'd trust him with my life, thought Lewis. It's got to be Kaspar's people, although I can't yet see why. Revenge? Not after so long, surely? But if I'm right, they'll make their demands and their reasons known fairly soon and then I can decide what to do. But until then I think the safest thing – for Grendel anyway – is to act as if I don't know anything's wrong.

He forced his mind back to the conference, and crossing the platform he wondered if this would be one of those occasions when he would receive a subtle but unmistakable invitation from a lady. It would be flattering, of course, but there was no room in his mind for seduction this time.

He came out of Bath Station and looked towards the taxi rank. It was almost five o'clock, and the rush hour was pretty well under way. Commuters were either setting out for home or just arriving back, and there was a queue for taxis. He hesitated, trying to remember how near to the station the hotel was, and wondering how much of a nuisance it would be to walk, and he was just making up his mind to stand in the taxi queue after all, when a youngish man wearing a dark jacket and a peaked cap vaguely suggesting a uniform, approached him and sketched a half-salute.

'Sir Lewis Chance? I'm from the Royal, sir. Their car's just over here.' He reached for Lewis's weekend case.

'I didn't realise I was being met,' said Lewis.

'Yes, sir. Cars for all the speakers at the conference.'

'How efficient.'

The young man deposited Lewis's case into the boot and held the rear door open. Lewis, getting in, said, 'This is very welcome. I was just cursing the lack of taxis.'

'It's a great problem at this time of day.' The man spoke with a slight accent, and Lewis, watching him get in behind the wheel, said, 'You aren't English, are you? Where are you from?'

Dark eyes met his in the driving mirror. 'The East.'

'Are you indeed? I was in the East many years ago.'

A cruel, remembered smile curved the reflected face. 'I know,' said the man softly, and as he switched on the ignition, the other passenger door was opened and someone slid in next to Lewis.

160

A voice said coolly, 'Whatever you are thinking of trying, Sir Lewis, do not. We don't want to shoot you, but we will do so if necessary.'

Lewis saw the gun before he looked at the second man's face, but he did not need to look. The voice, faintly contemptuous, strongly accented, was the one he had been trying to forget for twenty-five years.

Kaspar.

Two courses of action were possible. One was to attempt to escape. Lewis considered this briefly. He might be able to leap out of the car and yell for help, and he might just about bring it off, except that it was more likely that Kaspar would send a bullet into him before he had got the door half open. A solitary gunshot would never be noticed amidst all this traffic and impatient revving of cars and changing of gears. He might manage to stun Kaspar first and scramble out before the driver could do anything. The driver was probably armed as well, but no one, not even a le Carré hero or a James Bond could keep a gun levelled and negotiate rush-hour traffic. Lewis glanced at the car's controls: electronic door locks operated from the driver's console. Damn high-tech engineering!

The other course was to sit tight and listen to what they had to say, and hope it would lead him to Grendel, because Grendel's disappearance must be mixed up in all this. He looked at Kaspar. Kaspar was older by twenty-five years but the eyes had not changed and the thin curving smile had not changed either. Lewis felt a chill close about his heart, but he said, 'Well? What is all this?'

Kaspar smiled, but he said, 'Have you really forgotten the punishment graven on the Eighth Stone Tablet of the Decalogue?'

Lewis stared at him, a cold hand closing about his heart. The Eighth Tablet. The Tablet of Treachery and Betrayal.

'You remember it?' said Kaspar softly. 'Yes, I see you

do. We seldom invoke the Decalogue these days, Sir Lewis; but it still rules us. It will rule your trial. And if you are found guilty, the sentence will be that of the Eighth Stone. Exactly as it was twenty-five years ago.'

Lewis forced anger into his voice. 'What kind of trial?' he said. 'And for what crime?'

'The crime you committed twenty-five years ago,' said Kaspar. 'The murder of a religion. And this time we shall make very sure you do not escape.'

He brought up his left hand and Lewis caught the glint of a hypodermic needle before darkness rushed down.

Ginevra sat in Elinor's yellow and white bedroom and repeated to herself how absurd this all was.

The obvious deduction had to be that her aunt had gone off with Sir Lewis, but Ginevra found this completely incredible, because if Elinor had gone off with Lewis Chance she would have let somebody know, even supposing she was the kind of person to go off with a man, which she was not. And she had been expecting Ginevra: she had telephoned early on Friday morning, saying how much she was looking forward to the weekend, suggesting a visit to a street-market on Saturday afternoon, and asking Ginevra please not to travel by bus which would be unreliable and exhausting, and if there was any difficulty about the money for a train or coach to say so, because Elinor would pay it. You did not make plans to visit street-markets and offer to pay train fares if you were on the brink of an illicit passion. Anyway there was no such thing as illicit any longer, and Elinor and Lewis Chance were both free to do whatever they wanted.

Ginevra inspected the flat cautiously. Bodies under the bed? Axe-murderers waiting in the shower? No, of course not, you fool. Not even so much as a guilty lover cowering trouserless in the wardrobe. Elinor clearly occupied the yellow and white bedroom: her pale blue dressing gown hung behind the door – at least if she *had* gone off with a

162

man she hadn't taken that erection-crumpler with her – but the tiny bedroom next to it was half prepared for Ginevra's use. Fresh sheets had been put ready to make up the bed along with two thick bath towels and an unopened bar of scented soap.

There was food in the kitchen: tins of soup and beans in the cupboard and packets of muesli, and the fridge was stocked with cheese and salad and eggs. Two large chicken portions stood in a casserole dish, alongside a carton of soured cream and a small bag of mushrooms. That probably meant that Elinor had been planning to make one of her marvellous chicken curries for them: not one of Ginevra's sort where you sloshed in a tablespoonful of instant curry powder and banged everything in the oven and hoped for the best, but the one where Elinor ground up all the spices with a mortar and pestle, and simmered everything for about three hours and then stirred in the soured cream. Ginevra straightened up, frowning. Would anyone make all these preparations – a half-ready guest room, a complicated chicken curry – and then succumb to lust on a grand scale halfway through? Ginevra might do it herself, but she could not imagine Nell doing it.

She came back into the sitting room, and it was then that she saw Elinor's handbag on the small gate-leg table under the window. The bag was open, and doorkeys and purse were visible. Ginevra, aware of mounting fear, went through the bag's contents. It felt like the worst kind of intrusion, but it had to be done. Cheque book and cheque card were there; comb, tissues, a little make-up bag. Everything you would expect to find. Would anyone go off for a weekend without taking money and latchkeys and make-up?

Ginevra threw her few things into the wardrobe in the tiny bedroom, dragged a brush through her hair, and went down in search of the romantic poet.

'Of course I have reported the matter to the police,' said

Raffael, regarding Ginevra in the wooden-floored canteen which seemed to be the centre's heart, but which was completely empty now. Ginevra supposed people did not expect to receive hand-outs and help on Saturday mornings. During the week, this would be a rather lively, rather interesting place: filled with people serving or eating food, and wandering in for different reasons. But like this, shadowy and empty, it was a bit forlorn and creepy. Their voices rang out hollowly and when they crossed to the office, which was at the back, their footsteps echoed. It had begun to rain and there was the lowering darkness of late October. But once in the office Raffael turned on lights and flicked the switch of a coffee machine, and as the strong good scent of hot coffee began to permeate the room, normality returned.

'What did the police say?' Ginevra watched him setting out two mugs and opening a carton of milk while the coffee filtered. He was more attractive than she had remembered: dark-eyed and high-cheekboned. Middle-European? Italian? Even farther East? Those slanting cheekbones made you think of *Arabian Nights* tales and lost kingdoms: Scheherazade and Schahriar, and Omar Khayyám and the desert caravans going from Damascus to Mecca and Baghdad ... Nineveh from Ophir with ivory and apes and peacocks ... Now I'm back to English poets.

'The police were singularly uninterested,' said Raffael, pouring the milk and handing one of the mugs to Ginevra. '"A lady has not returned after a night, sir? And a gentleman is missing at the same time?"' A brief expressive gesture with the hands.

'Yes, but listen, her handbag's in her flat – money, keys, everything in it. Toothbrush and sponge in the bathroom. I think all of her outdoor things are there as well.'

The dark eyes flickered, and Ginevra, watching, thought: that's disconcerted him. Now why?

But Raffael only said, quite coolly, 'If your aunt has

164

gone with Sir Lewis, money would be the last concern she would have.'

'Oh I see. Well, yes. I suppose he'd buy whatever she needed.' Ginevra was not going to say that Elinor, with her brusque defensive shyness would have been horrified at the idea of her boss buying toothbrushes and combs for her. 'What about checking all through the house?' she said. 'She might have fallen somewhere and broken an ankle, or knocked herself out. I mean, you *have* searched the house, have you?'

Raffael said, 'Of course I have searched the house. There is no need to glare like an angry cat, Miss Craven.'

'I'm not a cat. I'm—'

'It was a compliment. I like cats. And you have tawny eyes and hair.'

He said it as one making a statement rather than proffering a compliment, but Ginevra felt a sudden tug of attraction. She said in a determinedly prosaic voice, 'Then if she's not in the house, what do the police suggest we do?'

'We are advised to wait for another twenty-four hours,' said Raffael. 'Perhaps until Monday morning. If there is no news by then, the police will send one of their men to talk to everyone here.' Another of the sudden pauses, as if he might be weighing something up in his mind. 'It looks as if you might be faced with a solitary weekend, Miss Craven.' Their eyes met.

'So I might. What about you? I mean – do you have to be here at the centre?' Ginevra was damned if she was going to acknowledge the implicit suggestion in the expressive eyes.

'I am around,' said Raffael. 'Sometimes I am here for several hours. There are no set times. This afternoon I will return to my rooms, which are nearby.' Another pause. 'But I shall come to the centre later this evening. Perhaps around seven.'

'Why?'

'It's one of my tasks to ensure the security of the building,' said Raffael, and again appeared to wait. The silence lengthened. It would be very easy indeed to say something like: 'Well, if you feel like it, come up for a drink.' Or even, 'Can you eat chicken curry?'

Ginevra said, 'I see. Thank you for telling me everything.' And stood up and went back up to her aunt's flat.

It would have been immensely intriguing to spend the night with someone who looked like Lorenzo the Magnificent or something out of Omar Khayyám, but there was promiscuity and there was outright madness, and to go to bed with someone she had only met a couple of hours earlier would be madness.

Ginevra sat down on the hearthrug, hugging her knees, and stared at the glowing bars of the electric fire. Raffael had said that the police had been informed about Elinor's disappearance, and Lewis Chance's, and also that he had searched the house. And while it was all very well to listen, rapt, to someone who looked like Lorenzo the Magnificent, Ginevra was not going to take Raffael's word for absolutely everything. What the hell was somebody who lived in a bedsit in Canning Town doing with a name like Raffael anyway?

She paced restlessly about the flat, peering into her aunt's wardrobe again – yes, all Elinor's clothes *were* here – and came back into the sitting room to stare out through the window. Rain streamed down in a ceaseless silver curtain, making it impossible to see across the road, and even at this time of day, it was dark enough for lights to be needed everywhere. It was important not to think that she was on her own in this brooding old house. She was not really on her own: there was a phone on the desk and she could walk out into the road any time she liked. She went determinedly into the tiny bedroom again and pulled on sneakers and the sweater she had worn on the train. She tied her hair back because it tended to tumble over her

166

eyes and it felt more comfortable to be tidy for a house search. Raffael had said she had tawny eyes and hair like a cat. Nobody had ever said that to her before.

She glanced at her watch. Two o'clock. Raffael had left for his rooms nearby, but he would return later.

There was plenty of time for her to make her own search of the house before he came back.

The old building was silent as she let herself out of the flat and locked the door, carefully pocketing the key, but the lights on the hideous iron stairway were on. Ginevra supposed there was some kind of time switch. She went systematically down, checking rooms as she went, unsure of what she was looking for but looking anyway. Elinor had said the place had been a music hall around the turn of the century, and even with the restoration it was easy to see how it would have looked. It was an interesting place and it might be fun to research into its past. There was a course in Theatre History starting next term; she might sign up for it and see if she could use this place as a study project.

The house felt shadowy and gloomy and there was a disturbing sense of eyes watching from the shadows. This was creepy but could not be paid any attention. Ginevra went firmly through the house, looking into offices and interview rooms, opening the doors of lavatories, because people had been known to pass out in the loo and lie undiscovered before now.

The ground floor was mostly taken up with the canteen and a couple of back offices, and there was no sign of Elinor anywhere. Ginevra went slowly down the iron stairs. Anything at the bottom? There was a kind of vestibule with cupboards opening off and a cubbyhole for cleaning stuff and Hoovers. And there was a door under the iron staircase, half open, with a dim light filtering out. Basement? Cellars? It did not look a very likely place, but it had better be checked. She pushed the door cautiously and went down the narrow wooden steps.

167

She had been expecting to see conventional cellars at the foot of the rickety wooden stairs: stone-floored rooms stretching beneath the old house: maybe the remains of a wine cellar, certainly heaps of junk and broken furniture.

The dank culvert with the eerie green waterlight sent a shiver of cold fear through her. The tunnel was deserted and silent save for the faint slopping sounds of water, but the sense of being watched and followed was much stronger here. Ginevra found herself glancing perpetually over her shoulder.

The tunnel was unspeakably nasty. Like a giant's drain. Anything might come creeping out of the shadows to meet you. Anything might be prowling stealthily along behind you.

But it was so clearly the kind of place where you might trip and break your ankle or knock yourself unconscious, that she forced herself to go on. Ginevra could not think of any reason why Elinor would come down here – why *anyone* would come down here! – but the image of her aunt lying helpless somewhere refused to be banished. She would go to the end of the tunnel and if there was no sign of Elinor, she would go back upstairs and think what to do next. To wait until Monday morning was out of the question.

Chapter Sixteen

Raffael had not liked leaving Ginevra alone inside Chance House, but she had stone-walled every attempt he had made to stay. Had she thought he was trying to seduce her? Now there's a thought, Father Raffael! An unwilling smile lifted the corners of his lips as he crossed the road to the corner where his ramshackle bedsit was situated. We might have guessed there would be a female in it somewhere, de Migli had said, coldly sarcastic. De Migli, unfortunately, knew the circumstances of Raffael's parting with the Church: he had been one of the Curia presiding over Raffael's case, most of whom had studied the details with the faint bewilderment of celibates, who know the sins of the flesh by name but seldom encounter them in any other form.

But de Migli had not looked bewildered. He had regarded Raffael with cold disgust and he had said very little throughout the entire hearing. Raffael had been raw and bleeding inside and exhausted from the weeks and the months of mental anguish, but he had eyed them all arrogantly, refusing to appear humble. He thought most of the Curia had recognised and understood this for exactly what it was, but de Migli had not and de Migli had never failed to plant a barb on the few occasions they had met since. So much for Christian charity. De Migli would never have understood that the female, who had figured so prominently at the hearing but whose face Raffael could scarcely now recall, had been a symptom rather than a cause. He would certainly consider Raffael to be

169

now hellbent on Ginevra's seduction, which said a very great deal about de Migli.

But twenty years separated him from Ginevra, and despite de Migli's cynicism, Raffael had not yet reached the age of leering at young females from behind a carapace of crapulous dotage. The alliteration of this pleased him and he repeated it to himself. But however good it sounded he was a long way from it yet.

He let himself into the house and went quickly up to his two rooms on the second floor. He hated the sloppily split old house, but it had provided him with exactly the right springboard to get into Chance House, which was what Cardinal Fleury had wanted.

'I'll leave the mechanics of it to you,' His Eminence had said. 'But I want you to get into Chance House and from there into the confidence of Lewis Chance or those close to him. It might be necessary to mingle with the poor creatures who attend the centre—'

'I imagine it might,' agreed Raffael, straight-faced. 'It will be a salutary reminder that I'm fortunate not to be one of them.'

'Things have perhaps – not been easy since you left us?' This had been Fleury's delicate way of asking if money had been tight, and Raffael had smiled inwardly, and had thought: Yes, but this mission is more timely than you know, Fleury.

'I'm not on the streets yet,' he had said.

'And you won't mind living in such a place for a time?'

'I've experienced worse.'

He had, but not much. The house's interior had appalled him and his two rooms were furnished with the most astonishing collection of things he had ever seen. But they were very convenient for Chance House and he had assumed he would become desensitised to peeling wallpaper and rising damp and the constant smell of cooking. This had not yet happened. The damp had etched green fungal swirls beneath the windows, and the cooking smells were always the distasteful ones of meals gone before, never the appetising drift of meals to come. They frequently mingled with a whiff of what might have been joss sticks burning, but which Raffael could by this time identify as cannabis or grass. When the smell was at its strongest, the thump of heavy rock music was at its loudest, as if the two were interdependent. There was never any giveaway smell of cocaine, partly because the consignments were delivered after dark to the basement flat, and partly because they were never there long enough to leave any evidence of their sojourn – into the dealer's hands and on to the street inside a couple of hours. When this strange business was cleared up Raffael was going to take enormous pleasure in informing against the basement tenants.

As he climbed the stair to the second floor the memory of the cool dim Vatican and Ambrosian Libraries flicked jeeringly across his mind. See what you lost? See what you exchanged that for? Toneless pop music and drug dealers and young men who sell their bodies in nearby pubs. One of the male prostitutes from the floor below him was just on his way out: Raffael nodded to him and they exchanged a comment about the fog. Yes, it was astonishingly like one of the old London smogs, and no, it was certainly not a night to be prowling the streets. The boy cracked the time-worn joke: still, better than working for a living, and Raffael smiled perfunctorily, because there was not really any answer to this that could not be bawdily construed. He could not even say something like, 'Make sure you stay well wrapped up,' because the boy would not be intending to stay wrapped up, in fact he would be unwrapping in the most basic of ways several times before the night was over. He would probably start off in the nearby Anchor, and go wherever the night took him, and if all Raffael had heard was true he might well have had ten men by 2 a.m.

The two boys had been off-handedly companionable to Raffael, coming up to his rooms to explain about leaving the main door on the latch so that the occupants could get in with their keys late at night, and warning him about the landlord's habitual trick of trying to get an extra week's rent when it was only a four-week month, sly old tosser. Raffael suspected they would ordinarily use a somewhat earthier word than tosser, but had refrained out of some dim sense of respect either for his years or some subliminal recognition of the authority he had once wielded. The pulpit still casting that invisible mantle of command?

They had appeared to accept him as some kind of eccentric – wasn't London full of eccentrics anyway, and one more made no difference – and shortly after he had moved in they had issued an invitation to supper. Raffael had imagined them saying to one another, 'Poor old sod, up there on the top floor all by himself. Let's ask him down for a meal, put him right about the ways of the house.' He had accepted the invitation, which he had thought would give him an insight into the kind of people who frequented Chance House, and after careful thought had bought four cans of bitter and four of lager to take with him. This had evidently struck the right note, and the supper – a huge greasy fry-up of sausages and eggs and hamburgers and chips – had been unexpectedly pleasant. Raffael had found himself relaxing, enjoying the sharp, *enfant terrible* humour of the two boys, and then had been annoyed with himself for his attitude. The Vatican's a long way behind you, Father, and you're a priest in reduced circumstances.

He went up the stair, his mind returning to the Decalogue. It would probably help to clarify his thoughts if he wrote them down. This was a habit carried over from his days in the priesthood and it still held good. The magnitude of the task still appalled him; it would not look any less appalling in writing, but it might help him define some kind of plan.

He let himself into his rooms. He had tried to improve them, covering the bed with a thick tapestry rug in cool blues and greens, and curtaining off the corner with the gas ring and the ugly Formica-topped dresser. He had arranged the two worn wing chairs in front of the gasfire, and bought a small table lamp with a thick parchment-coloured shade, and in the light of the lamp the room's dismal shabbiness softened considerably. It was not unpleasant to sit in one of the chairs with the gasfire popping in the way that old gasfires did. He would heat a tin of soup and drink it as he made his notes, and then he would return to Chance House and Ginevra.

It was then that he saw that the two wing chairs were occupied.

Several opening lines were possible, the most obvious being the classic: 'What the hell are you doing here?'

Raffael said, 'Who the devil are you? And how did you get in?'

At least the two men would not be intent on theft. There was nothing worth stealing in the room; in fact he would happily have assisted a burglar to carry most of the stuff out.

The men had risen at his entrance, and the taller one said, 'Father Raffael?'

'You're behind the times,' said Raffael curtly, crossing to the window and drawing the thin curtains before switching on the lamp. 'I haven't answered to that title for several years.'

'How do we address you?'

'You don't. You leave. At once.'

For answer the man resumed his seat, and after a moment the younger one did the same. 'We should like to talk to you,' he said, and this time Raffael heard the foreign intonation. They were both light-skinned, but with the pallor of non-Europeans, and the raven's-wing hair of the East.

Alarm bells began to sound in Raffael's mind, but he leaned against the thin window ledge and said, 'I'll give you five minutes. Talk.'

They exchanged glances, and then the tall man said, 'Admirably brief. We are here to request you to stay out of our people's affairs.'

'Your people?'

'We won't play games or prevaricate,' said the man. 'The people of Tashkara.'

'Ah,' said Raffael softly. 'So that's who you are. The League of Tamerlane, by any chance? Yes, I thought you might be. "Request" seems a trifle polite. How am I supposed to be in your affairs in the first place?'

'Firstly you want the Decalogue,' said the man, and the word dropped into the listening room with sharp clarity. 'That's why you're inside Chance House. We know that.'

'What we're unsure of,' said the second man, 'is who you're working for.'

'Why must I be working for anyone? Why can't I want the Decalogue for myself? Is it for sale?'

'It is not.'

'Are you sure about that? Most things have their price. Including men and women.' Raffael dwelled with brief amusement on de Migli's probable reaction if he were to be informed that it was no longer necessary to destroy the Decalogue, because the Vatican was going to purchase it. What would the figure be? Ten million? Several hundred million? Raffael would have given a great deal to see de Migli's face at such a piece of news.

'The Decalogue is not for sale under any circumstances,' said the man coldly, and Raffael regretfully banished the small fantasy. 'The Stone Tablets of Vengeance are priceless in the real sense of the word,' he said. 'And if you were thinking of stealing them—'

'Heaven forfend—'

'You should know that they are extremely well guarded and also very well hidden.'

'Then you have nothing to worry about,' said Raffael. 'By the way, we said five minutes and your time's running out.'

The tall man faced Raffael, and Raffael took in his height and the lean whipcord strength. Not one to oppose. Certainly not one to jump. 'It is not the Decalogue that is our prime concern,' said the man, 'although it would be better if your superiors abandoned their interest in it.'

Raffael's brows went up. 'I call no man my superior,' he said. 'Continue.'

'It is the boy, Grendel. In two or three days' time we shall take him back to Tashkara, and if you or Lewis Chance try to find him or follow us, we shall have you killed.'

Raffael's mind flinched at the cold threat, but a part of his brain registered the inclusion of Lewis Chance. Does that mean they haven't got him? He said, 'Why do you want Grendel?'

'As the Pretender to the Throne of our people. As their new ruler.'

Raffael stared at them, and then laughed. 'Forgive me,' he said, 'but this is purest nineteenth-century romance. And not very good romance at that.' He crossed to the nearest chair and sat down. 'Do go on. I can't wait for the denouement. And your five minutes have been extended. But do you think I could know your names – not because I particularly want to but it would make it easier to have something to call you.'

The two men exchanged glances. 'I am Timur,' said the spokesman. 'This is Iwane. We head the League of which you apparently have heard, and there are a number of our people in London with us.'

'Gathering to welcome the new Messiah?'

Timur stared at him coldly. 'It amuses you to mock us, doesn't it?'

'Enormously.'

'Did you mock your own religion?'

'Of course. That's why they kicked me out. Why are you really taking Grendel to Tashkara? What qualifies him to be your ruler?'

The sly cruel smile lifted Timur's lips. 'Grendel has a most remarkable ancestry,' he said. 'And the circumstances of his conception and birth—'

He broke off, and Iwane said, 'Twenty-five years ago Lewis Chance brought about the end of a religion. He splintered a line that had been unbroken for almost three thousand years.'

'Dear me,' drawled Raffael.

'As a result there was a division in our people,' said Timur. 'A schism. It started quietly and unobtrusively, but it grew wider and wider until seven years ago those of us who looked to find new ways formed the League of Tamerlane. We wanted to adapt, to make use of what we had instead of mourning what we had lost.'

'How admirable. And those who are outside the League – the traditionalists perhaps? – resisted? Yes, I see. Well, I have absolutely no interest in your petty palace revolutions or your minor civil wars, gentlemen. But I don't think I can let you take Grendel, you know. Not for all your ancient kingdoms.'

Timur leaned forward, his eyes hard and cruel. 'We have been watching Grendel and talking to him for several years now,' he said. 'Your word might be "conditioning". Lewis Chance knew that: it was why he continually moved the boy from place to place.'

'To evade you?'

'Yes. Because Grendel,' said Timur softly, 'has proved very receptive. And tomorrow night will see the climax of our years of work. Tomorrow is the ancient Feast of Sekhet, and at one hour before midnight Grendel will take part in the ritual of the Burning Altar. Everything is ready—'

'Ritual?' said Raffael sharply.

'Among our people it would be regarded as initiation.'

Raffael's mind was racing and his inner vision was seeing fragments of a macabre jigsaw slot into place, but when he spoke his voice was offhand. 'Human sacrifice?'

'Of course.' Timur regarded him. 'You with your

learning should know the ancient tradition that once prevailed in Egypt,' he said. 'That of hunting the gods and feasting on their cooked limbs.'

'I have heard of it,' said Raffael, his mind tilting in horror. 'Have you found gods here in London, then?' He was thankful that the words came out with just the right note of sarcastic disdain.

'We have certainly found victims,' said Iwane.

'Victims?' Raffael stared at them, and the mental jigsaw reassembled itself slightly. 'The prostitutes,' he said. 'That's what you mean, isn't it? The male prostitutes who vanished. It was your people all along.'

'They are very easy to take, your young men,' said Timur. 'And it was very easy to coax Grendel's natural instincts down the path we wished him to take. For several years now he has craved human flesh, and we have been happy to feed that craving.' A brief dismissive gesture. 'That is not important now. What is important is that our plans are not upset at the final hour.' His eyes never left Raffael. 'If you or Lewis Chance – or Ginevra Craven – try to stop us or follow us, or bring in your police, we shall simply remove you.'

'How?'

Timur smiled. 'You will die as all who try to interfere or spy on us die,' he said. 'And although we primarily use young and potent men out of respect for the goddess, we are not averse to sacrificing young fertile females occasionally. And she is very attractive, Ginevra Craven,' he said softly. 'But if you continue to hinder our plans, you will certainly see her die. She will burn on the Altar of our ancestors. And you will follow her.'

Extract from Patrick Chance's Diary

Tashkara, 1888

Finally able to leave Fenris's colony and start the journey into the forbidden city of Tashkara.

It's the very devil when your guts betray you, especially when they do it to such purpose, and particularly if you happen to be inside a leper settlement at the time with only a thunderbox perched across a stream by way of plumbing.

Theodore keeps saying things like, Serves you right, and, Always knew you'd come to a bad end, and muttering about Retribution and Divine Vengeance like some Old Testament prophet. I've refused to listen on the grounds that Divine Vengeance unlikely to manifest itself in such a sordid and undignified manner, and anyway none of the bad ends prophesied for me has taken the form of suffering disgusting version of dysentery in primitive mountain colony.

We bade an emotional farewell to Fenris and Sridevi and their people – at least I was emotional; Theo couldn't be emotional if he tried with both hands for a month – and I promised that once we were back in England we would arrange to send out whatever foodstuffs could be conveyed over such a long distance, along with medicines and blankets.

'I suppose your mind's running on impractical things like pears preserved in brandy and live poultry, together with a few cases of claret,' said Theo, afterwards. (It was.)

'You do realise,' he demanded, 'that between the exigencies of the journey, not to mention venal sailors and untrustworthy Sherpas, none of them would reach its destination?'

He's given to verbosity at times, that Theo, but on consideration have to admit he's probably right. The sailors would kill the poultry and eat them before they were out of sight of Plymouth Harbour and it's doubtful if claret would even get off the quayside. However, no reason why we can't ship out some cases of canned meat and fish – believe canning process much improved these last few years – and maybe some chloroform and morphia, or bromide mixtures. Should like to see a sailor purloining bromide!

We eventually set off two hours later than we had intended, hung about with various food packages from the lepers' small store – *tsampa* and dried fruit and salted meat – which they thought we might need on our journey. Accepting these was one more of those awkward and painful moments: the poor creatures had little enough for their own needs but to refuse would have wounded them beyond bearing, so we took it and expressed suitable appreciation.

'And a small leather flask of our special wine,' they said, presenting it proudly. 'We remember how much you enjoyed it.'

We threw the wine away the minute we were out of sight of the palace. It will probably render that square of ground for ever barren, and in years to come travellers will use it as a landmark and talk of it as the Patch Where No Thing Will Grow. I would rather bequeath a Patch Where No Thing Will Grow to Tibet than drink the lepers' wine again, however. The flask will be useful for carrying extra water.

At first I thought we weren't going to find anything. This valley is a strange silent place, not precisely desolate but locked in what I can only describe as the most immense isolation I have ever encountered. There is a *removed* feeling about it, as if it might have been sealed off from the rest of the world a very long time ago and has stayed sealed ever since. The mountains rear up on all sides, and there are odd whispery echoes everywhere. If you raise your voice even the smallest bit your words rebound off the rocks and bounce jeeringly back in your face, which makes you want to shout ribald expressions, only I didn't on account of offending Theodore's sensibilities and also in case we might be already inside

Touaris's realm and within hearing of any prowling lookouts she might employ. It wouldn't do to find ourselves labelled as people given to hurling indelicate epithets at the sacred peaks, although as Theo pointed out, it's unlikely that an ancient tribe of complicated ancestry and ambiguous religious persuasion would be able to understand ordinary everyday English, never mind Anglo-Saxon obscenities.

It was Fenris who had called the mountains sacred peaks, although the deeper we went into them the more they seemed like profane peaks to me. Remarked to Theo that if this was the path the renegade Bubasti tribe trod three thousand years ago you had to give them credit for perseverance at least.

'I'm not giving them credit for anything until I see them,' he replied sepulchrally, and added that he dared say the path had been easier in those days.

And then without the least warning the path wound sharply down, and as it curved to the right a splinter of brilliance from the noonday sun cut a slice of pure pale gold light across our path.

I think we could both be forgiven for thinking for a moment that we had stumbled across something from an *Arabian Nights* fantasy: an ancient walled city basking in the sunshine, its spires catching the light and throwing out dazzling spears of scarlet and gold. There was a sense of timelessness about it, and a feeling that it was not part of the ordinary world at all, but somehow beyond it and beyond Time as well. If the river at the gorge's foot was Kubla Khan's legendary Alph, this was undoubtedly Xanadu itself in its deep romantic chasm amid the dancing rocks. The sunlight poured over the mountains – pure soft light, streaked with crimson from the setting sun, and it was as if the entire walled city were lying inside a huge shallow dish fashioned from old gold and rose quartz and the sides of the dish were melting and

180

running down to immerse the city. It was the most breathtaking sight either of us had ever seen.

This was the ancient realm we had come to find: the hidden kingdom of the cat goddess of the Bubasti.

Tashkara, the forbidden city of Touaris.

Later. We have made a roughish kind of camp on the gentle slopes that look down on the city, and we can see it quite well from here; huge blank gates are set deep into the walls but beyond them are tantalising glimpses of buildings with the narrow vertical chimney structures that the Tibetans call *stupa* and paint with uncomfortably lifelike eyes to look out at the four corners of the world. At the very centre we can make out a kind of elaborate tiered palace with each layer gilded and japanned: scarlet and ivory and jade green.

It's almost dark now and we have eaten our supper (*tsampa* and strips of salted pork courtesy of Fenris's people), and each had a tot of brandy – well, actually we have had several tots.

Note: I seem to be spending this entire journey either drunk, dehydrated or in an advanced state of satyriasis, and whoever finally gets his (or her) hands on these pages will certainly have marked me down (or written me off) as an intemperate lecher by now.

Theo has undergone a complete volte-face (think this is result of brandy), and is filled with a pioneering spirit and reassuring me that we should simply walk in through the gates, since cultured and refined people would never refuse succour to benighted travellers, and also we are British, dammit. They will offer us food and shelter, he says confidently, and once we have eaten their salt they will be bound by the ancient laws of hospitality.

Unsure of what good being British and eating salt will do out here, and would not place too much reliance on the refinements of Touaris's people either, since defying the Pharaoh and indulging in licentious fertility rituals ever since does not suggest a particularly high level of refinement. However, am too grateful for Theo's optimism to argue and have given him another swig of brandy on strength of it. Suspect that Fenris blew the gaff about Touaris's four score handmaidens, and it's that that's cheering him up, because it's my opinion that he's rather susceptible on the quiet. I'm extremely susceptible and it's cheering me up no end.

(Must here record with *deep* thankfulness that the slight weakness I experienced inside the leper colony has proved to be of an *extremely* short-lived nature, and that as Shakespeare has it, my nobler part once again betrays my body's gross treason. In other words, I'm standing like an autumn crocus at the thought of the four score females of outstanding beauty, to say nothing of the licentious fertility rituals . . .)

All the same, I admit to a certain feeling of nervous apprehension about what is ahead of us.

Chapter Seventeen

Ginevra had drawn a complete blank in the underground tunnels, and she had drawn a complete blank everywhere else.

She had finally come back up to the flat, and had turned on the hot shower-spray, standing under it and trying to sluice away the smell of the tunnels. She tipped Elinor's scented shower essence over her and massaged rich creamy shampoo into her hair until her scalp tingled. I'm using up all your nice scents, Nell, and for all I know you're at the bottom of the river. Or are you bathing in Joy – the scent as well as the emotion – with the rich and fascinating Sir Lewis? I hope you are and I hope he's terrific in bed.

She roughly dried her hair and wrapped herself in her thick towelling robe, and then put the chicken pieces in the oven with a strip of bacon over each one. She had just put the kettle to boil for coffee and she thought she was really pretty calm, when there was a sharp knock at the door.

The unexpected sound and the abrupt realisation that somebody had come up the iron stairs without her hearing, betrayed the fact that she was not quite as calm as she had hoped. She jumped and spilled instant coffee over the sink.

'Who is it? Who's there?' It came out shriller than she had intended. 'Who is it?' she said again, and this time her voice sounded more normal.

'Ginevra? It's Raffael. Something's happened and I

think I'll have to bring you in on it. Can I come in? Or if you prefer, can you come out? We can even meet in the pub on the corner or something if you want.'

Ginevra hesitated for a split second. Most of her wanted to trust Raffael very much, but a tiny part was still unsure. Oh, what the hell! It was probably a time to go by instinct. And he had offered her the chance to meet him outside.

She said, 'Give me about ten seconds and I'll open the door. I was just in the shower.' She dived into the bedroom and pulled on jeans and a loose shirt and then padded across to the door in bare feet. If the romantic poet was about to turn into a ravening sex maniac – or any kind of maniac – it would not be a good idea to open the door wearing only a bathrobe.

But Raffael did not turn into a maniac. He sat in the chair by the window and unfolded the most remarkable story Ginevra had ever heard outside of fiction. She curled up by the fire to let her hair dry and listened to him, and thought: I was right about Scheherazade at any rate, except that tonight it's Schahriar telling the tale.

Raffael was not thinking about telling a good story; he was thinking about persuading this unusual girl that she was in danger and that the bizarre story he was about to tell was the truth. It flickered on his mind with grim irony that it was not so very long since no one would have thought of doubting his every utterance.

He had sat for a long time in his rooms after Timur and Iwane left, for once unaware of the cold shabbiness of the place, his mind in tumult, trying to see a way of reaching Elinor and Grendel. And of keeping Ginevra safe from Timur's threats.

The threats to the Catholic Church were on a different plane, of course; Raffael did not like them, but he thought that if he had to he could probably call on the might of the whole College of Cardinals. St Peter's Armies crusading all over again.

But threats to people were different, and seated

184

opposite to Ginevra in Chance House again he knew that he was going to tell her the whole story. She was a bit flippant and she was certainly a bit frivolous, but she possessed something of the same quality that Raffael had sensed in Elinor. Integrity? Inner strength? Whatever it was and whatever you called it, she could not be given half-truths or evasions, and the question of not trusting her was absurd. Raffael had not heard confessions from two generations of penitents or listened to the mild guilty secrets of struggling ordinands without knowing who could be trusted and who could not.

It was likely that Ginevra would disbelieve him of course, and it was even likelier that she would think he was crazy. But it was possible that she would believe him and ally herself with him. The word 'ally' gave Raffael a sudden feeling of warmth.

Ginevra, trying to sort the merely dubious from the downright incredible, thought this was just about the most astonishing tale she had ever heard. It was almost astonishing enough to be true. The Decalogue – the half-mythical, half-historical Ten Commandments of Satan – and the League of Tamerlane that the Vatican wanted to quench, and Timur and Iwane warning Raffael not to interfere – making that sinister threat against Ginevra herself in the process. Ginevra managed not to shiver or look stealthily over her shoulder, but it was a close thing.

Raffael related it all in such a quiet and understated way that despite her caution, Ginevra found herself believing him. She tested each separate fact carefully. Priceless old documents chronicling obscure fragments of history did exist, of course – and if not inside the Vatican vaults, then where, for goodness' sake? And strange pre-Christian religions did linger in remote corners of the world: the ancient cult of the exiled Bubasti tribe was perfectly credible.

The poor mad creature Grendel was credible as well. It was not so many years since people had shut away mad relatives in attics and kidnapping was a fact of life in any culture.

I don't want to believe any of this, said half of Ginevra's mind. But whether I want to believe it or not wouldn't stop it being true. I don't want to believe in nuclear waste dumping and Third World starvation and vivisection, but they all exist.

Whether she trusted Raffael and whether she believed him – whether this Tamerlane League really had threatened to drop Ginevra on to a grisly pre-Christian altar! – his presence in the flat was a charm against the growing feeling of menace. Ginevra returned to the kitchen, which was filling up with the everyday scent of cooking chicken and banged the cups around as she finished making coffee, deriving obscure comfort from the clatter. When Raffael took the coffee cup from her his hand brushed hers, and Ginevra repressed a sudden longing to reach out and touch him. Don't do it! I'll acknowledge this astonishing story, but I'm damned if I'll acknowledge anything else! Certainly not this sudden sizzle of attraction. Did he feel it as well?

But he had stepped back, and although there was a faint colour across his cheekbones, when he lifted the coffee cup his hands were perfectly steady. One-way traffic only, thought Ginevra, half relieved, half disappointed.

'This is a bizarre situation,' said Raffael. 'I've no idea how Lewis and Elinor's disappearance fits in – if it fits in at all.'

'It's a bit coincidental. Do you really believe that whatshisname – Timur – hasn't got Lewis?'

'I don't know,' said Raffael. 'Their culture's so wildly different to ours that it'd be difficult to know if they were telling the truth or practising some subtle form of deceit.' He paused, drinking his coffee. 'They were entirely open about taking Grendel and about guarding the Decalogue,' he said. He thought: and also about sacrificing you, Ginevra. But he did not say it.

186

'Is his name really Grendel?'

'Yes, why?'

'Just that it's an extraordinary name for anyone to have. Have you ever heard of the Old English poem *Beowulf*?' said Ginevra. 'It's one of those odd mixtures of Christianity and paganism and it's incredibly ancient – eighth century or something – but in it, Grendel's the monster who has to be slain, and after him his mother.'

'I do know of it, Miss Craven.'

'You can drop the formality, you know. I'm Ginevra to most people. Preferably not Ginnie, but occasionally Gina. What do you know about this cat goddess?'

'Touaris,' said Raffael. 'As far as I can make out she was some kind of immortal divinity. The Touaris of the Egyptians was the deity of fertility and childbirth – depicted as a hippopotamus and extremely ugly, I think. But this is a bastard version of the original Egyptian cult and it might contain all manner of things.'

'Including a few fragments of Christianity?'

'Oh yes, I should think so,' said Raffael at once. 'But if you scratch the surface of most religions you'll find a great many similarities; a lot of Christian festivals are based on pagan ones, in fact. The early monks were much cannier than most people give them credit for: they believed that if you put new wine into old bottles, eventually the new wine would smell of the cask. It's one of the ways they converted the Western world to Christianity.'

'You sound very cynical.' Ginevra rather prided herself on her scientific approach to religion – what you can't prove doesn't exist – but underneath was a sneaking hope that there might be something in it after all. But Raffael sounded as if he had believed and trusted and been let down, which was rather daunting.

'The cult of Touaris,' said Raffael, 'is far older than Christianity, Ginevra.' He smiled unexpectedly, and at once the austere ex-priest vanished, and in his place was a mischievous sensualist. 'Also,' he said, 'I suspect that it's a lot more physical than Christianity.'

'Tell me about Grendel.' It would not do to plunge too deeply into discussions about physical manifestations of ancient religions with an ex-priest, fascinating as the subject – and the ex-priest – might be. 'What's his condition?' said Ginevra. 'I mean – is it some kind of schizophrenia or dementia or what? I don't want that to sound flippant. I know very little about mental illness.'

'So do I. And I don't know if there's a medical term for what he has, or what he is,' said Raffael. 'But whatever he is, I don't think I can let Timur and his nasty little League take him. I certainly can't let them use him as a puppet in some wretched political coup, which is what I suspect they're planning.' He looked at her. 'And I certainly can't let them take you, Ginevra,' he said.

They stared at one another, and just before the silence crossed over into real intimacy, Ginevra managed to say, 'What about the Decalogue? What about your original commission?'

'Would you call it a commission? I'd say it's more of a suicide mission. But it still stands, of course. The whole future of the Roman Catholic Church is in jeopardy – if it ever came out that the Vatican had been guarding that document—'

'The *Maleficarum Decalogue*—'

'Yes. If it was known that such an evil document even existed, there'd be the most monumental outcry. The entire integrity of the Church would be thrown into doubt.' He looked at her sharply, and said abruptly, 'You do believe all this, don't you? Because if you're in the least doubtful . . .'

'There's no need at all—'

'I can arrange for you to meet Fleury and de Migli—'

'Truly it isn't necessary.' Ginevra thought that a Roman Catholic priest – even a dismissed one – was as much as she could cope with in one day; to add a brace of cardinals would be indigestible.

She said, 'Is this League of Tamerlane some kind of liberation front, do you think?'

'I've no idea. I don't know if there's anyone inside Tashkara who even needs liberating. Fleury thinks the League want to bring the place into prominence – but for all the wrong reasons.'

'Why shouldn't Tashkara be brought into prominence?' Ginevra did not much like the sound of Timur or the League, but she read the *New Statesman and Society* and was conscientious about attending Famine Relief rallies and open-air charity concerts for aid to Third World countries. 'Haven't we a duty to bring the plight of underdeveloped nations to people's notice? Parts of Tibet are pretty primitive.' This sounded quite good, but it did not really accord with ancient civilisations and cat goddesses and smuggled Stone Tablets. It certainly did not make her feel any braver about the Burning Altar threat.

Raffael said, 'Of course we have a duty to help them. In fact the Catholic Church gives more than most people realise. It just does it quietly, without rock concerts or TV marathons. If the Tashkarans wanted help it would be forthcoming, Ginevra, you must know that. A single TV documentary, and money and practical help would flood the country. Remember Geldof and Ethiopia and Live Aid? And Romania and Bosnia? Charity-raising is big business these days.'

'You're being cynical again.' Ginevra sat up on the hearthrug, prepared for a battle and Raffael grinned down at her. Ginevra wondered how she could ever have thought he was rough trade.

'I'm not being cynical, I'm being logical,' said Raffael. 'Timur's wretched League are out for themselves: it's why they're making use of Grendel and it's certainly why they're threatening to use the Decalogue.' He paused. 'Fleury believes if the Decalogue's existence becomes public it would be a deathblow to the Church.'

'Ah.'

189

Raffael smiled again. 'People don't set very much store by religion or Christianity any longer,' he said. 'But it's been going for a very long time, Ginevra. It's wearing a bit threadbare, but it must be preserved. That's why the Decalogue has to be destroyed or suppressed. It bothers you, doesn't it? My link with the Church?'

Ginevra said carefully, 'The thing is that I've never actually met a – a former priest—'

'Unfortunately there's a growing number of us these days. But I was only dispensed from my vows, you know, and it was more or less mutual. Defrocking's reserved for the really serious cases.'

'Serious?'

'I believe you have to be caught in bed with the bishop's daughter – or the bishop himself, of course – or actually intoning the Black Mass with the crucifix upside down and using consecrated wafers to—'

'I know that bit,' said Ginevra hastily, and then wondered why she was suddenly being prim. Everyone knew about devil worshippers masturbating on to consecrated wafers, for heaven's sake! 'What do you do now?' she said. 'I mean, what kind of job do you have?'

'I don't. But the Church uses me occasionally to deal with odd problems it can't acknowledge,' said Raffael. 'I'm a maverick. Brought in to mop up the unsavoury jobs.'

The cynicism was there again, and the faint self-mockery. Ginevra was trying to frame a suitable reply, when Raffael suddenly said, 'I think something's burning in the kitchen.'

The chicken was not burned, but it was a close thing. Ginevra arranged it on two plates, tipped lettuce, tomatoes and watercress into a shallow bowl and rummaged in the bread bin. It was no time to be worrying about *haute cuisine*, and it was no time to be wondering about seduction plots, either. If Raffael was trying to get her into bed he was going about it in the most bizarre fashion Ginevra had ever heard of. But she reminded herself very firmly of the isolation of Chance House and the loneliness of the flat. Still, if he pounces on me there's always the bread knife. But if he's a homicidal maniac I'll get me to a nunnery . . .

She found a loaf of French bread, foraged for butter and cheese, and carried the whole lot through to the gate-leg table under the window.

'The most sinister part about all this,' said Raffael, as they ate, 'the most worrying part – aside from Lewis Chance and your aunt's disappearance, and your own danger, of course—'

'Timur's reference to Grendel's initiation at the Burning Altar tomorrow night.'

'Precisely.' He smiled and Ginevra felt absurdly pleased, as if she had been set some kind of test and come through it.

'Would they really sacrifice humans?' she said, watching Raffael butter a wedge of bread. 'And then – eat their flesh?'

Raffael laid down the bread and looked very straightly at her. 'I know how it sounds, Ginevra, but it's what Timur said and I'm afraid it's probably true. Patrick Chance's diaries hint at the eating of human flesh inside Tashkara, and even Sir Lewis—'

'Yes?'

'I think Lewis knows more about Timur's people than anyone realises,' said Raffael, his tone deliberately non-committal. 'And ritual cannibalism – what Frazer's *Golden Bough* calls exophagism – is found in several parts of the world, even today.'

'What's exophagism? I mean what is it exactly?'

'Frazer interprets it as the eating of those outside of the tribe,' said Raffael.

'Oh.' Ginevra supposed she ought to have guessed that Raffael would have read up the background on his peculiar task. She said, 'What do we do? Do we tell the police?'

'We could.' Raffael cut a wedge of cheese absently. 'But I don't think those threats Timur made were idle ones.'

'Death on the Burning Altar.' Ginevra shivered.

'Yes. And if Timur really has got your aunt or Lewis Chance, or both of them—' He made a quick impatient gesture. 'I think we have to go on that premise, Ginevra.'

Ginevra leaned forward. 'Listen, if this were an ordinary case of kidnapping, what would we do? Wait for the demand, wouldn't we? It's usually money, although sometimes it's State secrets, or a contract to supply arms to somewhere outrageous, or even—'

'Stick to the point, child.'

'Well look, we've got until tomorrow night before the ritual starts – Timur said so. Can't we try to find the kidnappers' lair by ourselves? We've got one or two things to go on, and we could— Well, we could be a bit more unconventional than the police.'

Raffael looked at her thoughtfully. 'Half a day's acquaintance with you tells me that you've thought of a plan. And I suspect it's the plan I've thought of as well.'

Ginevra said, 'Shoot an arrow of the self-same flight.'

'Send out a decoy?'

'Exactly.'

The two young men who occupied the floor below Raffael's ramshackle rooms were wide-eyed with curiosity at finding themselves approached by their rather peculiar neighbour and his unexpected companion, but delighted to invite them in. It was only half-past eight anyhow, at least an hour before either of them would be going out, and they were both intrigued. Georgie said, and Baz agreed, that the very *last* thing either of them had expected was to see the top-floor tenant turn up with a cracker of a tart on his arm, although the word tart was a colloquialism as you might say, because both of them knew class when they met it. Ginevra Craven was class, always supposing you were that way inclined, which Baz was not, although Georgie had been known to experiment a bit.

They proffered coffee (Georgie had bought a new jar of Kenco only yesterday which was fortunate, and there was a packet of biscuits as well), and listened with round-eyed astonishment to the story that Top Floor had to tell. They had *never* heard anything like it, although Baz, who read the occasional paperback, said you wouldn't believe some of the things people dreamed up by way of a story, and this was exactly like something out of a book.

They knew about the disappearance of some of the laddies, of course, and they'd read the articles as well, which were a bit over the top, but pretty much accurate. One of the boys mentioned used to go into the Anchor which was where Georgie and Baz generally began their night, and they'd known him. No, not to say *well*, but enough to speak to, or have the odd drink with, which meant they had felt a bit peevy about Ralphie's possible fate, well, they'd felt very upset if the truth was told.

Despite the mounting fear for Elinor and for herself as well, Ginevra found herself enjoying the casual hospitality and the combined shrewdness and *naïveté* of these two. Their rooms were very much like a good many student flats, in fact the whole house was exactly like some of the split-up properties near the university, which had become a kind of student ghetto and which the stolider citizens of Durham said were little better than slums.

Raffael seemed to be pitching it about right. He had said nothing about the Decalogue or the Vatican – Ginevra was ready to bet their reception would have been a whole lot more guarded if he had – and he was laying all the emphasis on Grendel's kidnapping, and on the disappearance of Lewis Chance and Elinor. A cult, he said, stressing the word. They would know about these things, of course?

Well, of *course*.

'And,' said Raffael, 'you understand what we're asking you to do?' He saw them exchange glances, and said swiftly, 'The danger would be minimal. I won't cheat by saying it would be nonexistent, but you'll be followed and kept tabs on.'

The wariness surfaced instantly. 'Police?'

'No,' said Raffael, and saw them relax. 'I will follow you.'

Ginevra took a deep breath. 'And so will I,' she said.

It was not something to make a hasty decision about, but Baz said, and Georgie agreed, that they should do it. There was poor Ralphie to think about – well, there was themselves, too, if this cult thing was really rampaging through the district. Quite like Jack the Ripper it was, exactly as the newspaper had said. Georgie made a joke about kidneys for breakfast and then felt a bit sick remembering Ralphie.

Top Floor was quite honest about the danger. Minimal but not quite nonexistent, he said. They rather respected this frankness, because you got enough po-faced tossers telling you lies in this game. Come home with me and see what I can give you. Let me take you to the Riviera. The tossers who haunted Canning Town weren't the sort to take you to the Riviera; what they usually took you to was a seedy boarding house or the back seat of the car for a hand-job. You didn't get Riviera offers if you worked *Piccadilly* for heaven's sake, in fact you were more likely to get beaten up, especially on a Saturday night.

Georgie boiled the kettle for refills of coffee all round because it was only half-past nine, and they could set off a bit later than usual tonight. And although what Top Floor was asking was pretty risky – well, it was bloody suicidal in fact! – they began to think they would have a go. The plan was to do the rounds of the pubs and bars in their normal fashion, and try to get themselves noticed by these cult people. Raffael used the expression 'picked up', which made them laugh because 'picked up' wasn't a term anyone had used since – well, since Jack the Ripper was a boy, probably! In Canning Town you went bumming, blowing or wanking. They suspected they could have said this to Ginevra, but they jibbed at saying it to Raffael although neither of them could quite have said why.

'What we want you to do,' said Raffael, who was perfectly aware of all the expressions fashionable in Baz and Georgie's demi-world, 'is to ensure that you get – approached by this League of Tamerlane.'

Georgie wanted to know how they would recognise these people, on account of there being a good many foreigners in Canning Town, what with it being so near to the old docks and all. There were no working docks these days, but you still got the foreigners. He started to tell a joke about discharged seamen, remembered his company and trailed into abashed silence.

'You'll recognise them,' said Raffael. 'I'll be around to give you the nod, just in case.'

'And I'll follow you,' said Ginevra eagerly, leaning forward. 'Yes, I will, Raffael – these people can only have caught a glimpse of me, and I'll rig up a disguise so it'll be quite safe – and I'll see where you're taken. And we'll be in to rescue you before you can say—' Several apropos expressions occurred to her, but she said temperately, 'Well, before you can count to ten.'

'And when do we do it?'

'Right away,' said Raffael, looking across at Ginevra. They shared a thought: *we've got to find the hideaway before the ritual starts tomorrow night* ... 'Yes, immediately.'

'Like – tonight?'

'Like tonight.'

Chapter Eighteen

As the gaslight burned lower, Elinor's warehouse prison sank slowly into an eerie gloom, and a faint stench of corruption wafted from the culvert beyond the packing cases.

She had lost track of the hours. Her watch had been smashed when the cat-headed man, Timur, had knocked the candlestick from her hand, and she had no idea what time it was. But Timur had said that the Burning Altar ritual would start one hour before midnight on Sunday. Was it Sunday yet? Was it even Saturday?

The room was very quiet and although the gas jets were still flickering, a sickly green and purple twilight was creeping in. Elinor began to feel light-headed with fear and hunger, and several times she sank into a half-stupor in which the shadowy prison became alive with prowling nightmare beings, and reality and fantasy became indistinguishable. Once or twice a faint scrabbling beneath the trap door jerked her to full awareness, and she half started to her feet. Timur returning? No, too light and quick. Rats? If a rat gets in here I'll die of fright, thought Elinor, and then immediately: no, of course I won't, I'll be too busy worrying about Timur.

Grendel had prowled restlessly around his corner for a time, the chains slithering gratingly across the concrete floor, and then had seated himself cross-legged on the floor, apparently falling into some dark absorption of his own. From time to time Elinor glanced covertly at him, but as the hours slid away she began to be less frightened.

She had no idea whether this was because she had reached saturation point for horrors, or whether it was simply familiarity, or even whether she was catching a little of Grendel's own madness. This last began to seem entirely possible.

She had thought she was prepared for Timur's return, but when footsteps suddenly echoed along the tunnels, scalding fear rushed in again. There was the scrape of the trap door lifting and he was there, stepping up into the warehouse, a second man following him. As they lowered the flap Elinor huddled as far back in her shadowy corner as possible, praying to escape notice.

Neither of the men were wearing the cat heads, but she was fairly certain that the taller one was Timur. The build was right and the walk. They both looked to be twenty-eight or -nine and they were markedly alike: pale-skinned and with black straight hair and dark eyes and slanting cheekbones. Brothers? Whatever they were they went straight to Grendel, ignoring Elinor completely.

Grendel had curled into a small defensive huddle, his arms about his bent knees, his head down. The men exchanged glances, and then Timur bent down so that he was on a level with Grendel.

'Only a few more hours now, Grendel,' he said. 'Only a few hours before you join us in the ritual.'

Grendel raised his head at last and stared at Timur. 'The Burning Altar—'

'Yes. The way to Touaris,' said Timur. 'The thing you have been waiting for.'

'The thing we have been preparing you for,' said the second man.

Grendel lowered his head again, half covering it with his arms like a child frightened of the dark or of a blow. In a muffled voice so low that Elinor had to strain to catch it, he said, 'But not when I am *me*! It's only when *he* comes— *He's* the one who enjoys it!'

Elinor felt as if she had been plunged neck-deep into

black icy water. Schizophrenia. Wasn't it? Yes, surely the classic symptom was to refer to the alter ego as a separate individual.

'There is no *he*,' said Timur, and a note of cold implacability entered his voice. 'There is only you.' He exchanged a glance with the other man and Elinor saw his expression. They've miscalculated, she thought suddenly. Whatever they want of Grendel, he's jibbing. Because he's crossed the line back into sanity? And if he has, will it help me?

Timur turned back to Grendel. 'Remember all the things Iwane and I promised you, Grendel?' he said, and now his tone was that of someone taking infinite patience with a recalcitrant child. 'All the things waiting for you in Tashkara?'

'Your people waiting for you,' said Iwane.

'You have to lead them, Grendel. And the feasts – you will preside over the feasts at the Burning Altar.'

'You enjoy the feasts,' said Iwane. 'We showed you about the feasts. We taught you to enjoy them.'

'I did enjoy them—' But it was the half-ashamed admission of a child confessing a misdemeanour.

Iwane stood up and jerked his head towards the dead boy in the velvet jacket, and Elinor saw Timur smile and nod.

'Do we force him?' said Iwane softly.

'Only if we have to. But,' said Timur, in a low voice, 'we won't have to.'

Grendel had lifted his head and as his eyes fell on the body he flinched visibly. 'Don't make me do it again,' he said in a whisper, and pity spiked across Elinor's mind.

He's mad, of course. But he *knows* he's mad. She found herself wanting to bound across the room, knock the two men aside and comfort the poor mad creature who was so like Lewis that it hurt.

'You must do it,' said Timur. 'Just as you have done it before. You must be ready for the initiation at the Altar.'

'But when I am me,' whispered Grendel, 'I *know* how bad it is—' But the red glint was already waking in his eyes, and his tongue came out to lick his lips.

'But it's exciting,' said Timur very softly. 'Remember how exciting it is? Grendel, look at me. Remember the dancers? Remember the ceremonial cat-mask dance of the Bubasti?'

'The cat dance—' Grendel was staring at the body, half propped against the wall. His eyes narrowed and slanted, and the face that was so eerily Lewis's seemed to grow momentarily thinner. Excitement, raw and fierce, blazed up in his eyes. But he's fighting it, thought Elinor, in appalled fascination. I can feel him fighting it.

'Do it,' said Timur in a half-whisper. 'Do it, Grendel. Feel the flesh open under the knife, taste the rich soft taste—'

'There is nothing like it in the whole world,' said Iwane.

'There is nothing like it in the whole world,' repeated Grendel obediently.

'It's the way to Touaris, Grendel – it's the way to lead her people.'

'Yes, I remember now. I remember that it paints the blood pictures for me. In my head.'

'Then do it,' whispered Timur. 'Paint the blood pictures. But paint them *slowly*. Take all the time you want.'

'The blood pictures.' His eyes were blurred and inward-looking now, but when he looked up again, for a disconcerting moment, shrewd cold sanity showed. 'It's for Touaris,' said Grendel, staring at Timur. 'I shall lead her people. You promised.'

'I promised.' Timur reached out and took Grendel's hand, bringing him gently to his feet. But he's wary all the same, thought Elinor. He's braced for Grendel to do something unexpected. 'I promised and you shall have it,' said Timur. 'But first there is this. You must be worthy, you know.'

'I must be worthy.' There it was again, the heart-breaking humility.

Taking Grendel's hand, Timur led him forward to the prone body, moving with deliberate slowness as if fearing that an abrupt movement might shatter the dark spell he was throwing about Grendel. He bent down and pulled back the dead boy's cheap velvet jacket and then tore aside the thin shirt. The poor dead flesh was pale and flaccid, but here and there it was mottled with livid bruises where the blood had coagulated after death.

Grendel crouched down, his eyes on the boy, and after what seemed to be a very long time, he reached out, his hands crooked into claws. He raked both hands down the boy's chest, his fingernails gouging deep wounds and tearing away ribbons of skin.

Timur and Iwane smiled at one another over his head, and Grendel sat back, regarding his victim. Shreds of flesh clung to his fingers and there was a faint slick of not-quite-colourless fluid.

To Elinor's horror he lifted both hands to his mouth, licking them like an animal cleaning its paws. She shuddered, and then thought: but at least the boy was dead. Should that make me feel better? Is this what they'll do to me tomorrow night? But it won't hurt, my dear, because you'll be dead before we start . . . Oh God, am I back in the nightmare? If I'm not, I think I'm keeping hold of sanity, but it's getting to be a near thing.

Timur said in a low urgent voice, 'More, Grendel. Go *on*. You know what you have to do,' and Iwane said, 'The pictures, Grendel. The blood pictures. Make them come in your head.'

Grendel bent over the boy, burying his face in the gaping wound. There was a wet sucking sound, and then he lifted his head and looked up at the two men. His mouth and face were smeared with the leaking body-juices of the corpse, and his lips stretched in a crazed smile.

'Like this?' he cried. '*Like this*?' and Elinor shuddered, because at last it was the dreadful gloating voice of the dark demented creature. 'This is what you want, isn't it?' cried Grendel. 'The dark hunger of Tashkara! The feast of the flesh and the juice and the marrow of humans!'

Shreds of skin clung to his teeth and dribbles of glutinous fluid ran over his chin and it was impossible to escape the image of a feral, feeding beast, its jowls gore-soaked, looking up from its grisly banquet. Grendel held Timur's eyes and said, in a greed-laden whisper that sent prickles of revulsion scudding across Elinor's skin, 'I have the pictures. I have the cataracts of blood and the fields of bloodied bones, all pouring through my mind. I see them all. I *feel* them all. Bones squelching between my hands . . .' He held out his hands, opening and closing them. 'And blood dripping down my throat . . .' He drew in a deep breath, and then fixed his eyes on Timur. In a voice filled with thick purring menace, he said, 'And now give me the knife.'

Elinor had thought that nothing could possibly be worse than what had already happened, but when Grendel began to slice into the poor torn corpse with Timur's thin-bladed knife, she had to swallow very hard indeed to stop herself from being sick. There was an expression of intense concentration on Grendel's face, and although he was breathing harshly and droplets of sweat clung to his hair, the mad exultation had vanished and he appeared to be wholly absorbed in what he was doing. But when he finally held up a lump of flaccid flesh, his eyes were glittering with triumph, and he looked to the two men as if waiting for approval.

'It is very well done indeed,' said Timur. 'And now say it, Grendel. Say it as I taught you.'

Grendel said, 'I am the seed of the lost tribe who came out of the land of Egypt and into the land of freedom. I am the son of the Divine One of the Bubasti, who feast at the Burning Altar, and they shall take me for their leader, they shall forsake all false gods and fall down and worship me—' He broke off, bending over the repulsive lump of flesh, cradling it in his cupped hands, crooning over it.

Elinor thought she was not especially religious, but Grendel's glib obedient catechism of that travesty of biblical lore stung. *I am the son of the Divine One of the Bubasti, who feast at the Burning Altar* . . . Timur had sold him some kind of divine Messiah tale.

'Again, very good. And now you must eat.'

'Yes, I must eat,' said Grendel. He cupped the slab of flesh protectively, and crawled into the corner, half crouching, half kneeling.

Timur nodded to Iwane, who went across to the trap door and lifting the flap, went back down into the tunnels.

Timur watched him go and then turned to look at Elinor.

As his eyes met hers the gas jets sank lower, stirring the swelling shadows into eerie life and creating movement where no movement actually existed. It began to seem as if the whole cavern were alive with creeping shadows.

Timur's eyes were glittering with cold cruel lust, and there was a dreadful moment when Elinor felt his mind brush hers with sexual hunger. Oh God, he's going to rape me. I'm going to lose my virginity at last, but I'm going to lose it in this nightmare place with rotting bodies stuffed into a drain and a chained madman eating raw flesh within yards of us . . .

She said, as coldly and as disdainfully as she could manage, 'Has your jackal gone out to get more victims?' Her voice was cracked and dry because of not having spoken for so long, but it sounded fairly contemptuous.

'He's not a jackal, Miss Craven, but he has certainly gone out to find sacrifices. I see you understand something of what we are doing.'

'I understand that you're deliberately feeding Grendel's madness,' said Elinor. 'And that you're keeping me prisoner. You do know that I'll have been missed by now?

202

And that people will be searching for me?' This all came out much angrier and much braver than she had dared hope.

'No one will search for you,' said Timur. 'Lewis Chance is in Bath, and the centre is closed. And if anyone should start asking difficult questions – that meddlesome Raffael, or your pretty niece – we shall deal with them, as we have always done.'

Elinor stared at him in mute horror. Ginevra. Then she *is* here! But he knows she's here! And Raffael was meddling somehow! But her mind was unable to grapple with this, and after a moment, she said, 'What does – "deal with them" – mean?'

'If they try to find you or stop us they will die on the Burning Altar. As you will die tomorrow night,' said Timur. 'It was a pity you pried, Miss Craven, because we seldom use females in our sacrifices. But sometimes it is necessary, and unfortunately you saw too much. I'm sorry about it, but we can't risk letting you live. You will not die the sacrificial death, but that of a spy.'

'Is there a difference?'

'To die as a sacrifice to Touaris is honourable,' said Timur. 'To die as a spy is not.'

His voice held faint amusement and Elinor felt reality begin to blur again. Only I don't think I'm in reality; I think I must have slid back into the nightmare. *Please* let me have slid back into the nightmare. I'm going to die the dishonourable death of a spy.

The room tilted and whirled about her, and she fought to stay conscious, and then heard her voice say coldly, 'You'll be caught, of course. You really won't get away with this.' God, how conventional I'm sounding! But it's better than grovelling and pleading for mercy. Or is it?

Timur said, 'We shan't be caught. After tomorrow night my people and I will leave England and Grendel will go with us. You – assuming your body is identifiable – will probably be written off as one more of Grendel's victims.

We shall leave a few clues pointing to that, of course, and people will say, How very sad: but Lewis Chance was a great fool to think he could control that boy. And there will certainly be people to vouch for Grendel's mental state.'

As Timur spoke Elinor caught, on the rim of her vision, a slight movement, and realised that Grendel had turned his head to listen.

'The Burning Altar,' Timur was saying, 'is one of the oldest rituals in the world.'

By a supreme effort Elinor managed not to look in Grendel's direction. She kept her eyes fixed on Timur and pushed down the monstrous images his words were conjuring up, and said, 'I still don't understand what you're doing to Grendel. Or why you need him.'

'You don't need to understand. But I will tell you that our task has been made harder than we expected because Grendel is not quite as mad as we thought him. There are periods of almost complete normality.'

'Which doesn't suit your purpose,' said Elinor venomously. And look at me, Timur, *look at me* and keep looking, because Grendel's standing up, and he's listening very intently to what you're saying. And oh God, don't let me lose consciousness again!

'It does not suit it at all,' said Timur. 'We want Grendel very mad indeed, and we believe that tomorrow night will tip him once and for all into real insanity.'

'He seems helplessly insane to me,' said Elinor coldly. 'But perhaps our standards are different.' Anger flared in Timur's eyes, and despite her fear Elinor felt a spurt of triumph.

Timur said, 'As you saw just now, Grendel craves the taste of human flesh, but part of him is still desperately struggling for—'

'Normality? If you want Grendel for some kind of figurehead you must be a very strange crowd,' said Elinor. But keep talking, Timur, keep boasting about your mad plans, you horrible vain thing, keep your attention on me, because it's going to be your undoing . . . Only don't look round, because Grendel's creeping towards you . . .

Timur said, 'The madder Grendel is, the easier it will be for us to put him on the ancient throne of Touaris.' He paused, and then said, 'Mad, *really* mad, he will be easy to control. He thinks he will rule, but he will not, of course.'

'Who will?' This had to be the most fantastic conversation anyone had ever had. Ancient thrones and mad pretenders controlled by evil *éminences grises*. I'm in something out of Dumas or Anthony Hope, thought Elinor, *The Prisoner of Zenda* or *The Man in the Iron Mask*. Timur's probably as mad as Grendel, if the truth's known – no, that would mean I'm down here with two madmen, and I won't think it.

'The League of which I am leader will rule. Of course.'

'League?'

'The League of Tamerlane.'

'I've never heard of it,' said Elinor contemptuously.

'It is named for a leader of Tashkara who ruled a hundred years ago, and was known as Tamerlane the Avenger. And it consists of a group of activists who will sweep away the old superstitions and the narrow minds of Tashkara,' said Timur. 'And make a new enlightened people under a new leader.'

For a moment his tone was the unmistakable one of the fanatic pledging a better world, and Elinor stared at him and felt a sudden sensuous pull. A Redeemer, a Golden Race, a New Age . . . And then the fleeting evocative images vanished, and she remembered all those people vainly awaiting Redeemers who never came, and all those promises made by fanatics that turned out to be hollow. And Golden Races were only born out of the death agonies of slaughtered millions, and the only New Age that had dawned in the West this century was of half-gypsy travellers, most of whom worshipped nothing better than rock music and drugs . . .

'Grendel will serve the League's purpose – and therefore

my own – very well,' said Timur. He made a brief dismissive gesture in the direction of Grendel's corner, and Grendel froze into immobility at once. 'You have seen what he is,' said Timur, looking down at Elinor with amusement and cruelty in his expression. 'You see how near to the surface is the hunger. He can barely control it.'

'He's sick,' said Elinor bitterly. 'His mind's sick and you're deliberately making it sicker. You're forcing him down into madness.' *And little though you know it, Timur, you're condemning yourself with every word now.*

'Believe me, Elinor,' said Timur softly, 'Grendel needs very little forcing.'

Grendel was inching forward again. He had scooped up his chains in both hands, and he was paying them out as he went. But the steel linkage gave the chains a horrid life of their own and Elinor was excruciatingly aware that at any second there might be a telltale chink of sound. *He's a madman creeping up on another madman and if he fails, either of them or both of them will almost certainly kill me and they might do any number of appalling things to me first. Don't think about it. Concentrate on keeping Timur talking. Grendel's only got about another dozen more steps. What will he do? Strangle Timur with the chains? Knock him out? But supposing the chains aren't long enough? Oh God, what then?*

There was no time even to think this, because Grendel moved then, bounding forward, his lips drawn back in a snarl, the teeth gleaming wetly. *Like a huge cat,* thought Elinor, flinching as far back as her own chains would allow. There was a brief vivid glimpse of a face scarcely human and then Grendel had sprung on to Timur's back and looped the chains around his neck, jerking them tight. Timur gave an anguished grunt and his eyes bulged, and with his other hand, Grendel brought the bunched chains – looped, steel knuckle-dusters – smashing down on his skull over and over again. There was a sickening crunch of bone splintering, and there was an appalling moment when Timur was still struggling to get free, flailing at the air. He half broke away, and stumbled a few feet, but he was almost blinded and barely conscious. Grendel pounced again, dealing a final crashing blow, and Timur crumpled to the floor.

Grendel stared down at him, the bunched chains still held in his hands. 'You promised me the throne of Touaris, Timur,' he said. 'You *promised*. But you were going to cheat – I heard you say it.' He looked about him, scanning the dim warehouse, and Elinor pressed as far back into the shadows as she could. But when Grendel looked at her there was a vivid flash of sanity: a brief glimpse of a mind that was perfectly logical and perfectly normal. He has periods of almost complete normality, Timur had said. Yes, but how long do they last?

But when Grendel said, 'We must search his pockets for keys to the padlocks,' his voice was perfectly logical and normal, and when he said, 'And we must do it quickly!' it was almost Lewis's voice and Lewis's quick impatience. 'Iwane might come back at any minute!' said Grendel, and plunged his hands into Timur's pockets. Elinor waited, scarcely daring to breathe, and after a moment Grendel straightened up, frowning. 'Nothing,' he said. 'He was too wily to have kept them on him and brought them down here.'

'The trap door's not locked,' volunteered Elinor, forcing herself to speak in an ordinary voice. 'But we can't reach it. We can't escape that way.'

'No.' Grendel looked about him, and his eyes shone suddenly. 'But there is another way that we can escape,' he said softly. 'In a few hours Timur's people will assemble for the ritual of the Burning Altar.' He looked down at Timur. 'If they believe me to be Timur, they will do what I tell them. And that means—'

'What—'

'I must become Timur,' said Grendel. His eyes met Elinor's, and he lifted the glinting knife.

Chapter Nineteen

The knife caught the light as Grendel bent over Timur's prone body, and as he brought it slicing across Timur's scalp, blood welled up, thin, watery.

He was completely absorbed. After the first cut, he had taken up a position astride Timur, blocking him from Elinor's line of sight. But although she could not see what he was doing, she could hear. There was a wet squelch of skin tearing and once there was the indescribably sickening scrape of steel against bone.

After what seemed a very long time, Grendel moved back and stood looking down as if considering his handiwork, and for a moment Elinor was unable to make sense of what she was seeing, because there was only that wet mess of blood and the thread of white bone and teeth just beneath...

And then dreadful comprehension rushed in, and despite her resolve and despite thrusting a fist into her mouth again, a gasp of sick horror broke from her. I must become Timur, Grendel had said.

Where Timur's face had been was a huge bleeding wound. Like raw meat, thought Elinor. Like a shapeless lump of skinless meat. *Skinless*, oh God... If it had not been for the eyes – bulging pale globes no longer surrounded by their cushion of flesh and skin – and the unmistakable nose bone – white and jutting, like cuttlefish – the livid mass would not have been identifiable. Far worse than all else was the leathery flap of skin hanging from the scalp. He's removed his face! thought Elinor, appalled and sickened. He's peeled back the skin of his face, and it's hanging loose!

Grendel bent to his grisly task again, and as he did so, a dreadful moan broke from the man on the ground. Horror scudded across Elinor's skin, and Grendel recoiled at once, his hand frozen in the act of cutting the final shreds of skin away.

He's not dead! thought Elinor. Oh dear God, Grendel's taking his face off and he's not dead. This is the worst nightmare anyone could imagine. The coppery taint of stale blood gusted into her face as if something had breathed it and sweat broke out on her forehead. Concentrate. Don't throw up because you'll feel worse afterwards, never mind making a mess on the floor. And don't succumb to hysterics like some stupid Victorian heroine either.

She forced herself to remain seated upright, wiping her forehead with the back of her hand. Grendel was bending over Timur again, and there was a look of snarling satisfaction on his face, as if he were saying, Now you're definitely dead. I don't know what he's done, thought Elinor: I can't see, and I don't *want* to see! I suppose he's stabbed him through the heart or the base of the skull or something. And how mad is he really? Will he turn on me next? He can't reach me – I *know* he can't! – but supposing there was a key after all? Supposing he found it and he's about to unlock his chains and pounce on me? Would he jab the knife into my neck and then peel off my face? I wouldn't know he was doing it, but that's hardly the point. What if it's his obsession – like that horror film with Anthony Hopkins – where a mad serial killer cut off somebody's face and used it as a disguise.

Grendel straightened up again and there was an air of finality about him. Between his hands was something thin, and smeary and dripping with blood and mucus, which he held with extreme care. Grendel looked to where Elinor was hunched into a tiny fearful huddle, and nodded. Was he saying: The plan's going to work? Or was he saying: It's your turn next?

With the same immense care, Grendel lifted the grisly fragment of skin between his hands, and stood for a moment looking down at it. For the first time since Elinor had seen him, he appeared reluctant.

And then he seemed to take a deep breath and to square his shoulders. Moving slowly, he raised the torn-off skin and clapped it over his own face.

It stayed in place at once, but Grendel padded across to the wavery green mirror and stood before it, considering his reflection, pushing the grisly mask this way and that. He's forcing it into position, thought Elinor, unable to look away. I was right about it being like that film. He's wearing his victim's face.

Grendel did not look towards her again. He pulled the body of Timur into the shadows cast by the piles of packing cases, and began to strip his clothes off. Finally there was the scrape of the barred grille being pulled aside. Down among the dead men, thought Elinor. He's tipping Timur into the corpse drain. She heard the grille pulled back into place, and then Grendel reappeared. He had donned Timur's clothes, and the dreadful mask was in place. It clung to his skin and although it was ragged and bloody, in the dim uncertain light it gave him an astonishing resemblance to the dead Timur. It was overwhelmingly sinister. He sat down on the floor, facing the room, cross-legged, apparently withdrawing into the strange dark rapt state of his own once more.

Sweat had formed and dried on Elinor's spine. She had no idea how far Grendel could be trusted, or whether this might be part of some mad sick plan. *Let's sit down here together, my dear, with mutilated corpses scattered around us, wearing the faces I peel off my victims . . . And which one would you like to wear, Elinor . . .? You always said you were unhappy with the face God gave you, now's a chance to choose somebody else's . . .*

It was oppressively quiet. The gas jets hissed and spat, and once Elinor caught the scuttering of rats in the tunnels again. Once Grendel seemed to sigh and Elinor braced herself for an attack. But he remained where he was, the grisly visor drying on his face.

Waiting for Timur's people to enter the dim warehouse and begin the ritual of the Burning Altar.

Georgie and Baz had suggested the Anchor as the starting point for the night's venture, Georgie explaining that the pub was their usual Friday-night venue. He pronounced it *veen-yew* and was frowned at by Baz, who thought they ought to try to live up to Top Floor's company, never mind Ginevra Craven who was a very class act indeed.

Ginevra's classiness had worried them quite a bit, because as Baz pointed out, if she walked in to the Anchor looking all silk-knickered and Sloane she was going to stand out like a spare prick at a gang bang and *that* would finish everybody's chances of catching the villains! It was not, somehow, a question of clothes – Ginevra was wearing the most ordinary jeans and T-shirt and sweater – it was simply that she had an air of quality.

Ginevra, however, had already thought this one out. She had not brought many things with her because of it only being a weekend stay, and most of what she had brought was inside Chance House. But she plundered the boys' wardrobe and ended up borrowing the black leather bomber jacket which Baz had bought during his motorbike phase and not worn for six months, and a scarlet silk vest acquired by Georgie in a moment of rash self-indulgence. Baz pointed out that the jacket was not precisely leather and Ginevra grinned and said, 'All the better.' Georgie, never at a loss, said there was no knowing *what* might be in the pockets, and better let him turn them out first.

The jacket, over her ordinary jeans and the scarlet silk

vest, looked astonishing. She tried the vest with a bra and then without. Without, it clung to her breasts like wet tissue paper. No bra, then. She looked like a biker from the sixties, or a street-walker, which was the whole idea. The braless vest would give Raffael something to think about. Ginevra concentrated on Raffael's reactions, partly because it was an alluring idea, but also because it stopped her from dwelling too much on what might be ahead.

She twisted her hair into a tail on top of her head, leaving trailing strands all round, which gave her a faintly sluttish look. Thick make-up: industrial-strength eye make-up and lipstick like jam, and the earrings. Now she looked like the town harlot. 'In silk and scarlet walks many a harlot...' Or what about, 'It's a brave night to cool a courtesan' – *King Lear*, was that? She needed the English tutor to put her right – no, she didn't. Anyway, looking like this, leer was an appropriate word.

'Why is the League of Tamerlane only taking boys?' asked Ginevra, wandering around Raffael's rooms, trying not to think too much about what was ahead by guessing which were his possessions and which were the landlord's. The books were clearly Raffael's – no Canning Town landlord ever read Voltaire or Rousseau in the original French – and the table lamp and the very beautiful peacock-hued tapestry rug were probably his as well.

She said, 'I meant to ask about that earlier and I forgot. I don't mean why are they only taking prostitutes because that's obvious – easy prey. But why not girls as well?'

'I think it might be that the cult specifies young men.' Raffael was peering through an uncurtained window into the street below. He was still wearing the disreputable herringbone coat which flapped around his ankles and his hair looked as if it needed brushing, and with the drifting fog silhouetting him he looked like a displaced person; the kind you saw on old forties newsreels straggling out of

Poland or Czechoslovakia. He looked like somebody thrown out of Mother Russia for writing subversive literature or organising a revolution. He looked like anything other than a former Roman Catholic priest, and Ginevra wanted to reach out to him so much it was very nearly overwhelming.

'Remember, as well, that this is a tribe who worships a female deity,' said Raffael, still scanning the street.

'Touaris.'

'Yes. They might regard girls as *verboten*. But on the other hand it might be that females have been taken but not reported as missing.' He drew the curtains and crossed to switch on the lamps. A small core of warmth and light sprang up.

'And the press would be sure to play up the – the more sensational aspect,' said Ginevra thoughtfully. 'Or it might simply be that girls are cannier about who they go off with.'

'Or shrewder about spotting fakes,' said Raffael, and Ginevra grinned. 'Why are you dressed like a street-walker, by the way?'

'I'm going to blend into the background. I'm trying to look like somebody who frequents seedy East End pubs—'

'You look more like the Whore of Babylon, you ridiculous child. It's a good thing Fleury can't see you.' He went back to the window, and opened the curtain an inch, looking down again.

'Are you looking to see if we're being watched?'

'Yes. But I can't see anyone – in fact I can't see anything at all in this cursed fog.' He frowned. 'If we fail tonight we could make a search of the disused wharves tomorrow.'

'I hope this isn't going to turn into the classic race against time,' said Ginevra, trying to ignore the part about failing tonight. 'Or even the eleventh-hour-and-fifty-ninth-minute rescue.'

'Just so long as it *is* a rescue,' said Raffael. He looked back at her. 'You know, you shouldn't be here at all. I ought to make you go back to Chance House, only Timur's people are probably watching it—'

'Well, I wouldn't go anyway—'

'And you can't stay here for the same reason,' went on Raffael, as if arguing the matter out. 'It looks as if you'll have to come with me after all. What an exasperating infant you are.'

'Listen, we don't know what's likely to happen yet and you might be very glad I'm with you before tonight's over—'

'I am very glad you're with me,' said Raffael brusquely. 'Haven't you realised that yet?' And then, before Ginevra could think of a reply to this, he said, 'What about your family in Kensington? If we can flag down a taxi, would you go to them? No, all right, I can see you wouldn't.'

'I'm not going anywhere,' said Ginevra. 'Least of all Kensington. Jesus, they'd have a blue fit if they saw me looking like this, and—'

'Anyone would have a blue fit seeing you like that. And don't blaspheme.'

'I'm going into the Anchor to see if Georgie and Baz are followed,' said Ginevra firmly. 'And listen, if anyone ought to be skulking out of sight it's you; you'll spoil everything if Timur and his whatnot League see you.'

'They won't see me. I'll be with you, but I'll be out of sight,' said Raffael. 'Outside the Anchor – lurking in a doorway, somewhere.' He stiffened and motioned to her to switch off the light. Ginevra complied and padded across to the window to stand next to him. Thick yellow fog pressed against the glass and behind them the room was in darkness.

'What is it?'

'Someone standing on the corner,' said Raffael. 'Under the street light – see? You don't need to whisper, they can't hear us.'

214

'Sorry, overall furtiveness.' Ginevra leaned forward as far as she dared. 'I can't see anyone. Are you sure you aren't seeing things?'

'No, I'm not sure at all.' They were standing very close together because the window was quite small and because if there was anyone watching it was important not to be seen. Raffael leaned out again, and his hair brushed Ginevra's face. It might be uncombed, but it was clean and soft and there was a faint drift of masculine shampoo or soap. Her heart began to beat uncomfortably fast, but her mind said robustly that this was ridiculous: for one thing, he's twice my age. It wouldn't matter if he were four times it. And I don't even know if he's attracted to me – one minute he's tossing out declarations so wrapped up in allegories that you have to peel back the layers one by one to get at the truth, and the next he's cursing me for being in the way. And in a minute we'll be plunging into the fog to go after an ancient flesh-eating tribe and a sacrificial altar that roasts victims alive ... I wonder if anyone has ever had to cope with such a bizarre start to a relationship? I don't think any kind of relationship ought to start at all.

He suddenly pulled her round to face him, his hands on her shoulders. 'Ginevra, this is going to be appallingly dangerous,' he said. 'For the last time, will you let me get you a taxi to take you to your family's house?'

'No. Also for the last time.'

They stared at one another, and Ginevra's heart began to pound again. Here we go ... I think ... If he turns away now I'll know I misread the whole thing. One-way traffic only, kid ... Be grateful he's here at all.

But if his presence had been a charm, keeping the fear at bay, his touch was like a thousand-volt electric shock.

It seemed the most natural thing in the world to be pulled against him, and to feel his arms go around her. There was a faint comforting scent of masculinity again: fresh clean sweat and sharp male soap, and of course he was not rough trade, and even if he was she did not care.

There was nothing rough about the way he kissed her, although there was a kind of banked-down hunger, as if this was something he had been fighting to keep in check. Instant attraction, thought Ginevra, feeling an astonished spiral of delight soar. Then I was right after all. I only hope it isn't fatal attraction. She was aware of the most astonishing assortment of emotions, all warring for recognition. Thoughts like: I'd better not let this get as far as the bedroom. And then: I'd better not even let it get as far as the hearth. He's an ex-priest – yes, I'll remember that. I don't really care if he's a former devil-worshipper. He's Scheherazade and Schahriar, and he's Keats and Byron and the Medici princes all rolled up into one ... I've never met anyone like him – I don't think there is anyone like him. And he'll probably spoil me for anyone else, yes, I ought to remember that ... We certainly shan't reach the bedroom at this rate. I don't even think we're going to get as far as the hearth ...

It was the wildest blend of passion and spiralling romanticism and sheer frantic delight to find herself on the thick hearthrug in front of the popping gasfire – oh, we did get this far, then! – and to feel him reaching for her body, at the exact moment she was reaching for his. It was madness and it was ecstatic bliss and blissful ecstasy to see the dark eyes blaze up with passion, and to feel the hard thrust of helpless masculine need. I'm being screwed by an ex-priest while Elinor's in the hands of a gang of twentieth-century flesh-eaters! thought Ginevra, and then: no, I'm not being screwed at all! – I'm being *made love to*. I'd better not forget Elinor and the cannibals, though. Only I can't think about anything except what's happening ...

He made love with a kind of ferocious gentleness that drove out everything else, and when at last he lay back, his head on her naked shoulder, Ginevra, her spinning mind finally slowing into a deep intense calm, thought it was as if they had created an armour of warmth and safety. In a minute, in just another minute they would have to go out into the night. Only I'll be armoured. I'll have this to wrap around me. I don't know how long it'll last – the wrap, I mean – and I don't really know how effective it'll be, but I think it might last for quite a long time. I think I was right about being spoiled for anyone else, as well. I don't know whether to be glad or sorry.

Raffael raised himself on one elbow, and looked down at her. 'A benison,' he said, echoing her thoughts. 'A charm and a touchstone and a carapace against what's ahead, Ginevra.'

'Much better than Keats,' said Ginevra, and saw his eyes darken in half-amused perplexity. 'Just a thought. I'm glad you're original.' Some inner compulsion prompted her to say, 'This was a bit sudden for me. I mean I don't usually— Not within hours of a first meeting, that is.' Damn, why am I sounding so immature!

Raffael smiled. 'I'm glad to hear that, at least.'

And that's enough for the moment, thought Ginevra, firmly. Close the subject until after tonight, and then take another look at it. She said, in a practical voice, 'Is it time to go?'

'I'm afraid so.'

'Well then, let's.'

'Good girl.' He looked at her for a long moment, and then said in an ordinary voice, 'The fog looks quite thick – we'd better go hand in hand.'

Allegories again. Or was it? Ginevra said, 'All right.'

They stared at one another, and then Raffael said in a low voice, 'Because if I lose you in that murk I might never find you again.'

Chapter Twenty

The fog was still lying thickly over St Stephen's Road and the fake leather jacket was not meant for a cold October night with fog coming at you from all angles. But the carapace – what Raffael had called the touchstone – was still surrounding them, and Ginevra thought that like this she could walk into anything in the world and be unafraid. She could certainly walk into the Anchor and carry out the plan they had cooked up. Stay with me, Raffael.

The Anchor, when she pushed open the door, was filled with smoke and people and loud voices, and redolent with the smell of spilled beer and cigarette smoke and hot bar food. Ginevra had been wondering what type of pubs Georgie and Baz frequented on their rounds, but it would not have been polite to ask. She liked pubs as much as anyone, but she did not like smelly back-street bars with fly-blown mirrors and cracked plastic sofas, and evidence of people having been sick in the loo.

But the Anchor was not in the least sleazy or smelly and the seats were not ripped up by flick knives or stained with last night's vomit. It was lively and cheerful and bright, and at ten o'clock on a Friday evening it was very crowded.

Georgie and Baz were leaning against the bar, drinking lager and looking bright-eyed; Georgie had slicked his hair back with gel and put on a very snazzy striped shirt. They ignored her and went on with their conversation, which was part of the plan, and Ginevra pushed her way to the bar to buy a drink, which was also part of the plan.

House wine was available by the glass and a blackboard was chalked with the bar food available tonight. Somebody could not spell chilli con carne. Everything seemed so normal that she began to wonder if Raffael was the victim of a sick practical joke. But Elinor was missing and so was Lewis Chance, and so was his poor mad son. Get on with it, Gina.

She was jostled quite a bit, and several raucous suggestions came her way, which she countered by saying she was meeting someone. She thought she sounded pretty convincing and she thought she was blending quite well with the surroundings.

When her drink arrived she stayed where she was, leaning back against the bar and lifting her glass, which was the signal for Georgie and Baz to go into action. None of them had been sure if the plan would work, but Ginevra, sitting cross-legged in front of their gasfire, arguing the matter out and dealing with all objections, had won them over. Georgie and Baz could not just walk into the Anchor, or any of their other haunts, and expect Timur's people to approach them purely because they wanted it, said Ginevra, her eyes glowing with fervour. They needed to do something to make them stand out and to seem good targets to any of Timur's scouts. They needed to draw attention to the fact that one of them was going to be on the street by himself and therefore vulnerable.

Georgie and Baz had got quite fired up over Ginevra's idea. Quite a performance they'd have to give, not that they minded that, Ginevra was to understand. They began to tell one another what they would do and how they would do it and what the outcome would be. Baz found a notebook and wrote everything down, and Ginevra began to worry that they would go over the top.

They did not go over the top at all. They propped themselves against the bar and began to argue, quietly at first, and then more loudly. Georgie let his voice soar several octaves, which was astonishingly convincing and also remarkably penetrating. He said he was sick of being ignored, he was nothing but a doormat in fact, and he was very sick indeed of Baz screwing around. Anybody's, that's what Baz was, said Georgie, working himself up to a nice pitch of near-hysteria; anybody's for the asking, and very *belittling* it was as well! Ginevra, sipping her drink, listened appreciatively and sent a covert look about her. People had glanced in the boys' direction and one or two had smirked a bit knowingly, but on the whole nobody was paying much attention. She tried to see if any foreign-looking gentlemen were watching, but there was such a motley collection in here that it might as well be Commonwealth Day.

The argument was reaching its climax. Georgie was in the nail-biting, shoulder-hunching stage and Baz was trying to reason with him, looking around in an embarrassed way, laying a hand on Georgie's shoulder and being flung petulantly off. Academy Award-winning stuff, thought Ginevra. It would be a pity if they had to repeat this in too many pubs, because either the edge would go off it, or they would start putting in little embellishments – Georgie would certainly put in embellishments – and it would all ring false.

'—coming home at three in the morning—'

'—make a scene every time I speak to someone—'

'—know quite *well* who you've been with and all I can say is I hope I don't catch—'

'—getting pissed off with your jealousy—'

One or two people, clearly regulars who knew the pair, looked across and cheered them on. Somebody called out, 'Chuck him out, Baz,' and somebody else shouted, 'Toss him out and toss him off, Georgie,' which raised a raucous hoot of laughter. Ginevra hoped their credibility would not suffer too much.

Baz was saying, 'Well, you can fuck off if that's how you feel,' and Georgie was responding with, 'I will! I will fuck off, and I won't come back – *then* you'll see—'

220

'Who needs *you* anyway!'

Georgie slammed his glass down on the counter, and pushed his way blindly through the press of people. Behind him Baz shrugged and turned his back, leaning over the bar to attract the barman's attention for another drink, and Georgie made his way through the crowd, shrugging off one or two half-hearted approaches of sympathy – 'Leave me *alone*! – Take your frigging hands *off*!'

The street door swung open and he went out, pausing artistically in the doorway for a moment, turning up his coat collar and giving a realistic shiver at the cold night air outside.

Ginevra stayed where she was. It was too much to hope that they would hit the mark first time, and they would probably have to meet up in the second pub on their list. Baz, carefully efficient, had written it all down and even sketched a map, so that they could arrive by separate routes. Ginevra slid one hand into her pocket to check the list for the next pub, and as she did so two dark-haired men got up from a corner table, and went unobtrusively out after Georgie. Alarm bells sounded in Ginevra's head and she took a deep breath and set down her half-finished drink.

She gave it a count of twenty and then went out after them.

It was the classic walk through the fog-shrouded streets of London's East End. Ginevra could almost have imagined she had fallen into a time warp, because the mist hid all the signs of modern progress; it muffled the traffic and shrouded the telegraph poles and modern architecture, but it left visible the old Victorian buildings.

In some places they called river fog The Creeper. Ginevra wished she had not remembered this, because it sounded unspeakably sinister. She went determinedly on, the mist clinging to her hair and running down Baz's jacket in little rivulets. She could make out Georgie's shape up ahead, and she could see the outlines of the two men who had followed him. She hesitated and glanced back, trying to see if Raffael was behind her. There was no sound but that meant nothing because Raffael moved like a cat. And Baz would be following as well, so she was not really alone at all. It was only the fog that was making her feel isolated.

It was getting harder to see more than a foot or two ahead, but she was just keeping Georgie and the two men in sight. She thought they were definitely following him and although they might easily be – what would be the term – clients? – it seemed a pretty funny way of going about the matter. It was going to be a dreadful letdown if the men turned out to be a couple of punters soliciting Georgie's services for half an hour.

As she neared the corner of the road a thick squat shape came up at her out of the mist, and Ginevra gasped and threw out her hands defensively, and then gasped again in relief. A postbox, that was all. She had almost walked into it.

The trouble with fog was that it played tricks with your eyes, so that you began to imagine faceless beings crouching in its smoky depths, watching you. It played tricks with your hearing as well, and it created queer muffled echoes so that you began to think that someone might be creeping along behind you. At this point, Ginevra brought her thoughts to an abrupt halt and acknowledged what she had been aware of at another level for some minutes. Somebody *was* creeping along behind her.

It was a very bad moment indeed. She stopped dead in the middle of the street, and at once the footsteps stopped as well. Her heart began to pound. She went on, deliberately slower, and the footsteps slowed. Somebody genuinely lost, fumbling through the gloom? An echo of her own steps? She did the test again: walk fast and then suddenly very slow. Yes. Exactly in synch. This is

222

someone being very stealthy indeed. Padding through the night – no, that's a nasty way of describing it. *Walking* through the night.

It was almost certainly Raffael or Baz, of course, but it was a bit much of them to creep after her like this. Pursuit through the fog. It sounded like the title of a horror film: Jack the Ripper slinking through Whitechapel brandishing a dripping knife and being chased through the old river buildings, and finally falling into the river. They were not far from the river here, in fact they seemed to be going directly towards it: Ginevra could hear the muffled hoot of a barge.

It would be better not to think about Jack the Ripper. But Ginevra had long since discovered that thoughts can be stubborn and the more you try to dismiss them, the firmer they lodge in your mind. The more she tried to stop thinking about Jack the Ripper, the more she did think about him. He had cut out his victims' guts and stomachs and livers and made that macabre little banquet of one victim's kidneys. Not so very different from what's ahead of me now. Life's a circle, kid.

Georgie and the two men turned a corner and were abruptly hidden from view. There was a sudden shout of fear, abruptly bitten off with a kind of yelp, and then a different voice let out a muffled curse. Ginevra caught the sound of several soft thuds – blows? – and then of a scuffle. Footsteps rang out, not quite running, but going hastily and heavily and awkwardly.

She ran towards the sounds at once, swimming in and out of the swirling fog, praying not to run smack into postboxes or brick walls, or murderous assailants. She turned the corner into a narrow alley with high buildings on both sides. The road wound steeply down and the river sounds were suddenly much louder; she could smell the indefinable river-smell quite strongly.

She stood still, feeling rather helpless, wishing that Raffael would appear, and trying to penetrate the swirling mist. And then there was a sudden movement in front of her and the mist parted. A monstrous head, a nightmare head like a huge cat with snarling lips and yellow evil eyes peered down at her, and hands that were not hands, but greedy clawed paws reached out. Ginevra drew breath to scream, and from behind, a second set of hands closed over her mouth.

Chapter Twenty-one

Lewis struggled up out of misted unawareness to the realisation that he was half sitting, half lying in the back of some kind of large vehicle that was bouncing and jolting over a badly made road. He felt slightly sick and his mouth was almost unbearably dry, and he had absolutely no idea where he was or how much time had passed.

A voice at his side said, 'We are about two hours away from Tashkara, Sir Lewis. There is still a while to travel. And you are in the back of a Land Rover.'

Lewis, struggling for full consciousness, said, 'How did you—'

'Get you here? It was extremely easy,' said Kaspar. 'We took a plane from Heathrow to Beijing Airport. In your day, I think it would have been Delhi. And then from Beijing on to Lhasa.' A flask of distilled water was held out and there was the chink of ice cubes. Lewis drank gratefully; the iced water soothed his parched throat and helped to push back the drugged mists a little. He lay back trying to assemble his thoughts.

'I have no idea how you managed to get this far,' he said, and was pleased to hear that his voice sounded perfectly calm. 'But we shan't, of course, reach Tashkara.' The name came out in a kind of angry snarl, and he felt his mind flinch from it. Tashkara – Patrick's golden haunted road. And I'm going back. 'This is a kidnapping,' he said icily. 'You'll have been spotted.'

'No,' said Kaspar, and Lewis, still struggling for full awareness, saw that Kaspar was seated beside him, with two men in the Land Rover's middle and two more at the front. He thought the driver was the one from the car at Bath, but could not be certain.

'We injected you with diazepam,' went on Kaspar. 'Which you perhaps know better as Valium. It induces semi-consciousness and some amnesia. Believe me, Sir Lewis, although you don't remember it, you have made a very long journey with us, during which you have been perfectly docile. You have travelled in reasonable comfort and you have certainly not given anyone the impression that you were being kidnapped, or that you were making the journey unwillingly – in fact the airport staff and the stewards were extremely sympathetic about your illness. No one was so bad-mannered as to enquire as to its precise nature, but they were all anxious to help you. Especially the women,' he said. 'And particularly after they recognised you.'

'Recognised?'

'We took your passport from Chance House, of course,' said Kaspar, as if this should have been obvious.

Lewis stared at him. 'Your people appear to have progressed since I knew them,' he said at last, forcing a note of contempt into his tone. 'In my day you were all primitive savages.'

Kaspar laughed, and the two in front half-turned and smiled. One of them said, 'Our people were already cultured while your ancestors were still bartering and painting themselves with woad, Sir Lewis.'

'In the West, people are made use of by science,' said the other one. 'They become slaves to it, but with us, it's the other way about. We make science work for us. That enables us to live exactly as we please for most of the time.'

'To pursue the ways of our own people,' said the first.

'Nowadays,' said Kaspar, 'we send a proportion of our young men and women away to school and, if they are sufficiently intelligent, on to university. Therefore we are very familiar with modern medicine and modern travel and modern technology.'

'And Western languages,' said the one who had talked about the West being a slave to science. He said it sneeringly, as if Western languages were crude and inferior, and Lewis felt a stir of anger.

He said, 'I'm surprised to hear any of them come back to your peasant tribe.'

The man laughed. 'It's your religion that says, Give me a child until he is seven, Sir Lewis.' The dark eyes studied him and Lewis regarded him coldly for a moment before turning back to Kaspar.

'Well? Am I to be given the courtesy of an explanation?'

'Of course. I do not think,' said Kaspar consideringly, 'that there is a word, either in your culture or in mine, for the murder of a religion. But it is that crime you are charged with, Sir Lewis.'

'So you said in Bath. Are your heathens capable of setting up a trial? I don't expect a fair one, you understand; you've probably picked the jury and decided the verdict and agreed on the punishment already.'

'Oh, we can arrange the trial of miscreants if we have to,' said Kaspar, sounding amused. 'And if you are found guilty, the punishment will be carried out in accordance with the Decalogue's ruling.' He paused and then said, 'It is also possible that the punishment pronounced over you twenty-five years ago – the punishment you so narrowly escaped – will be revived. You have not forgotten that?'

'I shouldn't think anyone ever could forget it,' said Lewis. 'As an illustration of sheer barbarism it must be unparalleled.' This was surely the most unreal conversation anyone could possibly have. He wondered how much of it was due to the effects of the drug. He forced his mind to focus, and after a moment he said, 'Why now? Why have you waited all these years to bring me back?'

For the first time Kaspar appeared to hesitate. 'There is

some – unrest among the younger people of Tashkara,' he said at last. And then, as if imparting distasteful but necessary information, 'Seven years ago a schism occurred within our people.' His voice was expressionless, but his eyes glinted coldly. 'It is the first time in our history such a thing has ever happened, and it was then that the stone palace you knew was destroyed by a group of dissidents who call themselves the League of Tamerlane.'

'And who is Tamerlane?'

'The name is taken from one of my predecessors,' said Kaspar. 'But the leader of the dissidents is a young man called Timur. He and his followers made certain demands which I – and the elders of Tashkara – refused to accede to.'

'What kind of demands?'

Kaspar hesitated and then said. 'They wanted your son, Sir Lewis. They still want him. They want him as a figurehead ruler: a puppet leader to head their rebellion.'

He paused, and Lewis, his mind racing, thought: then the Tashkarans *have* got Grendel, only not in the way I thought!

Aloud he said, 'So you're facing a *coup d'état*. Well, you won't be the first puny ruler to do that, and your Timur won't be the first to grab some kind of cheap notoriety, either. Has he many followers?'

'Among the younger people he has many,' said Kaspar. 'Seven years ago they threatened to burn down the stone palace if I – if we did not agree to follow their ways.'

'One of them being to acknowledge my son as ruler?'

'Yes.'

'And you stood firm and they were as good as their word, and so the stone palace was destroyed,' said Lewis. 'Serves you right. I hope this Timur hounds you out for all he's worth. Is this League dangerous other than to your people?'

'Yes. Its people are about to make use of one of our prophecies,' said Kaspar. 'In the last century – during the time of Tamerlane himself – it was foretold that the

Decalogue would fall into the hands of Western leaders and Western power.' He glanced at Lewis. 'I do not wish to lose the Stone Tablets of my ancestors, and you would not wish it either, I think.'

'Rid yourself of that belief, Kaspar. I don't give a damn what happens to your bits of rock.'

'Not even if they were used to deal Western religion a lethal blow?'

Lewis met the dark eyes coldly. 'You're overestimating your rebels' importance,' he said. 'Western religion's taken far worse knocks than your tawdry little uprising could inflict.'

'Your Vatican does not think so.'

'Oh, bullshit. If Timur believes he can topple the Vatican he sounds closer to Adolf Hitler or Saddam Hussein than a peaceful liberator.'

'Timur intends to make use of the Tashkara Decalogue to bring himself to prominence.'

'In the West?'

'Or the East. He does not care which,' said Kaspar.

Lewis's mind was working furiously. 'In the Western world,' he said, after a moment, 'when men of power are threatened, they cast around for two things: a scapegoat or a diversion. Sometimes both. That's what you've done. I'm your scapegoat, aren't I?'

'If you are,' said Kaspar slowly, 'you have only yourself to blame. If you had not done – what you did all those years ago – this situation would not have arisen.'

'Balls,' said Lewis at once. 'You don't give a sod about Western – or Eastern – politics, or even about your precious Decalogue. You're protecting your own miserable skin and your own petty power.' He sat back in his seat. His head was still throbbing from the lingering drug and he was light-headed and dry-mouthed from the altitude, but he was somehow managing to maintain a cold contempt.

'You are not entirely right,' said Kaspar. 'But you are

right when you say I am going to use you to try to quench Timur's rebels. But there is also the question of Grendel.'

'What about him?'

Kaspar said, 'I would give up my own power for a worthy successor.'

'How altruistic,' said Lewis.

'But Timur is very unworthy indeed. Also, there is Grendel. And I would do anything in the world to stop Grendel from being given any kind of power in Tashkara.'

'Why?'

'Because he is flawed.'

'If he is,' said Lewis savagely, 'it's because of what happened at his birth. And it's because he inherited your warped lusts.'

'And yet once you shared in those lusts.'

'It was a question of eat or be eaten!' said Lewis bitterly, and thought: I don't believe I've just said that! He looked back at Kaspar. 'This Timur—'

'Yes?'

'Exactly who is he?'

'He heads the rebels.'

'So you said. What else?'

'As well as that,' said Kaspar, 'he is my son.' The dark eyes gleamed suddenly. 'It is an odd circle we complete, you and I. Your son and mine are trying to rule Tashkara, Sir Lewis.'

'I'm not completing any circles with you,' said Lewis.

As the Land Rover went deeper into the mountain desert, Lewis felt his courage slipping from him. All around them was nothing but dust and hard-packed roads, and the brooding Himalayas in the distance, smoky violet smudges against the skies. The vehicle would probably pass one or two of the primitive mud-walled farms, or an occasional hermit monk or nomad, but that would be all. The isolation was complete as it had always been out here, and there was no hope of escape and certainly no hope of sanctuary.

He felt the familiar dark cobweb-strands reaching out to entrap him once more. This is where I took part in that macabre ritual – where I supped on human flesh by leaping firelight – and this is where I entered the forbidden city.

And now I'm going back to face trial and if they find me guilty I shall certainly die under the ancient and grisly laws of Satan's Commandments.

The rope bridge over the gorge had gone, and a sturdier structure had replaced it, clearly intended to take vehicles but still perilously frail. The Land Rover jolted its way across and reached the other side safely, but Lewis, remembering the rough cart tracks leading to the saucer-shaped valley, thought they would almost certainly have to abandon it at some stage and finish the journey on foot. Would that be an opportunity for escape? A tiny shoot of hope unfurled. He would watch his every opportunity, and even if he had to hide in the hills and risk dying from starvation and thirst, it would be a better death than facing the vengeance of the Decalogue.

As they passed the burned-out ruin that had been the stone palace, he felt a shiver of cold fear, as if something evil and ancient had blown gently on his mind. What had once walked among those blackened and charred walls? And what might still walk, even today? Ghosts did not always come from the past.

'You see that it is quite ruined,' said Kaspar, following Lewis's gaze.

'I wish I'd thought of burning it down myself,' retorted Lewis. 'Your son and his League made a thorough job of it.'

'It was the protest of mutinous children, nothing more.'

'Whatever it was, it was a very substantial protest,' said Lewis.

He had thought he could make some kind of desperate run for the safety of the mountains when the four-track stopped, but he had reckoned without the lingering effects

231

of the drug, and of Tibet's altitude to which he was still adjusting. He had reckoned without Kaspar's men as well. When the Land Rover finally halted they were within a short distance of the once-shimmering city, and the four who had travelled in the front seats gave him no chance to get away. They bound his hands tightly behind his back even before they helped him out, and once he was standing up they looped a halter about his neck.

He was forced down to the ancient walled city, along the paths with the sheering rockface on each side. Cold dread closed about him as they approached the city gates – Patrick's fire-drenched gates of hell! Or was that the stone palace? Whatever it was, this time I'm going in as a prisoner.

As Kaspar's men half dragged, half carried him towards the shimmering tiered palace with the painted *stupa*, he said, with icy courtesy, 'Are you going to lock me up?'

Kaspar turned back to look at him. 'Of course we are. No one brought to face the Decalogue ever escapes, Sir Lewis.'

'I escaped twenty-five years ago,' said Lewis.

'And yet you are here once more.'

'Nearly a hundred years ago my ancestor escaped.'

There was an abrupt silence. 'Are you so sure of that?' said Kaspar.

'Yes,' said Lewis, meeting the dark stare levelly. 'Yes, I am sure.' He thrust down the insidious little voice that whispered: but did Patrick really escape? Didn't he come out of Tashkara so vastly altered that it was almost as if the real Patrick had died, and something had taken his place? 'Patrick returned to England,' said Lewis, 'and he lived on to write an account of his journey.'

'So he did. But,' said Kaspar, 'although you escaped us last time, there was one with you who did not.'

'Touaris,' said Lewis.

'Yes. She did not escape.'

'I do not forget it.'

Kaspar said, 'She suffered the extreme penalty for what she – and you – did.'

'I don't forget that either,' said Lewis very quietly.

The rituals inside the stone palace had gone on for a very long time and the images had printed themselves sickeningly on Lewis's mind.

After the macabre feast on what had been the guide Cal, there had been dances performed in the flaring torchlight, and songs and chants in the unfathomable language of Kaspar's people. Flagons of strong spiced wine had been passed round: Lewis drank several times, and watched the dances and listened to the chants. Nausea had been churning inside him, but he forced it back. His head was spinning and the scene before him was taking on the air of a surreal painting come to life: the mad whirling of the half-naked dancers, the glowing embers of the Burning Altar itself. A rich greasy aroma of roasted meat lay thickly on the air.

But the thrumming beat of the skin-drum pounded against his senses and underneath the repulsion he was aware that a dark fierce lust was stirring.

The dancers were pairing off as they had done during the feasting, sinking to the ground, unashamedly naked, and coupling with uninhibited openness. Lewis watched them, torn between self-disgust and the beginnings of helpless arousal, and when two of the women left the dancing and came over to him, caressing him sensuously, he pulled them to the ground beside him. Their thighs were taut and satiny, and beneath the triangular-shaped cloths about their waists they were naked. They reached between his legs with greedy delight and as their hands closed about him his body reacted strongly. It was like being caressed by the velvet paws of cats – like being stroked by little silk-mittened claws. They bent over him, and as their long hair brushed against his naked thighs, he felt their tongues, wet and slightly rough like cats'. He gasped and control spun away from him. Reaching for the nearest of the two girls, he forced her on to the ground and threw himself on top of her, driving between her sleek muscular thighs with hard violence. Beyond his own frenzied arousal and the women's delighted cries, he was aware of Kaspar's dark enigmatic eyes watching through the firelight, but by this time he was beyond caring. When the first girl shuddered and cried out in climax, he pushed her to one side and pulled the second one against him, taking her as crudely and as uncaringly as the first.

When he was finally spent, the women wandered back into the dance, as casually as they had left it, and Lewis lay where he was, his mind clearing slowly.

The smouldering carcase on the Burning Altar was a charred mass, blackened beyond recognition, and several of the older men were grouped about it, leaning over and plainly testing its heat. After several minutes they exchanged nods, and reached into the cooling remains, poking this way and that, causing a flurry of black crisp flakes to blow across the courtyard. Two of them lifted out a handful of small bones and, carrying them into a corner, squatted down and began to suck avidly on them, stripping them clean of the tiny shreds of meat that clung to them. Even through the thick smoky atmosphere, Lewis could see that they were finger bones, and the sickness he had been forcing back suddenly welled up. He staggered to his feet and stumbled blindly away from the circle of light, into the shadows. In a dark corner, he stopped and leaned over, retching and vomiting helplessly on to the ground, shuddering in self-disgust at the rich sweet taste of the regurgitated human flesh filling his mouth.

Chapter Twenty-two

The terrible Burning Altar was cooling and smeary as Lewis left the courtyard, and dawn was streaking the skies. A pall of greasy smoke hung on the air.

He returned unnoticed to the small room overlooking the courtyard; it was hot and fetid and it reeked of the dreadful feast but it was a temporary haven, and he leaned gratefully against the closed door, his mind in a tumult. His insides were still scoured with sickness and he felt tainted from the women's bodies. He thought he would never be able to forget the sights and the sounds and the scents of any of it. But he had escaped the Burning Altar, and somehow he would escape from the palace. Could he do it now, when Kaspar's people were exhausted from their feasting? He thought he had played his part sufficiently well to deceive them and no one had prevented him leaving the courtyard. But he dared not take any chances and so he moved quietly about the room, gathering up his things, and then, pausing to listen, inched open the door.

As he crept through the cool silent passages and galleries he expected every minute to be challenged; he certainly expected to be caught and taken into some wretched dungeon and confronted with the Burning Altar as soon as night fell once more – this time as the dinner rather than the diner. But nothing moved and no one came, and presently he was passing under the palace's inner gates and standing on the northern boundary.

With every step he took away from the palace, his spirits rose. It was still possible that Kaspar's people would hunt him down, but the farther he went, the less likely this seemed. The sun was high overhead and he was just thinking that he would pause and forage in his haversack for a drink, when he rounded a rocky crag, and there, in the light-washed valley below him, was the place that Patrick Chance had called the forbidden city of Touaris.

He started the walk down the slopes into the valley in brilliant sunshine, but by the time he neared the city, dusk was drenching it in twisting crimson and violet shadows and the immense gates were wreathed in darkness.

It gave him an unexpected *frisson* to know that this was the way Patrick must have come, in company with the cousin who had been his travelling companion. Had Patrick looked down on the shimmering city and felt, as Lewis was feeling, the absolute silence and the secret remoteness? But the lure for Patrick had been Touaris – that was clear from the early part of the journal – while for Lewis it was something very different.

He had no idea what had finally happened to Patrick, for Patrick, towards the end of his journal, had either been deliberately evasive or had simply expurgated his later travels. The affairs with women were still catalogued – some in astonishing detail – but the light-hearted insouciance that Lewis had found so attractive had vanished as abruptly as if a door had been slammed on it. Reading the brief, very nearly curt entries in the later pages, Lewis had been conscious of disappointment. Something had happened to Patrick that had changed him and it had been something so overwhelming that the irrepressible spirit had been completely quenched. The account of the journey back to England had almost been like reading a Baedeker.

If Patrick's ghost walked it did not walk here. Lewis had no sense of Patrick's presence, only a faint unease at trespassing on forbidden ground. He dredged up the few words of the Tibetan tongue he had managed to glean in Lhasa, and thought he was ready to meet any confrontation with polite explanations and a request to walk unobtrusively through the city and observe. He thought that no reasonable people could refuse this, and he steadfastly ignored the jeering little voice of conscience that said: and is that *all* you want to do? What about the Decalogue, what about those Stone Tablets that you've coveted ever since you first read about them? I would only look at them, rejoined Lewis, angrily. I only want to see if the story is true. Like hell you do! said his conscience derisively.

But as he approached the jade and ivory palace he found that he was not thinking of the Decalogue, but of Touaris herself. Immortality was a myth, it was a fairy tale for gullible romantics – he *knew* that it was! – but faced with this remarkable place it was difficult to cling to practicality. Lewis, staring at the soaring beautiful domes and the painted *stupa*, the golden-roofed pavilions, and shadowy courtyards with their aqua-tinted mosaics, felt as if he was entering a secret world where anything might be possible. He did not believe in immortal goddesses, but if immortality ever existed at all, it might well exist here. And if ever an eternal goddess's stronghold was built . . .

He had been wrong about Patrick's ghost as well, for as he entered the palace compound through a narrow roofed-in alley, he had a strong sense that someone walked with him. Someone who knew this place, and who was drawing him on and pulling him in, and guiding him to the centre. Patrick? Patrick's mischievous restless spirit pointing out the way, just as it pointed out the way to Tashkara?

The great hall at the palace's heart was so huge that it took his breath away. Lewis had stood in St Peter's in Rome and in the Basilica at Ravenna and felt the overpowering sense of immense space and antiquity in both those places, and as he went warily down the short flight of steps to a partly sunken chamber, he felt it again. Marble pillars, each one easily six feet in diameter, rested on great square granite bases and soared up and up, away from the vast lightless vault into the remote roof. The floor was set with more of the dim mosaic, depicting leaping cats, their eyes glittering with greenstones.

It was as he stood in the lee of one of the pillars that he caught a flash of something golden, as if something within the shadows had moved, and he turned to face it instantly, his heart leaping with fear. Something there? Something standing behind one of the columns, watching him? The feeling of dozens of pairs of eyes peering from the cool dimness clutched his mind and he spun around, scanning the darkness, his heart pounding. But nothing moved and if anything the silence was even more complete: it was a great oppressive weight pressing down on his lungs.

At one end of the hall was what in a Western cathedral might have been called an apse or a lady chapel, and Lewis saw now that it went far back into the shadows, and that within those shadows were rows upon rows of elaborate high-backed chairs, each one swathed in vivid scarlet and sapphire brocades and silks. Thrones. He moved nearer, his mind spinning with disbelief. Each throne was occupied. Each throne bore, seated upright, the life-size figure of a woman, clothed in an elaborate robe, with a rearing headdress bearing the snarling mask of a cat at the centre.

Statues: life-size statues – carved with the exquisite attention to detail and the remarkable jewel-like embellishments that Eastern craftsmen employed. Disturbingly lifelike, but nothing more than inanimate pieces of wood and stone and gilt. But even as the logical side of his mind was arguing this, a dark grisly knowledge was churning upwards.

Very deliberately and very calmly he stood still and counted the figures, taking his time. Get this right, Lewis. Don't lose track halfway through and have to go back and start at the beginning. People are driven mad doing things like that, counting the flowers on wallpaper, counting the tiles on bathroom walls ... And if ever there was a place to be driven mad in, this is it.

There were sixty-two figures. All were female and all were subtly different in the way that all people were subtly different. It was reasonable to assume that each figure represented a female who had ascended the throne of Touaris since Kaspar's people had brought the original goddess out of Egypt. If you allowed an average of fifty years for each life span, you had around three thousand years. Which took you to the very beginning of the cult that had come out of Egypt – *Out of the house of bondage, into the land of freedom* ... Egypt. The Egyptians had followed the practice of embalming.

I'm looking at the embalmed bodies of every earthly incarnation of the cat goddess, thought Lewis. I'm down here with the preserved corpses of three thousand years of a pre-Christian religion. He was seeing other things as well now: how some of the earlier figures were visibly deteriorating, how there were tiny, unpleasant indications that the embalming process was beginning to break down. They're regressing, he thought with horror. *Dust to dust* ... No, that's the Christian belief! He forced himself to examine the figures with detachment, seeing that several of the faces showed signs of inner decay: lips were drawing back from teeth, skin was shrivelling. Some of the features had fallen in where the nose and cheekbones had crumbled, and here and there the elaborate golden gowns were discoloured where corruption had evaded the embalming liquids and leaked through and dried, leaving dark stains. Loathsome masses of liquefying putrescence ... It was macabre and terrifying, but it was awesome as well.

As he stood looking at the figures, caught between revulsion and fascination, the glint of gold that had caught his eye earlier did so again. Something moving? He looked around and fear washed over him in a great breath-snatching gust.

The female seated on the newest of the thrones had turned her head and was watching him out of open living eyes.

Touaris had not originally intended to steal down into the Hall of the Goddess at all, because it would be easier to lie in wait outside and ambush the traveller running away from Kaspar's people. It would certainly be a whole lot safer, because to lure a traveller in front of the watchful eyes of all the long-ago goddesses would be regarded as sacrilege, and strictly speaking anyone found guilty of sacrilege was punishable by the fate graven into the Second Stone Tablet of the Decalogue, which was an especially nasty fate.

But sacrilege was only punishable if you were found out, and the Decalogue had not been invoked for centuries, well eighty years anyway, which sounded like centuries, and even then it had been for some kind of violation of the Sacred Temple.

Kaspar, that boring old adherent to custom, had sent the usual running boy to tell them about the latest traveller – an Englishman it was – who had appeared willing to join in the disgusting feasting of the Burning Altar, and then had skulked out of the stone palace at dawn, exactly as so many of them did. Touaris did not blame Kaspar's captives for skulking out at dawn, because anyone who had to witness the barbaric rituals in the stone palace, never mind join in, would want to skulk out at the first opportunity. The Burning Altar was a truly dreadful custom. It was all very well for Kaspar to say that these were the ways their ancestors had trodden and it brought them nearer to the goddess: cooking and eating human flesh was the most repulsive thing in the world. As soon as Touaris had coaxed more of the younger people into her way of thinking she was going to stage a revolt and have what the West called a *coup*.

240

Quite a few of her people had come out to the square below the palace to hear about Kaspar's escaped traveller, and they had all nodded in a serious-minded and responsible way, and said yes of course they would be on the watch for the fugitive, and of course they would send him back to Kaspar without delay. And then they had gone back to their houses to finish the preparations for tomorrow's procession, which everyone was looking forward to, and they had forgotten all about it.

Several of the older members of the community had viewed this with disapproval and said that in their day such casual behaviour would not have been permitted: Kaspar's miscreant would have been caught and dealt with, in fact it was not so very long since the Decalogue itself would have been consulted. There were people in the city today who knew from their fathers how the Decalogue had been invoked for two young Englishmen, a mere eighty years before. Ah, they had known how to deal with heretics and betrayers then, said the ancients, shaking their heads and looking doomful. They took themselves off to the wine shop in the square to disinter a few of the more stringent customs that had once pertained in Tashkara and discuss whether they might not resurrect one or two, although, as one of their number pointed out, what could you expect when the present incumbent of the sacred throne cut her hair short and used modern expressions, and wanted to bring in Western ways, never mind acting so flippantly that she might almost be suspected of indiscriminate relationships with travellers! Well, said the elders, torn between prim disapproval and prurient curiosity, they all knew the punishment that had once been extorted for *that* kind of misbehaviour!

Touaris, who had one or two relatively reliable spies, considered this very funny. She had had relationships with quite a large number of travellers, although to call her indiscriminate was unfair because she was very discriminating indeed, having a distinct preference for

European men and Americans in particular. Western men treated you exactly as an equal, which Eastern men did not, and the Americans had taught her all kinds of colloquial expressions, never mind highly entertaining variations on love-making. Most of them asked afterwards, with a kind of anxious courtesy, whether you had been satisfied, which Touaris thought extremely polite. But none of it could be called indiscriminating, never mind what the boring old farts of elders might say. It would serve them right if she started to carve notches on her bedpost, or took to flinging discarded lovers out of her window into a fast-rushing river the morning after a night of passion as a queen of Ancient Greece was supposed to have done. But her bedposts were all solid silver, which was difficult even to dent, and you did not get many fast-flowing rivers at the bottom of a valley, well, you did not get any.

Touaris had not, so far, actually had an Englishman, which made the news about Kaspar's newest escapee particularly interesting. Englishmen were supposed to be very good lovers indeed if you could get beneath their surface reserve.

She sneaked down to the Hall of the Goddess as dusk was falling, and donned her ceremonial robes, which were amazingly uncomfortable but effective for dazzling a potential lover. Her heart was beating uncomfortably fast, because this was absolutely the most dangerous thing she had ever done. Even putting on the robes was a great risk, because they were only supposed to be used on formal occasions, such as the procession tomorrow night, which everybody except Touaris herself was looking forward to. Once you had seen one ceremonial dance you had seen them all, and also, Kaspar's tribe had had to be invited, which meant no shred of pomp could be omitted on account of Kaspar's people being stupidly sensitive and apt to think themselves slighted if you forgot the tiniest ritual. Touaris sighed to think of the hours of ceremonies that would have to be got through, and thought she deserved a small treat by way of the English traveller beforehand. If you could not squeeze the occasional treat from being a goddess, you might as well go and live on the hillsides among the nomadic tribes.

It was a reasonable assumption that unless the English traveller was confronted at the city gates – which was not very likely – or spotted crossing one of the courtyards – which was even less likely since most people were either in the wine shop or their own homes by now – he would find his way to the Hall of the Goddess. This was one of the slightly eerie things about Tashkara that Touaris had never been able to explain. It was as if the Hall held some kind of magnet for travellers, and it was as if they were compelled towards it. She had occasionally even entertained the fancy that Touaris – the real undying Touaris – sometimes walked in the shadowy hall and drew the travellers in, and to someone bred in the reverence of the goddess, this was rather an uncomfortable idea.

Usually the travellers glanced furtively and fearfully inside the hall and then took to their heels. Occasionally, greatly daring, they stepped inside and examined the mosaic floor and tried to make knowledgeable remarks about the workmanship. The few who stayed long enough to discover the Death Temple where the embalmed bodies sat in endless state, generally beat a hasty retreat on discovering that the bodies were mummified corpses. Touaris had never been able to decide if this was simply because the travellers found the sight of so many corpses disturbing, or if it was the disintegrating condition of the Middle Centuries ones, which were admittedly getting a bit unsavoury on account of the embalming processes of that era being a bit slipshod.

The Englishman who had escaped from Kaspar's clutches did not conform to any of these patterns. He moved around the hall, clearly interested in the carvings and the mosaic floor, and although he was plainly aware of

243

the strange lingering echoes down here, he did not seem to be overly afraid of them. This was unusual, and Touaris, watching from the throne where she would one day sit in embalmed state herself (but not for a *very* long time!) found him unexpectedly attractive. Something to do with the eyes, which were intelligent but cynical, as if he might have trusted life and been let down by it. Something to do with the mouth, as well: mouths were a far better guide to character than eyes, and the Englishman had sensitive fastidious lips. Part satyr, part sinner, part aesthete. *Very* interesting.

Touaris waited until he had entered the Death Temple, gave him long enough to realise the truth about the embalmed figures, and then very deliberately turned her head to look at him.

He caught the movement at once and turned to look unerringly back at her. Touaris thought his perceptions were either very acute to start with, or had been heightened by the timeless quality of the Hall of the Goddess. She leaned one elbow on the arm of the throne and cupped her chin in her hand, watching him. He would probably either run out in terror, or shriek in fear, and if he did he was not worth bothering with.

But he did neither. He stayed where he was, subjecting her to a long level scrutiny, and then said, in careful, rather erratic Tibetan, 'Good evening. I come here only to observe.'

Touaris got down off the throne, and said, in her most down-to-earth voice, 'Yes, that's what they all say.' There was the satisfaction of seeing his eyes widen with surprise and then narrow in appreciation. A sense of humour as well! Very good indeed. And he had been courteous enough to take the trouble to learn a few words of the Tibetan language. Her interest, stirred at the outset, now awoke in earnest. This one was going to be worth luring.

'You speak English,' said the man. 'Thank heaven for that, at least.'

'We are not savages here. I am not fluent but I will mostly understand you. I think you are the traveller who escaped Kaspar.'

'I am. But whether I'm about to fall into another much worse fate—' He looked around the Death Temple and then back at her rather quizzically.

Touaris said, 'Well, not as far as I'm concerned. But you do realise we're in one of the most forbidden places in the entire city?'

'I thought we might be.'

His eyes met hers, and Touaris felt a spiralling tingle of desire. Was she picking up his emotions, or only her own? She remembered that some men found danger physically arousing, and so with the idea of testing this, she said very softly, 'We should not be here. If we are caught we will be punished.'

'You sound as if you would almost relish it.'

'I get so bored, you see.'

'With obeying the rules?'

'With being a goddess.'

There was a sudden silence. 'Ah,' said Lewis, 'I thought that might be it. Ought I to kneel at your feet or something?'

'You could. But only,' said Touaris, slanting her eyes at him, 'if you think we would both enjoy it.'

Unexpectedly he laughed. 'I have no idea what I should call you,' he said, 'and I certainly don't believe in immortality. But it's a pity that my ancestor who came this way about eighty years ago didn't encounter you, because he might have met his match. I'm Lewis Chance. And you, of course, are Touaris.'

'Of course I am.' Touaris regarded him. 'Did you come here to find the city, or to find me?'

He paused, as if considering his answer and Touaris felt something wholly unfamiliar tighten about her heart. Yes, very attractive. Oh, I can't let this one go.

Lewis said, 'As a matter of fact, I came here to find the Tashkara Decalogue.'

The silence closed in again, a thick charged silence, binding them into sudden intimacy. Then Lewis said, 'Well? Can you show it to me?' And then, challengingly: 'Or perhaps you don't know where it is kept.'

'Certainly I know.' Touaris stopped and bit her lip, because of course he had goaded her into the admission. 'But to enter the Chamber of the Decalogue is the most forbidden thing in all our laws,' she said, staring into the clear grey eyes – like quicksilver, like frosted water in the bleakest of winter dawns. 'Only the elders of the city, or the head of Kaspar's tribe are permitted, and even then only when there is sentence to be pronounced.' She stopped, and felt the Englishman's intense concentration. He's willing me to do what he wants. To take him down into the ancient vaults. A shiver of fear, mixed with excitement scudded across her skin, and without warning a huge recklessness surged up.

She said, 'We would have to be very quiet and very careful—'

'We will be.'

'If we are caught—'

'We won't be caught.'

'If we are caught,' said Touaris seriously, 'it will be a very dreadful punishment for us both.' She studied him again. 'Will you risk that, Lewis?'

'Yes,' said Lewis, staring at her. 'Yes, I will risk it.'

Chapter Twenty-three

Patrick Chance's Diary

I'm writing this in a narrow dim room with a wooden floor and a faint scent of sandalwood on the air. Through the window is a view of the jade and ivory palace, infuriatingly remote and impossibly beautiful.

By contrast, I'm in a low-roofed flimsily built structure just beyond the city gates. There's a table and chair and a kind of rush mat on the floor, and around the walls prance a series of murals that beat anything London's seamiest brothels ever displayed hands down. Suppose they must be *thankas*, which is the Tibetan word for the wall paintings that adorn some of the monasteries out here. Apparently a good many *thankas* are believed to be imbued with such immense power that the lama monks consider them only fit to be exposed on the holiest of holy days. The *thankas* in here are only fit to be exposed to a roomful of men intent on a bawdy night in a brothel, because they depict several men in astonishing positions with huge cats, most of which I should have thought physically impossible although that might only indicate the paucity of my experience. The men are perpendicular with arousal – the cats are pretty rampant as well – and if the paintings were taken from life it looks as if Fenris hit it square on when he talked about unbridled licentiousness. Halfway around, the pictures change to show a solitary female lying naked on the ground before another of the cat-creatures, plainly waiting to be ravished by it. After that they become progressively more explicit, ending (predictably) with the lady being penetrated, although judging by the size of the beast's accoutrement, impaled might be a better word. If that's the legendary Touaris I may have to rearrange my ideas.

All of which forcedly flippant garrulity is designed to put off the moment when I must write down what has actually happened during the last two days, and when I must face how extremely afraid I am. It's an Englishman's duty not to show fear under any circumstance, of course, but I'll bet the Englishman who coined that one was never imprisoned in a stone room with his very own scaffold being built under his window and nothing but painted copulating cats for company! I don't know yet what these barbarians are going to do to me on that scaffold, but judging by what I've seen so far, they won't be short of ideas.

In the past half-hour the light has begun to fail, and although shadows are stealing across the floor the small bronze lamps in the wall niches have been lit (yak oil again!) and I can see quite well to write this. I'm trying very hard to ignore the shadows, because they're beginning to look like black disembodied hands, feeling their macabre way across the floor to where I sit. That's just nerves, of course; they say that prisoners start to imagine things after a time. Maybe I'm succumbing to gaol fever. To wake up inside Newgate would be the greatest relief ever, in fact just to wake up would do.

I'm locked in. That's the first thing to admit, and it looks just as awful written down as I thought it would.

The locking in was done with immense courtesy –

they're very courteous, the natives of Tashkara – but it was also done with a silent implacability that was absolutely bone-chilling. I've no idea where Theodore is: they took him off somewhere, but I suppose he's locked in as well. And probably indulging in an orgy of I-told-him-so's. No, that's unfair; he'll be worrying himself into apoplexy.

I've been allowed my writing things. A small bamboo table was carried in about an hour ago by two men, and arranged under the window. (More of that granite-faced courtesy.) It might have been a concession to a privileged prisoner, but it felt more like the condemned man being given the tools to set down his last wishes. Write it down in a good firm hand that I bequeath my worldly goods to the ladies of London Town and my body to medical research... Or should it be the other way about? They've angled the table so that as I sit at it I'm looking straight at the last wall painting: the one showing the cat-thing in the very act of ejaculating fountain-like across the unknown lady's thighs.

As far as I can make out I'm to be taken at midnight to face something called the Punishment of the Decalogue. I haven't yet discovered what this is, but it sounds extremely severe and it looks regrettably public: for the last two hours the courtyard below my window has echoed to the sounds of hammering, and if I look out I can see a wooden platform being built. It's that that bears such a sinister resemblance to a scaffold and if I could place any other connotation on it, I would.

Later. The hammering stopped about twenty minutes ago and the resultant silence is brimful of a very unpleasant expectancy. In the privacy of these pages I admit that I'm by now extremely frightened. There's a sense of growing menace everywhere, and – worst of all – an impression of excited anticipation. What-ever they're going to do to me they're going to enjoy it.

I've tried the door at five-minute intervals and I've tried smashing the lock as well. All to no avail. The only window is the slit-like affair which is halfway up a sheer stone wall and has a drop of forty feet. Six brass Buddhas, wreathed in yak-oil smoke, are watching me with sphinx-like imperturbability from the alcoves, and all round the walls cats are fornicat-ing with humans. How in God's name did I get into this?

How in God's name am I going to get out of it?

There are five hours to midnight.

Entering the walled city was easy enough to make us suspicious, particularly Theo, who's naturally suspic-ious to begin with.

The walk down the slopes took longer than either of us had expected – distances out here are deceptive; it's the pure, thin air – and by the time we stood at the gates the sun was sinking behind the peaks and the walled city was plunged into a sullen crimson glow. Theodore shivered, for which I didn't blame him, although it was unnecessary to say it was like descen-ding into hell and we ought to turn back. I ignored the rest of his doomful utterances, since could not seriously believe in the practice of clay-potting unwary travellers' heads in ovens, which Theo swore was standard procedure in these situations. Told him he had read too many Rider Haggard novels and had missed his vocation in life: clearly he should be writing adventure stories for bloodthirsty youths of fifteen.

But when we found that the city gates were ajar, even I stopped in my tracks. We glanced uneasily at one another, but at last, I said, 'I dare say it doesn't mean anything other than that they're always happy to receive travellers.'

'No, but people who go to the trouble of walling a city and building huge gates to keep the world out don't normally leave those gates open for enterprising enemies to stroll in,' said Theo. 'But still, since we've come this far we may as well go on.'

Beyond the gates it was like a small town. There were various buildings, all plainly used for different purposes. Some were quite grand, as if they were occupied by the élite of the community, others were so far from grand as to be shanty-like. Dotted here and there were small temples, each with the characteristic tiered pagoda roof, some with tiny doll-like bell towers. A roughish road wound its way into the city, and as we set foot on it we both felt that we were being watched. The *stupa* on the palace and on several of the temples are painted with the flat enigmatic eyes intended to symbolise Buddha looking out on the four corners of the world, but as Theo and I entered the forbidden city it felt more as if the eyes were thinking: be blowed to the four corners of the world, let's concentrate on this pair of adventurers. It was very disconcerting.

By tacit agreement we made for the jade and ivory palace, on the grounds that if Touaris existed at all, she probably existed inside it. Also, I was damned if I was going to get into a forbidden city and then be satisfied with plundering and raiding shanties. If there was any plundering going to be done, it might as well be done in the palace.

'Although God alone knows what's in there,' said Theo, staring up at its soaring walls and pavilion roofs. His tone suggested he would not be surprised to find that the palace housed an army of blood-quaffing murderers still smeared in the gore of their victims, or devil worshippers dancing naked under the full moon.

Once or twice we thought we glimpsed movements, and once Theo stopped dead and turned to peer into the shadows.

'What's the matter? What can you hear?'

'Nothing. There's no one there.'

'Well, that's all right then. And no one's come out to challenge us, have you noticed that?'

'I had noticed it, Patrick,' said Theo. (There may well have been a note of sarcasm in his tone.)

It was getting dark by this time and only the occasional flicker of light from the various buildings enabled us to see our way. It was absurd to find ourselves trying to avoid the *stupa*'s eyes, but we did. It was mad in the extreme to imagine that the eyes followed us, or that they flashed messages to one another across the pointed rooftops: *The intruders are entering your territory now . . . Bait the traps, tighten the tripwires, dig the pits . . . Get ready, they're almost with you . . .*

I started to play that ridiculous childhood game: if we can reach the building on the corner without being seen we shall be all right. And then if we can get past the high wall on the left and not be challenged, we shall be safe.

We were nearing the palace compound, and I was just saying: and if we can cross that inner courtyard we shall be safe, when I caught a slithering movement from the nearest rooftop. I stopped dead and looked up, and the next minute a thick grey net, like a huge mosquito net, was dropped over me.

I fought wildly, but the more I struggled the more entangled I became. The impression of having been neatly and efficiently staked out and captured, in the manner of big-game hunters capturing wild animals, darted unpleasantly across my mind.

Something rapped me sharply across the head with the same neat efficiency, and the last thing I heard was Theo shouting my name before I crumpled into unconsciousness.

I have absolutely no idea of how long it was before I fought back to awareness.

There was a slight dull headache from whatever had hit me, but the smothering layers of net seemed to have vanished, and I was lying on a warm and very comfortable bed. I opened my eyes.

I will admit that I had only a quarter believed Fenris's tales of a vaguely immortal cat goddess and her four score female attendants and I had certainly not given much credence to the veiled hints about licentious ceremonies. But unless I was still unconscious, or unless someone had secretly fed me De Quincey's opium or Shakespeare's poppy and all the drowsy syrups of the world, it looked as if I had tumbled straight into Touaris's lair, or at least that of the handmaidens. And a lair thick with fleshly lusts it was.

(Should here mention that although I might have been drugged *then*, I'm not drugged *now*, and I can state with absolute surety that that place was so brimful of sexuality and sensuousness that the very air throbbed.)

The room was long and low-ceilinged, and firelight cast eerie shadows on the walls so that in those first moments of consciousness it felt as if I had tumbled into some kind of subterranean hell.

But hell and its fire-drenched caverns were presumably never furnished with silken cushions strewn about the floor or with low velvet-covered divans. And hell never had the drifting, quarter-soothing, three-quarters-exciting scent of musk and sandalwood and of warm soft femininity.

The leaping firelight came not from conventional brick hearths in the wall, but from scooped-out holes

253

in the floor so that they burned at the room's centre, the smoke spiralling upwards into smoke-holes cut in the ceiling. Slender sinuous female forms moved in and out of the warm slumberous glow. After a few moments I raised myself carefully on one elbow and looked around. There was no sign of Theodore, but the room was peopled by ten or twelve females, all of them young, all of them extremely good-looking. And all of them watching me.

Now I have no idea what anyone else would do in that situation, but in my defence certain things should be taken into account.

To begin with, I had been netted in a kind of giant fishing net and knocked unconscious, so that I was slightly confused and a bit dizzy. On this count alone I was completely at the mercy of my saviours. (Apologise for any biblical connotation that may be inferred here, and stress NO religious context meant.)

On a second count, if I was not precisely fed opium or mandragora, I was certainly given some extremely strong (and very delicious) wine.

Finally (and I do feel that here we reach the real crux of the matter), all of the ten or twelve females were so scantily clad they might as well have been naked.

Some of them were curled into graceful heaps before the fire, blinking in the warmth and occasionally sipping wine from jewelled goblets, and some of them were padding about the room on little bare feet. They were astonishingly alike: all with black silky hair, growing rather low on their brow and worn loose about their shoulders, and they were dressed in the thinnest of white gowns and nothing else. When they passed in front of the fire the gowns might as well have been transparent, and speaking as someone who cut his sexual teeth on laced corselets (extraordinarily complicated to remove those things, never mind getting tangled up in the lacing), it was loin-stiffeningly erotic. If these were the mythical four score handmaidens of Touaris the myth might have exaggerated the numbers, but it had not over-rated the attractions.

Their faces were paler than most European girls, and although they had the slanting cheekbones of the East, they had large black-fringed green eyes and short curving upper lips. Like cats. The simile was impossible to avoid.

They bent over me, offering sweet potent wine and bringing bowls of warm scented water for cleansing. It was immensely soothing but it was also immensely arousing to lie in the glow of the firelight, the heady scents of the room washing over my body, feeling little silk hands, like velvet paws caressing my skin . . . I challenge anyone, short of an octogenarian Trappist monk, to find himself stripped of his clothes and washed by six half-naked females, all plainly hellbent on seduction, and *not* respond in the most basic of ways.

Even so, I did not give way all at once, in fact I tried quite strenuously to resist. I certainly tried to think what might have happened to Theo and what I had better do about it, and whether there was any way in which I could communicate with these people.

But after about ten minutes of intimate exploration by those velvet-skinned hands (to say nothing of being within prick-ing distance of the sensuous gleaming thighs), Theo was relegated to the back of my mind . . .

I didn't manage the entire twelve.

What I did manage was a *very* energetic five hours, starting off with a stand as rampant as any I ever had in my life, which took about five hours to gradually dwindle to wrung-out impotency.

It was intriguing, as well, to discover that it was perfectly possible to caress between the thighs of *two* females with my hands – one on each side, one hand to each – while a third bestrode me, and not lose any synchronisation of movement. That experience on the railcar earlier must have helped, or perhaps I simply have a natural sense of rhythm.

By the time dawn was lightening the low-ceilinged room, that portion of my body which is the most sensitive, was as raw as if it had been flayed with sandpaper and was clearly going to need several hours (if not an entire day) to recover. Some of the blame for this must be laid at the door of my companions who continued their attempts to coax a final few drops of passion, long after it must have been obvious that the last drops had been shed, and very agonisingly too, towards the end. However, I'd be interested to know how the achievements of Giovanni Casanova compare, because I refuse to believe *anyone* capable of making love *satisfactorily* to twelve women in five hours.

I had fallen into an exhausted sleep when there was a commotion outside, and the sound of marching feet and sharp commands in an unfamiliar tongue. The girls leaped up in panic and huddled into a corner of the room, chattering in terror and clutching one another. Plainly something castigatory was about to take place, and from the look of them it was going to take a very unpleasant form.

I grabbed my discarded clothes and scrambled into most of them – it's an Englishman's duty not to be caught naked in ladies' bedchambers, no matter how bizarre the bedchamber or willing the ladies – and was fastening my trousers when the door was summarily flung open.

Eight men stood there, all of them armed with glinting wickedly sharp spears.

The armed men half dragged, half carried me out to a dawn-washed square, which seemed to be at the centre of the jade and ivory palace, and thrust me unceremoniously before four more of the black-haired men, who were standing in the courtyard's centre with the palace behind them. Four sets of *stupa* eyes looked down.

There was a rather nasty air of hasty tribunal about the whole thing, and cold fear began to churn in the pit of my stomach. What had until now been a hazardous but intriguing adventure was beginning to slide into something very much darker and very much more frightening. I wondered if it was unreasonably optimistic to hope that Theo might have escaped.

All of the men bore a strong resemblance to the ladies in the firelit room – the black, low-growing hair appears to be a strong racial characteristic among them: it's rather attractive but combined with the lean sinuous build it gives them an uncanny resemblance to huge cats, and it was the most unnerving experience in the world to be hauled before four men who looked as if they might bound forward on all fours at any minute and savage me. What was worse was that they looked as if they would *enjoy* savaging me. The cold knot of fear tightened.

I marked their leader out before he spoke. He radiated such authority that the air about his head positively sizzled and I was not in the least surprised when he stepped forward to address me. His teeth were slightly prolonged, and the upper ones were discernibly pointed.

Incredibly, he had a smattering of English. I won't reproduce the vicissitudes we had to resort to in order to understand one another, or attempt to describe the sign language employed to reach precise meanings, because if an author's licence is permissible any-where, it's permissible here. So I will simply set down the approximate gist of the conversation.

There was some kind of ceremonious exchange of bows – our version of a handshake, probably – and then the man, whose name is apparently Tamerlane after some long-ago conqueror of Samarkand, said, 'You have entered the sanctum of Touaris's hand-maidens and violated them.'

I thought this was a bit much, since any violating had been instigated by the handmaidens themselves, and I said so, quite forcibly. I'm aware that this is contrary to all laws of chivalry which decree that gentlemen don't kiss and tell (and certainly don't fornicate and tell), but these things shouldn't be carried to excess and chivalry is no good to anyone in the face of four savage-looking gaolers, to say no-thing of eight guards brandishing spears.

I also pointed out that if Tamerlane's people don't want guests they shouldn't leave their city gates open and unattended, and that in my country the laying of mantraps is against the law. (Think I may have been on shaky ground there, but Tamerlane unlikely to be familiar with the niceties of English law.)

'The handmaidens will be punished according to our law,' he said. 'They are allowed to take prisoners, but they are required to bring them all to me.' He paused. 'They are greedy and selfish, and they are aware of the punishment.'

'Well, could I be aware of it as well, please?'

Tamerlane studied me and then said, 'They will be brought to the Burning Altar at midnight.' His hard green eyes glittered like bits of glass, and the thin cruel smile curved his lips, reminding me un-pleasantly of the sharp long teeth. 'As for you, English traveller,' he said softly, 'you, also, will be brought to the Burning Altar at midnight.'

'Why?' I said, with more insolence than I was actually feeling.

'You have offended against the Decalogue,' said Tamerlane. 'You have intruded into our city, and you have sinned against the Eighth Stone of Treachery and Betrayal. Because of that, you will suffer the punishment graven thereon.'

He nodded to the spear-carriers and I was taken away from the square.

I have set my watch on the edge of the table and I'm watching the minutes tick away. It's like one of those dreadful timing devices where thin sand trickles slowly but inexorably from one glass funnel into another.

Just over one hour remains until I'm to be taken out to face the punishment of the Eighth Stone Tablet, and God alone knows what it'll be. Cannot decide if it would be better to know, or if ignorance until the last moment is preferable.

There's still no sign of Theo, and I'm torn between hoping he managed to escape and wishing he were here with me. (This last utterly selfish, but true. I never felt so alone in my life.)

I can see the scaffold structure quite clearly, because Tamerlane's people have set blazing torches all around the square, and the flames are washing over the palace walls, drenching the entire building with leaping flames. The glow is tinting the night sky, and it's as if we're at the centre of a huge bloody wound that's leaking its gore upwards into the darkness— No, I daren't think like that!

The guards are bringing out what looks like an immense table, easily ten feet square and covered with vivid scarlet and jade silk that ripples gently in the night air, so that there's the impression of unnatural life under the silk. I find this unspeakably sinister.

Hell and the devil, I find the entire thing so utterly terrifying that I don't know how I'm managing to write this down!

The square is lined with wooden seats – had not noticed them when I faced Tamerlane, but they're three and four deep and set around the edges in tiers like the auditorium of a theatre.

Fifteen minutes to go, and something's happening.

About five minutes ago I became aware of dozens of human voices intoning a rhythmic chant and from my window I made out the flickering lights of a torch procession: a line of people walking slowly through the palace, each one carrying either a candle or a small burning cresset that spilled light through the palace windows. As they approached my heart began to beat erratically.

And then they were pouring into the square, through a door at the far side, chanting as they came: appearing in pairs but separating as they emerged, the men taking seats on the left, the women on the right. Tamerlane's people – for all I know, Touaris's people as well – the cruel beautiful dark-haired tribe of the forbidden city, all assembling to see the punishment of the Decalogue dealt to the English intruder.

I haven't counted them but there must be at least a hundred and fifty. They're all in place now, and the chant's filling up the whole palace: a dark mesmeric rise and fall of human voices that thuds sickeningly against your mind and rakes at your senses. Somewhere within it is a soft steady drumbeat and I'm dreadfully afraid that it's a death knell.

Two minutes to midnight and I can hear footsteps approaching along the passage outside.

The guards are coming for me.

Chapter Twenty-four

As Lewis followed Touaris across the Death Temple to a dim corner beyond a groyned arch he was aware of mounting excitement.

This is it. I'm about to descend to the Stone Chamber of the Decalogue. I'm about to see the Stone Tablets – Satan's Ten Commandments – that the long-ago tribe brought out of the pharaohs' Egypt. He watched his extraordinary companion – was she really the present Touaris? – lever up a square trap door sunk into the floor. It came up with a faint screech of protest, sending the accreted dust of years scattering across the mosaic floor. A dank tomblike odour gusted upwards, as if an ancient coffin had been unsealed. This is the breath of something timeless and something that has lain down here for thirty centuries, Lewis thought. He blinked and pushed the showering images aside. Because as well as all that, this is a forbidden place, and if you're caught there'll be a reckoning.

Beneath the trap door was a narrow flight of stone steps winding down; they were shallow and worn away at the centre and Touaris, looking at them with fascination, said, 'That wearing-away has been made by my people descending to the crypt to consult the Decalogue.' She looked back at Lewis and he felt the tension between them. Because of what we are about to do? Or from some other cause altogether? Touaris kneeled to brush the dust from the floor back into the yawning aperture.

'Covering our tracks?' said Lewis, bending to help her,

half amused, but uncomfortably aware of a knot of nervous anticipation at the pit of his stomach.

'Of course. We truly must not be found here.' She stood up and looked at him and Lewis felt a sudden twist of physical desire. He quenched it instantly, because that would be mad, that would be the maddest thing yet— She was astonishingly beautiful, fine-boned, and with the silky black hair and the striking pallor that was neither quite European nor Eastern, but a sensuous blend of the two. He thought she was about nineteen or twenty.

'Ready?'

'Yes.'

'It will be very dark. We should take lights.'

'I have a torch in one of my knapsacks. Or would that be—'

'Sacrilegious?' Warm amusement showed in her eyes. 'I think we have already gone beyond sacrilege, Lewis.' She had an unusual, rather attractive way of pronouncing his name. Lewis reminded himself that all he intended to do was take a look at the Stone Tablets – if possible copy out any inscriptions – and then beat it. Like a bat out of hell? said a jeering inner voice. Well, maybe not quite. Maybe it would be worth talking to the lady for a little. Oh sure, said the voice sarcastically.

'You will take the torch,' said Touaris, suddenly becoming practical. 'And I will take the candles.' She paused, and then said, 'You understand that it is necessary to be very silent and very careful?'

'Yes, I understand.' They looked at one another.

And then Touaris said softly, 'Shall we go down, Lewis?'

If the Hall of the Goddess and the strange grisly Death Temple had felt timeless, descending to the crypt was like stepping outside of time altogether. Lewis felt a cold prickle of fear brush the nape of his neck, and as they descended it was as if they were slicing down and down through the centuries... Down and down through the hundreds of years, stretching back and back. There was a dry ancient smell: old damp stone and brittle timbers.

He directed the torch carefully, the cold modern electric beam cutting through blue-grey shadows, disturbing the silence and the solitude. The steps wound down into the darkness, curving as they went. At one point Touaris paused at a kind of half-landing and held the candle up, indicating a low crumbling archway. Lewis shone the torch and made out low-ceilinged chambers, snaking away into silent blackness. There was a brief glint of wall paintings.

'Through that arch is the buried city of the first Bubasti,' said Touaris, and Lewis saw how her eyes looked into the pouring darkness with a mixture of fear and awe.

'Your ancestors?'

'Yes. They built that city three thousand years ago, but now it is only a heap of rubble and dust,' said Touaris. 'I went in there once – I wanted to see the original city entrance, which our chronicles say was one of the most beautiful things ever built by man, and which was supposed to have ranked with the Hanging Gardens of Babylon and the Temple of Artemis at Ephesus.'

'The Eighth Wonder of the World,' said Lewis, staring through the arch.

'Yes, but now it is probably in ruins like all the others,' observed Touaris, becoming practical again. 'And in any case, the walls of the tunnels had fallen in and also some of the roofs, so I did not find it, which was a pity.'

'Yes.'

'Yes, but for me to have got buried for ever would have been a greater pity.'

They went on down, and after what seemed to Lewis an eternity, the steps debouched into a wide cavernous tunnel with immense *thankas*. They were executed in soft glowing colours, with all the exquisite attention to detail he had come to recognise, but none of the *thankas* he had seen in Lhasa were remotely like these.

'Some of the images are what are called Tantric Deities,' said Touaris, as Lewis paused to inspect them. 'They symbolise the Kalachakra Wheel of Time, which is so complex that only those who have studied it for their whole lives can understand it, and even then only partly. Other images are past incarnations of Touaris, and some are future incarnations.' She indicated an enigmatic figure portrayed in cool peacock shades. 'This one depicts a Touaris as yet unborn. She holds one hand to her heart in the Buddhist gesture of turning the wheel of teaching but the other is extended to reveal the thumb and first finger in the symbol of eternity.'

'They're very beautiful,' said Lewis, studying the paintings as if he had all the time in the world, and as if his heart were not thrumming with the anticipation of what was ahead.

He looked back at Touaris. She was standing a little ahead, the candle flame illuminating her face from below, scooping out dark hollows, and it was as if her eyes peered calculatingly out from black caverns. Lewis felt a stab of fear. I'm alone, below an ancient city with a creature who claims to be the incarnation of a long-ago cat goddess. Supposing she's one of Kaspar's Flesh-Eaters; supposing it's all a plot? I must have been mad to follow her.

He said abruptly, 'Are we near to the Decalogue yet?'

'Yes, we are almost there. Can you not feel it?' She smiled, and the candle flame danced and the light danced in her eyes, and it was again the half-mischievous, half-imperious lady who had arrayed herself on the sacred throne and lain in wait for an unwary traveller.

Even without Touaris's words, Lewis thought he would have sensed the Decalogue's closeness. It was as if they were approaching an immense powerhouse or the magnetic centre of a vortex. The cold tomblike stench seemed stronger, and when Touaris spoke again she lowered her voice as if she were afraid of being overheard.

'One of the legends tells how after the Decalogue was created it was carried forth from the darkness of hell's nether-world, and sent spinning through the cold wastes of time until it came to rest in a mystical kingdom in a remote part of the world.' She glanced at him and the urchin grin lit her face. 'It has a good sound, that?'

'Very.' The grin was that of a pleased child, saying, aren't I telling you a good story! but the words themselves were astonishingly evocative: Lewis's mind had received a vivid darting image of dark storm-torn mansions through which faceless creatures stalked and held dreadful courts. Because we are approaching something that really was forged in hell's dark satanic halls? I don't believe any of it. No? Then why are you down here in the first place?

'The words are written in one of our chronicles, and I liked them myself,' said Touaris, brushing cobwebs off her arms. If you were about to seduce someone you did not want to do so with bits of cobweb draped all over you. 'The chronicle tells how the Stones dragged with them an immense dust-cloud that had gathered as they spun through the dark silent skies beyond the world,' she said. 'As they plunged to earth the ancient dust shrouded half the land and blinded those who tried to look at it.' She sent him another of the half-mischievous, half-enigmatic glances. 'Your Christian Bible refers to it,' said Touaris. 'Although not quite in the same words.'

'The dense darkness that fell over the land? The Ten Plagues of Egypt?' Lewis forced lightness into his voice, because he was damned if he was going to show any sense of awe.

'I think it was called that,' agreed Touaris, in the deliberately offhand voice of one who is enjoying herself immensely but determined not to show it. 'Does that disturb you, Lewis?'

'Not in the least,' said Lewis untruthfully. 'Are we there?' For Touaris had stopped before an iron grille: thick

265

black bars had been driven into the rock floor and they stretched up and up until they vanished in the shadowy roof.

'Yes, we are there. But we cannot get any farther than this, because the gates are locked.'

'You have no keys?'

'No.' Touaris considered briefly whether it might be possible to steal the keys and take Lewis into the inner chamber. No, it would be impossible. She said, 'There are seven sets of keys which have to be used in strict sequence, and each key is with one of the elders. Kaspar holds the first.'

'He would,' said Lewis drily.

Touaris grinned and said, 'If we go right up to the gates and set your torch down and light several more candles, I think we shall see very well indeed.'

As they lit the candles, Lewis felt his heart pounding with anticipation. In a moment I shall see it: I shall see the legend-drenched Stone Tablets of the ancient fable. Forged by the devil in furious response to God's bequest of the Ten Commandments to Moses, cast down to earth countless centuries ago – *carried forth from the darkness of hell's nether-world . . .?* Do I believe that? No, of course I don't. But I think I believe the rest of it: how they were originally in the possession of the pharaohs, and how they were stolen by the rebellious worshippers of the divine cat goddess and smuggled into Tashkara.

As he set down the last candle, embedding it in its own small circle of dripping wax, his mind received a vivid glancing impression of a vast exodus: many, many people travelling slowly across arid deserts under fiercely hot skies – the exiled heretic worshippers of Touaris driven out of Egypt, the jeers and the curses of Amenemhat's people echoing about their ears.

For ever damned . . . For ever cast out . . .

The cries were so clear that Lewis glanced over his shoulder towards the tunnel, thinking that after all they

266

had been followed. But there was no one and there was nothing, and the silence and the dust were undisturbed. The Decalogue lay in its secret stronghold, exactly as it had lain for centuries.

But it will not for long stay undisturbed, for tonight fifty of our youngest, strongest men will plunder the Pharaoh's most guarded apartments... We shall cheat the High Priests, for when the skies have fallen to their darkest hour, we shall carry the Stones of Vengeance out of Amenemhat's palace while sleep is upon him and the harlot who denounced us is at his side...

For the harlot and the High Priests feared Touaris, and they spied on us... And tomorrow, when the sun is at its highest point, they will slay us for practising the Forbidden Religion... They will slay us one by one, using the punishment of the Stones, reading aloud the ancient and terrible vengeance to be inflicted on those who defy their laws... The only way to save our people and to hand on the true beliefs, is to flee...

So we have bribed the guards who stand outside the miserable prison where we are incarcerated, and while Amenemhat's city sleeps, we shall escape... And we shall have our own revenge, for when we go, the Stones of Vengeance will go with us...

Lewis gasped and put out a hand to the rock wall to stop himself from falling, and at his side, Touaris said softly, 'I think you are hearing the echoes, Lewis.'

'I – am?' Lewis straightened up. 'How do you know?'

'Because I hear them sometimes as well. It is something that happens,' said Touaris pragmatically. She set down her own candle and indicated the black bars. 'Now here is what you wished to see,' she said, and Lewis turned slowly round. A great stillness fell on him and for several moments he could not speak.

Ever since he had come across that tantalisingly brief reference in Patrick's journal, he had visualised the Decalogue as a beautiful golden thing: each tablet perhaps adorned with symbols and incantations, all of them alive and alight with vibrant thrumming potency. The reality was so different as to strike disappointment through him.

The Stone Tablets were plain circular wedges of thick rough stone, each one about six feet from rim to rim, and some three feet thick. They rested against the far wall in upright positions, and as the torchlight and the flickering flame of Touaris's candle fell across them, it was almost as if they were huge lidless eyes endlessly staring out of the deep blue shadows.

The carved symbols Lewis had visualised were there, but they were like no symbols he had ever seen and they were not recognisable as any language or any form of writing he had ever encountered. I'm disappointed, he thought. Is this all they are?

But as he stared at the massive Stones, the disappointment began to fade and an immense awe took hold of his mind.

The Stones were plain; they were very nearly ugly. They're like giants' chariot wheels, thought Lewis. But they're the most breathtaking things I have ever seen. Ogres' millwheels ... *Sent spinning through the cold wastes of time until they came to rest in a mystical kingdom* ... I was wrong to be disappointed: they're awe-inspiring and soul-subduing. They're awe-ful in the real sense of the word.

The engraved symbols must be so immeasurably old that their origins would be buried in the world's genesis. It would be impossible to decipher them, and it would be absurd even to try. But I wonder if I can possibly copy them? he thought.

He had reached this point in his thoughts when Touaris came to stand by him, and said in a voice like melted honey, 'And now, Lewis, don't you think I deserve a small reward for having brought you down here?'

Touaris had been growing more interested in the English

traveller, and as they opened the trap door, the thought had just nudged her mind that it would be the most amazing experience ever to seduce him actually in the Decalogue Chamber itself. Delighted shock rose up at once because the Decalogue was the most absolutely sacred thing of all; Kaspar and the boring old elders spoke of it with hushed reverence.

The trouble was that once a thought had entered your mind you could not unthink it. You could banish it – she did try to banish it – but you could not pretend it had not been there. That being so, it would not hurt at least just to take a look at the idea. Touaris took a look and found it hugely alluring and probably the most original experience she would ever have.

It would not really be so very dangerous. No one ever came here, and even if anyone did skulk down the stair, there would be plenty of warning, because *nobody* could descend to the Decalogue Chamber – even skulkingly – without making *some* noise. And if Kaspar and the elders came they would huffily stomp their way down, and there would be plenty of time to uncouple and scramble into clothes, although it would be a pity if the uncoupling had to happen precipitately.

They had lowered the trap door in the Death Temple before they began to descend the stair, which made it even safer. It made it seem as if they were shut away together. A delicious spiral of anticipation began to uncoil, and when she said to Lewis, 'Don't you think I deserve a small reward,' her voice was so laden with purring promise that there was absolutely no mistaking her intention.

Lewis did not mistake it. He had been aware, since approximately ten minutes after their meeting in the Death Temple that this was a lady hellbent on seduction, and it had not been a question of whether he wanted to respond, but of how safe responding would be. I'm about to screw a sacred goddess, he thought, in fascinated amusement. Am I? God, yes, I think I am.

When Touaris issued her velvet-voiced suggestion, he did not hesitate. He pulled her into his arms and brought his mouth down on hers.

What surprised Touaris was the soaring sweetness and the strong gentle authority in Lewis Chance's love-making. What had been intended as a quick adventure – well, all right, a quick adventure in a forbidden place! – started to unfurl into something much deeper and much closer and something that fastened about her mind and fired it to violent longing at the same time that it was firing her body.

She had thought she knew quite a bit about making love – not everything, but quite a bit. But this was nothing like those snatched lusts on the mountainside, this was worlds and years away from all of the brief tomorrow-forgotten encounters. This was real and solid and warm. The thought: how on earth am I ever going to want anyone else after this? slid treacherously into her mind.

Lewis's hands moved over her, leaving tiny trickles of scorching desire everywhere they touched, and Touaris arched her back in purest delight. There was no undressing – no *time*! she thought, tumbling deeper and deeper into the dizzying delight – but there was sudden surprised gratitude because this one did not fumble: there were no awkward gropings and fingerings, and no laboured chancy culmination as there had sometimes been on dark mountainsides, or standing up against the city walls. Touaris had more than once found herself on the receiving end of premature ejaculation – which was complimentary but *messy* – or incomplete arousal – which was insulting. And both were *embarrassing*.

Lewis succumbed to neither of these insulting or messy embarrassments. When she reached down to enclose him with her hand he gave a deep groan of longing that sent white-hot desire slicing through her. But although he was more strongly aroused than she had ever known any man to be he was unexpectedly gentle, and as his hands caressed her breasts and moved between her thighs Touaris thought that she might easily faint from longing.

The gentleness vanished when he thrust into her and she caught his passion at once: a sweeping joy closing about them in the candlelit cavern. Touaris pulled his head down, kissing his mouth – oh yes, sweet! – and felt his hands cup her face as if he wanted to drink her all in, and as if he wanted to learn her and absorb her through the pores of his skin so that he would never forget her.

There was an explosion of emotion and delight, unlooked for, astonishing; he tightened his hold and she knew he had shared it. In the dying candle flame she saw his eyes darken as if he had found something he had been searching for over many years, and he pulled her against him, clinging to her with painful intensity.

As if he would never let her go.

Chapter Twenty-five

The pounding of feet overhead jerked them both abruptly out of a drowsy half-sleep, and the sudden opening of the trap door rasped against senses still drifting in a hazy half-world between sleep and awareness.

Lewis sprang up at once, dragging at his clothes, but Touaris was still dazed and half-bewitched and she was slower. She stood up, the pale lidless eyes of the Decalogue behind her, the black bars of the cage framing her body. Her cheeks were flushed, her eyes were slumberous and her hair was tumbled, and even at such a moment, with most of his attention focused on the people plunging down the stair, Lewis had time to register how blazingly beautiful she looked. Incandescent. Don't think about it now. Concentrate on what's about to happen.

When Kaspar and six of his people entered the cavern, Touaris was still pulling ineffectually at her gown, but even without that Lewis thought there could be absolutely no doubt about what had taken place between them.

There on the floor, in the dust of God-knows how many centuries, and in the shadow of something ancient and implacable and vaguely menacing . . . I've screwed these people's divine goddess, he thought, and then in the same instant, but that wasn't screwing, that was making love. Whatever name it's given, I think there's about to be a reckoning.

Kaspar regarded Touaris for a long moment, but when he finally spoke to her, he spoke in what Lewis assumed to be their own tongue. The words and the cadences bore no

272

resemblance to any language he had ever heard, but the cold contempt in Kaspar's voice did not need interpretation.

Touaris heard Kaspar out with sudden regal courtesy, and then looked across at Lewis. He saw at once that the imperiousness was a perilously thin veneer, and that behind her eyes was a very deep fear. 'Kaspar says we have defiled the Sacred Place of my ancestors,' she said.

'How predictable of him.' Lewis managed to inject a note of cold arrogance into his tone. 'Well, so what?' he said.

Kaspar looked at him with angry dislike. 'You have offended on three counts, Mr Chance,' he said. 'You have intruded into the forbidden city of Tashkara, which means you have committed the offence we call overlooking. That we might have forgiven, but you have also committed an offence that has only once before been known here.'

He paused, and Lewis, dredging up every ounce of courage he possessed, said coolly, 'How annoying that I wasn't the first. What is the offence?'

'The defilement of the goddess,' said Kaspar, and his eyes narrowed with glittering hatred. 'And for that you will receive one of the most extreme of all our punishments.'

Lewis leaned back against the wall and folded his arms. 'Do go on,' he said. 'You have such interesting customs here, although on second thoughts, archaic might be a better description. You referred to three offences: what's the third?'

'Blasphemy,' said Kaspar. 'The deceit you practised in the stone palace.'

'The Traveller from the West,' said Lewis, regarding Kaspar with cynical amusement. 'The prophecy of the one who would save Tashkara from a great catastrophe. I thought it was rather good, myself, and I certainly wouldn't have used the word blasphemy. But perhaps you don't see it from the same viewpoint. You weren't really naïve enough to believe it, were you? Ah, I see you were. How astonishing.'

Kaspar said, 'For blasphemy there is also a punishment.'

Lewis regarded him thoughtfully. 'You know, one of your weaknesses, Kaspar, is your complete absence of any sense of humour,' he said. 'Still, I expect you've got any number of barbaric punishments lined up for intruders and blasphemers and – what was the other one? – oh yes, defilers. Don't let me interrupt you.' And now shut up, said his mind. Don't taunt the creature further by suggesting half a dozen possible tortures, because you'll end up hoist with your own petard! It would be Kaspar's idea of a very neat vengeance to use your own ideas against you.

Kaspar turned to the men standing with him and there was a brief consultation in the Tashkaran language. Lewis watched Touaris's expression, trying to guess at what was being said from her reactions, but could not. She was pale and her eyes were huge dark circles in her little white face, but she was composed.

Then Kaspar nodded, as if confirming some agreement, and turned back to Lewis. 'You will be imprisoned here for one month,' he said. 'At the end of that time, you will be brought to the Hall of Judgement at the centre of the city, where you will be tried and sentenced.' His eyes flickered to the silent stones, and Lewis felt fear crawl across his skin. Ten punishments for ten offences. And every one of them certainly terrible. I wish I'd been able to decipher the hieroglyphs on the Tablets. No I don't, I'd rather not know. Does Touaris know? Yes, of course she does. He looked at her again, and saw that she appeared to be listening to the interchange with detached interest. He was suddenly immensely grateful to her for maintaining the cool arrogance; he wondered if any of the liberated Chelsea females he knew would have behaved so well or whether they would have crumpled into hysterics by now.

He said, 'Why the delay? Or is that another part of the punishment?' and for the first time Kaspar smiled.

'Now you are the one who is being naïve,' he said. 'And for an English traveller and a gentleman of the liberated 1970s that is as astonishing to me as my belief in prophecies was to you.' He paused, and Lewis thought: get on with it, you bastard!

'There is surely,' said Kaspar, 'the possibility that a child has been conceived.' He paused and as Lewis stared at him, he said softly, 'Well, Mr Chance? I am right?'

Lewis, his mind in tumult, thought, what the hell do I say? Could he be right? Yes, of course he could, you fool, you forgot about all the restraints or, if you're honest, by the time you reached that point you didn't want to remember them. And you certainly didn't come down here with your wallet stuffed with contraceptives! My God, if it has happened I'll have turned their odd remote world upside down, and they'll probably rend me limb from limb! But I'll be bloody unlucky if it's happened on a one-off! he thought. And then, with a small secret spiral of delight – yes, but what a one-off it was!

Kaspar had turned to regard Touaris, and when he spoke again, Lewis heard the dislike in his voice. Kaspar said, 'Touaris has committed the greater offence. And even though it was never believed that the goddess would demean herself in this way, there is a due punishment.'

Lewis felt the faintest tremor of fear from Touaris, and forcing cold boredom into his voice, he said, 'It's pushing it a bit to expect me to believe that none of your goddesses has ever broken out. In three thousand years? Come off it, Kaspar! Who's being naïve now?'

'Nevertheless, it is true. The tradition is of a virgin goddess.'

'More likely they didn't get found out,' said Lewis caustically. 'And what if there is a child? What then?'

'The punishment would be deferred until after it had been born,' said Kaspar. 'We do not kill unborn children.'

'You surprise me,' said Lewis politely. 'In Ancient Greece a little feast of new-born baby was considered a delicacy. I would have expected your cannibals to follow that example with enthusiasm.' He felt Touaris flinch, and thought: yes, that was a savage thing to say! But this is a savage situation.

'But this would be the child of a goddess,' said Kaspar. 'It might be something to revere.'

'"Might"? What else "might" you do with it?'

'If Touaris does not survive the Decalogue's punishment, and if the child is a girl—'

'You *might* train her up for the next Touaris?'

'It is not necessarily as simple as that,' said Kaspar. 'But it could be possible.' He frowned, and for the first time since Kaspar's entrance, Touaris spoke, turning to Lewis.

'Each time the reigning Touaris dies,' she said, her small face intent and serious, 'a search is made for a girl child, no younger than two, no older than four years, in whom must be recognised the reappearance of the goddess.'

'And they say religion is never derivative,' murmured Lewis.

'The search for the replacement is nearly always long and complex,' broke in Kaspar. 'And the tests are very stringent. There must be the recognition of objects belonging to the original goddess; there must be prescribed similarities of face and feature and above all there must be certain race memories,' he looked at Touaris, 'as there were with you.'

'Yes.' For a moment the mischief flared in the dark eyes. 'There was no doubt about me, was there, Kaspar? And it kills you to admit it. But there was never any doubt, for all you tried to promote your daughter.'

'Did he really do that?' said Lewis promptly. 'I'm shocked. Intriguing for power? Dear me, Kaspar, I wouldn't have thought it of you.' He grinned at Touaris encouragingly, but his mind was shuddering from the implication that she might not survive the Decalogue's sentence. Looking back at Kaspar, he said, 'This is a wholly hypothetical discussion, but – if the child were to be a boy? What would happen?'

'A boy could be put to interesting use.' The cold cruel smile curved Kaspar's mouth. 'There are certain ceremonies involving the Burning Altar, and use of a newly born boy-child,' he said. 'As you foresaw.'

Damn! thought Lewis furiously. But surely I didn't need to put that idea into their evil warped minds! Isn't there any way out of this?

He glanced to the guards standing behind Kaspar. Was it remotely possible that he could knock them aside and beat it up the stair and out into the night? But there were six or eight of them, and they were all muscular and strong. They were not armed in the way Lewis, with his twentieth-century outlook, thought of as armed, but they carried glinting knives. And the stair was impossibly narrow and as far as he could see there was no other way out of the Decalogue Chamber. Then I'm trapped. And there was Touaris – it was unthinkable that he should leave her to face this alone. He ground his teeth silently, but when two of the men seized him and began to force him back up the stone stair, he went without a struggle. He would save any struggles for later, for when he had formulated some kind of plan. It was inconceivable that he should submit docilely to these people, and it was even more inconceivable that he should let Touaris do so.

But panic was flooding his mind, and he thought: I'll never escape from these people! I'll never be able to fool them, or bribe them, or reason with them—

But Patrick escaped, he remembered suddenly. Patrick eluded them all those years ago, and returned to England.

A tiny voice tapped against the surface of his mind like brittle icicle fingers on a freezing cold dawn, and the memory of Patrick's strange metamorphosis, so clear from the journal, slid coldly into his mind. A treacherous little voice deep within him, said, Did Patrick really escape?

Chapter Twenty-six

Patrick Chance's Diary

Tashkara

Only a sense of tidiness (uncharacteristic but infuriatingly persistent), and an awareness of a task left uncompleted has forced me to turn to these diaries again.

I made a half-flippant comment in England (in another life and another world), about writing a bawdy account of my travels, and publishing it in the face of my father and everyone else's displeasure. The more I look back on what has happened, the more this seems less of a flippancy and more of a possibility. Could it be done? Would I do it? I believe I would.

But as for what was done to me in the courtyard, in the grisly shadow of the Burning Altar— No, that's not for telling to the world. What I write down about that is for no one's eyes except my own.

I believe that some stage performers insist (with varying degrees of coyness) that they experience something akin to orgasm when they step on to a lighted stage and face their audiences. When I stepped into the torchlit square at Tashkara's centre and faced *my* audience, orgasm was the last thing I was about to suffer, although there was a strong possibility that I might disgrace myself with the same part of my body, but in a very different manner. However, it's yet another duty of Englishmen to control bladder and bowels *no matter the situation*, and at least that humiliation was spared me. Not much else was.

The scaffold was unspeakably sinister. It was positioned directly in front of the altar and the honours for sheer malevolence were divided pretty much equally.

The scaffold was not the flat platform I had thought, but a rectangle of wood about ten feet long and half as wide, with chains driven into each corner. Manacles. Whatever they were about to do, they were going to chain me down while they did it.

It was being tilted by six of the men, and it was horribly clear that once a prisoner was chained hand and foot to the wood, he would be practically vertical, splayed out on the surface, facing the assembled people. The twisting flames from the flambeaux fell across the grisly oblong, suffusing it with crimson. Like the floor of a coffin, soaked in blood.

Of Theo there was no sign, and I could not decide if this was hopeful or not. On the one hand he might have escaped and be bringing help, but on the other he might be cooped up in some miserable dungeon, about to face all manner of fates.

The people taking their places on the seats surrounding the square were attractive in the way that Tamerlane and his guards were attractive: tall and well-built, all with silky black hair worn rather long, and although they had the high slanting cheekbones of the East they had the wide-open eyes of the West. It was an arresting blend of several cultures and I spent some minutes wondering about their ancestry because anything was better than speculating on the purpose of the coffin floor.

I had just reached the point of remembering Fenris's

story about the renegade Egyptian tribe, when a single plangent note from somewhere inside the palace rang out. It pierced the air and shivered on the night long after it had been sounded, and my skin crawled with absolute and abject terror, because I had never heard anything so implacable and so *pitiless* as that sound. If I ever get as far as hearing the Last Trump that's precisely the kind of sound it will make. Imperious and bone-chilling. *Marrow*-chilling.

The men and women on the seats had been murmuring to one another – it was impossible to avoid drawing comparisons with a London theatre audience waiting for the curtain to rise! – but at the sound of the note they stopped as if a door had been slammed, and an immense silence closed down. Every head turned to a door at the square's northern side, and my heart began to beat very fast. Something was coming. Something tremendous and powerful was approaching. Something connected with the silent sinister altar? Or with the coffin-floor rectangle of wood?

By this time, I should not have been surprised to see anything from a hooded Jack Ketch, to a whole battalion of black-robed Inquisition torturers, brandishing white-hot flesh-tearing tongs and dragging a medieval Scavenger's daughter behind them. All the better to crunch your bones, my dear . . .

The steady drumbeat started up again, and, as if they had received a signal, the audience began the low chanting I had heard earlier. The sound lifted the hairs on the nape of my neck. Cannot even begin to describe how creepingly menacing it was; there was a kind of relentless implacability about it, and a pulsating blood lust and the thought: *it's my blood they're lusting for!* snaked around my brain and tightened. For several seconds it was difficult to breathe and a great weight pressed down on my mind. The rectangular scaffold and the crouching, silk-covered altar swam in a red mist.

Into the square came not hooded Inquisitors or black-masked hangmen, but eight rippling-haired girls – plainly Tashkarans – each wearing a thin white robe with a scarlet silk girdle. The torchflames stirred as they passed them, throwing huge elongated shadows across the wall of the palace directly behind them so that for a moment the square seemed alive with monstrous prowling shadow-beings. They bore, at shoulder height, an immense ornate throne, ivory and silver and jade, slung between two golden poles, and seated on it was a figure dressed in stiff ceremonial brocade: scarlet and gold, with an elaborate headdress of gold and jade that glinted in the flickering light.

Not the Scavenger's daughter. But from the look of her, very possibly the iron maiden.

Touaris, the ancient cat goddess of the renegade Bubasti of Egypt.

She was older than I had been expecting – probably around forty or fifty – and she was *huge*. I don't mean she was fat – fatness is quite different and can be rather jolly. The creature on the chair-throne was a massive-framed, large-boned female with a heavy hippopotamus face and little mean lizard eyes that constantly darted from side to side. Boadicea in avenging mood, or one of the majestic black-browed Furies . . . Tamora feasting on her own sons in that grisly *en famille* banquet, or the murderous Clytemnestra— I pulled my thoughts up. If I was facing death – or even merely mutilation – and wandering amidst Shakespeare's villainesses and Greek Tragedy for comparisons, I was nearer insanity than was safe. I stole another glance at the creature.

281

I would allow her the divinity status, but this was not a face men would sack cities for.

It would be wrong to say that after ten minutes of the ceremonies following Touaris's entrance I was bored – I defy *anyone* to be bored whilst awaiting torturing and/or execution – but my attention was certainly erratic. Sacred goddesses and pagan ceremonial dances are all very well in their place, but suggest that their place is *not* as the curtain-raiser to an execution, and especially not when it's mine. In fact, as the dance spun out and out I started to feel aggrieved. I don't think I'm any more egocentric than the next man, but if you can't be the centre of attention at your own execution, when can you?

It's possible that but for the sense of gathering malignancy, never mind the guards' presence, I might have derived some small interest from the dance. I certainly might have taken notice when the male dancers donned monstrous masks fashioned like the faces of snarling cats and buckled about their waists huge leather belts with immense jutting phalluses of pale polished leather. They began to dance again, faster now, leaping and prowling around the silent altar, their shadows prancing fantastically across the square, so that it was as if each dancer had a dark giantish alter ego mimicking his every movement. (Have to say, however, that if this was Tashkara's idea of an orgy it was a bit tame, in fact I had seen bawdier behaviour in St Stephen's Road Music Hall. I had *taken part* in bawdier behaviour.)

The dance reached its all-too-obvious conclusion. The men each took one of the dancing girls, and the phalluses were duly driven home between the girls' thighs. Very predictable. I glanced at Touaris and caught a disdainful, rather pitying smirk on her granite features. I was unclear whether the dancing was intended to be arousing – personally I had never felt less aroused in my life – but my viewpoint was necessarily warped. But if that was the quality (never mind *quantity*) of sexual attention these Tashkaran women were used to, I might as well not have bothered scraping myself raw last night, because the false phalluses were absolutely *huge*. I wondered how aroused the men actually were inside the leather prongs and hoped they were all rampant to strangulation point.

The watchers were cheering them on, and a section of the younger people had started up some kind of chant on their own account. I had no idea what they were singing, but it sounded like an old-fashioned round song and it was obviously pretty Rabelaisian in content. Tamerlane, the killjoy, sent a frowning glare at them, and they straggled into abashed silence.

The single plangent note rang out again, and that astonishing abrupt silence fell once more. The dancers stood up, and the lady in the elaborate throne walked regally towards me, Tamerlane at her side.

She was so immense that she did not walk, she waddled. It ought to have been laughable, but there was such an air of menace about her that she was not laughable at all. A fragment of a half-forgotten verse – something about the ground shakes as they walk the world, and the air trembles with the fee-fo-fum wind of their speech – went through my mind.

She appeared neither to speak nor understand English, but I had not been far wrong about the iron maiden part, because if ever a female was getting ready to enjoy a torturing, this one was. She was practically licking her lips over it.

Tamerlane spoke in his halting imprecise English. (Again, will not set down our rather tedious roundaboutations, but will simply convey the essence, and, saving the mark, the *flavour*.)

'You have witnessed our ritual of the cats, English traveller,' he said.

'And very explicit it was too.' I was damned if I was going to give this barbarian – or the hatchet-featured female at his side – the satisfaction of seeing how afraid I was.

'It is in homage to the cat goddess Touaris, and it precedes all of our solemn ceremonies,' said Tamerlane.

'I'm glad to know I'm taken solemnly. What happens next?'

The cruel smile curved Tamerlane's lips. 'Next,' he said, 'we bring out your companion. And to add a little refinement to your own punishment, you will witness his sentence and punishment.'

I felt as if I had been flung, neck-deep, into black, ice-cold water. Theo! Hell and damnation! But I said, very coldly, 'Sentence? Punishment?'

'You have defiled Touaris's handmaidens and for that you will suffer the punishment of the Seventh Tablet of the Tashkara Decalogue handed down and down by our ancestors,' said Tamerlane. 'It is a punishment not carried out for many centuries.'

'I'm glad to provide you with something out of the ordinary. What about my companion?' Whatever else Theo might have done he would certainly not have done any defiling.

Tamerlane said, 'He is to suffer the punishment reserved for those who overlook the Secret Domain of Tashkara – you would call it intruding, I think.'

'Not necessarily. We might call your reception of us discourteous and hostile. But go on.'

'The punishment reserved for those guilty of overlooking is that of the Sixth Tablet of the Decalogue,' said Tamerlane. 'It is a three-fold sentence.' He paused, and then went on, obviously quoting. '*The loss of hands so that the guilty one shall not write of*

284

what he has seen . . . The loss of feet so that he shall not walk in the world to tell of what he has seen . . .'
He stopped and I stared at him, my mind reeling. 'But,' said Tamerlane, softly, 'we do not extort the full sentence any longer.'

'How very merciful of you.'

'But since we believe him to be your servant and therefore under your orders, we shall inflict the third part on him,' said Tamerlane.

'And that is?'

Tamerlane exchanged a look with Touaris, who smiled. I had the feeling that she knew precisely what was being said and that she was enjoying it immensely, the bitch.

When Tamerlane spoke again, his tone licked over the words gloatingly. *'The tearing out of the tongue so that he shall not speak of what he has seen . . .'*

There was absolutely nothing I could think of that would save Theo. Wild ideas of breaking away from the guards and creating some kind of diversion so that he could run, tumbled through my mind, but the instant they brought him out I saw that it would be pointless. He was heavily guarded and his ankles and wrists were manacled, so that even if he had understood sufficiently quickly, he would not have got six feet before they caught him.

I knew at once that he was very frightened, but I knew as well that he was determined not to show it. Good for you, Theo. I had the awful feeling that when it was my turn I would struggle like a mad thing.

Whether he knew what was about to be done to him I had no idea, but he knew that it was something extremely nasty. By this time the dreadful waiting silence had descended on the Tashkara people again, and as Theo was taken to the centre of the square they were so still they might have been carved from stone. Only the flickering torch-flames gave an air of life to the terrible scene, and when the soft thrumming of the drumbeat started up again it was so exactly in time with the pounding of my heart that for a moment I did not realise the sound was outside my body. A thrumming tension was building, and the watchers were leaning forward avidly, and murmuring in anticipation. Sweat broke out on my scalp.

The guards snaked the chains about Theo's wrists and ankles, pinning him to the wooden board, and then – this made me shudder in sick horror – they passed two iron circlets about him: one around the upper part of his head like a travesty of a coronet, the other around his neck. The ends were driven into the board and his head was held absolutely immobile, with the neck brace almost choking him, so that I found myself swallowing convulsively. Was it better to half strangle than to have your tongue torn out? Hold on, Theo. I'll get you out of this somehow. I'll think of something. But I knew I wouldn't; there was nothing I could do against so many and even if I could outwit the guards there were easily three hundred people on the wooden seats. Theo would have to endure the torture, and after they had finished with him it would be my turn.

I looked at Touaris. She was standing with Tamerlane; her eyes were fixed on Theo and the avidity was easy to read, even from where I stood. She was an ogress, an eater of children. *The ground shakes as they walk the world, and the air trembles with the fee-fo-fum wind of their speech . . .* She protected herself by posting a leper colony at the entrance to her city, and trapped travellers and tore out the tongues of intruders.

Two men, both wearing plain black garments, approached Theo, and anticipation, very nearly sexual in quality, sizzled across the firelit square. The men moved as if performing the steps of a frequently rehearsed dance; without appearing to consult, one stood behind the board, reaching around it and thrusting his fingers knuckle-deep into Theo's mouth, dragging it wide. Theo jerked and let out a cry of mingled surprise and pain, and a trickle of blood ran from the torn corner of his mouth. The other man stood in front of him, his lips curving in a smile, a jagged-edged clamp with serrated edges held in his hands. They're savouring him, I thought, and as the man held the clamps up before Theo's eyes, black fury rose within me because they could have spared him that, they could have kept the torture instrument hidden until the last moment. If I could have got free for ten seconds I would have torn the smile from the man's face with my nails.

The man behind the scaffold had thrust some kind of wedge into Theo's mouth, forcing it impossibly wide, and I felt the muscles of my own jaw clench with cramping pains in sympathy. Theo's eyes were straining from his head and sweat was running down his face, gluing his hair to his forehead. In the crimson torchlight his skin had taken on a greyish pallor, and I clenched my fists, digging my nails into my palms, praying for something – anything – to intervene. I would have summoned Satan and his entire hierarchy of demons if I had had the means, and if I had thought they would arrive in time. The drumbeat was increasing and the tension was building up and up, like an elastic thread stretched to breaking point.

And then the drumbeat quickened perceptibly and as if a signal had been given, the man holding the steel clamp stepped forward and thrust it down into Theo's mouth.

I could no longer see what they were doing,

because they were bending over him, but I could see that he was struggling against the chains, and I could hear him choking and gagging as well. Dreadful to have those pitiless iron pincers forced to the back of your throat. Unbearable to realise their purpose. Theo was flinging himself against the restraints, but the chains held firm.

And then there was a cold snapping sound that grated against every nerve-ending in my body, and a low moan of triumph went through the watchers. Theo screamed again, but the sound was different – it was guttural, *grunting*; the cry of a creature no longer able to form words— I thought: they've done it. They've torn out his tongue. My mind spun with the agony of it.

The guards stepped back and triumphantly held aloft the terrible steel clamps. A dripping fragment of dark red flesh, faintly slimy, hung from it, and at once the watchers yelled in delight.

Theo was flailing weakly against the restraints, and thick blood and great clotted strings of saliva spilled out of his mouth. He began to retch with dreadful unformed grunts, vomiting phlegmy blood that spattered over the upper part of his body, and I felt my mind swing between churning pity and shameful repulsion. His mouth was bruised and swollen, distorting his face, making him a nightmare thing, and as the torch flames flickered and washed over him, he opened his eyes and stared around the square. For a terrible moment I saw only the distortion, so that it was not Theo who was chained there but something monstrous, something out of one of the ancient grisly fables of the world's dark ages: macabre half-humans with men's bodies but beasts' heads: one of those aberrant lumpish blendings of animal and human that occasionally shamble pitiably through freak sideshows ... How must it feel to be so hideously deformed that you must needs live in a twilit half-existence, seeing the world flinch from you?

I forced the images away and as Theo was untied, he turned his head and through pain-wracked eyes saw me. Half-coagulated blood still ran from his mutilated mouth and his clothes were wet with vomit and saliva. He tried to lift one hand in acknowledgement of some kind.

Tamerlane's soft voice at my side said, 'And now, Englishman, it is your turn.'

Chapter Twenty-seven

Patrick Chance's Diary continued

I can vividly remember my emotions as Tamerlane's guards led me to the scaffold; I can remember how my heart was thumping, and how sweat was trickling between my shoulder blades.

They had started up the drum-roll again, and it tapped its insidious message against my mind. Yes, yes, you're going to die . . . My guts began to clench and unclench with agonised panic, and I found myself walking in exact rhythm with it. I was about to face the punishment of the strange ancient Decalogue and I was trying to mark time as I walked!

Tamerlane walked ahead, Touaris at his side, the sacred cat goddess of Ancient Egypt leading me to my fate. It was so utterly extraordinary as to be almost unbelievable. She turned her head from side to side as she went, the dark basilisk eyes flicking over the watchers. Every gaze was upon me, and I felt as if I was at the heart of a seething bubbling cauldron of lust-filled anticipation.

I had expected to be chained down as Theo had been and so I was, but I had not expected to feel such abrupt repulsion. The wood was hard and uncompromising, and it was slippery from Theo's blood and still warm – oh God, his spilled blood was still warm! The thought: I can't bear this! gripped me, and then I remembered that Theo had had to bear it. I scanned the square trying to see if he was still here, but I could only see the rows of greedy-eyed Tashkarans and the flat smile of Touaris herself. I would have to submit to these barbarians, and if I died in screaming agony the last thing I was going to see on this earth was the hungry-ogre face of this bitch goddess.

The structure had been lowered once more, and as the guards forced me on to it a tiny night wind blew across the square, stirring the torch flames into life. The stench of stale blood and drying vomit gusted into my face, and my stomach lifted and I swallowed convulsively. Forgive me, Theo. The chains clamped about my wrists, but as the guards bent to secure the leg shackles, Tamerlane said something that appeared to stop them.

He looked straightly at me. 'You are ready?'

'No.' This is it, I thought, my heart racing. 'I'm not ready at all. But we'll get on with it, shall we? I find your ancient Decalogue very tedious, Tamerlane, and the sooner I can be out of reach of it and its melodramatic punishments, the better.' This came out so convincingly that it gave me an unlooked-for edge of courage. I would probably be screaming for mercy in ten minutes, but it need not prevent me from hurling insults now.

For the first time since Theo had been dragged from the square Touaris spoke, and every head turned to her instantly. I had no means of understanding what she said, but as her harsh voice cut across the listening square I saw a gleam of something very sly and very calculating come into Tamerlane's expression.

'What does she say? Hell's teeth, man, if this delay is part of your wretched torture—'

Tamerlane said, 'She says you have spoken against the Decalogue.'

'Of course I've spoken against it. If I knew where

you kept it, I'd smash it to splinters and fuck the entire female population of Tashkara on the pieces! What did she expect!'

'She says you speak against the Decalogue, but that one day in the future the Decalogue will speak against you and against your Western civilisation. The Decalogue is an instrument of deep and ancient vengeance.'

'How interesting,' I said sardonically. 'But she's missing the mark; it's wreaking its deep and ancient vengeance now.'

Touaris spoke again and Tamerlane listened with intense concentration, and then, apparently translating for my benefit, said, 'The hands of those who have power over their inferiors will one day wield the knowledge of the Stone Tablets of Tashkara.'

'I've never heard such meaningless bombast in all my— Oh, or is she feeble-minded, poor creature?' I laced my tone with such heavy sarcasm that even Touaris herself must have understood. The cruel eyes rested on me.

'She occasionally has – I think your word is precognition,' said Tamerlane. (This was a term I arrived at later.) 'She has glimpses of the future.'

'How amusing for her. Listen, if you're not going to do anything to me do you think I might be allowed to get off this thing, because it's starting to give me appalling cramp—'

'That is to say,' went on Tamerlane, ignoring the interruption, 'that the Decalogue and all it stands for will one day be revealed to your world and used by power-hungry people to gain sway over the weak.'

'Well, I'm sure the world will survive. It's survived the rise of empty dictators before.'

'Would your Western religions survive?' said Tamerlane. 'Perhaps you do not know that your

Roman Catholic Church fears the Decalogue's legend so much it has suppressed all knowledge of its existence for twenty centuries?'

'Listen,' I said, 'I don't give a damn about *anybody's* religion at the moment and I don't care who knows about your accursed Decalogue and who doesn't. Will you either unfasten these chains or get on with your punishment and tell your hippopotamus-faced goddess to stop poaching my limelight?'

He could not have interpreted this very clearly but he undoubtedly got the gist of it. So did the lady. She fixed me with that basilisk stare and lifted an imperious arm to the guards. They moved forward and Touaris rapped out a command.

Tamerlane looked at her and then said to me, 'The guards have been told to remove your clothes. The sentence is about to be carried out.'

'Why am I to be undressed?' But dreadful comprehension was struggling upwards, pushing aside the forced arrogance. The Seventh Tablet of the Decalogue. The punishment for defiling the handmaidens... For *defiling*... And according to the laws of the renegade Bubasti, according to the rules of their strange Devil's Commandments, all punishments had to be strictly in relation to the offence.

Tamerlane said, 'Your punishment is twofold, English traveller. Since you lay with the handmaidens of the Temple you will be deprived of the organ that caused the offence. You will be castrated.'

He paused and then said, 'After that, because you looked on the forbidden inner Temple of the Goddess, your eyes will be torn out.'

The firelit courtyard and the avid-faced watchers blurred and fused in a whirling vortex, and I felt myself being sucked down into the spinning heart.

When my senses cleared the terrible scaffold was being raised to a near-vertical position again, and I was facing the Tashkaran people on their wooden seats.

I was naked although I had no memory of them undressing me, but that was the least part of anything now. My ankles were chained to the outer edges of the rectangle, stretching my legs wide, and the guards were spreading sawdust directly beneath. The scent of it rose up: grotesquely reminiscent of homely ordinary things: carpenters' workshops and newly sawn apple branches; stables and freshly laid timber floors. Yes, and the grim operating rooms of the old barber surgeons who had strewn sawdust beneath the table and rendered their victims drunk on cheap rum before subjecting them to the torments of the knife . . .

Castrated and then my eyes torn out – the words were etched on my brain. I fought to get free and scoured my mind to think of anyone who might rescue me. But the only person who knew where I was was Theo . . . Despair and panic closed about my mind. Theo and I might finally survive and be able to return to England, but it would be a pitiful survival indeed. All of the unthinking aphorisms about the blind leading the blind lashed against my mind, but for us it would be much worse – it would be the blind leading the dumb, and the dumb leading the emasculate . . . I struggled to summon the whirling unconsciousness again. Let me faint, or at least let me drink mandragora, the drowsy sleep juice, or even the cheap rum of the barber surgeons . . . Let me wake up and find it all over!

Only once it was over I should be *blinded* – Out, vile jelly! Where is thy lustre now? And once it was over I should be castrated. A gelding.

I tried to pretend it did not matter which they did first. It could not count whether I was forced to watch while they tore my manhood out by the roots –

knowing that once it was done, I would be thrust into eternal darkness – or whether the darkness came first. Darkness . . . I would be sightless. *Eyeless*. Put out the light and then put out the light. My reason spun crazily out of control, and real madness hovered. If I could be mad – truly mad – if I could embrace uncaring, *unfeeling* dementia and babble of green fields and childhood ways – at least I should not know and I should not feel . . .

Chained to that appalling scaffold, all these things tore through my mind, and my reason spun crazily at the end of a spider's web, so that for several minutes I had no clear idea of where I was. Hysteria, Patrick. Push it away. Hang on to that cold insolence you dredged up earlier. It won't save you but it might stop you from breaking and it might stop you begging for mercy.

I don't think I did beg for mercy, and in any case, no mercy was forthcoming. The two men who had carried out Theo's sentence came to stand before me, and for a wild moment I thought they were to use the same instrument they had used on Theo. The torches were burning lower in the twisted iron wall brackets now, and the ancient crimson-shadowed square was growing perceptibly darker.

The instrument was not the same. The flames glinted on it, and I saw with sick dread that it was an elaborately worked clamp – either bronze or gold – adorned with the head of a snarling cat. The two shanks were hinged at one end, and there was an oval ring— I stared at it, mesmerised.

Tamerlane said, 'You will see that this is not total castration. The oval ring draws up the phallus, allowing only the removal of—'

'Yes, I see it.' Sanity was spinning dizzily out of my grasp, but the part of my mind that still retained some hold on logic shied from embarking on another of the

295

involved discourses to establish a precise meaning. They were going to cut off my testicles and leave my prick in place. Sufficient unto the day thereof.

Tamerlane said, 'The eyes will be removed afterwards.' And nodded to the guards.

The feel of the cold bronze clamp between my thighs almost broke my resolve, but I fought for mastery. I tried to remember that in some lands and in some cultures this was regarded as a mark of distinction; I tried to think of the silver-voiced castrati who submitted willingly to this, and of the Christian martyrs who suffered self-castration to remove carnal temptations. But I did not want carnal temptations removed!

The clamp was closing about me – I could feel the guards' hands adjusting it in dreadful intimacy; their fingers brushed against the inside of my thigh, and there was the rasp of a rough hangnail on my skin. It was suddenly intolerable to have to suffer the irritation of someone's ill-kept nails at such a moment.

The skies were closing in and closing down, and there was the sensation of breathable air draining slowly from the firelit square. The night wind whipped across the square again, and several of the low-burning torch flames guttered so that dark shadows leaped forward and there was the acrid tang of smoke. I felt the hinged clamps being adjusted—

There was the snapping of serrated teeth as the clamp came down, and pain exploded into my body, ferocious scarlet pain, violent agony made up of biting teeth and jagged claws ripping upwards into my stomach ... I cried out and tried involuntarily to double over but the chains jerked me back and held me vertical. Grinding agony rushed in, swamping me ... Screaming torment – unbearable ... There could not be so much pain in the whole world. The lower half of my body was a raw open wound and thick viscous fluids were running down my legs and dripping on to the ground. Waves of sick blackness closed over my head.

I was dimly aware of voices nearby, but a mist was obscuring my sight and blurring my senses. I thought the guards thrust something between my legs to stanch the blood – soft cool cotton waste or lint – and the thought, at least they don't intend me to die! skittered crazily across my brain.

There was the sensation of a huge darkness moving across the square, and from a great distance I heard the low menacing thrum of an approaching storm. Like marching feet coming through the mountains.

There seemed to be some kind of consultation going on; the guards were saying something to Tamerlane, and Tamerlane was indicating impatiently to them to continue and holding out a thin long-handled, long-bladed knife. For a moment the pain and the sick unconsciousness receded. The knife's end was honed to glittering razor sharpness, but it was formed in a curious spoon shape. This was what they were going to use to scoop out my eyes. They were going to hold me down and dig out my eyes. Put out the light and then put out the light . . . And afterwards I should truly be an outcast: blind and impotent, forced to sniff my way through the world . . .

Only four of the flambeaux burned now, and the night skies were heavy and lowering as if the storm were pressing them down on to the valley. The sense that something was creeping towards Tashkara from the purple-smudged mountains increased, and I caught again the soft low-pitched sound from the east. Thunder rolling forward across the valley. Like the low murmuring of dozens of people. *People.*

A tiny green shoot of hope forced its way through the pain, and I struggled to listen. People coming through the mountain pass, shouting as they came?

Was it possible? Wild visions of Theo having escaped and summoned help whirled through my mind, and then I remembered that there had not been time for Theo to get away, and even if he had there was no one in this remote enisled valley but the Tashkarans.

But there was someone. There was an entire colony of someones living on Tashkara's borders. The leper colony: Fenris and his people. I forced my mind to concentrate. Had I really heard it? Or was it only a gathering storm and my own mind betraying me into false hope?

The iron circlet they had used for Theo was being passed around my neck: I struggled and at once the guards tightened it almost to throttling point. They nodded as if satisfied but their unease was apparent; several times they glanced in the direction of the east, and one of them pointed and said something. I tried to follow the direction of his pointing finger, but my sight was blurred with tears and agony, and red lights were dancing before my vision.

Red lights. I blinked and tried to focus, and this time I saw more clearly and my heart gave a huge bound of hope. A thin strand of moving lights – torch flares! – was coming through the mountain pass towards Tashkara! I struggled against the restraints again and was slammed back against the wooden scaffold by the iron neck-brace and the chains. But I knew I had seen it: people were coming, they were approaching the walled city. But how near were they? And if they were truly the lepers what could such a pitifully weak people do against the Tashkarans? A different agony rose up.

The watchers were pointing to the lights and murmuring uneasily to one another, most of them looking towards Tamerlane and Touaris as if for guidance. Touaris's heavy-jowled face was unreadable but Tamerlane looked angry. He gestured impatiently to several of the guards and rapped out an order which sent them running from the square. To close the city gates? Dear God, was I to be so near to rescue and be cheated of it? I was still swimming helplessly in and out of huge waves of pain, but I tried to beat them back and think of a way of delaying Tamerlane's men.

The guard was lifting the grisly spoon-shaped knife and behind him two more were replenishing the wall brackets. Lighting the torture yard so that they can see to conclude their work ... The flames burned up, reflecting in the eyes of the guards and the watchers. Red-eyed devils watching me. Hell's demons grinning as I go down in screaming agony once more.

There was a sound of shouting from the far side and into the square, determinedly holding aloft the torchlights they carried, came the shambling, limping figures of Fenris and Sridevi and the lepers.

Every single one of them was there. Their heads were uncovered and in the glowing light of the flambeaux their diseased faces were mercilessly revealed.

The outcasts. Ishmael himself, but an Ishmael whose eyes glowed with bitter hatred. Fenris leading his people to the rescue of one who had shown them a brief surface kindness. They had dragged themselves here with God knew what agonies – many of them leaned heavily on sticks, and the trudge through the mountain pass must have been torment to their poor failing bodies. But they had come doggedly and unflinchingly to rescue me, purely because I had shared their exile for a few nights and because I had accepted their poor hospitality and listened to their stories. I felt stupid tears of weakness and pain well up.

They moved slowly, but they moved purposefully, as if a plan had been carefully thought out and was being followed. They simply separated into little groups and converged on the Tashkarans, holding out their eaten-away hands and pushing back their robes to display the ravages of their bodies. It was terrible and pitiful, and through my own pain and exhaustion I felt a great gut-clenching spasm of something akin to awe.

They were fighting not with swords and pistols and clubs, but with the only weapon they had: their own disease. Each group cornered a clutch of shrieking frightened Tashkarans and reached out to them, touching, stroking ... Two of the women fell on Tamerlane, winding their arms about his neck, one holding him down, the other leaning forward and breathing into his face.

Fenris stood at the centre like a general marshalling his forces. The light from the torch he carried cast a glowing mantle about him, and as he looked around and saw the Tashkarans fighting to get free, squealing in fear, his spoiled face took on an expression of such cynical bitterness that the remembered anger for them and about them rose up in me, and for several astonishing minutes the pain withdrew its claws.

Tamerlane had broken away and was whisking through one of the courtyard archways, and of Touaris and her attendants there was no sign. The guards were scattering, and the men and women who had lined the square and who had watched with such silent intensity as Theo and I were mutilated, were fighting to get through the northern arch.

I became aware then of Sridevi standing at the foot of the scaffold, looking up at me with unexpected gentleness in her expression.

'I am sorry,' she said, 'that we did not get here sooner, Patrick.'

'For Christ's sake, find Theo,' I said. 'And get me down from here before I pass out altogether.'

Chapter Twenty-eight

Elinor was becoming light-headed with fear and hunger, and she was dimly aware of swimming in and out of consciousness.

She was no longer sure which was the nightmare and which was the reality, but when the sound of doors unlocking pierced her awareness, sick realisation flooded back. All real. All true.

She had not known that the warehouse had conventional doors in addition to the trap door, but as they were flung open there was a glimpse of hazy smoke-filled darkness, and an achingly elusive scent of the real world drifted in. There was a flick of movement as Grendel darted back into the shadows cast by the packing cases, but Elinor's eyes were fastened on the two men silhouetted against the night. Something's about to happen, she thought, her nerves jumping. Have we reached Sunday night and the ritual?

And then the doors were slammed, and two men came in, carrying the inert body of a young boy between them. As they moved under the glow of one of the gas jets, Elinor saw that he looked to be in his early twenties. He did not look dead, but he was certainly unconscious. Another street boy for Timur's gruesome ritual?

The men deposited him on the ground and chained him to a stake in the wall, exactly as they had done with Elinor. They moved swiftly and efficiently, and when they had finished, one of them looked around him and called out, 'Timur? Are you still in here?'

'I'm here.' The voice came from the shadows, echoing slightly in the huge warehouse, and it was so like the dead Timur's voice that the hairs prickled on the back of Elinor's neck. But at least they're speaking English. Out of courtesy to the land they're in? Or to keep in practice? I wonder what Grendel would have done if they hadn't used English. Or does he know their tongue anyway?

'I'm still here.' There was a movement, and the dreadful false face looked out of the dimness. 'There is a very great deal for me to do yet,' said Timur's voice that was not Timur. Elinor clenched her fists, but the men nodded, and one said, 'Iwane is bringing one more from St Stephen's Wharf and then we shall have enough.'

'Good,' said the voice. 'Very good indeed.' Elinor caught the faint hint of the greedy purr again, and she thought one of the men looked up. He took a step towards Grendel and her heart lurched. And then there was a scuffle of sound from the main doors again, and the one she recognised as Iwane came in.

'The last victim?' said the man who had called out to Timur.

'The last,' said Iwane, and as he passed under the circle of light from the gas jet, Elinor saw that in his arms was Ginevra.

And from the look of her, she was either drugged or dazed.

Or dead.

Raffael spent most of the night scouring the streets around Chance House and St Stephen's Wharf, trying to find Ginevra, or at the very least trying to find a clue.

Around four a.m. exhaustion and cold drove him indoors, and he and Baz brewed coffee in Baz's untidy rooms, and sat over the gasfire, which was identical to Raffael's own but dirtier. They discussed what to do next, although Raffael found it difficult to concentrate; mentally he was still out in the fog, trying to see if there was a street or a doorway or an alley he had missed. There would have been several dozen, of course; the fog made it impossible to see more than a few feet in any direction. It had hidden him from his quarry which was probably as well, but it had hidden the quarry from him very thoroughly indeed.

Bitter self-blame scoured his mind. You should have picked her up and carried her out of the entire thing, said his mind angrily, never mind if you had to knock her out to do it! But you didn't; you let her stay because you wanted her around, and you made love to her because you'd wanted to do it ever since you saw her! What happened to all that hard-won selflessness, Father? What happened to self-denial and self-restraint? Out of the window, along with all the rest of the vows made and broken!

And afterwards, said the persistent nagging voice, what must you do afterwards, but talk that ridiculous romantic rubbish about being armoured and creating touchstones and charms? Who did you think you were – some kind of pseudo-Arthurian knight? Something out of Tolkien? Grails and charms and nine-fold rings and magical swords! It'll serve you right if she's gone for good, and if you never find out what value she accorded all that frantic lust on the bare hearthrug! But it wasn't just lust, said his mind. Oh no? said the inner voice jeeringly.

Baz had spent almost as long searching the streets as Raffael, and had even tried several of the pubs on the list made earlier, on the grounds that the people who had taken Georgie and Ginevra might still be prowling for victims.

'It was worth trying, but I'm afraid they've got their shoal,' said Raffael. 'I'm afraid we've lost the trail.'

They reviewed what had happened – 'For about the millionth time,' said Raffael wearily – in case they had forgotten something that might provide a lead. There had been that sudden scuffle just out of sight, which both of them had heard, and then the sound of running footsteps.

303

Raffael thought there had been more than one set of footsteps, but he could not be sure. Neither of them could be sure in which direction the footsteps had gone, although Baz thought the scales weighed just very slightly in favour of their having gone towards the disused quayside. He was inclined to rail against himself for not keeping Georgie in better sight, but Raffael, pushing down his own agony, said, 'Self-blame's a waste of energy. We lost them in the fog, and now we've got to find them and that's all we're going to think about. All right?'

Baz said all right, and tentatively asked about calling in the police which Raffael recognised as an indication of how worried the boy was.

But Raffael said, 'We can't. We daren't. I don't suppose it matters telling you the whole thing now.' He made an impatient gesture and then said, 'Timur threatened that if I tried to prevent them taking Grendel, or brought in the police, they would sacrifice all the prisoners on their accursed Burning Altar.' He paused, and then said, 'And that they would take Ginevra.' He made an abrupt angry gesture. 'Which is exactly what they have done. If we make a wrong move now, they'll all die – Ginevra and Elinor and Georgie and anyone else with them!' He frowned, and then said, 'The only thing to do is find Timur's hideout before midnight tomorrow.' He glanced at his watch: five a.m. 'Tonight, rather. It's Sunday morning.'

'But it could be anywhere.'

'No, I think it's likely to be very near,' said Raffael.

'Why? Why can't they have just chucked the prisoners into cars and driven off somewhere with them?' This came out a bit more belligerently than Baz meant, but he could not bear to think of Georgie, silly old tosser, being offered up as a sacrifice on some grisly altar.

Raffael said, 'I don't think they'll dare use cars.'

'Why not?'

'For one thing cars can be traced. Number plates can be

noted down and traced back to owners, or to hire companies – to people stealing them even, although I don't see Timur's famous League of Tamerlane as car thieves.'

'Too risky?' Baz sounded a bit surer of his ground here.

'Too far beneath them,' said Raffael caustically. 'But also if they're operating around here – and we've already seen that they are – they don't need cars. All the dozens of narrow alleys and tiny courtyards – a car would actually be a hindrance.'

'Docklands,' nodded Baz. 'Disused jetties and quays.'

'Victorian docklands as well,' said Raffael. 'Absolutely ideal for their purpose. There must be dozens of abandoned wharves and warehouses and cellars around here. They're near to us, Baz, I can feel that they are. I can almost smell that they are.'

They looked at one another, and then Baz said, 'What do we do? Search? Until we find them, or until—'

'Until we find them,' said Raffael. He looked at his watch again. 'We've got about eighteen hours to do it.'

They quartered the area around Chance House and St Stephen's Docks – 'Like an army manoeuvre,' said Raffael – and Baz suggested that they separate to explore, but meet up once an hour to share information. 'Else we might find one of us has discovered something and the other's wasting time still looking.'

'That's a very good idea.' Raffael regarded Baz approvingly, and Baz felt rather pleased, because peculiar as Raffael was, he was somebody you would want to think well of you. 'We'll have an hour's rest first,' said Raffael. 'I don't suppose either of us can sleep, but we should try. And as soon as the shops are open I'll get an A to Z – newsagents usually stock them, don't they? In the meantime, you draw up the checkpoints. You know the area better than I do.'

Baz said with a kind of bitter anger that this was the sort of thing that Georgie would have relished. 'Thrown himself into it heart and soul,' he muttered, blowing his nose vigorously, and then by way of covering up such an unmacho display of emotion, said aggressively that it was just like Georgie, silly sod, to bollocks up the entire plan, pardon for swearing.

'Swear away,' said Raffael, stretching out on the battered sofa, and thought: did you but know it, my friend, I could match your profanity in three languages!

The brief rest refreshed them slightly and they set off, concentrating first on the streets surrounding the quayside itself; partly because Baz thought the footsteps had run off in that direction, partly because of all the deserted wharves and warehouses there, but partly because, as Raffael said, they had to start somewhere.

The fog still clung everywhere, shrouding the streets, so that even by daylight there was a shadowy, faintly sinister feeling. Raffael, who had not lived here long enough to become very familiar with the area, found it chilling and desolate. It might have been practical to have hired a car or a taxi for a few hours, but a car would have been noticeable and he was very strongly conscious that Timur's people could still be watching him. And as he had pointed out to Baz, there were too many places where a car could not go.

He moved methodically along the designated streets, looking in doorways, peering into alleys – some of them still with the old cobblestones of the previous century – and looking through the grimed windows of deserted buildings. Nothing. At intervals he and Baz met, as planned, and then went off to scour the next portion.

At one o'clock they stopped for soup and sandwiches in a small café, which Baz said was mostly used by early-morning shift workers wanting breakfast. The place had a faintly seedy air, but the tables were clean, the bread fresh, and the soup piping hot. It was a small oasis of light and warmth and rest and Raffael was grateful for it.

As they drank mugs of strong tea, cupping their hands about them for warmth, Baz said, 'How much is left to search?'

'Let's see.' Raffael dragged the A to Z out of his pocket and opened it, his heart sinking at the amount of streets still to cover. They would never do it in time. For the first time defeat closed about his mind in cold sick waves.

Then Baz said, 'We can't call in the police – I understand that. But there're people who might help.'

'Who?'

'Friends,' said Baz, a bit defensively, and then, in a rush of explanation: 'People who go to the Anchor and the other pubs round here. People who knew Ralphie and some of the others who got taken. They'd help with searching. And they know the area.' It was not necessary to explain to Raffael about territories and boundaries, and how you got beaten up if you strayed on to someone else's patch by mistake.

'Can we trust them?' The words were out before Raffael had time to consider them, and he could have kicked himself.

But Baz only said, 'Not all of them and not any of them with the whole story.' He looked at Raffael across the table. 'But we could tell part of it, if we were a bit choosy. I could put the word around.' He paused, remembering his company, and said, 'But you mightn't want to associate with such people.'

'I'd associate with the devil and his entire hierarchy of demons if it would save Ginevra,' said Raffael.

If it had not been for the nagging anxiety and the awareness of time slipping away, Raffael would have derived a wry amusement at finding himself patrolling the streets in company with a group made up mostly of male prostitutes, with three or four female hookers for good measure, and a brace of barmen. Some of them were almost certainly part-time small-time thieves and others would be receivers and fences. Some probably had sidelines in such things as forged MOT certificates and Social Security allowance cheques.

But it's the brotherhood of the streets, he thought; the community spirit that some politicians and most newspapers would have you believe no longer exists. Whatever it is, thank God for it! As the search began again, he thought with sudden irrepressible irony: I wish de Migli could see me now, scouring London's East End with a gang of thieves and forgers and rent boys!

He never quite sorted out the component parts of the motley collection called up by Baz that day. He thought that several people donated an hour and then went off on various and probably nefarious ploys of their own, but that others took over from them – the twilight shift. Fagin's pickpockets swarming London Town, or the raucous colourful felons of Scott's Alsatia – the seventeenth-century Whitechapel sanctuary for miscreants. Alsatia had long since gone – Raffael thought the area was mostly occupied by publishing houses and printers now – but its descendants were still here: they looted TVs and video recorders instead of gentlemen's fobs and guinea-purses, and they stole microchips out of computers to order, but beneath the skin they were not so very different.

It was almost five o'clock before he began to search the quayside proper, and darkness was closing in. His eyes were aching with peering through the fog, but he turned up the collar of his greatcoat and went cautiously down the steps. Behind him reared deserted-looking buildings with tiny mean windows set near to their roofs and directly ahead of him was the river: he could not see it for the mist, but he could hear the muffled hoots of river craft – probably barges – and he could smell the dank wet river smell. His own steps conjured up phantom ones – ghost footfalls coming after him. Someone following him? Someone *really* following him, not just his tired brain and disordered imagination creating sounds? He tripped over a stone mooring and swore, and then paused, trying to get his bearings. The phantom footsteps had vanished and he had the sense of being entirely alone now. At his feet were wet slippery stones and scatterings of debris: odd lengths of rope and sodden bits of unidentifiable rubbish. There was the occasional sound of a barge still, and blurred discs of smeary lights from moored crafts.

To his left was a second stair that probably went down into the river and was probably used for maintenance of the river wall and access to sluice gates. He looked back at the empty buildings. Were they really empty? Supposing he had missed one, and supposing that was the very one holding Ginevra and Elinor and Georgie? There're too many questions altogether, thought Raffael, and began to descend the steps.

It was then that he saw the leather jacket Baz had lent to Ginevra, lying sodden and rather forlorn halfway down.

'It might be a false trail, of course,' said Raffael, as he and Baz retraced his steps. 'Because it's pretty unlikely that Ginevra's captors didn't know she'd thrown it down. But it might be a real clue, and anyway—'

'It's the only clue we've got.'

'Precisely. Be careful where you step – that's the quayside wall on our left, and I think this is one of the really old river stairs – probably Henry VIII came down here on his way to Greenwich.'

Partway down the steps a narrow ledge branched off into a jutting shelf that appeared to extend along the quayside wall, about halfway down. Raffael caught the glint of dull green water below, and stepped back at once.

Between the swirling fog and the encroaching darkness it was difficult to see if there were hiding places large enough for two men carrying an inert body, but there might be any number. He began to walk along the brick shelf, keeping his back against the wall, praying not to miss his step. The ledge was wider than it had looked from the stair, but it was still perilously narrow. He had gone about ten feet along when he stopped, and in a low voice said, 'Baz. Come and look at this.'

'What? Where?'

'A circular hole with a brick surround. It's cut into the quay wall itself.' He moved closer until he could see the opening more clearly: it was eight or ten feet across and it yawned blackly.

'It looks like the opening to a tunnel,' said Raffael, as Baz came along the ledge. 'At a guess it's the overflow outlet of a disused sewer. About a hundred years ago the effluence of most of London's East End probably discharged into sewer pits inside there. When it reached a certain level it simply overflowed and gushed out into the Thames.'

'Through that outlet?'

'Yes.'

'I always said the Thames was a shit-hole.'

Raffael grinned, and Baz said, 'That's the way we've got to go, isn't it?'

Raffael frowned. 'Supposing the jacket was a red herring,' he said. 'Supposing they've gone farther along this ledge? Or even left the jacket there guessing we'd find it and walk into a trap? No, I'm seeing too many sides to the situation. If you start counting up "supposings" you never stop.' He bent down and peered into the dimness. 'Shall we just take a brief look in here to see if there're any more clues? If not, we can explore the ledge a bit farther.'

'How much time have we got?'

'It's half-past six.'

'Five hours, then.'

'Less. If they've set their hellish ritual for midnight, they'll probably start preparing at least an hour beforehand.' He paused, and then said, 'I think we should assume we've only got three hours left.'

Baz said, 'Do you think they're both still alive?'

'I'm praying so.'

Ginevra was not dead, but she was unconscious for so long

that Elinor's mind swung between black helpless despair and sheer mindless panic at least a dozen times.

Iwane had chained her at the far side of the warehouse from Elinor, which had made communication almost impossible. Elinor had not dared call out to Ginevra because Grendel would be listening, and she still had no idea of how far Grendel could be trusted, and also because Timur and Iwane's people were constantly in and out of the warehouse now, preparing for tonight's ritual.

Grendel kept to the shadows. He managed to convey the impression that he was attending to some vital part of the ritual in his own corner of the warehouse, and if anyone approached him, he spoke off-handedly over his shoulder, but each time this happened Elinor was dreadfully aware of how perilously near to discovery he was. She was appallingly aware of Grendel's own fragile sanity.

She was increasingly weak with hunger and thirst, and the dizziness was worse, and from time to time she lost track of what was happening. But as the hours crawled by, the preparations for the evening built up and a sense of anticipation began to sizzle on the air. She forced herself to remain alert. She watched Timur's people bringing in food and wine, and tried to count them. They were all similar in appearance, but she thought there were no more than twelve or fourteen, and roughly half were women.

Ginevra was not dead. She looked pale and dishevelled, but she was unquestionably alive, and Elinor was so hugely relieved that for a time she nearly forgot what was ahead. If she had been hit over the head she probably had a headache, but knowing Ginevra she would manage to shrug this off.

As night approached, the hours that had been crawling suddenly began to race. We're almost there! thought Elinor, and as if on cue, Grendel moved out of his shadowy corner.

The main doors of the warehouse were flung open and

from out of the night, arriving in silent orderly procession, came the cat-headed people.

They wore plain dark clothes, and they were supple and sinuous and lithe. Elinor saw that her estimate of their numbers had been right, but as they moved into place she had to remind herself that the cat heads were false. It would be very easy indeed to imagine that she had tumbled into a mad surreal nightmare, where half-human things walked upright like men and donned a thin veneer of civilisation, but beneath it slavered hungrily for human flesh— Stop it, Elinor!

But the blood was drumming inside her head because this was it, this was the moment when Grendel's macabre disguise would be put to the test; in the next few seconds he would *have* to come out of the concealing shadows. She remembered with silent anguish that he was still chained.

But as he stood half in, half out of the shadows, a cursory glance would show him to be Timur: build, hair, stance even, were all Timur's. The face was most dreadfully Timur's. But the instant he stepped into the flickering light they would see the distortion: they would see that Timur's face looked as if it had *slipped*, as if it had been held over a furious heat and had melted and run, and then had hardened into a faintly warped cast.

Iwane said, 'We are ready to start, Timur,' and from the shadows Grendel said, 'Then start! Bring in the Burning Altar!'

He stepped out of the darkness.

Raffael and Baz had returned to Raffael's rooms to get torches and a coil of rope, which Raffael thought might be useful if there were any descents to be made into drains.

'And chalk,' said Baz, foraging for the pieces he and Georgie used when it was darts night at the Anchor. It always raised a bit of a laugh because Georgie insisted on

312

using coloured chalks for the scoring, and always took his own along.

'Why chalk?' began Raffael, and then: 'Oh, to keep track of where we've been and where we haven't. You're right – it'll probably be a maze in there.'

The sewer had obviously long since been abandoned. It smelled very nasty indeed and after the fog it was close and hot. They spoke in whispers but their voices were picked up by a dank dull echo. A faint light trickled in from somewhere.

They were about a dozen yards along when they came to an abrupt halt. In front of them, stretching from the floor of the tunnel to its ceiling, was a pair of ancient sluice gates, the centre sections solid age-blackened oak, the top and bottom thick spiked iron.

Raffael stared at it, his mind grappling with this new obstacle, but Baz was less daunted. He shone the torch, and after a moment said, 'There's a mechanism at the side for opening them – a kind of pivot arrangement. See it?'

'I see it, but it doesn't mean a thing to me. Can we operate it?' Raffael stared rather helplessly at the machinery.

'Well, not without the key.' Funny to think such a poshly educated person could look at a piece of machinery and not have a clue how it worked. 'You need the key,' said Baz.

'Yes, you said that. But I still don't—'

'The key turns that wheel,' explained Baz patiently, because it was apparent that Raffael hadn't a clue what they were talking about. He pointed to the immense wheel, set horizontally at the base of the mechanism. 'It works like –' he sought for examples – 'like opening a giant tin of corned beef or sardines.' This was probably not the most elegant of comparisons, but at least it was one that could be understood. Everybody in the world had opened a tin of sardines at some point in their lives for heaven's sake, hadn't they? 'You slot the spline of the key

313

down here – it'd be a couple of feet long – and then you can rotate the wheel.'

'And that would open the tin, I mean the gates?'

'Yes, they'd roll back, or maybe they'd roll up. At least,' said Baz, 'they would if we had the key.'

'Can we force it to – rotate?'

'Not without a lot of noise. And it'd take time and maybe equipment.'

'What kind of equipment?'

'Plumbers' stuff. Those massive pliers that plumbers use. Monkey wrenches and maybe a jack. But I might be able to get the lend of some stuff.'

It was probably better not to ask where Baz would get this at short notice late on Sunday afternoon. Raffael did not much care by this time, anyway. 'The trouble is,' he said slowly, 'that we still don't know if we're following a false trail.'

'No.'

Raffael studied the immense gates, his mind working. They could waste time breaking through this forbidding Victorian portcullis arrangement, only to find nothing on the other side save a few sewer rats. On the other hand, if Ginevra and the others were there—

'How long would it take to get the equipment?' he said at last.

'Say an hour, an hour and a half at most.'

'As quickly as that?' The brotherhood of Alsatia and Whitechapel again, but working at top speed this time.

Baz grinned briefly. 'I put the word out,' he said, 'and one person will tell two, and those two will tell three each. They'll all know inside an hour, and the tools'll be here.'

'And – you could open the gates?'

Baz, kneeling down to inspect the mechanism in more detail, thought he could. It wouldn't be easy, on account of not knowing how long it was since it had been used, but he reckoned he could work it. They'd pour some freeing oil on it, like you did for seized-up car brakes and such.

314

'You may not need it,' said Raffael, pointing to a thin trickle on the ground. 'These gates have been oiled recently. I think we're on the right track, after all.' He straightened up. 'But we've got less than three hours to get through.'

Chapter Twenty-nine

When Grendel finally began to walk out of the shadows, every head turned, and ice and fire chased down Elinor's spine.

Even with the terrible skinned face it was easy to see that Grendel's eyes were glowing with fervour, and he stared at the Burning Altar like a man finally looking on a consummation longed for over many years. Despite the danger Elinor felt an unexpected pang. Lewis's son, walking towards what might be his own death. Did he know that? Did he sense it with that curious mad intuitive mind? Whatever was ahead, he was certainly going into the hands of people who would use him without compunction.

The Altar had been set up by several of the men, who had dragged it from a dim corner and arranged what looked like clay bricks across the top. They had fired it from beneath – Elinor thought it worked on roughly the same principle as an ordinary garden barbecue – and it was already glowing with heat. Sentinels had been dispatched: two to guard the main outer doors, two more below the trap door into the tunnels, and inside the warehouse a sense of immense expectancy was building, as if the cat-headed people were saying: Nearly there! Nearly time!

Elinor dared not take her eyes from Grendel. He was standing at the Altar's head, but he was treading a line so appallingly fragile that it might snap at any second and precipitate them all into disaster. The heat burned up suddenly, lighting the macabre distorted face, and a murmur of shock went through the watchers. This is it, thought Elinor in panic. They've seen that something's wrong. They're realising. Oh God, what will Grendel do?

As if he had caught the thought, Grendel lifted his hands and deliberately and slowly peeled back the grisly mask. It came away stickily, like tearing a bandage off a wound still wet, and beneath it his face was caked and smeary with dried blood. Elinor caught a movement from Ginevra and saw her put both hands over her mouth as if forcing back a cry of horror. There was a moment of appalled silence, and then Grendel seemed to take a huge breath and plunge straight into the centre of it.

'Behold your ruler!' he cried, and his voice echoed and spun around the lofty-roofed warehouse. 'I am the one brought to preside over the Burning Altar of Touaris!' He paused, his breathing harsh and ragged with emotion, and there was a low murmur of hostility.

'Grendel . . .' The single word growled through the echoes.

'Yes, I am Grendel.' He spun round to face Iwane, his eyes showing the red light. Remember that he's mad, thought Elinor, staring at him. Only a madman would have deliberately walked straight into their midst, so don't depend on him to get you out of here. But he's got this far; he fooled Timur and killed him, and although these people are hostile they're listening to him. They're not pouncing on him. She sent a quick look to Ginevra and saw that Ginevra was half-kneeling, her eyes fixed on Grendel.

Iwane said, 'Where is Timur? Grendel, where is Timur?'

'Dead.'

'At your hands?'

'Yes. But he was expendable and I am not. I am your ruler.' Grendel's voice was logical and calm, as if he was explaining facts to a witless child.

'Touaris is our ruler!' cried Iwane, and behind him, someone murmured, 'Imposter!' and a snarl of assent went through the others.

'You are our creature,' said Iwane. 'Nothing more. If Timur is dead, I take his place. But you are *ours* to use as we please!'

'A cipher!' cried one of the women.

'A puppet!' shouted another.

'An imposter,' said Iwane again. He swung round to face the Tashkarans. 'And imposters,' he said, 'should share the fate of all false prophets!'

'Burn him!' shouted the Tashkarans at once. 'Burn the false one! Feed him to the Altar!'

There was a soaring note of blood lust in their voices and Elinor shivered. On the other side of the warehouse, Ginevra was dragging fruitlessly at her chains. It would be like Ginevra to somehow break free and go helter-skelter into battle, heedless of the consequences, and have to be rescued, upsetting a lot of plans in the process. Blast you, Ginevra, stay where you are! thought Elinor in silent anguish.

The Tashkarans who had stared at Grendel with that cautious respect, were staring no longer. They were circling about him, like monstrous feral cats, and the warehouse was echoing with their shouts.

'Bring him to the gods' table!'

'Let him burn!'

'Feed the Altar! Feed the Altar . . . the Altar . . . *the Altar . . .*'

They began to close in, and the fierce heat of the Altar showered them with glowering crimson.

'Bring forward the prisoners!' cried one, and at once the others took up the words, a dreadful rhythmic chant that beat painfully against Elinor's senses.

'Bring the prisoners! Bring the prisoners!'

Four of the men stepped forward to snap open the padlocks holding the chains, and Elinor and Ginevra and the young man with her were dragged forward to the searing heat of the Burning Altar.

* * *

The brotherhood of the streets had worked with the efficient swiftness that Raffael was coming to recognise, and in just over an hour they had an assortment of tools that Baz said should be enough to knacker the Aswan Dam for ever, never mind break through a half-rusted sluice gate.

They had decided to do this part alone; Baz had said that bringing along the Anchor crowd, never mind that rabble from the Wayfarer, would balls up the whole thing on account of the noise.

He apologised for swearing again, and Raffael said, 'I think we'd better set the record straight once and for all – I don't give a tuppenny fuck how much or how violently you swear. All right?'

Baz said all right, thought that people never ceased to amaze you, and got down to work. It was a bit awkward to free the spigot and get down to the wheel-crank itself, and not being able to make any noise made it even worse. There was no trick to the job, of course; you just stripped the wheel down until you reached the turning mechanism. Like picking a lock. He did not say this aloud, however, because some things were best left unsaid.

What with the darkness and the ban on noise, it took longer than either of them had thought, and Raffael was drenched in sweat by the time Baz straightened up and said he thought they were there.

Raffael glanced at his watch: just on ten o'clock. Timur had said the sacrifices would take place at midnight, but there might be all manner of rituals leading up. Ginevra might be facing death even as they stood here.

Baz began to spin the wheel, and at once there was an answering grating of metal which made both of them jump and look uneasily over their shoulders. The ancient sluice gates began to unfold and Raffael said softly, 'This is where we impose complete silence, I think. Once through those gates we daren't risk being heard.'

'What if there's guards? On the other side, I mean? Is that likely?'

'I don't know. Yes, it might be possible.'

'Do we knock them out?'

'Could you?'

Baz thought about Georgie's possible fate and Ralphie's and all the other laddies who had vanished, and he thought about the very classy Ginevra Craven who had gone so enthusiastically into this. He said he would be very happy to disfigure the whole bunch of evil wankers for life, and this time made no apology for his language.

'Good,' said Raffael, pocketing the heaviest of the small spanners. 'That's what I hoped you say.'

A breath of old sour air gusted into their faces as they moved through the darkness, but there was still a faint thread of light from somewhere. I'm going towards the light, thought Raffael, caught between fear and sudden exhilaration. I'm going towards the light and I'm going towards Ginevra. His hand closed about the heavy-headed spanner in his pocket. Knock out any guards, he had said. If it comes to it, will I really do it? Violence is never justifiable, Father. Yes, it bloody is! thought Raffael.

The tunnels were not as maze-like as he had feared; there was a main passageway with a curved roof and groyned brick archways buttressing it. Small intersections branched off the main tunnel, and several times they had to step over noisome iron grids. At each intersection they paused for Baz to make a faint chalk mark on the walls to keep track of where they were and where they had been.

Even with the thin ingress of light it was still very dark and they did not dare use the torches. The tunnels picked up every breath of sound and magnified it over and over, so that Raffael kept thinking they were being followed, or that they were being watched, or that someone was crouching up ahead waiting to pounce . . .

And then the whispering echoes suddenly coalesced into pounding footsteps, and two men, dark-clad and wearing some kind of nightmarish snarling-cat heads, erupted out of the darkness.

For several seconds Raffael and Baz both stood stock-still, unable to believe their eyes. And then they shared the thought – only masks! –and met their attackers head on.

Baz, child of the East End docks, swung out at once, aiming the wrench not at the protected head, but at the shoulders. There was the sickening crunch of steel on bone and the man yelped and fell back, one arm hanging uselessly at his side. Baz launched forward instantly, ripping away the masked head, the wrench lifted to deal an even more disabling blow.

Raffael had been knocked to the ground, and his attacker had pounced on him, one hand pushing into his throat, the other raised, ready to smash down. Raffael brought his knee up and rammed it hard into the man's groin, and he gave a grunting sound and doubled up at once, rolling away, clutching himself in agony. Serve you right, you bastard! thought Raffael, but for all that, he was glad that it was Baz who again lifted the wrench and dealt the second blow, aiming at the base of the neck. The man crumpled into unconsciousness, and Raffael scrambled to his feet, slightly shaken, but feeling not the least trace of guilt.

'What now?' said Baz, staring down at the two prone bodies. Raffael was bending over his attacker, but he looked up and grinned briefly.

'They've given it to us on a plate,' he said. 'We don their identities. We put on the cat heads and we go into the lions' den.'

As the Tashkarans made to fall on Grendel, Ginevra started forward as if to help, but Elinor dragged her back.

'Stay where you are!'

'But—'

'If we try to escape now they'll tear us to bits and throw us on to that thing!' said Elinor in a furious whisper.

'Oh.' Ginevra swallowed and collected herself. 'Er – this is Georgie. He's been helping us—'

'Good,' said Elinor impatiently, without looking at the boy, her eyes still on Grendel.

It was then that Grendel began to speak, and at his first words the Tashkarans froze. The hair prickled on the back of Elinor's neck.

'Clio sings of famous deeds and restores the past to life.
Euterpe's breath fills the sweet-voiced flutes.
Thalia rejoices in the careless speech of comedy
While Melpomene cries aloud with the echoing voice of gloomy tragedy.
Terpsichore with her lyre stirs and governs the emotions.
Erato bearing the plectrum harmonizes foot and song in the dance.
Urania examines the motions of the stars.
Calliope commits heroic songs to writing;
Polymnia expresses all things with her hands and speaks by gesture.
The power of Apollo's will enlivens the whole circle of the Muses—'

Grendel paused, surveying the Tashkarans, and for the first time there was amusement and arrogance in his expression. When he resumed the strange, apparently patternless chant, he did so with cool deliberation.

'But Touaris, fiery cat-blooded Touaris, dons the masks of them all:
Taurt she is and Apet; Hesamut she is and Smet;
Shapuit she has been and Hathor she will be.
She sits with Horus, with Thoth at her right hand and Osiris at her left,
And consorts with Khnum and Ptah, the creators.'

He stopped again and the Tashkarans stared at him, apparently stunned into silent immobility.

'It's some kind of key,' said Ginevra softly. 'Elinor, it's a – a password of some sort.'

'Whatever it is they recognise it.' Elinor looked around the warehouse frantically. Was now the time to make a run for it? She glanced towards the trap door. Could they be down the stairs and through the tunnels and out into St Stephen's Road? No, a watch had been posted. Even with the thought, she saw the trap door lift, and the two guards stepped up into the warehouse, and stood on each side of the open hatch. Don't want to miss any of the fun, thought Elinor bitterly, and turned back to Grendel.

Grendel was facing Iwane and he seemed to be waiting. The silence stretched out and when Iwane finally spoke his voice was slow and unwilling. He said, 'You have the race-memories of our ancestors.'

'I have. The exodus from Egypt, the building of Tashkara's first city in the valley that stands beyond time . . .' He paused, and again the fearful murmur brushed the watchers. 'The city gates that were ranked alongside Artemisia's mausoleum at Halicarnassus and the lighthouse of Alexandria and the Temple of Artemis at Ephesus,' said Grendel, softly, and then said, clearly quoting, '"We shall raise up our city in the wilderness, and there we shall pursue the worship of the One True Religion and the blasphemies of the world shall never prevail against it . . ."'

'"We will build two gates to the city,"' said Grendel, and now the soaring note of exultation was unmistakable. '"And one will be of sawn ivory and one of horn . . . And where the ivory gleams there will be my people and my truths . . . And where the burnished horn shines, there will be my enemies and their falsehoods."'

He smiled at Iwane. 'You see,' he said. 'I know what is written in the Chronicles of my people. And I know the secret chant of the goddess. As you have just heard.'

'You could have found that out.'

'How? Where?'

'There might be ways—' Iwane stopped and then said very deliberately and very slowly, 'Are you the messenger that stands before the face of the gods?'

'I stand at the door and knock,' said Grendel, and a ripple of emotion stirred the watchers.

Iwane said, 'The gods are athirst.'

And again Grendel responded: 'I will raise up a Table in the Wilderness and my people shall hunt the gods and feast on them and therefore feast with them.'

It was like a dark catechism or a travesty of a religious litany. Question and answer. Challenge and response. And whatever it means, he's giving the right responses, thought Elinor. And it's shocked them.

'You could *not* know that,' said Iwane, staring at him, 'not possibly. Not unless—'

'Not unless I had the spirit of the goddess reborn?' Grendel smiled and began to advance on Iwane, and Elinor heard Ginevra gasp. She looked back at Grendel and her stomach churned with fear. Grendel's face, bloodied and slimed as it still was, was unquestionably changing. The dark slavering thing surfacing . . . Like this he's a match for Iwane, and he's probably a match for any of them. But he's still chained . . . Oh God, I'd forgotten that he was still chained . . .

Grendel leaped on to Iwane, the curled fingers of both hands reaching for his throat. The chains jerked taut and Iwane flinched and tried to pull away but it was too late; Grendel had caught him, and the nails of both hands were gouging deep into his jugular veins. Blood spurted, spattering Grendel's face.

'Doubter!' screamed Grendel. 'Disbeliever!' His nails tore into the thin cloth of Iwane's shirt, and ripped it aside in maniacal fury, and with a cry of triumph he pushed Iwane back on to the Altar. The most appalling scream Elinor had ever heard tore through the warehouse, and then there was a fierce hiss of heat as Iwane fell into the centre of the fierce glowing heat.

The Tashkarans surged forward at once, holding out their hands to pull him clear, but the heat was too intense, and they flinched back, throwing up their hands to shield their faces and eyes.

Iwane was lying on his back across the Altar's surface, his face contorted, his hands flailing helplessly at the air as he struggled to get free. His mouth was stretched in an endless scream and his eyes were starting from his head, the whites suffused with crimson. Hissing curls of steam rose up all around him, enveloping him. This is the moment, thought Elinor wildly. If ever the attention was away from us, it's away now. She looked about her. To run to the main doors at the far end? But that meant going straight through the centre of the Tashkarans. And behind them, although the trap door was open, it was guarded. Elinor stared at it in despair and at the two guards. Had she imagined it, or had the nearer of the two made a small, almost imperceptible gesture of beckoning? No, there it was again.

At her side, Ginevra said in a whisper so low that Elinor barely caught it. 'Elinor. Start edging back to the trap door.'

'Why?'

'Because that's Raffael.'

Elinor stared and then said, 'Are you sure?'

'I'm sure.'

'All right. But *slowly*. Inch by inch. Keep your eyes on what's happening and if anyone looks our way, freeze.'

The Tashkarans were still grouped about the Altar, vainly trying to reach the squirming dying Iwane, and Grendel was raising his fists above his head in maniacal triumph. Madness, stark and wild, glared from his eyes, and he began to laugh, great insane peals of terrible mirth tearing through the crimson-lit warehouse. He's covering us, thought Elinor, suddenly. Dear God, I believe he really is! He's forcing the madness to the surface so that we can get free! Here we go. I hope Ginevra's right about this guard being Raffael.

Holding hands, they began to retreat towards the waiting square of darkness, going so slowly that Elinor found herself wanting to scream to them to hurry, because at any minute the Tashkarans could look up and catch them. She fixed her eyes on the scene before her, and concentrated on moving slowly and noiselessly.

Grendel was still in the red glare from the altar, exulting over the dying Iwane. 'Scream!' he cried. 'Scream until your throat bursts! Scream until your lungs shred and you vomit them on to your cooking body! When you are done, I will feast on you, I will *eat* you, shred by shred! And then I will rule from my mother's throne!'

Elinor saw the shudder go through the watching people. But in another minute they would remember their prey . . . How near to the trap door are we? Ten paces? I think we're going to make it.

And then they were there, and the two guards who were not guards at all, were grabbing them and almost throwing them down the stair.

As Raffael reached up to pull the trap door down over their heads, the last thing Elinor saw was Grendel standing over the squirming screaming body of Iwane, still laughing with demonic delight.

Chapter Thirty

They ran through the subterranean passages with the sounds of the Tashkarans' shouts of fury echoing after them.

'Outrun them!' cried Raffael. 'We must! They'll be after us within minutes! Through here!'

'How do you know that's—'

'We marked the tunnels as we came,' said Raffael, grabbing Ginevra's hand and pulling her along with him. 'Along here and as fast as you can!'

Ginevra flung breathless scraps of information at Elinor as they ran: something about finding Elinor's handbag in the flat, and something else about Raffael working for the Vatican and employing the two boys, Georgie and Baz, as decoys to find the warehouse.

'And it worked splendidly, didn't it work splendidly, Georgie?'

The thin, faintly weasel-featured Georgie was understood to say that it had worked too bloody well.

Raffael was moving ahead, scanning each intersection of the tunnels as they came to it. Leading us out of the darkness, thought Elinor, and as if he had caught this, he looked back at her. He seemed somehow less disreputable than she remembered, but he still looked untidy and haggard. He said, 'It's all right, Elinor – you're safe. We'll get out.'

'Well, of *course* we'll get out—' Ginevra retorted.

'Are they following us?' said Elinor abruptly. 'I can't hear anything, but—'

'No, that's because we're making so much noise ourselves.'

'Do hush, you abominable child,' said Raffael, and Ginevra subsided at once. 'Listen.' He held up a hand for silence, and they listened. Nothing. No sound save the echoes of their hurrying footsteps and the faint dripping of water from somewhere. But Timur's people had known these tunnels, and at any minute the dank sewers might fill up with the cat-headed creatures— Elinor shut off the thought abruptly. Safe. This is safety. We've been rescued.

She said, 'Surely they'd come straight after us? It might be a trap. We might get to the end of these tunnels and find them waiting for us.' Panic rose in her voice and she quelled it at once.

'I think they'd have to remove the evidence,' said Raffael. 'They'd assume we'd go straight to the police and they'd be more concerned about their own skins. Also,' he said thoughtfully, 'they've still got Grendel, and that's probably their main concern.' He glanced at Ginevra, and Elinor saw something flicker in his eyes. 'But I don't think we dare go back to Chance House,' he said. 'That's the first place they'll look.'

Elinor shivered but managed to say, 'Then where?'

Raffael grinned suddenly, and in the dim light, the years fell away. For a moment he looked like a gleeful child who has outwitted his elders. He said, 'Unless Baz and I muffed it earlier on, we'll come out into an abandoned sewer in the docks.'

'At any minute,' affirmed Baz, pointing to a faint chalk mark on the brick wall.

'Lovely,' said Georgie in a sepulchral voice.

Raffael laughed. 'It's all right, Georgie, from there we're going into asylum. Into sanctuary.' And then, as they stared at him, 'The Roman Catholic Church has ever looked after its own,' he said.

And Georgie said, in a voice of extreme horror, 'Oh Jesus Christ, he's taking us to a frigging church!'

The Underground had stopped running, but once clear of St Stephen's Wharf there were several cruising taxis and they hailed one and fell thankfully into it. Elinor felt a layer of the horror peel away, and a thin carapace of safety begin to form. With every mile, I'm farther away from it. With every minute, I'm a little bit safer.

At her side Ginevra said, 'Where are we really going, Raffael?'

'Bloomsbury. The house of friends.'

'In a minute you'll pat everyone's hands and say, "*Trust me*," in a patronising tone.'

'No, I won't. But you can,' said Raffael. 'I mean you can trust me.' He sat back, looking through the taxi windows at the night streets. From the forward seat Georgie remarked that it was to be hoped they had enough money between them to pay for the journey, and was told to hush by Baz.

But when the taxi pulled up in front of the tall Bloomsbury house Raffael pressed four ten-pound notes into the driver's hand and said brusquely, 'You have not seen any of us tonight.'

'Not on the run nor anything, are you?' demanded the taxi driver, scanning Raffael's face suspiciously.

'No, we are on the side of the angels, but we are not permitted to say any more,' said Raffael, to which the man shrugged, pocketed the notes, and said equably that what the eye never saw the heart never grieved after.

'Secret Service,' said Georgie approvingly, as they stood on the steps of the house and rang the bell. 'Or a hint of Government Intelligence, always supposing the Government ever has any – intelligence, I mean. *Very* classy, as well. I said you were a class act, Raffael, didn't I say that, Baz?'

'Several times.'

'I don't expect,' said Ginevra, eyeing the shuttered windows and drawn curtains doubtfully, 'that there'll be anyone up, will there? It's after midnight.'

Raffael said, deadpan, 'For those who wish to enter, the door is always open,' and from the bottom step Georgie was heard to observe that if this was a church it was a very stylish one.

It was at that moment that the door swung open to let them in.

Fires burned in the quiet comfortable first-floor room, and lights were lit and the curtains were closed against the night.

Elinor had stopped shivering and she had stopped feeling light-headed at last. She thought it would be several hours, or even several years, before she would be able to blot out the memory of the gaslit warehouse or the Burning Altar, but she was managing to keep a kind of ballast by concentrating on the immediate present and shutting everything else out.

She and Ginevra had been shown to a large bedroom on the top floor. It had the air of a guest room kept in permanent readiness: it was comfortable but rather anonymous, and there were brushes and combs on a dressing table and a small bathroom adjoining.

'You'll find the water hot and fresh towels laid out,' explained the young man who had let them in and who seemed to recognise Raffael and to see nothing in the least improbable about their midnight arrival. 'His Eminence will expect you in his book room in – shall we say an hour? Coffee and sandwiches are being prepared for you.'

Elinor said, 'Thank you very much. Forgive me, you are?'

'Brother Robert,' said the young man. 'I'm attached to His Eminence's staff while he is in England.' He glanced round the room again. 'If there's anything you want I'm just down the stairs. Give me a call.' He smiled at them both with incurious acceptance and went quietly out.

The hot water gushing into the deep-sided bath and the thick thirsty towels were the most marvellous thing Elinor had ever experienced. It would have been even better if she had been able to put on fresh clothes, but at least Ginevra had had a shoulder bag which had not been lost when she was knocked out, and Elinor borrowed a dab of make-up.

'I've never met an Eminence,' said Ginevra, seated before the dressing-table mirror, brushing her hair free of smog and cobwebs. 'I hope he doesn't think I'm a hooker.'

'I should think he might. What on earth are you doing dressed like that?'

'It was part of the plan.'

'Well, don't make any bad jokes about bishops and actresses.'

Ginevra looked at her in the mirror. 'Do you want to talk about it?'

'I don't think I do, not yet,' said Elinor carefully. 'What about you?'

'I don't want to talk about it either. I might later. But for the moment I think I'd like to have just ordinary things.' Ginevra thought she should have known that Elinor would understand without needing to be told. After a moment she said, 'I expect we'd better go down now, had we? This is a very lush place for a cardinal. What do I call him by the way?'

'"Your Eminence" I think. If in doubt, say "sir".'

'I've never called anyone *sir*,' objected Ginevra, the socialist.

'Then start now.'

In the event, it was extremely easy and not in the least formal. Raffael was already in the book room, and as they entered he drew them forward and simply said, 'Eminence, this is Miss Craven – Elinor – and this is her niece, Ginevra.' And to the two girls, 'This is Cardinal Fleury.'

'Ladies.' There was a gentle handshake and a very ungentle scrutiny from cool intelligent eyes. As George and Baz came in, Georgie bright-eyed and curious, Baz wary, Raffael turned to them.

331

'And these, Eminence, are the two young men who so bravely helped us. Georgie and Baz.'

'We are extremely grateful to you both,' said Cardinal Fleury, and Georgie was so entranced at being presented with such style and ceremony to a prince of the Church that he forgot about being vaguely atheistic, and returned the handshake warmly, saying it was an honour to be here and they'd been happy to help out. Baz shook hands and said how do you do.

To Elinor the warm room and the fire burning up in the hearth and the leather spines of the books strengthened the feeling of safety. Now I'm really all right. Now those people really can't reach me. It was inconceivable that violence and terror and ancient blood rituals could find their way in here. This was a place where everything was orderly and civilised; where people studied and held quiet, scholarly discussions, and contemplated theological mysteries: the meaning of the Gospels, and how many angels can sit on a pinhead. It's a place where very *good* people live, thought Elinor. I wonder if I'm feeling the goodness because I've just come from a place reeking of such extreme evil?

The hot strong coffee and the chicken and ham sandwiches set out on large platters tasted better than the finest *haute cuisine* banquet. Elinor drank two large cups of coffee and ate some sandwiches and began to feel better. She tried to remember how long she had been in the warehouse and when she had last eaten, and failed. Cardinal Fleury brought a square-necked decanter and poured generous measures of brandy into heavy, cut-glass goblets which he handed round.

'You will find it warming, Miss Craven. And if you should require medical attention after your ordeal—'

'No, truly not,' said Elinor, rather alarmedly visualising the efficient papal machinery summoning a battery of doctors there and then. 'I wasn't attacked in any way, you understand. I just need to – get back inside my skin.'

'Ah. And – Ginevra?'

'The same,' said Ginevra. 'Thank you, though.'

'There will certainly be a degree of reaction for you both,' said Fleury. 'We will give you whatever help you need. The modern custom is to analyse unpleasant events and ordeals for several weeks with trained counsellors, of course.' He paused, and Elinor waited. 'But,' said the cardinal, 'it is my belief that such a course can sometimes simply serve to prolong distress.'

From his own chair, Raffael said, 'Tragedies and pain can sometimes be better coped with by overlaying them with small, quite ordinary things. Have some more small and ordinary food and with it a large and extraordinary brandy.'

Fleury, who had finished dispensing coffee and brandy had by now seated himself in a deep armchair, and was tranquilly sipping his own coffee which he took black and unsugared. Ascetic, thought Elinor, and then saw the brandy standing at His Eminence's hand.

It was a little like a semi-formal meeting of some committee or work group, and when Raffael said, 'And now we should decide what to do next,' this feeling increased. They had all been rather silent, letting the terror and the horror of the last few hours slough away. Ginevra was hunched over her coffee cup, her hands curling around it as if to draw warmth from it, and the two boys were silent and tired-looking. Georgie had slid down in his armchair until his head was nearly level with the arms. It was to be hoped he would not so far forget himself as to put his feet up on the inlaid walnut table which held the sandwiches and the coffee pot.

But at Raffael's words they all seemed to sit up and to look more alert. Elinor, who still felt raw and vulnerable so that every nerve ending was ultra-sensitive, thought a sense of gratitude went through them. Someone's going to tell us what happens next, they were thinking. She glanced at Ginevra. Ginevra was leaning forward, her hair tumbling about her face. Her eyes were fixed on Raffael and her cheeks were faintly flushed. Oh *dear*, thought Elinor. That's a complication I didn't bargain for. But perhaps I'm wrong; perhaps it's only nervous reaction or something – hers or mine. I wouldn't know the difference at the moment. She tried to concentrate on what Raffael was saying. His voice was rather attractive. He was not English, of course; she could hear it plainly. Had she known he was not English?

She sat up a bit straighter, fighting off the warm drowsiness, turning over and over the knowledge that she was safe and that the cat-headed creatures could not get to her here, and trying not to think about what might have happened to Grendel. The thought: I wish Lewis were here, formed without warning and so strongly that for a moment it drove out everything else. It suddenly seemed unbearably wrong and fiercely disloyal to be here with this extraordinary assortment of people, forging the bonds that did form between people sharing danger, and not to have Lewis there.

It was of Lewis that Raffael was speaking. Something about the Tashkarans having taken him: something about rival groups and uprisings deep inside the remote part of Tibet. Elinor, by now struggling against the overwhelming need simply to curl up in a dark warm place and let sleep close down, heard something about stone tablets of incalculable age.

The last thing she heard before she gave way to the beckoning folds of sleep, was Raffael saying, 'And therefore the only thing we can do is go to Tashkara and find Lewis Chance.'

'If he is there.'

'Yes.'

'And,' said Fleury, 'destroy the Tashkara Decalogue.'

'The original mission,' said Raffael, and Elinor was jerked out of the smothering tiredness for a moment. She looked up to see him regarding the Cardinal very levelly.

After a moment Fleury said, 'I am glad you have not forgotten it, Raffael.'

'Oh no,' said Raffael softly. 'I have not forgotten.'

Chapter Thirty-one

Lewis came up out of a leaden sleep and for a moment could not think where he was.

And then memory flooded back and despair clawed upwards into his mind.

I'm inside the forbidden city. I'm in the hands of Kaspar and his people, and quite soon I shall be facing a trial for murdering a religion, exactly as I faced a trial for defiling a goddess all those years ago. Only that time I escaped, and this time I think they'll make very sure I don't escape.

He raised himself cautiously on one elbow and looked around. They had brought him to a small but not unduly bleak room with stone walls and a timber floor laid with a square of pale woven matting. Brass oil burners stood in niches in the wall. In one corner was a chair and table, and in the other was a washstand with bowl and ewer, and bucket beneath. The door would be locked, of course, but he tried it anyway. Not only locked, but from the feel of it, bolted as well. He stood very still and felt time slither and blur, so that he might have been back in that other captivity, waiting for the pronouncement of the elders, waiting for the judgement of the Stone Tablets. Only that time Touaris was with me . . .

He crossed to the slit-like window. There was still a feeling of mental dislocation and a lingering weakness, but he had no idea if this was due to the injected drug, or to the altitude, or if it was because he was feeling the past stream forward to engulf him.

The room was high up, and Lewis could look across the

strange secret valley and see the thin dawn trickling out of the skies. Clear unearthly light spangled the ground with glistening cobweb strands and touched the ancient palace with rose and gold. He stayed where he was for a long time, watching the dawn light, and the feeling of having fallen through a tear in time into a lost world stole over him, exactly as it had done twenty-five years earlier. But the twenty-five years had touched the palace in a way that the thirty preceding centuries had not. Twenty-five years ago this vast timeless citadel had been alive and alight with life and people, and humming with ordinary day-to-day living; now it was silent and brooding, and there was a forlorn air of neglect. Lewis, leaning out as far as he dared, had the impression of gardens untended and cobwebs left to thicken into shrouds, and of crumbling stonework and decaying timbers. The dust on antique time unswept . . . That was a chilling and desolate image, however you looked at it.

He leaned his chin on his hands, staring out. Did I do this? Were the seeds of this decay present in that past I travelled through, and was I the catalyst? Oh Lord, now I really am hallucinating! It's as well I don't know anything about Einstein's theory of relativity or I'd probably start quoting that as well!

But the sense of the past reaching out to fasten soft blighting hands about the present persisted. The brightness faded from the air . . . yes, that described it exactly. How did the rest of the line go? Something about queens dying young and fair, and dust hath closed Helen's eye. That describes it as well, thought Lewis wryly. Because Touaris is long since dead. She died under the most appalling torture, and I was powerless to save her.

And now it looks as if I'm going to die as well.

After a while he had lost track of time in the underground rooms where Kaspar's guards put him after they had caught him in the Decalogue Chamber with Touaris.

337

They had not treated him especially harshly; there had been food and water – even books and writing materials. He had tried to keep a kind of diary-cum-calendar, although the entering of the diary had been grimly reminiscent of Patrick. Had Patrick been here in this shadowy subterranean prison, facing God alone knew what horrors, somehow clinging to sanity? If Patrick could survive then so could Patrick's descendant.

The underground prison was deep beneath the Death Temple, close to the Decalogue Chamber itself, and as the weeks went by, Lewis became more and more strongly aware of the malevolence emanating from the Stones. He lay awake, hearing rustlings and stirrings; several times he thought he heard strange dragging footsteps going past his door and on down into the ancient bowels of the palace. Once there was something that sounded like huge leathery wings beating on the air, and on another occasion he woke to hear what he thought were faint whisperings as if several people were speaking very quietly in an unknown tongue. Satan's dark bequest, the pharaohs' Stones of Vengeance waking, taking on substance in the dark? Rubbing their invisible hands at the thought of another victim?

He had no idea where they had put Touaris, but he knew, with helpless fatalism, that there would be a child. That shared moment of surprised delight; that sudden soaring explosion when the sombre surroundings had receded and something incandescent and luminous had enveloped them both, could not have had any other culmination. It was a moment and a memory to hold on to, and to store away in a safe secret corner of his mind. A touchstone from which to draw strength throughout whatever was ahead.

When Kaspar's guards finally came to take him out, he was angry to find himself weak and dazed by the burning torches that lit the passages and confused by the noise of the guards. For the first time he understood that his sight and his hearing had become dimmed from living for so long in the shadowy underground apartments and bitter impotent fury blazed up in him. He supposed his senses would adjust once he was in the ordinary world again, and then he remembered it was unlikely that he would ever see the ordinary world again, and panic and despair rushed in. I'm going to die, and I'm going to die at the hands of these murderous cannibals. And so is she.

The guards took him not up into the Death Temple as he had been expecting, but down through the flame-lit stone passages, and Lewis realised for the first time that his trial and sentence – yes, and probably the execution – would be inside the Decalogue Chamber itself. Horror lashed against his mind. It's to be there! There, before those evil pieces of rock. A tiny part of his mind that was still retaining a tenuous hold on logic argued that it did not matter – a man could suffer screaming torture anywhere – but Lewis was nearly beyond logic by this time.

This was the death walk, this was the last journey of the condemned man. But I haven't been condemned yet. I wonder which of the devil's commandments they'll invoke? Patrick, did you take this walk and if you did, how did you come out of it with a whole mind?

Entering the huge cavernous crypt was like entering one of the hells of Dante or one of Brueghel's painted devil-ridden scenes. I'm walking into hell. The deepest most fire-drenched cavern of all – where demons prance and goblins dance: where torment rules and agony holds exultant crimson court.

Shallow bronze dishes set on stone plinths held twisting spirals of flame, and the chamber was filled with people. As Lewis was pushed forward, every eye turned to him, and hostility and anger reared up like a solid wall.

But inevitably he looked first towards the Decalogue itself. The huge stones were as silent and as inanimate as when he had first seen them, but they were implacable and terrible. Lidless, sightless ogre eyes, watching from the shadows. Lewis stared at them in helpless fascination before turning to take stock of his surroundings.

Kaspar and some dozen or so men were grouped at the centre of the chamber – Lewis supposed the other men were the elders – and Kaspar's dark eyes were filled with what Lewis could have sworn was amusement. He's enjoying this, the bastard!

He looked about him for Touaris, and when Kaspar said, 'Touaris has given birth to a boy. That is why we are assembled,' Lewis made a gesture of acceptance and said, 'Of course.' His voice was cracked and husky from having spoken so little for so many months, but he managed to return stare for stare, and to look about him with disdain. This gave him a tiny spurt of courage. I'm acquitting myself reasonably well so far.

But when they brought Touaris and the child in, Lewis's thin shell of resolve broke.

Touaris had not enjoyed the wearisome months of captivity, and she had certainly not enjoyed being violently sick every morning and suffering leg cramps and backache and a hundred and one other ailments.

What she had enjoyed was thinking up ways of scoring over Kaspar and the boring old farts of elders. After she had got over her indignation at being locked in her rooms – *guarded* as well, for heaven's sake! – she began to cast about for means of alleviating the boredom. Seducing the guards was the first and most obvious thing – there were never less than two outside the door, and if you counted the duty changes there were actually eight in total, which was not a problem, of course – but on closer inspection it was not such a good idea on account of not being sure of their loyalties. Also Touaris had no idea if you were supposed to seduce people when you were pregnant. It might turn out to be dangerous or harmful. When she considered the idea further she found that it was unexpectedly distasteful to think of seducing anyone other than

Lewis. This was a feeling that might change, of course, although Touaris was not sure whether she wanted it to change.

What would be fun and what would disconcert Kaspar and the elders would be if she could come out with a few nicely depressing prophecies. Prophesying was something that you could sometimes get away with if you were a goddess. There had been quite a famous Touaris around the turn of the century, who had had the much-quoted vision of how the Decalogue would one day be revealed to the world, and how Western Christianity would rock on its tottering throne as a result. She was known as Touaris the Seer (although among themselves the younger ones called her Touaris the Hippopotamus-faced, which was disrespectful but if the embalmed corpse was anything to go by, highly apt), and she had lived about seventy years ago, which meant there were still people whose fathers – well, all right, *grand*fathers – remembered her. Touaris thought that a seer might be quite a good person to model yourself on, although you would not want the hippopotamus face.

She practised a few suitably sonorous sentences and tried out one or two glassy-eyed trances before the mirror, which they had allowed her to have after she had threatened to burn the palace down. You could exist in captivity for a while, but you could not exist anywhere without a mirror.

In the end the prophecies struck quite a gratifying response, because while no one entirely believed them, no one quite dared disbelieve. She predicted several undignified fates for the elders, described how Tashkara would crumble into ruins, and rounded it off with Kaspar himself being ignominiously toppled by his own bloodline, and being forced to live out his days in a hermit's cave. It was all very satisfying.

When she ran out of prophecies she substituted being abruptly sick all over whoever brought her breakfast. This was quite a good diversion as well, and she became expert at timing it, but after a while they caught on and simply pushed her breakfast inside the door and beat a hasty retreat.

She was not especially frightened at the thought of punishment, because she did not think the elders would do anything unpleasant to her. Probably there would be some kind of reckoning, and probably Lewis would have to share in it, but once it was all over life would go on very much as before. Except that there would be Lewis and there would be the child.

The birth, when it finally began, jerked her out of her half-dreamlike security, into a cold and dreadful reality. She had known – hadn't she? – that birth was a painful messy business, but no one had prepared her for the clawing agony that tore through her womb over and over. Between spasms she understood dimly that no one had prepared her because no one had thought it necessary. She was the inviolate incarnate Touaris, the immanent one, the virgin goddess. The relevant adjective was 'virgin'. Some virgin, thought Touaris, swimming in and out of the pain. Some goddess. If Hippo-face had gone down in the annals as the Seer, she herself would go down as something very different. Touaris the Defiled. Touaris the Whore. Was it better to be remembered as sinned against or sinning? She cried out as another sickening vice clenched her lower body, and when one of the hovering women told her to take deep breaths and try to relax, Touaris shouted at the woman to sod off, which was a very satisfying curse she had learned from an American journalist. Touaris the Shrew.

The pains rose to unbelievable unendurable intensity, and there was the feeling of something tearing deep inside her. The room wavered and grew blurry as if she was looking at it under water, and the voices of the hovering women became faint. This is it: I'm dying. Probably as well, really. Touaris the Martyr. She gave her life for the child of the only man she ever loved . . . The *child*.

342

From the far end of a long echoing tunnel she caught the thin wail of a child and somebody murmuring something about a boy. A boy. Lewis's son.

Be blowed to dying, thought Touaris, struggling back into consciousness.

For a truly dreadful moment Lewis did not recognise the girl half lying, half propped on the litter carried in to the chamber. Touaris's hair was flattened to her head with the sweat of the agony; her skin was pale after the months of captivity and there were violet smudges under her eyes. And then she looked across at him and his heart lurched in precisely the way it had lurched all those months ago.

He understood that the birth had only just taken place, and he thought: they might at least have allowed her to recover a little. They might have washed her face and brushed her hair free of the sweat. He looked at the child lying next to her, and a slow strong anger began to burn. My son and hers. And they will take him for one of their macabre rituals. Not if I can help it.

The elders had been murmuring together, and several of them had glanced several times at the Decalogue. As they came to stand at the cavern centre their faces were grave and stern, but their eyes, glittering in the leaping light of the bronze fire dishes, betrayed them. The watchers pressed forward eagerly and Lewis's heart lurched. This is it: they're about to pronounce sentence. I wish it wasn't so hot in here; it's difficult to concentrate when it's so hot. I wish there weren't so many eager-eyed people crowded in as well. The cavern was stifling and there was a rising stench of human sweat and of whatever had been set to burn in the bronze saucers. Lewis began to feel sick. He looked across at Touaris, and tried to signal to her to stare them down – although had Touaris ever needed telling to stare anyone down? – but she was looking down at the child lying beside her. Something wholly unfamiliar fastened about Lewis's heart.

And then Kaspar began to speak.

He spoke first in the Tashkaran language but he spoke swiftly, so that Lewis, who had managed to pick up a very little of the language during his captivity, could not follow. But Touaris had raised her head and was listening with intense concentration, and Lewis watched her and saw the gathering horror in her eyes. Whatever they've pronounced it's terrible. It's so terrible she never imagined it could happen. There was a drumming in his ears as if he might at any minute faint, but unexpectedly it was the absurdity of this that helped him keep hold of consciousness. I can't faint just as I'm about to learn how I'm to die!

Kaspar switched to English, directing his words to Lewis, and Lewis felt the hatred of the Tashkarans, whose goddess he had taken and whose sacred Decalogue Chamber they had together defiled.

Kaspar said, 'Your punishment is twofold, English traveller. It is in strict accordance with the laws of our people which decree that all punishments must be in exact measure to the offence.'

Gilbertian, thought Lewis wildly. In a minute he'll say something about letting the punishment fit the crime and then I really will lose all grip on reality. This is hell, of course: the real thing. I'm down in the fire-drenched caverns, I'm at the exultant crimson court of agony – no, I'm not, of course I'm not! Damn you, Kaspar, get it over!

Kaspar said with slow deliberation, 'Since you committed the sin of fornication with the goddess, you will be deprived of the organ that caused the offence, in obedience to the Seventh Stone Tablet.' He looked at Lewis and Lewis stared at him in disbelieving horror. Kaspar said, 'You will be castrated.'

The too-hot cavern with its fetid stench of sweating, excited humanity, and the flickering torch flames all began to whirl about Lewis's head. But Kaspar's voice cut through the spinning panic.

344

'After that, because you have overlooked the Secret Domain of Tashkara – your word would be spying or trespassing – we shall invoke the punishment of the Sixth Tablet, which is a three-fold sentence.' He paused again, as if savouring the words, and then said, *'The loss of hands so that the guilty one shall not write of what he has seen . . . The loss of feet so that he shall not walk in the world to tell of what he has seen . . .'*

A murmur of horror and triumph went through the cavern, and Lewis, clinging to awareness by a thread now, heard Kaspar continue in the same measured tones.

'As for the lady who was our goddess, she will suffer with you,' he said, and Lewis heard his own voice, hard and harsh, saying, 'Well? What barbarity have you and your savages reserved for her?' He turned to Touaris, and saw that the colour had drained from her face, leaving it so white that she looked like a corpse. *She knows. He's already said it for her, but he's going to say it again, and he's going to* enjoy *saying it again. I've never seen such cold merciless gloating in any living creature's eyes.*

He waited, and after a moment, Kaspar said, 'Hers is the greater sin, for she had the awareness of her rank and the awareness of the ancient undying spirit of the goddess. She sinned in the full knowledge of what she did. She sinned against the First Stone Tablet of the Decalogue, which states, *The office of the gods shall be inviolate.'*

'That,' said Lewis, angrily, 'can be interpreted in at least a dozen different ways. Get on with it, Kaspar.'

Kaspar said, 'For her, too, the sentence is a form of castration. We shall destroy her womb so that it can never betray her again. We shall force into it the ceremonial phallus of the ancient cat people, which was crafted two thousand years ago and intended for the punishment of any Touaris committing the sin of fornication. Until tonight it has never been used.' He looked at Touaris, and using their own language, which Lewis managed to follow, said, 'You are about to create history, my dear.'

345

Chapter Thirty-two

Touaris was furious with herself for fainting in front of them all within minutes of hearing her punishment, and she was furious with Kaspar for being the cause of it. She held on to the fury for as long she possibly could, because if you were filled up with fury, there was no room for any other feeling.

She had struggled up out of sick unconsciousness to find herself still in the Decalogue Chamber, and that moment of realisation had been the worst thing she had ever experienced. Still here. Still in the suffocatingly hot Decalogue Chamber with everyone watching, with the faces of the elders stern but excited at what was ahead. Secretly gloating over the punishment.

The punishment. The barbed and cusped phallus: the monstrous rearing symbol made of silkily polished wood, but fletched like an arrow down its sides, so that although the entry would be smooth and relatively painless, the removal would tear cruelly into your flesh. Shredding your womb to tatters. It was at this point that the fury began to drain, like water trickling out of a sieve, and fear began to pour inexorably in.

It was going to happen. A punishment born in some sadistic brain two thousand years ago and never until now invoked, was going to be inflicted on her and there was absolutely no way of escaping it. They were going to do it, and they were going to do it *now*, with her womb still aching and bruised and unbearably vulnerable from the birth. No one was going to stop them and no one was

346

going to rescue her, because the only person who might have rescued her was here in the chamber with them, held by four of Kaspar's guards.

She met Lewis's eyes across the suffocatingly hot cavern, and saw her own horror mirrored in them, and with the horror, bitter frustration that he was helpless to save either of them. Touaris managed a tiny smile. Sorry, Lewis, but it looks as if this is it: they're going to castrate us both. We might survive and then again we might not. I hope I was worth it for you. You were certainly worth it for me. And there's the boy. She glanced down at him and for an astonishing few seconds she forgot about the approaching agony, and a brief smile curved her lips. That brief time of undiluted joy with a stranger, and there's another little life in the world. Except that Lewis had never been a stranger.

Kaspar's musicians were starting the low beating of the skin-drums, and the sound thrummed relentlessly through the cavern. Some of the younger ones had begun to sway rhythmically, their hands linked, their eyes half-closed, and Touaris hated them. She had managed to drag herself into a half-sitting position by this time, but she felt light-headed and there was a deep ache between her thighs like an open wound.

Into the cavern came six of the ritual dancers – Kaspar's tribe again. Was Kaspar setting himself up as Tashkara's ruler? In other circumstances Touaris would have rebelled instantly; she would have *enjoyed* rebelling as well, perhaps getting together some of the younger ones and challenging Kaspar, and seeing him routed.

The dance was what Kaspar's people called the Harbinger and it preceded all Decalogue executions – no, not that word! The men wore the obscenely fashioned loin belts and the macabre cat heads; they were thrusting and moving to the drumbeat and working themselves to frenzy pitch. It was the kind of thing that might even give you a slightly warped kick if you were feeling so inclined. If you

347

were waiting for your own punishment you were more likely to throw up on the ground. Touaris wondered if she could still do this to order, and whether if so it would delay the sentence. No, they would simply fetch a pail of water and sluice it away and then get on with things.

The dancers circled her and Touaris shrank back on the makeshift litter, wondering if she could fight them – gouge out their eyes as they approached, bite their hands. And then two of the guards grabbed her arms from behind and jerked her back, and she knew there was to be no fight and no escape.

They pulled the litter to the centre of the chamber, and the flames in the bronze dishes danced and leaped as the current of air stirred them. Above the scent of the burning myrrh was the mingled stench of human sweat and human excitement, and above that was a steadily mounting anticipation, so thick and so real that if you reached out you could plunge your hands wrist-deep into it.

A shadow fell over her and Touaris raised her eyes fearfully and saw Kaspar standing over her, the immense ceremonial phallus held in his hands.

Lewis had been half hoping that Touaris would faint again and put herself beyond most of the pain, but as Kaspar walked towards her with the appalling wooden phallus he saw that she was fighting to remain conscious and she was certainly fighting to stay defiant.

There was absolutely nothing he could do to reach her and he could think of no means of saving either her or himself. He was being forcibly held by three guards and at least six more stood nearby. He considered a sudden bound across the chamber but discarded it almost at once. They would not let him get more than four paces.

The ceremonial phallus with the barbs down its length appalled him, even though he could only guess at the degree of pain it would inflict. Would it be anything like the pain he would shortly suffer himself? Castration and

348

then the hands and feet to be removed . . . And what afterwards? Would they tend his wounds or would they leave him bleeding and mutilated on the floor of the cavern, unable to walk, barely able to crawl? I can't endure it! he thought. There must be a way out!

They were spreading Touaris's legs and Lewis felt a knife turn in his gut as he saw how she was struggling against them. Kaspar was looking down at her, the carved phallus grasped between both his hands and Lewis felt the sexual arousal irradiating from the man. Deep hatred flared up. One day, Kaspar, there will be a reckoning for all of this!

The people were crowding forward, craning their necks to see, but from where Lewis stood he had a clear view. As the drumbeats quickened their pace, a low moan, unmistakably sexual in quality, broke from the watchers.

Two of the women moved the child from Touaris's side, and Kaspar bent down and began to slide the impossibly huge phallus between Touaris's thighs.

Touaris was clinging to consciousness by a thread so fragile that it might at any minute snap and plunge her into blessed unawareness. But she was hanging on for Lewis's sake, because when this was over Lewis would be put to his own torture, and it was unthinkable that she should not try to share his pain with him as she thought he was now trying to share hers. She could feel his mind reaching out to her, and there was a faint comfort in the knowledge.

She sensed, as well, Kaspar's sexual excitement, and as he lowered the phallus between her thighs their eyes met. It was a travesty of a lover's embrace, a warped version of intimacy. She thought she said, 'I hate you,' and she thought Kaspar replied softly, 'I know,' but her whole being was so concentrating on staying aware and on not breaking down that the words might only have been inside her head.

349

The first touch of the phallus was cold and hard, but whoever had crafted it had polished the wood to a silken finish. As Kaspar began to force it into her, the cramping pains that had been still vaguely ebbing and flowing intensified, and Touaris instinctively tried to hunch over, only to be jerked back by the guards.

Kaspar knew what he was doing. Touaris, fighting the pain, was dimly aware that he was moving with the assurance of one very accustomed to female bodies and this was something that would ordinarily have been interesting – Kaspar a womanizer? But the pain was blotting everything out; it was getting worse by the second: the phallus was huger than any man's could possibly be; it was a giant's, an ogre's . . . Touaris gasped, and then clamped her lips tightly shut because she would not give them the satisfaction of hearing her cry out. She would stifle the cries somehow. Touaris the Stoic.

The pain was building to an impossible level and she could feel soft vulnerable flesh tearing and bruising. Despite her resolve, she began to gasp aloud. But the real agony's ahead – the moment when they drag the thing out, that'll be the real torment. Kaspar gave the phallus a vicious push, and Touaris cried out helplessly. It was all very well to be high-minded about stoicism and silent martyrdom but when it came to the reality, you found yourself yelling your head off. A stronger wave of pain clawed upwards, and she gasped. Do it, Kaspar, curse you, *do it*. Drag the wretched thing out and get it over with! A thick mist was obscuring her vision; sweat was streaming down her face, stinging her lips, and the pain was by now so fierce that she could no longer move. She was shrinking to a single concentrated pinpoint of white-hot pain, and the slightest movement was beyond her.

Kaspar gave a sudden final thrust – and Touaris moaned in agony. Her sight was blurring, but there was a moment when she focused on Kaspar standing over her, his hands still moving with unbearable intimacy between her thighs, his eyes blazing with lust.

And then he pulled hard on the wooden phallus, dragging it down at last, and pain – excruciating unbelievable pain – swamped Touaris's entire body. A huge darkness swung down, pressing on her lungs and blotting out the light. From a distance, Touaris heard her own voice trying to scream, making weak mewling sounds like a kitten.

On the other side of the cavern Lewis moved.

Lewis had several times tried to break free, but each time the guards had jerked him back and pinioned his arms behind him. He was almost frantic with the desire to reach Touaris but he was helpless.

Until the moment when the child was moved to a corner by himself, and Kaspar began to force the phallus in.

Lewis made a lightning calculation. The attention of every person in the cavern was focused on what was happening and if ever there was a moment to move, this was it. He looked at Touaris, and knew she was beyond his help; she was bleeding heavily – dark thick blood that flowed down her legs and dripped on to the ground. She was still gasping and crying weakly, but her eyes had filmed over and her skin had taken on a dusky pallor. Dying, thought Lewis, and a bolt of pain slammed into him. No time for that now.

Summoning every ounce of strength and courage, he jerked out of the guards' hands. It was done so quickly that the guards were taken off balance, and Lewis had a clear run and took it. He snatched up the child, holding him aloft.

'Come near me and I'll dash his brains out on the stone floor!' yelled Lewis, backing towards the stair, his eyes blazing with fury. 'I'll do it, Kaspar, so call off your damned jackals!' On the rim of his vision he saw Touaris scrabble weakly at the sides of the litter. Searching for the child. Even like this, even dying in that appalling agony, blind and deaf with pain, she sensed that the child was gone. The knife twisted in his guts again, and he shouted, 'Touaris! Listen to me! I have the boy safe! I won't let them take him!' He thought she made a half-gesture as if of acknowledgement and acceptance, but the litter was soaked with her blood and she had barely the strength to lift her hand. 'I'll take him away and look after him!' cried Lewis. 'You have my word!'

He began to retreat to the stone stairs that led up to freedom, holding the child tightly, keeping his eyes on Kaspar, but aware of the others as well. Kaspar had halted the guards with a single imperious lift of one hand but his eyes were wary. He said, 'This is an absurd and arrogant gesture. And you will not escape us.'

'Touch me and I'll smash this child's skull like an eggshell and spill his brains on the floor!' shouted Lewis. 'And then where will your ritual be?' Kaspar made an involuntary movement and Lewis raised the child above his head. God, don't let him push me because I could never do it. But he doesn't know that! He said, 'A girl to take Touaris's place; a boy for the Burning Altar – wasn't that it, Kaspar? It looks as if you've lost Touaris, and if you try to stop me now, you'll have lost your precious sacrifice as well!' He moved back another step and saw the uncertainty in Kaspar's eyes. Confidence poured into him. He believes I'll do it! He wanted the boy for his savage ritual –the sacrifice of the first-born. Oh God, yes *of course* – and he doesn't want to lose him! He pressed the child closer to him. Not this one, Kaspar. Not Touaris's son and mine!

There was a white dint of fury on each side of Kaspar's thin mouth. He said, 'You will never get far enough away. Even if you get out of Tashkara we will hunt you through the world!'

'Do so,' said Lewis at once. 'And I'll see every one of you inside a British prison on counts of murder.' He glanced behind Kaspar to where Touaris lay silent and still.

Butchered to death, and it was my fault. Unbearable. But I'll grapple with that afterwards. And if I can save her son I'll have atoned a very little. And I'll still have something of her—

He had reached the stair and he felt for the first step with his foot. Almost there. Can I turn and run? No, not yet. He ascended two steps and there was a low angry growl from the Tashkarans. Lewis cast a frenzied glance around him, and without knowing he was going to do it, reached up with his free hand and snatched the nearest of the fire dishes from the stone plinths. There was a searing pain as the heat blistered his palm but he flung the dish into the centre of the Tashkarans. There was just time to see it tip and spill licking tongues of flame and sizzlingly hot oil in several directions, and to see the Tashkarans fall back in alarm. Lewis felt a surge of exultation. That's for Touaris and for Cal and for all the other poor creatures who fall into your paws!

As he raced up the narrow stair angry cries followed him, Kaspar's voice rising above them, screaming in his own tongue. They would quench the small fires almost at once, but it would take them a few minutes, and those few minutes were all he needed.

He scrambled through the trap door into the Death Temple, gasping for breath. It was lit by more of the bronze, fire-filled dishes and there was the pungent scent of burning oil and the hush of extreme age that he remembered. Lewis, his sight still vulnerable but adjusting, kicked the trap door down into place, and turned to scan the Temple. In another minute they would be swarming up the stair and they would push the trap door open and be on him. Unless he could bar their way.

His body moved ahead of his mind again. He darted across to the doors, and flinging them open, laid the child carefully on the floor. So far so good. Now for the side temple. The sightless eyes of the embalmed goddesses stared implacably down at him and he took a deep breath and reached up to the nearest. It came easily, toppling forward out of the elaborate throne, the dry dead arms falling about his neck, the brittle hair brushing his face. He gasped and shuddered, but set his teeth and carried the grisly thing to the trap door. It felt light and empty, husked dry of life ... Don't think about it. And one isn't nearly enough. He went back a second time and a third. I'm going back and back, I'm defiling the goddesses of at least a century. But I've already been found guilty of that, so I might as well be hanged for a sheep as a lamb, only they weren't going to hang me, they weren't going to do anything so merciful as hanging. Are they coming up the stair? No, they're still tramping about trying to quench the fire, I can hear them.

The last one he took was one of the half-rotting ones, and Lewis felt his fingers break through the badly mummified skin and sink into soft pulpiness, like too-ripe fruit in autumn. Dreadful! Yes, but if it gets me free it's worth it! He piled the last body into place, and it was then that the scattering of tiny winking gems fell from the rotting fabric, and spilled over the ground.

Lewis wasted seconds he did not have in staring at the bright droplets of colour. Real? Yes, of course they'd be real, you fool! A fortune – several fortunes, probably! – lying there for the taking. And if you don't take them you'll regret it for ever! But if you do take them, you'll have stepped over one of your own self-imposed boundaries. Like father, like son. Don't be such a prig, said Lewis to Lewis. Grab the things now and beat it before they come swarming up out of that devil's cavern!

The feel of the sharp fiery jewels in his hands gave him a kick of such power that it knocked him almost off balance, and the sight of them fastened seductive hands about his mind. Deep vibrant red blazed against glowing sensuous emerald and against warm pulsing amber and fiery diamonds. To do it? To take what he could in these final crowded minutes, and then get out? Or to relinquish it all, and return to England with a clear conscience? Yes, and with empty pockets, and a zero bank balance! And there was the child. If I do it I'll do it to provide for him, said half of his mind. Oh sure, said the other half, sarcastically.

Be damned to it, thought Lewis furiously. If I'm going to commit the classic plundering of the ancient temple, I'm going to do it in style! He tipped the scattered jewels into his pockets, and dived back to the side temple, snatching at the shining jewels on the robes, and the elaborate rings on the dead fingers. His mind was whirling and part of him was shuddering, but his hands were perfectly steady. Like father, like son.

It took minutes only, but during those minutes a kind of madness possessed him, and only the awareness of the Tashkarans below the trap door stopped him from taking far more. He came back to the piled-up bodies, and protecting his hands with a torn piece of one of the robes, he lifted the nearest fire dish and carried it to the tumbled heap of ancient corpses. What had worked once, would work a second time. He threw the dish and its contents into their midst and at once a sheet of flame tore upwards. Lewis dodged back, but not before he had seen the bodies seem almost to rear up in the heat, their blazing hair on end, their gaping eyes starting from their heads. He stared for a moment, and then turned away, and taking up the child, stepped out into the pouring dusk beyond the Temple. The immense city gates were directly ahead – hell's gates and I'm coming out of hell. Delight began to unfold. I've come through and I'm almost free. And with me is Touaris's son, and also with me are the jewels of a lost civilisation!

He stood for a moment, looking across to the sweep of the mountains, tasting the cold clean night air, thinking nothing had ever tasted and smelled and felt so good in the entire world.

As he walked through the gates, towards the purple and blue horizon, a wry humour rose up without warning. I'm in the middle of the most desolate country in the world, and

I'm carrying an hours-old child, and I haven't a clue of what to do next, or where to go from here.

Yes, but I'm rich once again.

Chapter Thirty-three

Extract from Patrick Chance's Diary

Tashkara, 1888

If Fenris and the lepers had not stayed with me and with Theodore after they rescued us from Tamerlane's savages we should probably have died from our wounds. God knows, there were times when I wished that I had died.

It's difficult, at this distance, to recollect the exact sequence of events after they unchained me from that appalling wooden scaffold; it's difficult, as well, to separate nightmare from reality.

The reality was what Tamerlane's butchers did to me – and to Theodore – in that fire-drenched square inside the forbidden city; the nightmare's now.

The memories are blurred and fragmented, and trying to set down a record is like lifting the lid of a grisly Pandora's box. Several times since sitting down to complete these diaries, I've been attacked by doubt. Isn't it better to leave the lid tightly closed, and seal the memories up for ever?

But the trouble with memories is that you never do quite seal them, not completely. They have a way of suddenly forcing up the lid – generally when you're least expecting it as well – and spilling out into the light, as fresh and as hurting as when they were made.

No matter how much you think you've pushed them into a dark cobwebby corner of your mind they don't die; they stay in a dry embalmed state like something caught in amber. Like pressing a flower between the leaves of an old book and going back to it years later, and still being able to smell the fragrance. Only my pressed memories don't smell of flowers: they're blood-soaked and gore-crusted and they're gibbering, bleached-bone corpses that won't die, and that come gibbering and clawing at you in the night watches . . .

I think I feel better for that outburst, which may prove my point: drag the wretched things out, Patrick. Draw their teeth and lay the ghosts once and for all. Here I go, then.

The journey out of the forbidden city and into the leper colony was somehow achieved with makeshift litters, and with the endless patience of Fenris's people. I was still swimming in and out of consciousness, but I remember the amazing gentleness of Sridevi, whom I thought then, and still think, is one of the most truly beautiful human beings I ever met. It was Sridevi who taught me that the outer covering doesn't matter: it's what's within that counts.

I remember Theo's appalling agonies as well, and his struggle to come to terms with his mutilation, first by writing on a slate, and later with sign language. It was only afterwards, when we were in England again, that I heard how Sridevi and two of the other women had fed him thin soup and goats' milk and melted honey: spoonful by patient spoonful because his mouth was so dreadfully wounded that for several weeks he could barely swallow.

And through it all was my own agony: jagged shards of clawing torment splintering my mind. I lay in the small stone room on the outskirts of the leper colony, staring up at the low ceiling and although at the start there was no thought beyond that of the pain, eventually the pain receded, and there was space for bitter despair.

Emasculate. A gelding. A half-man. I thought: I can't bear it, and knew in the same heartbeat that it had to be borne. I could not begin to imagine how I should feel, once out in the world again. Did the desire die along with the ability? What about all the drivelling old men who married girls a quarter their age and spent their days fumbling and fondling and very little else, regret in their eyes for the whole world to see? And what about the real *castrati*, what the Ancient Romans had called the *spadone*? I had seen them as well – the silver-voiced singers. They became coarsened, thickened. Their voices became eternally soprano – Unbearable. Oh God, why didn't I die in that hell-ridden palace!

For a long time, the stone room was my whole world. I drifted in and out of awareness – occasionally rousing sufficiently to eat and drink. Between times Fenris and Sridevi talked to me. Sridevi had the kind of eyes that made me think of all those lyric poems about wine-dark seas (Homer?) and black and brilliant stars, and tranquillity filling up the wine-cup of the universe. The disease had ravaged her, but she had a gentle irony and the deep unshakeable faith and trust of the true mystic. I think the lepers regarded her as what the East call a twice-born. An old soul in the truest and most exact sense.

'We spend as little time with you as possible,' said Fenris on one occasion.

'But not,' put in Sridevi, 'because we would not like to,' and when I said if it was because of the infection they need not bother because I didn't give a damn any longer, she said, very severely, 'Do you think we risked all we did only to see you die? How ungrateful of you. You will not die, Patrick; you will live. I – I *order* you to live.' And then she said, 'What was done to you was truly terrible, but there is no need for anyone in your world to ever know about it.'

'Who would tell them?' added Fenris, rather sadly.

'Become an illusionist,' said Sridevi, and for a second a grin lit her face.

I stared at them.

'Listen to me,' said Fenris. 'You do not think it now, but one day you will take pleasure from living again.'

'I can't begin to imagine how it will be—'

'But you will do it,' said Fenris.

And at his side Sridevi said, 'Patrick, you should remember that we are here to help you, as you tried to help us. You should lean on us until you are strong.' She paused, and then said, 'Among my own people we have very wonderful writings of a philosopher and a visionary who lived in Persia many centuries ago. His name has long since been lost, but fragments of his teachings live on. And when he wrote about friendship and love, he wrote these words.' She paused, and then said, very softly, '"Throw me your nightmares, beloved, and watch me spin them like a juggler, and one by one exorcise them of their devils and return them to you with their fangs drawn and their red poison sucked out."' She paused again, and then went on in her soft voice that the disease had not yet marred, '"And then you will see how the nightmares will depart; they will slide back across the silent black waters of the oceans and usher in the light."' She smiled at me. 'Love and friendship drive back all the nightmares, Patrick.'

'And the world feasts on illusions,' I said, my own eyes never leaving hers. 'We have a poet as well, Sridevi, an Englishman who lived nearly a thousand years ago, and who said that life is a thoroughfare full of woe, and we are but pilgrims passing to and fro.'

'That is also good,' said Sridevi, listening absorbedly. She made one of her rare gestures of taking my hand. The lepers tried never to touch anyone, but her hand lay cool and strong in mine for a brief moment. 'You will do it, Patrick,' she said. 'You will survive and you will drive away the nightmares and you will fool the world and there will be some happiness for you.'

In the face of their patient acceptance of their own lot it's difficult to argue the point.

We left the colony, Theo and I, after a space of time that might have been several weeks or months, or several worlds.

Sridevi's words about fooling the world stuck in my mind and lodged there, and I returned to them over and over, using them like a touchstone. No one need ever know. The only other person who knew the truth was Theo, and if I could not trust Theo, I could not trust anyone.

I would become an illusionist, I would wear false colours to the world. Sliding back the nightmares ... I would even doctor my travel journal to fool people. Edit, wasn't that the word?

'Back into the world,' I said to Theo, and he made the sign that meant *Yes*, followed by *Good*. It occurred to me for the first time that I was better placed than he was to throw up an illusion. Let's face it, even if you've been castrated you can still *pretend* you're as rampantly capable as the next man (unless, of course, the next man actually demands proof, in which case you're lost), but you've either got a tongue to speak with or you haven't.

As we neared Lhasa and the first outposts of civilisation again, Theo scribbled the question: 'Would you have preferred your sentence to be carried out the other way round?'

Blinded and saved before the castration? Yes, but you don't need your sight to make love. I said, 'I don't know.'

It was in Lhasa, in the hotel that had seemed spartan on the way out but now seemed luxurious, that I recalled the prophecy made by Touaris. It's true that at the time I hadn't been in any case to appreciate the finer points, even if Tamerlane's translation could be trusted which was debatable. It's also true that that hippo-faced old goddess had probably only been trying to steal my thunder, but all the same—

All the same, prophecies sometimes have an unpleasant way of turning into threats, and threats have more than once erupted into full-blown quarrels.

After we dined in the hotel's sparse dining room that first night, and sat sipping Lhasa's idea of brandy, I suddenly said, 'Theo, I've reached a decision.'

He looked up, and I smiled for the first time for what seemed a very long time. 'There's something we've got to do. And we've got to do it quickly.'

He waited, and I said, 'We're going to Rome.' And, as Theo looked startled, I said, 'We're going to see the Pope.'

We didn't get to the Pope, of course, but we got pretty close.

We were received by some kind of aide, who treated us with exquisite courtesy, although for all I know he might simply have been a lowly priest with nice manners, kept on tap to deal with freakish people who turn up insisting they've had a vision of the Risen Christ, or attention-seekers announcing that the world's going to end next Tuesday. Theo and I probably came outside both these categories – neither freak nor fowl nor good red herring.

Father Karyl listened politely to the story of the Tashkara expedition and I gave him a severely pruned version of the events in the palace square, because it seemed a bit tasteless, not to say discourteous, to talk about castration and enforced celibacy in the presence of one who was celibate from choice. So I merely said that Theo had suffered the greater burden of punishment, and that the lepers' rescue had been timely. Karyl probably knew there was more to it: real *religeux* have a disconcerting way of looking at you very directly as if they can strip away the verbiage and hear the truth, but his good manners forbade prying. Also it was nothing to do with the Vatican whether I was Casanova and Rabelais and Aretino rolled into one, or whether I was as impotent as a mule. Which I was.

But when I related, as accurately as I could, the odd prediction that Touaris had made, Father Karyl leaned forward, his face alight with much more than politeness.

'She actually said that, Mr Chance? That one day in the future the Tashkaran Decalogue would speak against Western civilisation?'

'Well, as near as I can remember, she did. It wasn't exactly a situation where you record every word.'

'No, quite.' He sat back, frowning, and then said abruptly, 'I wonder if it would disrupt your plans to stay in Rome for a few days? You see, although it is almost certain that there is nothing in what the lady said, one is inclined to remember the parable of the wheat and the chaff.'

'So one is.' I gave him the address of our hotel. (Theo indicated afterwards that it would not have been out of place to have suggested that the Vatican footed the bill for the extra few days' sojourn, but this was only Theo getting back on form, the old miser.)

'I shall report this to the appropriate section of the

Curia,' said Father Karyl, and I waited for him to say, 'But of course, these things take a very long time to consider.'

'Of course,' said Father Karyl, 'A thing like this will be looked at very quickly indeed.'

It would probably be three months at the most optimistic calculation. Six would be nearer the mark and a year the likeliest.

Father Karyl said, 'You will hear from us within two days,' and ushered us out.

I spent the next two evenings getting thoroughly drunk on several very palatable bottles of Chianti, and falling into conversation with the mandatory lady-travelling-alone in the hotel (there's always at least one), who on this occasion was on the shady side of thirty-five, spoke not a word of English, but had polished the art of predatory flirtatiousness to a diamond-hard brilliance. It was a grim reminder of Tamerlane's butchers, but it gave me a chance to try out my own skills as an illusionist.

I think they passed muster. I think she believed my excuse of a vow (unspecified) that precluded my accepting her skilfully veiled suggestion. The excuse wouldn't have done for an Englishwoman (will have to think up something more suitable when I reach London), but they're very down-to-earth about vows in Rome; it's the proximity of the Vatican.

I think, also, that if anyone ever reads my entirely fictional account of our activities in her bedroom, they will find it credible, although on reflection I may have overdone the part with the lighted candles.

In these very private pages, however, I can admit that when her bedroom door closed it closed with me outside it, and the sound had such a chilling ring of finality that bitter despair closed over my head afresh. This was what it would always be like from now on. There was as yet no indication that the nightmares might be starting to slide back across Sridevi's silent black waters.

Of the ushering in of the light there was no sign at all.

Cardinal Gregory was most apologetic at having detained us on our travels, which he appeared to see as the outside of discourtesy, and seemed to think it necessary to make up for the solecism by giving us a kind of potted tour of some of the private sections of the Vatican before repairing to his own apartments.

It stretches for miles, of course, this seat of Roman Catholicism, and we only saw a minute part. But it was a remarkable experience. It's a curious and not-always-pleasant blend: sumptuous grandeur and ancient history, and achingly beautiful statuary and *objets d'art*, which they refer to in the most casual way imaginable. Gregory didn't quite say things like, 'Don't trip over the Michelangelo,' or, 'Those Botticelli frescoes blot out the light a bit,' but I had the feeling he might.

There are unexpected little tucked-away chapels and oratories and tabernacles so that you keep falling into sudden pockets of extreme calm where the very walls are soaked with goodness and prayer, and then descending abruptly down odd dark passages where anything might have happened (and probably did). It's disconcertingly impossible to forget all those frequently greedy and sometimes bloody battles that went on for power, and if the shades of any of the unscrupulous, power-seeking cardinals do walk in the Vatican, I'll swear they walk in a particular stretch of corridor near the old Borgia apartments. Workmen had just started to restore the marvellous frescoes which Pinturicchio painted for Alexander Borgia and which later generations primly covered up, but even with dust sheets and bottles of linseed oil, and trestle tables tripping you up every few yards, the place had a dark sinister aura.

But beneath all that there's an innate and very orderly tranquillity, and more than once during that brief tour I felt as if a huge calming hand had laid itself across my mind (sliding back the nightmares at last, Sridevi . . .?). For some reason I could never explain, I didn't ask Theo for his reactions; for myself I kept remembering the part in the New Testament where Christ commanded Peter the Fisherman to build a church on a rock and never to permit the gates of hell to prevail against it. They'd struggled to keep the gates locked and at times they'd struggled to keep them merely closed – physically as well as metaphorically – but the rock was still holding firm. So far, anyway.

We crossed a small, sun-drenched quadrangle, leaving the ghosts behind with the turpentine and irreverently whistling workmen, and Cardinal Gregory led us into a low, ivy-covered wing with small heavily latticed windows. There was the good scent of old leather and even older timbers and a feeling of quiet unassuming scholarship. Our host seated himself at a desk, explained that we were in a small wing of one of the libraries, and invited me to tell my story again. Theo passed me the notes we had compiled in the hotel the previous evening (before the wine-drinking, you understand, although after the apocryphal episode with the Italian *signora*), and I plunged in.

Gregory listened absorbedly, making a few notes, and apparently taking it at face value – presumably the Old Testament had familiarised him with much more bizarre tales of visions and fiery prophecies – although he posed a number of very searching questions afterwards, which I struggled to answer.

'I truly can't be more specific, Your Eminence,' I said, at last. 'And I'm sorry that I can't remember Touaris's exact words. But for one thing they were in

366

an unknown tongue, and for another we both thought we were facing death.' At my side Theo nodded to indicate he should be identified with this.

'Yes, it would concentrate the mind, to be facing execution,' said the cardinal, without batting an eyelid, and I remembered that the Roman Church was as familiar with violent death and bloody martyrdom as it was with prophets. Gregory said, 'But Father Karyl who reported to me, thought you had the spirit of the prophecy, if not the letter.'

'I think we have.'

'Then if I have understood correctly, the prophecy was both general and specific. The generality was that the Decalogue was an instrument of ancient vengeance, and that one day it would be revealed to the world.'

'Yes.'

'The specific was that the hands of those who have power over their inferiors would one day wield the knowledge of the Stone Tablets of Tashkara.'

'Yes,' I said again. 'I interpreted that to mean that some power-hungry despot might seize on it as a bargaining tool.'

'It is a risky business to interpret prophecies, Mr Chance,' said Gregory, but he smiled and at my side, Theo scribbled a question: 'Does the Vatican take prophecies seriously these days?'

'Well, we usually try,' said Gregory. 'It's always tempting to write certain people off as hysterics, of course, but it's as well to approach these things with an open mind. Neither of you seems to be at all hysterical, by the way.'

'Thank you.'

'On the other hand, it's entirely possible that your extremely unpleasant experience warped your judgement,' said His Eminence, showing that even the Church liked to hedge its bets. 'I'm assuming you know the legend of the Decalogue, do you?'

'About Satan casting it down to earth to rival Moses?' It sounded entirely natural to say this in Gregory's quiet room; although I wouldn't want to put such a sentence to the test in Simpson's or even – heaven forfend! – somewhere like St Stephen's Music Hall! 'The lepers knew something about it,' I said. 'And Father Karyl gave us more detail. It's a – remarkable legend.'

Theo scribbled a second question: 'How much credence does the Vatican give the story?' and for the first time Gregory hesitated.

'You didn't see them?' he said. 'The Stones of Vengeance?'

'No.'

'Ah. Well, we have never known how much was legend and how much was truth,' he said. 'But it is quite true that in our vaults is a certain extremely ancient document purporting to describe the ancient Stone Tablets brought out of Egypt by the Bubasti tribe nearly three thousand years ago.'

'That part's true?'

'Oh yes, I should think so,' said Gregory. 'There *are* some unexplained things in the world, of course – I wouldn't be in God's service if I didn't believe that. But there are also a great many explained but extremely ancient and valuable artefacts in the world, and I believe that the Tashkara Decalogue is simply one of them. But,' he said thoughtfully, 'that would not stop someone making use of the legend and in the process damaging Western religions.' He looked at me. 'I think we have to treat this very carefully, Mr Chance.'

I leaned forward. 'What are you going to do?'

It's an odd feeling to know that you've contributed to what the Vatican calls the Secret Apocrypha

Writings, but that was what we appeared to have done.

Gregory was of the opinion that the prophecy made by Touaris must be recorded in what he referred to as the Codex Vaticanus Maleficarum, and that his successors should be made aware of its existence.

'We have our own spy network, Mr Chance,' he said, as he bade us farewell. 'It is gentle but efficient. We shall watch Tamerlane's people, quite unobtrusively, of course, and we shall ensure that the knowledge of the Decalogue does not get out.'

'Well – I'm glad,' I said.

Gregory's eyes rested on me thoughtfully. 'I will pray for you both,' he said unexpectedly.

'I – thank you.'

'Whatever was done to you, Mr Chance – to both of you –' he included Theo in his look – 'you will finally come to terms with it.'

'Will we?'

'Certainly. God never sends more suffering than His children can bear.'

'It's sometimes – very difficult to bear it, however.'

'I am sure it is,' said His Eminence. 'But who told you that life was intended to be easy?' He shook hands, and then sketched a minute gesture over us both, which I took to be the Sign of the Cross.

Allowing for the difference in religion and nationality, it's the same sentiment that Sridevi and Fenris expressed. I find it remarkable that the only things helping me to cling to life at the moment are the philosophies of a Tibetan leper and a Roman Catholic prelate.

I suppose I should be hard-bitten and cynical and say I don't give a damn what happens to a few bits of ancient stone, and that it doesn't matter to me if Western religion is dealt a deathblow in some unimaginable future.

But I find I do care. I find myself hoping that Gregory's successors will take Touaris's prophecy seriously and that if necessary they'll take steps to prevent the knowledge getting out – even if it means destroying the Decalogue itself. As I drifted into sleep that night, for the first time I was thinking not of my own miserable mutilations, or Theo's, but of the Stone Tablets of Tashkara: Satan's Ten Commandments.

I wish I'd seen them.

Chapter Thirty-four

'I wish,' said Cardinal Fleury rather wistfully, 'that I had seen the Decalogue.' He looked at Raffael, and at Elinor and Ginevra as he spoke. 'Especially since you're going out there to destroy it.' He frowned. 'It's against all my inclinations, you know,' he said. 'The deliberate destruction of one of the world's oldest legends – I wish there was some way of preserving the Tablets. Safely preserving them.'

'So do I,' said Raffael, and Elinor glanced uneasily at Ginevra in case she might suggest taking colour photographs, which would be frivolous. Or would it? 'We'll do our best,' said Raffael.

'I should very much like to come with you to Tashkara,' said His Eminence thoughtfully.

'Well, you could—' began Ginevra, who was curled into one of the cardinal's most comfortable chairs, sipping coffee, but Raffael instantly said, 'No, you could not. The journey will be extremely arduous and we have no idea what we'll find at the end of it.'

'Lewis Chance? That poor tormented creature, Grendel?'

'Both of them, I hope,' said Raffael, and glanced at Elinor, who said, a bit diffidently, 'Grendel tried to save us from the Burning Altar and Timur's people. He truly did.'

'Yes, but we still don't know how far he can be trusted,' objected Ginevra. 'Whatever he might have done, he's still roaring mad. I don't mean that to sound hard.'

'Also, we don't know how safe Grendel himself is,' said Raffael. 'Those savages might have accepted him as their leader, but they might as easily decide to make him pay for the death of Timur and Iwane. Elinor, that weird little catechism ceremony you saw – did it make them accept Grendel?'

'Yes, what's your opinion of their intentions, Miss Craven?' said Fleury.

Elinor said, 'I wouldn't trust any of them an inch. I certainly wouldn't give tuppence for Grendel's life, puppet-leader or no.'

'And Sir Lewis?' said Fleury. 'Do you really think he's been taken to Tashkara, Raffael?'

'I do.'

'Why?' said Ginevra. 'I mean – what would Sir Lewis's value be to them? They looked on Grendel as some kind of figurehead, but they wouldn't look on Sir Lewis himself in the same way, would they? Or would they?'

'I don't know. But he's Grendel's father and it appears that their goddess was Grendel's mother, and— Sorry, Elinor, you were going to say something?'

'Well, it's probably not of any value, but I wondered if they might have taken Lewis as a – a counter-attraction to the rebellion.' Elinor said this hesitantly, because she was not very used to putting forward an opinion and having it listened to. But Fleury looked at her with approval.

'That's a very perceptive suggestion, Miss Craven,' he said.

'And although we don't know much about what happened in Tashkara twenty-five years ago, we do know one thing,' said Raffael. 'We know that Lewis Chance had – what were Iwane's words? – that he had *splintered a line that had been unbroken for almost three thousand years.*'

There was an abrupt silence. 'Revenge?' said Fleury. 'They've taken him for revenge?'

'Don't you think it's possible?'

'Yes. Dear God, yes. And these people's idea of

372

vengeance—' He broke off and Elinor felt the warm safe book room grow momentarily cold. Lewis at the mercy of those people who worshipped at the Burning Altar. Because he had lain with their goddess and fathered a child on her. I don't care what he did twenty-five years ago. Yes, I do.

Fleury looked across at her. 'You're going into a very dangerous situation, Miss Craven,' he said gently. 'Won't you reconsider your decision? It'll be no place for ladies.'

How sweet of him, thought Elinor. How beautifully old-fashioned and chivalrous. He doesn't know that it's impossible for me to stay here if Lewis is in danger. She said, 'It's kind of you to be concerned. But I must accompany Raffael.'

'It's not that you fear you're trespassing on my hospitality? Because that is not a consideration—'

'It isn't that,' said Elinor. 'I could go back to my parents' house and be perfectly safe.' Fleury would see this as the logical move; he would not know that Elinor had no intention of going back there, not now, not ever. She said, 'I do know that those people might try to find me to stop me from talking. I know that it's why you're trying to stop me going back to Chance House, and you don't have to spare my feelings because I'd worked it out for myself.' It sounded brusque and ungracious but it was better than sounding frightened; and she was covering up the fear fairly well so far.

She had slept for twelve hours after the astonishing escape from the warehouse, and had eaten a late and delicious breakfast by herself in the dining room of the Bloomsbury house. It had been rather touching to discover that in the meantime Ginevra had sallied forth to buy for her aunt a toothbrush, along with underwear, tights, two pairs of trousers and two sweaters.

'Church benefices,' Ginevra had said, gleefully tipping the booty on to the bed in their room. 'The Eminences were insistent so I had a binge on your behalf.'

'I can't possibly accept these—' The trousers were the kind that Ginevra herself wore, which was to say extremely modern. The sweaters were loose and soft and fashioned from open-weave, dishcloth-type material, although at least Ginevra, who would undoubtedly have worn them with only the skimpiest of bras, had added a cotton shirt to go underneath. Everything had designer labels; one of the sweaters was a deep vivid emerald, the other the colour of rich bronze autumn leaves. Beautiful. The thought: if Lewis could see me wearing these . . . surfaced, only to be pushed down.

'I can't accept them and anyway I don't wear things like that,' said Elinor. 'The trousers – for heaven's sake, I can't wear those.'

'I don't see why not. You've got absolutely the figure for it. I think you'll look a knockout,' said Ginevra. 'And you can't go to Tibet in twinsets and pearls.'

'I don't wear—'

'Metaphoric twinset and pearls. The underwear's Janet Reger, by the way.'

'So I saw,' said Elinor caustically, and thought: this is bizarre. In two days' time I'm going into one of the most remote and desolate parts of the world; I'm going to find Lewis, assuming he isn't already dead, and I'm going to help destroy an ancient legend which might end in all of us being killed by carnivorously inclined savages. And I'm sitting here discussing clothes!

'The cardinal's funding the entire Tashkara expedition,' said Ginevra defensively. 'Well, not to say the cardinal personally, but the money's coming from wherever cardinals get money. Plane tickets, visas, hotels, guides, everything. He's somehow rushed the visas through *and* some kind of temporary passport for you and me.'

'I've got a—'

'Yes, but it's in Chance House,' objected Ginevra. 'I haven't dared ask how he's managed that side of things, but I'll bet he's put the screws on the Chinese Embassy.

He told me to get suitcases and whatever clothes we both need for the trip, and not to stint. He's a pussycat, isn't he?'

'Well—'

'And what you had on in that warehouse was pretty well shredded to threads.'

'That's not the point,' said Elinor, unsure whether it was more irreverent to describe a prince of the Roman Catholic Church as a pussycat than to suggest he might have coerced the Chinese Ambassador.

'Well, you can pay it back when you get hold of a cheque book again,' said Ginevra, and Elinor remembered that everything she owned was inside Chance House. It was astonishing how vulnerable you felt without money or bank cards or latch keys or your address book, and even without your own familiar bits of make-up and deodorant and aspirin bottle. It was as well she was not on the pill or anything like that.

Ginevra was saying, 'Wait till tomorrow, Nell – we'll have a real splurge then. You can't go three-quarters across the world with only two sweaters and a spare pair of knickers.'

'I suppose not,' said Elinor, who would have gone barefoot across burning hot coals if Lewis were alive and waiting for her on the other side. She managed not to say this, but she stuck to her decision to accompany Raffael to Tibet. If he refused to take her she would go by herself, she said. She would get her own visas and tickets and she would hire a guide to take her into Tibet's interior, because if Cardinal Fleury could hire guides so could she. In the end they had given in, and since Fleury thought, and Raffael agreed, that it would be unsafe and inappropriate for Elinor to go alone, Ginevra, fizzing like uncorked champagne, was going to accompany them.

'But,' said Raffael sternly, 'you will phone your tutor at Durham and explain that you are detained on a private family matter.'

'Oh yes, of course I will.'

'And you will ask for details of assignments and lectures and you will bring whatever notes you can with you.'

'Oh yes.'

'Well, go and do it now.'

It struck Elinor that Raffael was speaking to Ginevra rather in the way one would speak to a wayward but much-loved child. There was reprimand in his voice, but it was an indulgent reprimand and there was a look in his eyes that was not a reprimand in the least. And he had agreed to Ginevra's accompanying them with unexpected acquiescence. As for Ginevra, she was agreeing to everything with guileless obedience, but with such mischievous delight curving her lips that Elinor, glancing from one to the other of them, thought, as she had thought on that first night: but that's quite unsuitable. And then: or is it?

Baz and Georgie had returned to their lodgings, on the threefold score that none of the Tashkarans would be looking for them and anyway did not know where they lived; that they had their living to earn (begging pardon for mentioning it), and finally that they would not journey to Tibet if somebody paid them a thousand pounds apiece. Georgie was sick crossing the ferry to the Isle of Wight, for heaven's sake. Baz said very firmly that it would be better if they bowed out at this stage, and Georgie hoped they could be told what the outcome was, because it had all been so exciting, hadn't it been exciting?

'A riot,' said Raffael, deadpan, and the boys grinned and said, Well, they would like to hear what finally happened. Georgie said they were both *ever* so trustworthy, they would give their absolute *word* not to talk.

'Of course we'll tell you,' said Ginevra. 'We'll all go out to dinner somewhere immensely expensive and posh, and we'll tell you everything. Lewis Chance can foot the bill,' she added, and hugged them both before they left, which Elinor thought rather pleased them.

The banter and the acquiring of visas and foreign

currency and clothes and a small medicine kit helped to cover the creeping fear. Elinor was beginning to feel that every hour until they could set off was a crawling nightmare that must somehow be lived through, but she thought she was keeping it reasonably well hidden, because you could not just hop on a plane at Gatwick and go to a place like Tibet without the proper arrangements. Cardinal Fleury – or his minions – was being amazingly quick but a tiny pulse was continually beating against Elinor's mind: we-must-hurry, we-must-hurry... Occasionally it changed to: we-may-be-too-late. But I won't let it be too late. Hold on, Lewis, we're coming. And I don't care if you've had fifty goddesses and a hundred children.

'Don't we have to have any inoculations?' demanded Ginevra.

'Apparently not, there's no smallpox or malaria or anything like that.' I'm sounding all right, thought Elinor. I'm having ordinary sensible discussions, and nobody's guessed what I'm feeling. Except – I wonder why Ginevra bought that expensive silk underwear for me? No, that was only Ginevra's extravagance.

She said aloud, 'Raffael's getting something called Norfloxacin in case any of us drink impure water, and something else – I forget the name – to help against altitude sickness.'

'Won't it be cold? Isn't it their winter?'

'Yes, we'll have to dress in layers as much as possible,' said Elinor. 'Trousers and sweaters and anoraks, and jogging shoes or even boots.'

'I said we'd have a binge.'

'Yes, but not in Knightsbridge. There's nothing wrong with Marks & Spencer or the Army & Navy Stores.'

They checked in at the Holiday Inn in Lhasa, showered and changed, and then met for a meal which was late dinner as far as the hotel was concerned, but which felt more like breakfast.

'It's very lavish,' said Ginevra, surveying the dining room with pleasure. 'I thought we'd be in a yak-shack.'

'You may get your wish sooner than you think,' said Raffael repressively. 'We're only here for two nights anyway; Fleury thought we'd need a respite to acclimatise.'

'And didn't see why it shouldn't be a comfortable respite,' nodded Ginevra. 'I see his point.'

Elinor took her seat at the table abstractedly. It was difficult to adjust to the time difference and the altitude, but what was far more unbalancing was the feeling that they had stepped across an invisible demarcation line. We're beyond the point of no return, we're through a curtain or a watershed. The die's cast, and we're across the Rubicon . . . no, I'm all wrong, the Rubicon is really a small river somewhere in Italy. This feels more like the River Jordan.

She chose something from the unintelligible menu more or less at random, and heard Ginevra and Raffael talking as if from a great distance. I know what this is, thought Elinor suddenly: it's the Lethe River, the fabled River of Unknowing. We're going into the labyrinthine waters whereof who drinks forgets his former being . . . I dare say we'll all forget our former beings before this is over. That's if we don't get eaten instead. She sat up a bit straighter. Altitude sickness, Elinor. Or jet lag. In her most pragmatic voice she said, 'How long will it take to reach Tashkara?'

'I haven't the least idea.' Raffael grinned suddenly. 'How long does it take to find Samarkand or even Elysium or Valhalla or the Isle of Avalon?' He stopped abruptly, and Elinor stared at him, because his thoughts were so exactly in line with hers that it was almost as if he had caught the echoes. She remembered that he had been a priest, and wondered if he had heard confessions. How would it feel to pour out your sins to someone who looked like this? If he hurts Ginevra I'll kill him.

378

Ginevra said, 'Do you realise that between us we've ordered enough to feed the five thousand? I hope we're having rice wine with it – I've never drunk rice wine.'

The feeling that the past was streaming forward and merging with the present stayed strongly with Lewis as he lay in the small room in the ancient palace, awaiting trial at the hands of Kaspar's people.

The feeling that he was not alone persisted as well. Patrick? Are you with me now, just as you've been with me all along? And if you are, what's the end going to be? Will they revive the original punishment? Castration and then that second sentence. Can I remember the words of it? Yes, of course I can, I never stopped remembering them. *The loss of hands so that the guilty one shall not write of what he has seen . . . The loss of feet so that he shall not walk in the world to tell of what he has seen . . .*

I escaped once before, but I don't think I shall escape this time. I think I'm going to have to face it, because they're certainly going to pronounce me guilty. Kaspar's scapegoat.

He fell into a blurred uneasy slumber in which he was no longer sure who he was. Patrick Chance, impudently setting out on that long-ago journey, but returning so changed, so different that it might have been another person who had written those last journal entries? Or his own younger self – the hounded son of the disgraced banker, fleeing England, following in an ancestor's footsteps, half motivated by curiosity, half by shame? And, let the fact be faced, by a tinge of greed as well. I wanted to see the Decalogue, and I wanted to see if it could be brought out of Tibet. I didn't bring the Decalogue out, but I brought out the jewels of a dozen immortal goddesses.

The sound of people gathering in the square below his window roused him. This is it. They're assembling to pronounce judgement exactly as they did before. Only that time it was the defiling of their goddess, and this time it's the murder of their religion. Forgive me, Touaris. I never forgot you, my poor lost love, although I can't in honesty say I was faithful to your memory. But if you'd lived, you certainly wouldn't have been faithful to mine, you witch.

But I saved your son, Touaris. And for what? jeered his mind. For that guarded half-existence, locked away in discreet homes, shut away in cellars. Always fighting Grendel's taint, always struggling to protect him. Always hoping that one day the slavering maniac would fade, and the bright intelligence so indisputably near the surface would emerge.

The Tashkarans would revive the original sentence; Kaspar would make sure of it. Lewis had no idea whether he would survive, and if he did, he had no idea how much he would care. All those women – not as many as Patrick had apparently had, but a good number. And he could not bring any one of their faces to mind. Chance House and the people in it were far more vivid. People like that remarkable man he had engaged to guard Grendel – Raffael. People like Elinor Craven. Astonishing that of all the women he had known Elinor should be the one he was thinking about now. He had the unexpected thought that if he should survive Kaspar's butchery and return to the world, he would not mind Elinor knowing what had been done to him. He could imagine her saying something brusque and unemphatic, and then assuming that they would get on with the work of Chance House. How very sad, and now what about the meeting with the Drugwatch organisers? The longing to hear Elinor say something like that was suddenly extraordinarily fierce.

The Tashkarans were assembling in the courtyard below his window, and when he looked out, he saw a number of the men lighting the wall torches.

The trial was about to begin.

Chapter Thirty-five

It proved more difficult than Raffael had thought to find a guide to take them into the wild remote valleys beyond Lhasa, but in the end the hotel produced a young, slightly furtive-eyed man.

'He seems to know the area,' said Raffael to the two girls. 'But he's apparently charging us at least double his normal rates.'

'Why?'

'I can't find out. But in the absence of anyone else, he's our best bet.'

'It sounds as if he's our only bet,' observed Ginevra. 'Still, if it comes to a tussle it's three to one.'

The guide was silent as he piloted the Jeep across the wild Tibetan landscape, and although he seemed nervous, he was not overly sinister. Raffael relaxed his concentration sufficiently to take in their surroundings, and felt the extraordinary serenity and the unending desolation wrap about his mind like cool silk.

He vaguely recalled having read somewhere that Tibet's remote valleys were so soaked in silence and in the numberless centuries of meditation and prayer, that the entire country was like a vast open cathedral. He had always thought this an exaggeration, but even bouncing along in the badly sprung Jeep with the guide hunched broodingly over the wheel, he saw that it was very far from an exaggeration.

Ginevra and Elinor were standing up to the arduous journey far better than he had dared hope. Ginevra, of course, was seeing it as a huge adventure; she knew about the urgency and the mounting need to get to Tashkara and Lewis Chance and his son, and she shared in it. But Raffael knew that beneath it all a tiny guilty part was revelling in the helter-skelter journey and drinking in the breathtaking sights. She was trying very hard to hide it, but Raffael could feel her mind sizzling with delight. It was not new to him, this awareness of another's mind, but the intensity and the sudden and complete *rapprochement* was very new indeed. It's nothing to do with the physical thing, he thought, and then, with relentless self-honesty – or is it? But he knew it was not. The honourable action – the *generous* move – would be to bow out now, to leave her to some boy nearer her own age. Shall I do that in the end? What boring lives honourable men must lead.

Elinor was far more difficult to read. Raffael studied her covertly during one of their halts for food and rest. She was not his idea of beauty: she was too stern and too defensive. But there was a curious allure, for all that. A challenge. And like this, her hair tousled and the outlines of her cheekbones whipped to vivid colour by the wind, she was almost better than beautiful. Somewhere beneath the brusque exterior and the black-bar brows and wary eyes, was an elusive will-o'-the-wisp light of something very unusual indeed. Ginevra was wilful and mischievous and lovely – she could have sat to one of the dramatic slumberous Pre-Raphaelite painters who would have brought out the reddish glint in her hair and the creamy pallor of her skin – but the only painters who might have wanted Elinor were the heavy brooding Dutch masters. They would have understood and depicted her uncompromising stare and the sudden tantalising glimpse of smouldering emotion behind it. Raffael did not know, not definitely, that Elinor was blind and deaf to every consideration except that of finding Lewis, but he sensed it, and he thought it a pity Chance could not see her now.

It was not until the second day that the guide pointed

out the gorge that Patrick Chance had once likened to Kubla Khan's fiery Alph, and said, 'There ahead, is where you wanted to go. Tashkara.'

'You will take us down there?' said Raffael.

'No.' He moved back at once, and sent a hunted glance about him. 'There is a bad place. I take you anywhere else. But not there. No one of us ever goes there.'

'If we were to offer you more money—' began Raffael, and Ginevra murmured something about Rome's open-handedness.

But the guide said vehemently, 'No, I do not go there. You should not go there, also.'

'Why not?'

The guide sent another of the furtive, fearful looks about him. Then he said, 'Tonight in that valley, when the sacred peaks are in darkness, is the celebration of the feast of an ancient time.'

'What kind of feast?' said Elinor sharply.

'The Feast of Bast,' said the guide. 'And when it is dark every person in these valleys will lock his doors and stay by his fireside.'

'Why?'

'Because it is told how the people of Tashkara come out into the mountains and the hill farms to catch sacrifices,' said the guide. 'People vanish on the Feast of Bast. Young men who are taken to feed the goddess. I will not go into Tashkara on the Feast of Bast if you pay me a million dollars.'

Elinor stared at him, cold fear clutching her heart. She saw Raffael frown, and then he said to the guide, 'In that case we must go on without you. We'll take supplies and fuel to last us for—'

He glanced at Elinor, who said, 'Two days? Three?'

'Two.' Raffael looked at the guide. 'You understood that?'

'I understand it, but sir and ladies, you should not go on—'

'We have no choice,' said Raffael curtly. 'If you won't come with us, will you return here in two days' time?' There was the rustle of money, and Elinor saw the guide's hands close greedily about the wad of notes. 'I'm trusting you not to let us down,' said Raffael. 'But I'm only half-trusting you because I'm only paying half your fee. You won't get the other half unless you come back.'

'I understand. I do not like, but I will come back here. In two days I will come back.'

As the guide began to reverse the Jeep on the narrow rutted track. Ginevra said, 'What do we do if he doesn't return?'

'Face a long walk.'

Elinor, who was looking down into the valley, said, 'There are lights burning down there, can you see? There's a cluster of buildings at the centre of the valley – on its floor, in fact. You can just make out the outlines.'

'It looks like firelight,' said Ginevra coming to stand by her. 'Is it the Feast of Bast beginning? What is the Feast of Bast?'

'I've no idea. But I haven't forgotten how they celebrated the feast of one of their other gods,' said Raffael grimly, and Elinor turned to stare at him.

'Sekhet.' It came out in a whisper. 'They celebrated the feast of the lion goddess Sekhet in England – they were using it to give Grendel his initiation. They set up the Burning Altar – or they set up a makeshift altar.'

'This won't be makeshift,' said Raffael. 'This will be the real thing. If these barbarians really have got Lewis Chance, and if they really do intend to take some kind of mad vengeance for what happened all those years ago—'

'They'll never miss the chance of doing it on the feast of their pagan cat goddess,' finished Elinor.

Lewis felt the heat from the wall torches the minute the guards pulled him into the courtyard, and he felt, as he had felt once before, the hatred and the animosity and the sheer hunger of the Tashkarans focused on to him. As he entered the square the hateful skin-drum was beating its soft relentless tattoo – *Yes, yes, you're going to die...* and he saw at once that there were at least three hundred people assembled around the square. Standing before them was Kaspar, his eyes glittering with triumph.

As Lewis was brought forward the skin-drum stopped abruptly as if a signal had been given and silence, thick and stifling, descended. Lewis met Kaspar's eyes squarely, although the blood was pounding in his ears and icy sweat was sliding down his spine.

Kaspar said, in his soft accented voice, 'You are here to have sentence pronounced on you.'

'I thought I was here to stand trial,' said Lewis coldly. 'I should have known you'd cheat, you deceitful bastard.'

A low growl of anger broke from the watchers; Lewis supposed they had not Kaspar's fluency in English, but they had sufficient understanding to know what had been said.

Kaspar was unmoved. He said, 'The trial was held three days ago.'

'While I was kept a prisoner inside the palace?'

'Yes. It was held in our own language, of course, and even if you had been present you would not have understood what was being said.'

'How convenient,' said Lewis. 'And the verdict?'

'Guilty.'

'Of course. I didn't expect anything else. You always intended that I should be found guilty. I'm your scapegoat, aren't I? By punishing me you hold on to your grubby bit of power.' He looked at the watchers. 'Are they all gathered to witness more of your barbarism?'

'You must understand, Sir Lewis, that you are responsible for a situation that we have never before known. The killing of a religion is an offence never until now encountered.'

'I didn't kill your religion, you stupid savage!' said

Lewis. 'Your religion died of inanition! It died of narrowness and your own bigotry! It folded in on itself because you wouldn't look beyond your own tiny valley and your ridiculous legend!' He felt anger welling up, and he grasped it gratefully. Hold on to the anger because it's the only thing that's going to get you through the next few hours.

'With all your so-called civilisation, Kaspar, have you never heard of the principle of dynamism?' said Lewis. 'Dynamism is movement: it's progress and change. *Life*. Its opposite is stagnation and regression and eventually death. Things have to change to survive, Kaspar, and nothing's changed here for nearly three thousand years! That's why your religion's dead! Not because of what I did twenty-five years ago!'

Kaspar regarded Lewis coldly. 'You are the one who does not understand,' he said. 'When you left Tashkara all those years ago you had ended the unbroken line of a goddess's earthly incarnation.' The dark eyes were unwavering. 'You splintered a line that had been intended to be eternal.'

'Not intentionally. And nothing is eternal.'

'The intention is irrelevant, it is the deed and its results you have been judged on.' Kaspar paused, and then said, 'You will remember how, in each generation, the goddess is selected? The recognition of certain items belonging to the first Touaris of all. The race-memories; the Chant of the Goddess which is guarded in such strict secrecy that only one person in each generation knows it—'

He broke off, and Lewis said in a bored voice, 'I suppose you'll get to the point eventually, will you?'

'After Touaris died,' said Kaspar, 'we thought we would find her new incarnation easily. Our people went out and we scoured the hill farms and the valleys. But after several years we had to face failure; for the first time for three thousand years no girl child had been born with the essence of the goddess. And in the end we came to believe that the last Touaris – *your* Touaris – had been cheated of a great many years of life. That she had died before the goddess was ready for rebirth. You cut her life short, Sir Lewis.'

'Crap. Touaris died because you inflicted that grisly punishment on her!'

Kaspar said, 'Touaris died because it was the law. But she died before her time and that was your fault! And ever since there has been dissent among us!' He swept a hand about him, indicating the majestic ruins and the decaying grandeur. 'You have brought us to this!' cried Kaspar. 'And that is why you must die!'

His voice rose in shrill frenzy, and behind him the crowd murmured its eager assent. Lewis stared at them and then at Kaspar. He's quite mad, of course. But he's sweeping the people along with his madness. I might be looking on an ancient biblical scene: Elijah or Moses or Aaron, whipping up the twelve tribes of Israel, filled with the light and the fire, preaching the Word of their all-powerful God ... He blinked and shook his head, and reason reasserted itself, because this was very far from the fiery old Testament prophets. This was the shadow-side: it was not the light and the fire, it was the warped underside; the tainted charisma of an Austrian dictator laying greedy hands on half of Europe ... the Holy devil Rasputin, mesmerising the Romanovs, bringing about a dark and bloody revolution ... It was every deceiving power-hungry cult leader ever born.

Kaspar said, 'To begin with we considered reviving the original sentence against you – you will remember what it was?'

'Don't be ridiculous,' said Lewis. 'Of course I remember.'

'But,' went on Kaspar, 'we were agreed that something more was needed.'

'I'll bet you enjoyed debating that. Get on with it.'

Kaspar said, 'In your world – the world of the West –

you have only simple straightforward punishments because you are simple straightforward people. The breaking of murderers' necks, or the gassing or electrocuting or beheading of them. Even your most tyrannical kings could not think beyond breaking bones on the device called the rack, or crushing limbs in vices.'

'Compared to you we're saints and philanthropists, in fact.'

'My people are not of Tibet, or of the lands adjoining Tibet,' said Kaspar, as if Lewis had not spoken. 'But over the centuries something of those cultures has spilled over, and we have absorbed a little of Eastern ways and ancient Eastern methods of punishment. We have adopted some of those punishments, just as we are adopting one for you now.' He stopped, and Lewis though: dear God, they're going to come up with some kind of appalling refinement of torture from the Japs or the Chinese! Wild fragments of stories from the Second World War whirled through his brain: the brutality of Japanese soldiers in the jungle; recalcitrant prisoners of war shut into tiny cramped boxes and left to boil in the heat . . . Women raped by bamboo sticks; water tortures and tiny cages, and skins slit and smeared with honey to attract mosquitoes and ants . . .

Kaspar said, 'There is a punishment used many centuries ago by high-born Chinese for those found guilty of offences of dishonour. You have been found guilty of the highest dishonour imaginable in Tashkara, and we have decided that the mandarins' ancient method of execution will be a fitting death for you. It is that which we have spent the last three days preparing. Also,' he said, softly, 'this is the Feast of Bast, one of Touaris's incarnations, and as such a fitting night for your execution.' He nodded to the waiting guards.

The twisting flames of the wall torches were blurring before Lewis's eyes and the blood was pounding so loudly in his ears that he thought he might faint. But he could see that the guards were carrying something in, and although

388

he could not make out its purpose, a shiver of awed horror stirred the crowd. Lewis looked back at Kaspar. The Tashkaran leader was standing in the direct light of the torches, the flames lending him a diabolic appearance, and he was watching the guards' approach with a half-smile.

'This method of execution,' said Kaspar, looking back at Lewis, 'was known to the ancient mandarins as the Iron Cage of Ten Agonies.' He stepped back and as the guards moved into the light, appalled comprehension began to dawn on Lewis's mind. As the guards seized him with avid hands, and stripped him of his clothes, sick despair closed down. *I think I know what this is, and there's nothing I can do to escape it: there are no bronze fire dishes to tip up this time, and there's no new-born child to snatch up and use as hostage . . .*

The skin-drum was beating again, mingling indistinguishably with the blood pounding in his head, and Lewis fought for control. But horror and panic were mounting. *The Cage of Ten Agonies . . .*

As the guards moved into his line of vision, his mind began to spin into a half-swoon, and he struggled to plunge into its merciful darkness. *Let me faint, let me pass out very early on. Those poor wretched Chinese victims probably counted it an honour to stay aware as long as possible, but I'll bet it didn't save any of them! Well, sod honour, if I can go into unconsciousness and miss the whole thing I'll bloody do it!*

But unconsciousness eluded him, and he watched with growing terror as Kaspar's guards brought across something so fearsome, and so imbued with horrid malevolence, that a ripple of awe stirred the watching Tashkarans.

It was an immense man-shaped iron-mesh cage, hollow and hinged so that it opened to admit a man's body. The device was fashioned intricately and minutely, with curving calf muscles and rounded head portion, and with individual fingers, and shaped genitals . . . The legs were

389

divided, so that whoever was inside would be forced to lie or stand with his legs wide . . .

As they forced him inside and clamped the hinges shut, Lewis realised that the frame was in fact divided by slotted gates. Ten of them . . . Yes, of course there are ten, Kaspar would never get something so basic as that wrong . . . And I can feel them: I can feel that my feet and calves are divided, and that my knees and thighs, and hips and groin . . .

He was dimly aware of being carried, and then of the terrible cage being nailed down to a half-horizontal platform, tilted so that it faced the watchers. The sound of the nails being driven into the wood almost broke his resolve, but after it was done, Kaspar said, 'You are inside the Cage of the Ten Agonies. You begin to understand a little of their purpose now, Sir Lewis?'

'No,' said Lewis.

'Well, you will be aware that the cage is sectioned,' said Kaspar. 'And in a little while, rats – starving rats, deliberately deprived of food for the last three days – will be brought in. At exactly midnight, we will introduce them into the lower sections – the ones holding the feet and calves. The mandarins who ordered this method of execution allotted names to each of the divisions, and the first ones they called the Gates of Dawning Agony.'

'How descriptive,' said Lewis through sweat-soaked lips.

'After one hour,' said Kaspar, 'the second and third gates – called the Gates to Approaching Night, and covering your knees and thighs – will be removed to allow the rats to crawl higher up your body.' He paused. 'There is no record of anyone ever surviving beyond the fourth and fifth gates,' said Kaspar. 'Those are the sections covering the groin and hips, and the ancients called them the Gates of Exquisite Torment. It will be interesting to see if you are the first person to endure beyond them, Sir Lewis.'

The cage restricted Lewis's vision and muffled his hearing, and he could only see the torchlit square through the closely woven mesh – like looking at a fire-soaked hell from behind thin iron bars. I'm trapped. I'm a rat in a cage – oh God, no not that – yes, but in a very few minutes the rats will be trapped in here with me. Starving and deprived of food for three days – Will I die from shock or pain or loss of blood or what? Will they eat into a vital organ? The fourth and fifth gates ... Well, you'll see your damned castration sentence after all, Kaspar! But I'd have preferred it some other way.

He could not see what was happening very clearly, but he was aware of someone standing over him, and of a warm feral stench. There was a sudden high-pitched squealing.

Rats! Leprous rodent creatures: carriers of disease and filth. Scuttling sewer-dwellers.

And then he heard the teeth-wincing scrape of metal as Kaspar lifted the first of the gates.

Chapter Thirty-six

As Raffael entered Tashkara, he was more strung up than he could ever remember being in his entire life. Nothing, not ordination, not facing the Curia for the dispensing from his vows, had touched him so deeply or stirred his soul so overwhelmingly. *I'm entering the Forbidden City of the ancient cat-worshipping Bubasti. I'm approaching one of the most ancient legends in the world's history: the Ten Tablets revered by the Pharaohs as the Stones of Vengeance, and used by them to mete out justice. The Stones believed to have come to earth at the same time as the biblical Commandments vouchsafed to Moses on Mount Sinai.*

And I've got to find a way to destroy them.

At his side Ginevra shivered suddenly, and Raffael ached to put his arm around her and warm her. He did not – no more physical distractions until all this is over! – but he tightened his hold on her hand. On his other side Elinor was so calm she might have been carved from stone. To an outsider she might have been devoid of all emotion, but Raffael could feel emotion irradiating from her, so intense, that he could nearly see it slicing through the darkness like arcing electricity.

They had been exchanging low-voiced remarks as they walked hand in hand into the valley, but as they passed under the huge stone arch and entered the once-great city they fell silent. Ginevra, staring up at the towering walls, lichen-crusted and jagged-edged, felt a tug of regret that all that remained of Tashkara were these sad dust-strewn ruins. How must it have been to have entered this place before decay overtook it – to come in through the massive iron-sheeted gates that had shut out the world and shut in the inhabitants; to be aware of the endless spun-silver cord of the legend stretching back and back?

As they went deeper the evidences of decay were everywhere. Most of the houses were empty and rather sad; there were buildings that must have been meeting places or small temples, and what looked to be the equivalent of taverns or wine shops. The silent cautious walk began to take on a dreamlike quality, as if they had tumbled out of the ordinary world with its ordinary problems and loves and hates and petty nuisances, and fallen down and down through a tear in time's fabric until they were caught in a lost world. The Bermuda Triangle where planes vanished, thought Ginevra; or that patch somewhere in Northern Tibet – oh God, yes! – where travellers disappeared and then occasionally reappeared looking strange. Or am I mixing that up with fiction? I don't know if I'm through a Tear in the Curtain like that old John Buchan book, or whether I'm through the Looking-Glass or down the rabbit-hole, or even whether I'm in a Stephen Hawking-type Black Hole somewhere in space.

She was hugely grateful for Raffael's presence, because if she had to share this with anyone, she would want it to be Raffael. Faithless wench that I am, she thought, remembering the English tutor. But if he had been here, the predictable old bore, he would have been quoting *Hassan* by now – The Golden Road to Samarkand – or Omar Kháyyam, or maybe Southey: The curse is upon thee. For ever and ever . . . Yes, he would certainly drag that one up. Ginevra rather wished she had not dragged it up herself, because if she started to think about curses she really would be frightened. She wondered if Elinor was frightened. Elinor was not showing it, but then she never showed anything. The jacket and boots suited her;

Ginevra thought she had never seen her aunt look quite so stunning and she was conscious of a strong wish that they should find Lewis Chance and that Elinor should go on looking like this for him.

Elinor was not thinking about how she looked, and she was not thinking very much about being frightened. She was intent only on one thing, and that was finding Lewis. She understood about destroying the Decalogue, and she thought, in a remote way, that it would be rather a pity. But until they knew if Lewis was here – until they knew he was *safe* – she had no thoughts for any other mission.

They were still some way off the burning lights when Raffael held up a hand to stop them, and pulled them into the deep shadow of a high building.

'Listen,' he said, speaking very softly. 'We haven't the least idea what we're going into, but so far we haven't come across a single soul.'

Elinor said, 'I think they're all together in that place where we can see the lights.'

'It's a reasonable assumption,' said Raffael thoughtfully.

'Will it be an advantage or the reverse?'

'I've no idea. But supposing we simply go openly through the streets—'

'Openly?' said Elinor, and then, 'Oh – because they don't know any of us, and if we're caught we can say we're ordinary travellers, a bit off course, looking for somewhere to spend the night.'

'Exactly. And if we're challenged we might just get away with it. What we've really got to do, of course, is search the city.'

'Separately?' said Ginevra in rather a small voice and despite himself Raffael grinned.

'No, my child, we must stay together now if ever we do.'

'Hand in hand and shoulder to shoulder, and into the valley of death and—'

Elinor said in a cross whisper, 'If you dare to say, "All

for one and one for all", I will personally strangle you and drop your body over the nearest gorge.'

'Was I being flippant?'

'Yes.'

'Well, I'm sorry.'

'Don't do it again.'

'Well, I won't.'

'We're searching for three separate things,' said Raffael, sounding faintly amused. 'Or for clues about any or all of them.'

'Lewis,' said Elinor at once. 'And Grendel. Don't let's forget Grendel.'

'I'm not forgetting him, Elinor.'

'And the Decalogue.' This was Ginevra.

'Yes. I seem to have come a long way from my original mission for Fleury and the Church,' said Raffael. 'Or maybe I'm getting closer to it.'

He looked at them both and Ginevra said softly, 'But you never lost sight of it, did you?'

'Not for the smallest instant.' Raffael stared at her and then in a different tone said: 'Are we ready?'

'Yes,' said Elinor.

'No,' said Ginevra. 'But let's do it anyway.'

'Remember that if what's going on within those lights is a – a gathering of some kind, there might be spies about.'

'Spies? Why would there be spies?'

'He doesn't mean a gathering, he means a ritual,' said Elinor flatly.

'Well, why can't he say so?'

'Chivalry. He's afraid of wounding our delicate sensibilities.'

'I don't think I've got any delicate—'

'We know that,' said Raffael. 'The point I'm making is that nobody holds a ritual without posting lookouts.'

'I wish you'd say what you mean. It'd make things much easier.'

As they walked through the deserted ancient city,

Elinor began to have the sensation that eyes were watching them from the deserted buildings, and that deep within the shadows people were rubbing their hands together and grinning with dreadful anticipation. She began to imagine that low throaty whispers hissed through the night: *Three for the Burning Altar . . . That one for the roasting pot and that one for the clay oven and that one for the gridiron . . .*

She was not really hearing anything at all, of course. It was only nerves. The whispers were inside her head or it was the altitude again, or maybe it was the memory of Grendel in that warehouse. Eating human flesh – *raw* human flesh. Yes, but inside here they cook them first. Humans for roasting, victims for the Altar.

Yes, yes, English travellers, victims for the roasting, meat for the ovens . . . Three choice morsels, three juicy human sacrifices . . . Come inside, my dears, come inside and be EATEN . . .

She was not seeing eyes any more than she was hearing whispers, of course. The eyes were only the flat painted eyes on some of the doll-like towers. But she might be hearing echoes of some kind. The centuries-old ghosts of all those people who had lived here and worshipped their strange goddess here, and hunted humans for sacrifice for the Burning Altar . . .?

Yes, yes, the echoes of all those travellers caught and offered up . . . Just as you will be caught and offered up . . . We're lighting the ovens for you, my dears . . .

If the Tashkarans caught them they would all be burned alive and then eaten. But they were not going to get caught. Raffael was right about walking innocently forward; if they did that they would be all right.

They had just crossed a small square and the soaring pale building where the lights burned was directly in front of them, when Raffael's hand tightened, and Ginevra said, 'What is it?'

Raffael said, 'There's someone coming towards us.'

It was a very bad moment indeed. They could all hear the footsteps – several sets of them – coming purposefully towards them, and short of turning and running away, there seemed to be nothing for it but to hold to Raffael's plan.

It was in that crowded instant that Elinor knew, quite definitely and quite overwhelmingly, that Raffael's plan was wrong. The logic was sound – there was absolutely nothing wrong with the logic – except that it would not work. The Tashkarans would never believe that they were ordinary travellers, and even if they did it would not matter, because they would see the three travellers as manna from heaven, sacrifices for their horrid rituals – *meat for the Altar . . .*

As the footsteps came running towards them Elinor drew breath to call a soft warning and at the same time moved back into the shadows of the marble-pillared temple.

The warning was never uttered. Six Tashkaran men erupted out of the shadows and fell on Raffael and Ginevra; Elinor, by now hidden from view, knew a split-second of indecision: go forward and try to save them, or stay back and hope not to be seen?

But there were six of the men and they were strong and muscular. One man and two women against them would have no chance at all, and for Elinor to pitch in would only result in them all being captured. But if she could stay free she might manage to follow unseen and stage some kind of rescue. She pressed back into the shadows, her heart racing and forced herself to remain absolutely still. Raffael was saying something about travelling through Tibet and, 'Your interesting valley,' – at least he and Ginevra could be trusted not to give Elinor's presence away! – but the Tashkarans ignored it. There was another bad moment when they scanned the shadows and a look of puzzlement flickered across their dark features. Elinor, hardly daring to breathe, braced herself for discovery, but the men shrugged and one of them said, 'Two only of you.' There was a faint question in his voice and his English was heavily accented.

Raffael said, 'Yes, two of us. What is this? Where are you taking us?' His voice held the exact right note of indignant bewilderment.

'We are taking you to the courtyard at the city centre,' said the man and grinned suddenly, his teeth gleaming in the moonlight. 'You will witness the execution ceremony which is about to start. And after that you will provide a small feast for us.'

Elinor shrank back into the doorway of the temple, her mind swinging between panic and frantic calculation, the guard's words hammering against her senses. Execution. An execution ceremony about to start. Lewis? Oh God, don't let it be Lewis!

There was no point in following the guards until she had thought out some kind of a plan and there was no point in trying to get into the lit square until she could rescue Ginevra and Raffael.

She had not taken any notice of the temple building behind her, but she turned now to survey it. It was a huge, rather ornate place, better preserved than the rest of the city, and beyond the marble pillars were massive double doors with strange symbols and hieroglyphs carved into the surface.

Elinor hesitated, wondering if it was worth exploring, wondering if the temple might provide another route to the courtyard. Or would it lead into a trap? Supposing the guards who had taken Ginevra and Raffael were only one of several similar patrols? It might be safer to find a hiding place while she tried to think what to do next. She pushed the temple doors cautiously and felt them swing noiselessly inwards.

If echoes had trickled through the darkened streets earlier, in here they had coalesced. Elinor, trying to adjust to the shadow-wreathed, partly sunken temple, felt them at once. Centuries upon centuries of unbroken serenity and silence, and of seamless tradition. Like an endless tapestry, like an enchanted carpet, stretching back and back, and then going forward and forward: spinning its own threads as it went, scooping up little fragments and snippets of living events and weaving them into a great glowing pageant . . .

Her feet made no sound on the pale mosaic floor, and as her eyes grew more accustomed to the dimness, she saw the small side temple where, about twenty-five years earlier, a mischievous, slightly bored girl had dressed in the elaborate gown of a goddess and set out to seduce a young English traveller.

Staring up at the embalmed bodies of the long-dead goddesses of Tashkara, caught between awe and repulsion, the beginnings of an idea stirred deep within her mind. Something to do with Grendel in the warehouse; something to do with him skinning Timur's face and wearing it as a disguise to fool the Tashkarans.

A disguise to fool the Tashkarans.

There was a moment when her mind whirled in a dizzying snowstorm of fragments of thoughts and snatches of conversation and tail-ends of knowledge: the huge reverence the Tashkarans had for each Touaris, the Tamerlane League's kidnapping of Grendel to replace his mother . . . They had to have Grendel because there's no Touaris now, thought Elinor. Have I got it right? Because if I have . . .

The plan dropped into place, its edges trimmed and its surface buffed smooth and Elinor saw the way very clearly indeed. And it was a way that would work perfectly so long as two factors held.

One was that the Tashkarans were as superstitious about, and as much in awe of, the earthly Touaris as Elinor believed them to be.

The other was that Elinor herself had sufficient nerve.

Over the first she had no control whatsoever, but over

the second she had absolute control. And if her nerve failed, it meant that Raffael and Ginevra would certainly die – and very soon – and that Lewis would probably die as well. She did not know, not absolutely, that Lewis was at the centre of the execution ceremony, but she sensed it.

'There's no contest.' said Elinor firmly, and began to walk along the serried rows of the embalmed goddesses.

Several of what looked to be later thrones were unoccupied and she passed them by. The vital thing was to be quick but to be convincing. Which of them?

She could feel the minutes slipping away as she scanned the rows of set stiff figures, discarding most of them, aware of mounting desperation. An execution and then a small feast. And the feast small because there are only two victims tonight – Ginevra and Raffael. And Lewis . . .? Oh God, I must be quick and I must get it right!

With the framing of this last thought she heard, faintly but definitely, the sound of a drumbeat from the square. A death knell? The heralding of the Burning Altar being brought in – the real thing, not the makeshift affair she had seen in the warehouse near Chance House! Don't let them start the ritual yet, don't let them start the execution. Lewis, I can't have got this close and then lose you! Oh God, which of these can I use?

And then she saw the small rather slender figure near the door, and she knew at once: that's the one!

It was unspeakably gruesome to pull down from its throne the light, sucked-dry body, and remove the stiff formal gown, but Elinor did it. She had the uncanny feeling that the girl had not been very long dead, and that she might at any minute open her eyes and look up at this clumsy western traveller who was vandalising what was probably a sacred temple.

But I can't help it! sobbed Elinor, struggling with the thick heavy brocade and velvet and the jewel-crusted skirts of the robe. Please forgive me whoever you are! I can't think what else to do, and if you knew what was at stake you'd understand, I'm sure you would! She was trying not to look at the face, but she had seen that the girl was much younger than the other bodies – scarcely older than Ginevra – and although she was wearing a gold and bronze headdress like the rest, there was somehow a modern look to her.

The drumbeat was quickening as Elinor flung down the small backpack she had been wearing, and stripped off her own things: trousers and jacket and the thick sweater. Underthings? No, you fool, no one will see them! There was a moment when the cold air brushed her bare arms and thighs and then she was pulling on the vivid jade-green gown with the crusting of jewels at the neck and cuffs that might be emeralds, and with silver and gold embroidery on the front. It was the kind of gown that under ordinary circumstances you would rather enjoy trying on. It was exotic and startling and Elinor thought with irony that she would probably never again wear something that made her look as good.

She took the jewelled headdress from the dead girl and pushed her own hair out of the way beneath it. The headdress felt cold and hard, but it was not as heavy as she had expected. Anything else? What about shoes? Panic threatened again. I can't stomp into that courtyard wearing thick-soled boots under this get-up! The dead girl had been wearing little gold-tasselled slippers – they would be absurdly flimsy and thin-soled for the cold night ground outside, but Elinor would happily succumb to pneumonia or pleurisy when this was all over. How good a fit were the slippers? Not at all bad; you can go to the ball after all, Cinderella. How did the whole thing look? She dived into the haversack and pulled out a tiny oblong of mirror. It was not marvellous but it was not bad. It ought to fool a pack of savages by torchlight – at least, she would hope so.

She took a deep breath and stepped out into the street, and turned in the direction of the rhythmic drumbeat.

Chapter Thirty-seven

The feel of the warm squirming rat bodies against Lewis's skin was the most appalling thing he had ever experienced. The feel of their teeth tearing into his flesh was the grimmest torment in the entire world.

Through the tearing agony he was dimly aware of people being brought into the courtyard by the guards, and of the Tashkarans murmuring in delight. But pain was driving out every other sensation and he barely acknowledged it.

He tried to see through the mesh head-cage, but there was only the confused impression of a great many people watching him with hot avid eyes, and of Kaspar standing over him. The torch flares blurred before Lewis's sight until he was staring through a swimming crimson mist that threatened to close over his head.

The harsh bristly fur pressing against the inside of his ankles and the thin twitching tails brushing his skin made him feel so physically sick that he had to bite his lip to suppress a rising nausea. I won't be sick, I won't give way. I'll survive and I'll see these bastards punished.

Kaspar was bending over him, his face so close that Lewis could see it clearly through the steel latticing. 'One hour has passed, Sir Lewis. We are about to remove the third and fourth gates. The Gates to Approaching Night.'

Lewis thought he managed to say, 'Damn you, get on with it,' but he no longer knew whether the words were only inside his mind.

Kaspar gestured to the waiting guards and at once there

was the grating sound again, and the excited scrabbling of the rats, swarming up his body, their ravening teeth sinking into the flesh of his calves. Rat saliva, warm and slightly sticky, dribbled over his thighs and he smelled the hot feral excitement of the creatures. Because they're nearer. The agony was lapping up his body, and it was so intense that despite his vows of fortitude he cried out.

He clenched his fists – I *won't* give way and I *will* survive! – but he could already taste the blood of his bitten lip. And it's only the start: as the night wears on each gate will open ... Is the Fifth Gate the next? Exquisite Torment. That's what they're all waiting for, of course. I'm going to die here in this terrible place. Black unconsciousness came smotheringly down, and he swam helplessly in and out of awareness. Time was blurring and becoming meaningless, but the minutes must be sliding past. Like sand trickling through an hourglass. Like tiny scuttling creatures with pointed teeth. Gnawing away at the hours. Has the second hour passed, yet? How close am I to the Gate of Exquisite Torment, the Gate no one has ever survived? This is going to be a terrible way to die—

The drumbeat quickened and Lewis was aware of Kaspar leaning over him again, the hard cruel smile curving his lips – sharks' lips, rats' lips. His hands were closing about the Fifth Gate.

Without the least warning the drumbeat cut off, and a cry of fear went through the courtyard. Kaspar turned his head, and the gloating smile changed to a look of the most abject fear Lewis had ever seen.

Ginevra had fought the guards every inch of the way – even biting one of them at one point – and in the end they had simply picked her up and carried her through the dark streets and thrust her into the lit courtyard, Raffael beside her.

The scene that met her eyes was so unbelievable that for a moment she thought something had gone wrong with her sight. The courtyard was lit to glowering life by the flames spiralling from dozens of wall brackets, and at least two hundred people were grouped around the square, some of them seated on wooden benches but most of them standing. At the centre, with grim-visaged Tashkaran guards at its head and feet was something so appalling, so inhuman, that Ginevra forgot about her own danger and about what Elinor might be doing, and stared in horror.

A man enclosed in a huge steel-mesh, man-shaped cage that had been nailed to an immense oblong of wood, and then raised to face the assembled people. Raffael's voice said very softly, 'Dear God, it's Lewis Chance,' and pity and fear washed over Ginevra afresh.

Even through the iron latticing it was possible to see that the lower half of Lewis Chance's body – from his feet to halfway up his legs – was a heaving mass of twitching brown fur, and as Ginevra and Raffael were pushed to stand alongside him, they saw that blood was already staining the cage.

Raffael said softly, 'Rats – rats inside the cage. Dear God, they're *eating* him!'

'Section by section,' whispered Ginevra, beginning to shudder with sick repulsion.

As Kaspar bent to remove the slotted gate Raffael tried to shake off the guards, but they only held him more firmly. Ginevra was shivering, half with fear, but half with anger, because how dared these people treat any human being like this? She looked about the square, trying to see if it might be possible to create some kind of diversion, and it was then that the drumbeat faltered. A cry of fear rang out and every head turned to the far side of the enclosed square.

Into the firelit scene, walking slowly, walking as if she had all the time in the world and as if that world was arranged solely for her pleasure, was a small imperious figure, garbed in dazzling emerald green, glinting with diamonds.

The fearful murmur went through the Tashkarans again, and this time the man overseeing Lewis Chance's torture stopped in the act of raising the slotted gate. He turned his head and as he saw the small figure, he flung up a hand in front of his eyes as if suddenly dazzled by a brilliant light. Ginevra heard him whisper 'Touaris,' and the word was taken up by the crowd.

Touaris. The reincarnated goddess of the ancient rebel tribe; the immortal female deity whose genesis was older than Christ, whose history was so closely woven with that of the pharaohs that it was no longer possible to separate it.

As the figure moved forward, the Tashkaran leader fell back, his eyes bolting from his head, and at Ginevra's side Raffael said, very softly, 'Ginevra. Get ready to run.'

Ginevra, her eyes on the glittering figure, said, 'What—'

'Elinor,' said Raffael softly. 'You do know it's Elinor?'

'No, I – I mean, yes—'

'She's trying to create a diversion,' said Raffael, still speaking in a low urgent whisper. 'Clever. There'll be a moment when they'll forget we're here – any second now. When I give the word, run for your life while I get Chance.'

'All right,' said Ginevra, who had no intention of running for her life and leaving the others to face these evil creatures, but who was not going to waste time arguing.

The Tashkarans had fallen to their knees, moaning softly and rocking to and fro. The guards fell with them, their prisoners momentarily forgotten. Ginevra was just drawing breath, because this had to be the moment, when Raffael said, 'Now!' and as one they fell on the steel cage, dragging it open.

The hinges gave easily, and the cage opened, but as Ginevra saw the prisoner inside, there was a brief instant when she thought they were too late: Lewis was so white and still that he was surely dead. And then his eyes flickered open and he looked straight at her. His eyes were pain-filled but they were sensible.

Ginevra said hastily, 'It's all right – we're friends – we're going to get you out,' and cast a hunted glance over her shoulder, and thought: yes, but *how*?

405

The rats had scuttled to the ground, squealing in fury, and crouching malevolently, their little red eyes glaring evilly, their tails twitching. Lewis was alive after all, but his legs were in bloodied tatters and Ginevra caught the white glint of bone. Behind her, Elinor had come to stand between two of the wall torches, half in shadow, and she was raising her hands as if she were about to give some kind of command. Diverting their attention, thought Ginevra. But I don't think it's going to be enough. I think that at any minute they'll see that it's a trick, and then we'll all be in the shit—

'Imposter!' The word rang out harshly, and then was repeated in the strange Tashkaran tongue. Kaspar bounded across the courtyard, seizing Elinor and staring down into her face. He dragged her to the centre of the square and a stream of unintelligible words broke from him. At once the Tashkarans rose and began to surge angrily forward.

Elinor was fighting Kaspar, but he held her firmly, and two of the guards had already run to his side. Four more had sprung on to Ginevra and Raffael, pulling them away from Lewis and the crowd were shouting and jeering. Some of them were climbing over the wooden benches and starting forward. Ginevra shrank back, staring at them in horror.

'Leave them to us!' cried Kaspar. 'Leave them to face punishment, and leave that one –' his hand was outflung, pointing at Lewis – 'leave that one to finish the sentence! The Agony of the Ten Gates! He *shall* suffer it! The Cage! Close the Cage!' He gestured to the guards, but they were already closing down the hinged cage again, and Lewis was still inside.

'Gather up the rats!' screamed Kaspar. 'And then bring in the Burning Altar! Because when we have finished with the creature who murdered Touaris,' he cried, 'then we will burn his collaborators!'

A cry of assent came from the crowd, and Kaspar turned to the prisoners. His eyes were suffused with a mad red glare and spittle flecked his chin. 'You will burn!' he cried. 'All of you, starting with the insolent creature who put on Touaris's mantle and walked in Touaris's footsteps! You will die on the Burning Altar! We shall offer you up in the ancient sacrifice of our people on this Feast of Bast, and you will feed the goddess!'

As the drumbeats started up again, despair slammed into Lewis's mind so violently that his hold on sanity slipped.

There had been a space of time when he had felt the cold night air on his skin, and he had seen Raffael without the least surprise; the *rara avis*, the *sui generis* I found in London. It seemed entirely natural that Raffael should be here, fighting Kaspar's people.

And there had been that other moment – astonishing, unforgettable – when he had stared through the flickering torchlight to where a figure stood half in shadow, half in firelight. The dark half was Touaris, *his* Touaris, somehow with him again, but the other half – the half caught by the light – was someone else altogether, and Lewis could not bring this someone else quite into focus. It was someone he knew very well and someone whose presence was suddenly immensely strengthening. As Raffael tore aside the cages, Lewis struggled to make the two halves of this person into one coherent whole, but his mind was still awash with pain and it was beyond him.

It was then that Kaspar screamed that hate-filled cry of 'Imposter!' and the guards dragged Raffael and his companion back, and three of them seized the girl who was half Touaris and half not, and Lewis understood that the confused rescue attempt had failed. Sick bitterness swept over him at the cruelty of it.

As they brought in the Burning Altar a sigh went through the square, and as the guards bent to fire the clay bricks the drumbeat quickened and the Tashkarans began the rhythmic swaying that Lewis remembered. The years splintered and he was once again in the Stone Palace, watching the young guide dragged screaming to the white-hot table and flung on to its surface. But by the time they do that to me I shall be dead! he thought in bitter anguish. And then: but the others won't!

The drumbeats stopped and an intense silence fell on the courtyard again. They're waiting. They know what's about to happen. The Fifth Gate – Exquisite Torment – the one that no prisoner ever survives! His eyes met Kaspar's and then Kaspar reached down to draw up the gate. Lewis clenched his fists and into his mind came the ridiculous thought that now he would never know the identity of the firelit Touaris. He was about to die in screaming agony and he did not know who she was, and it was suddenly overwhelmingly important to know—

As the Gate began to lift, into the square, running hard and brandishing flaming torches and swords and knives, their eyes blazing, came upwards of fifty young Tashkaran men and girls.

The League of Tamerlane.

And at their head was Grendel.

Lewis was swimming in and out of sick unconsciousness, but he was aware that hands were pulling him free of the appalling cage, and he knew that this time it was going to be all right.

His sight was still blurred with tears and sweat and exhaustion but he could see Grendel, and although Grendel's eyes were blazing with that astonishing fervour and his face was dust-smeared and his hair sweat-soaked, his eyes were clear.

Touaris's son leading the rebel separatists; entering into the ancient land of his people, but doing so violently and angrily, and with murder in his eyes and his heart. This was the final reckoning; youth against age – the dissolving of a once-indissoluble people who had fled for their lives from the Pharaoh Amenemhat a thousand years before Jesus of Nazareth... The old order changing, giving place to the new . . .

There was a brief blinding moment when he felt time slither and dissolve again, and he was aware of a pattern being repeated. I was here like this once before, he thought confusedly; and I was as near to death then as I am now. But there was a rescue that time as well . . .

He was dimly aware that Grendel's followers were falling on the Tashkarans and hacking at them with knives and makeshift spears, and thrusting flaming sticks of wood into their faces, screeching some kind of furious battle cry as they did so. The courtyard began to ring with screams of pain and anger as Kaspar's people scrambled over the wooden benches and fell on the intruders.

Lewis felt himself being lifted and carried away from the screaming tumbling carnage and he heard someone nearby say, 'Try not to hurt him.' Someone else was pressing a wad of cloth against his poor mutilated legs and he cried out in pain, and then a female voice said, 'Only one thing for it – we'll have to go into the Temple and barricade the doors.'

Lewis tried to ask what was happening, but his voice was so weak that he could hardly make himself heard over the shouting and the screams. Raffael bent down and said in his ear, 'Grendel and his people are fighting Kaspar and the guards, Sir Lewis. But you are safe and we are getting you away. You understand?'

'I – yes.' Lewis managed to clutch Raffael's hand gratefully. 'Thank you. *Sui generis* – recognised it at once. Can't talk – say it all later . . .'

He thought Raffael said, 'I've never been called that before,' and he thought there was even a note of wry amusement in Raffael's voice. And then he fell gratefully into blessed unconsciousness.

As they ran through the darkened streets, leaving the courtyard behind, Elinor wanted to scream at them to run faster. Because we have to get clear, we have to get to safety – to *sanctuary*. The old word, that had once meant so much more than just a hallowed place, rang through her mind. To enter sanctuary had once meant to step on to sacred ground and be instantly and unassailably protected from pursuers. And there was only one place here that might afford them a temporary respite, and that was the Temple.

Raffael had wrapped his jacket around Lewis; he had his arms about Lewis's shoulders and chest, and Ginevra, who had been nearest, had taken his feet, wrapped in the makeshift wadding to stanch the bleeding. Elinor ached to push them both aside and fling her arms about Lewis and cry, but it was not a time for being emotional; it was a time for being practical and quick-thinking and for reaching safety. If they got out of all this – *when* they got out of all this – she would have the noisiest breakdown ever.

The ancient Temple with the mummified goddesses was ahead of them, and Elinor conjured up in her mind an image of the immense doors with the huge bolts on the inside. The Temple would not give them shelter for very long – Kaspar and his people would be after them within minutes – but it might give them a breathing space.

The Temple was cool and dim and the sound of the bolts being driven home from inside was the most comforting thing any of them had ever heard. The bolts were immense iron struts, each one as thick as a man's forearm, and the doors themselves were massive affairs of solid silver, strengthened with iron staves and inlaid with panels of marble and gold. Raffael, gasping, laid Lewis on the floor and turned to inspect them.

'All right?' said Elinor, meaning the doors.

'Yes, better than I thought. A battering ram would have a difficult job against these, and I don't think even fire would get through all that silver and marble. Good girl.'

Ginevra said, 'There're tiny spyholes up there as well – can you see? I can't imagine why they were put there, unless this was once under seige, but at least we can see

410

what's happening outside.'

'We'll hear what's happening outside,' said Elinor grimly, as Raffael rummaged in the haversacks for candles and matches. Tiny glad flames burned up, vividly red and orange in the dark vaulted hall, and she dragged a spare shirt out of her own bag and tore it into strips to bandage Lewis's wounds more thoroughly. There was antiseptic cream in their small medical kit and Elinor spread this thickly on the bandages, strongly conscious of the futility of these measures. She was sick with fear when she thought about the danger of infection and blood poisoning, but for the moment there was nothing more that could be done. The important thing was to get free and get him to the nearest hospital. The overwhelmingly important thing was to get free.

Ginevra had crushed three aspirin tablets in a plastic cup of Evian water and was holding it for Lewis to drink, and Elinor felt a sharp gratitude to Ginevra who did things without needing to be told. She started to ask about searching for other entrances or exits, when the sound of loud knocking rang through the Temple.

They all spun round at once, and Elinor's heart began to thump. The knocking was on the main door, the huge silver doors they had so firmly bolted only minutes earlier, and to hear it through the thickness, whoever it was must be using a metal weapon of some kind. Kaspar. Kaspar and his people trying to get in. Trying to penetrate this flimsy sanctuary.

Raffael held a finger to his lips and padded silently across the cat-mosaic floor to the tiny glass spyholes halfway up the doors. Elinor felt her fists curling into balls, the nails of her fingers digging into her palms. Don't let them get in, please let us be safe, please let us escape.

Raffael said, 'It's Grendel,' and dragged back the bolts.

Grendel was hunched against the door, bleeding from at least a dozen different cuts, and he fell through into the

411

Temple gasping and sobbing. The stone he had been using to beat on the door fell from his hands.

Raffael said sharply, 'Tell us what's happening,' and in a perfectly sane voice Grendel said, 'I ran away. They lied to me—'

'Never mind that. How badly hurt are you?'

'Cut. Only a bit.' The smile that was so uncannily not his own showed briefly, and Ginevra heard Elinor draw in her breath. 'They said I would find Touaris,' said Grendel and for a moment his eyes held the bewildered hurt of a child. 'That's why I came with them. But they lied to me,' he said again. 'And so I ran away.'

'They're bad men,' said Raffael gently. 'It's all right now. We'll talk about it later. But now we have to get away from them, do you understand that, Grendel?'

'Yes. Get away.' He looked trustfully at Raffael.

Elinor had been dragging on the discarded trousers and sweater and boots. She passed the remains of the torn-up shirt across almost automatically, and Grendel wiped the blood from his cut arms and hands. There was a moment when he stared down at the blood, and seemed to pause. Something flickered in his eyes, and Elinor felt a lurch of terror. But then Grendel put the cotton strips into a pocket and the moment passed.

Raffael was walking around the immense Temple, clearly trying to find other exits and it was then that Lewis put a hand out and clutched Elinor's arm. His skin felt hot and dry and feverish, but when he spoke his voice was weak but perfectly rational.

'We can – hide in the ruined city,' he said, and pointed to the corner by the groyned arch. 'There's a trap door that leads down to the original city of the Bubasti, and to the—'

'To the what?' said Raffael sharply. 'Sir Lewis, what's down there?'

Lewis focused on him with difficulty. 'The Decalogue Chamber,' he said.

Chapter Thirty-eight

The frenzied descent down the narrow dark stairs with Raffael and Elinor carrying Lewis was awkward but they managed it.

Grendel went ahead, using the strongest of the electric torches, and Ginevra brought up the rear with the small pencil-torch.

'And very appropriate too,' she said, with a touch of slightly too-emphatic flippancy. 'Anything that comes creeping along after us will get me first. What happened to chivalry?'

'It's leading the party carrying the best torch,' responded Raffael shortly.

Lewis smiled weakly up at Ginevra, who blinked and then smiled back, but thought: hell's teeth, if he used to look at Nell like *that*, no wonder she's come half across the world for him! I wouldn't have minded knowing him twenty years ago – I mean if I'd been the same age. I'll bet he could tell some stories. Oh *dear*, thought Ginevra, unaware that she was mirroring Elinor's own thoughts about Ginevra herself and Raffael. Poor Nell.

When they reached the break in the stairs Lewis pointed to the low cobweb-swathed opening with beyond it a Stygian darkness. 'Through there. The ruined city of the first Bubasti— If you'd put me down for a minute you might find it easier.'

Ginevra caught the note of angry impatience in these last words and understood that Lewis was fighting the pain, but that he was also fighting frustration at slowing them down. As Raffael and Elinor set him down she scrambled past them to where Grendel was clearing away the fallen stones.

'It looks as if part of the roof's caved in at some time,' observed Raffael, regarding the small archway.

'Well, let's hope no other parts cave in until we're through.'

Ginevra had hesitated for the fraction of a second before going to help Grendel, and then she saw, as Elinor had seen earlier, that Grendel was intent only on clearing a way through. She quashed the prickle of unease and kneeled by him, dragging at the piles of broken bricks and stones, and said in what she hoped was an ordinary voice, 'This is a hellish place, isn't it?'

'Yes, but beyond this we'll be safe,' said Grendel, nodding to the piled-up rubble. 'And there are beautiful wall paintings to see.' Ginevra felt the breath catch in her throat for a second – how does he know *that*!

Lewis said, 'If you can pile the debris on to the stair behind us it might delay anyone coming after us.'

'Will they get this far?' asked Elinor, helping Raffael to carry two huge boulders that still bore traces of carved hieroglyphs on one side. 'Won't the bolts on the Temple door hold?'

'Yes, but let's block every avenue we can,' said Lewis, and then, 'Damn, I'm lying here giving you all orders—'

'Oh, order away,' said Ginevra promptly. 'We're the poor down-trodden proletariat, slaving under the yoke of bloated capitalism.'

'I think,' said Raffael repressively, 'that we can get through now. The archway's very low and there are more stairs leading down – do you see them? But we'll have to go very carefully. I wouldn't trust an inch of this place.'

As they passed under the low crumbling archway the stench of mould and damp breathed into their faces, and as they went down towards the ruined apartments there was a stifling sense of ancient darknesses and of old, old

414

evil. Ginevra shivered and glanced across at Lewis to see how he was coping.

Lewis was clinging to consciousness and calm by the frailest of threads, but as they descended into the dark, stale-smelling void the pain receded briefly, and the years fell away. He half closed his eyes and for a leaping moment he was his own younger self, descending these stairs in the wake of the mischievous-eyed lady who had dressed up in a goddess's regalia and was beckoning to him.

And now I'm making the same journey, but this time I'm being carried. And even though I'm trying not to think about it, I'm probably halfway to some disgusting form of blood-poisoning, and even if I escape that I'm probably crippled for life—

And Touaris was dead, her womb ripped to shreds by the sentence of the First Stone Tablet which stated that the office of the gods must be inviolate. But Touaris's son was here, leading the way, his torch cutting an arc of cold twentieth-century light through the pouring darkness, sweeping aside thick swathes of cobwebs. It was an eerie experience to watch Touaris's son pushing back the centuries, exactly as his mother had done all those years ago.

Grendel's face was in shadow, but once or twice Lewis caught a glint from his eyes, and once when Grendel paused and looked back over his shoulder Lewis felt a shiver of new fear. For a second the planes of Grendel's features had seemed to sharpen, and there had been the sly sideways glance from inward-slanting eyes and the thin cruel smile. If he pounces on one of those girls in this cramped space— I'll have to watch him closely, thought Lewis, and I'll have to be ready for anything. Then pain seized him again, and he remembered with fresh bitterness that if Grendel's dark insanity surfaced now, he would be helpless. Be damned to that! he thought angrily. If he attacks Elinor I'll drag him away with my own hands! This struck him as an extraordinarily emotional reaction.

The passage was so impossibly narrow that several times they had to stop and clear a path through fallen masonry. In places they had to bend almost double to go beneath the low roof, and the ground everywhere was strewn with fallen stones and dangerously uneven. Once Ginevra twisted her foot in a deeply rutted section and almost went headlong and once Elinor gasped with sudden pain as a jutting spur of rock scraped her shoulder. Sandstone columns supported the roof at intervals, but most of them were eroded almost to dust. Here and there were gaping holes in the ground and on one occasion they had to edge around a well-like void from which a dank sour stench gusted upwards.

'Horrid,' said Ginevra, helping to hand Lewis across this. 'How far down until we reach the actual city part?'

'I've no idea.'

'Do you know how near we are to the Decalogue Chamber?' asked Raffael.

'Not very near. In fact I think we're going away from it. Why – is it important?'

'It was,' said Raffael rather drily. 'But I think there are other priorities just now.'

The air was becoming very stale, and Lewis felt the beginnings of tightness about his chest. Heart attack pending? No, you fool, lack of oxygen!

Several times the sweeping torch beams showed up crustings of pale fungoid growths on the roof's underside, but several times as well they caught the glint of wall paintings that owed nothing to the grafted-on Tibetan culture but were wholly Egyptian in execution. We're nearing the original part, thought Lewis, and through the tidal waves of pain a little pulse of excitement began to beat in his mind.

Grendel stopped by one of the columns and ran the flat of his hand almost reverently over one of the wall paintings. 'That is the Bubasti people carrying the cat goddess out of Egypt,' he said, tracing the faded beautiful outlines. 'Taking with them the Stones of Vengeance.'

Lewis caught his breath. He's recognising this place, he thought, his eyes on Grendel. He knows it, not because he was here himself, but because he's inherited the memory; he's inherited a whole bank of memories and he's reaching down and down, and back and back into them. I think he's more your son than mine, Touaris. But I think he always was.

Grendel shone the torch on to the fresco which was faded and dim, but whose colours and outlines were still discernible. Rows of figures, drawn and painted in the formalised style of Egyptian art, some with their heads turned back as if looking to whatever place they were leaving; others pointing ahead as if to the destination. The central figures were driving oxen yoked to immensely thick wheel-shaped objects.

Raffael said softly, 'The exodus of the renegades.' He touched them lightly with one hand.

'And rows of hieroglyphs,' said Elinor. 'I wish we could know what they say.'

Grendel said, 'I know.' He paused, and then said,

'Since the time of the ancestors –
The gods who were before time –
Who rest in their pyramids . . .
Their place is no more.

'It's from the Eleventh Dynasty and it was the mocking Bubasti jibe at the Pharaoh Amenemhat and his descendants.'

The two girls stared at him, and Elinor started to say, 'How do you—' And then stopped and looked around, as if she had caught a sound.

Lewis had caught it as well, but he thought it was not so much a sound as an awareness. Something long dead, something so far back in time that it was almost impossible to catch the echoes . . . Something nearby seemed to shiver and sigh, and a dry, softly warm wind breathed into his face. The exodus, he thought. The desperate journey out of Egypt. But beneath the desperation – flee before we are caught and taken back to face death! – had run an exultant current of triumph.

Because although we are leaving the rainless land, we are taking Satan's Commandments that were forged in the deepest fire-drenched caverns of hell and cooled in the snow-capped mountains of the world ... We are taking them from the land of oppression into the remote, mountain-rimmed East, and there we shall found our own civilisation and indulge our own worship – Touaris, goddess of true immortality, who was once Bastet and also Apet and Hesamut and Rert ... And one day, when Amenemhat's splendour is in dust and the pharaohs' names lost to the world, our city will still be standing and Touaris will still live and our people will endure ...

But for now we must think only of the journey, and we must hasten to outrun Amenemhat's jackals ...

We must run, thought Lewis, confusedly. We must outrun Amenemhat's jackals ... The suffocating darkness of the ruined passage closed about him, and he blinked and felt the present click into focus once more.

But the eerie echoes lingered for a moment longer, and although he had no means of knowing what they were or where they came from, he thought they were another of those inexplicable shards of time that occasionally break and lodge in the present. Splinter-echoes of the beleaguered Bubasti tribe from three thousand years ago? More likely I'm becoming feverish from the rat-wounds, he thought angrily.

But the urgency was still crowding in, and there was still the sense that it was imperative to go on and go quickly lest they were overtaken. He started to say something to Raffael about moving faster – when Ginevra whipped round, staring into the darkness.

Elinor started to say, 'What—' And then stopped and

looked back as well, because they could all hear it now.

And this time it was not a thin faint echo of the past. It was people dragging open the trap door of the Death Temple.

There was no point in going deeper in, but there was nowhere else to go. Elinor, trying to protect Lewis from the worst jolts of the frenzied scramble through the tunnels, scanned the darkness frantically, searching for somewhere to hide. It would be appalling to get lost down here, but it might be better than being caught by Kaspar. And then she remembered that their supply of torches and candles was limited, and that the haversacks held only a couple of days' food and bottled water. Was it preferable to die from hunger and thirst in the dark than to be flung summarily on to the Burning Altar and roasted alive and eaten? And the danger's down here with us anyway, she thought suddenly. It's running alongside us – I can *feel* that it is! It's with us in these gruesome passages and it's much closer than any of us suspect ... stalking through the darkness ... prowling the tunnels alongside us ... Don't be ridiculous!

The Tashkarans had reached the second stairs and they were pouring into the tunnels; Elinor could hear them shouting furiously in their own tongue. The ground was shuddering under the impact of angry running feet and little flurries of dry red sand were dislodging from the roof. From somewhere deep in the bowels of the ancient city came a faint menacing growling, echoing hollowly. Like standing on a deserted Underground station and hearing a train approach, thought Elinor wildly. Did the ground shudder as well? No, I'm imagining it. But the feeling that something deep and ancient and awesome had been disturbed persisted.

It was then that Grendel turned back. He had been leading them and the arc of light from his torch turned with him, so that there was a moment when he was standing behind the light, wreathed in shadows. And then there was another moment when the shadows twisted about his face, sharpening the features, lengthening the lower lip. Elinor stared at him and knew why she had felt that sense of danger walking with them: the danger was here, it was barely two steps away. Grendel – Lewis's son, who had his father's eyes and hands – who had been so helpful about clearing the blocked tunnels and had shown them the cool lovely wall paintings, was changing: he was metamorphosing into the slavering, hungry-eyed thing Elinor had seen chained in the warehouse below Chance House.

As Grendel pushed past them, Ginevra fell back against the wall and Raffael's arms went out to her automatically. Lewis, his face contorting with pain, struggled to stand, reaching out to Grendel as if to stop him. But Grendel made an angry gesture of repudiation, and then brought both his hands up to clutch his head as if forcing back some deep inner torment.

The dull growling came from beneath the city again, and this time large stones broke away from the ceiling and began to shower down. Elinor sent a nervous glance at the low uneven roof and saw a faint ripple of movement, as if a giant breath had blown across the surface.

Down the dark tunnel came a flood of red torchlight, and from out of the shadows, their eyes wild with the ancient blood lust of their ancestors, their feet pounding on the hard-packed earth floor, burst the Tashkarans. Elinor and Ginevra shrank back, and Raffael made as if to lift Lewis again. But we're outnumbered! thought Elinor frantically. And we can't possibly outrun all these!

Grendel shot forward, his hands lifted above his head, the fingers curving into claws. His upper lip curled back and his teeth gleamed in the flickering torchlight, and Elinor understood then that Grendel was channelling his own insanity: he had forced it back earlier, but now he was unleashing it. Kaspar's people had cheated him and the Tamerlane League had cheated him and he was deliberately summoning up his cruel inner self. As he went towards Kaspar he was like the avenging god of some ancient myth.

Elinor felt a chill of primeval fear. He was terrible and awesome, but against the Tashkarans and against whatever lived in the bowels of these tunnels, he would stand no chance. She started after him but Lewis grabbed her arm and jerked her back. She thought he said, 'Let him go, Elinor,' but the ground was shuddering beneath them now and the sandstone pillars were shaking and it was becoming difficult to hear or see or even think.

Grendel was in the centre of the tunnel, sandstones and pouring red dust cascading about him. The torches lit him to surreal life, and he hunched forward, lowering his head. Thick pale mouth-fluids ran from his mouth and dribbled over his chest, and his eyes showed red. Huge splits appeared in the roof, dirt and rocks pouring down, and Elinor threw herself against Lewis, forcing him against the wall, shielding his body with her own. She was totally unprepared for his arms to come instantly about her, and she was even more unprepared for the startling response of her own senses. It was a reflex action, of course, it was absolutely nothing more than that, but her eyes flew up to meet his, and she said a bit jerkily, 'I'm trying to protect you from the stones and – and things.'

'I know,' he said. His eyes were still cloudy with pain but they were perfectly sensible. His arms stayed tightly round her and as he held her against him something fastened about Elinor's heart and mind that had nothing to do with panic or fear and that had everything to do with sudden soaring hope and surprised joy.

The present came rushing in again almost immediately and Elinor thrust the moment down because it was not to be believed and it was not to be relied on. He was half delirious with pain and they were all half mad with fear and panic. But if they ever did get free, it might be one of those moments to be stored away with immense care, and only unwrap and look at when you were absolutely alone. We'll get out of here if I have to tear down every brick in this crumbling place, thought Elinor fiercely. We'll beat those devils if I have to strangle every one of them with my own hands!

As if in echo of this last, Grendel gave a low snarling sound – inhuman, bestial – and fell on Kaspar, knocking him to the ground, sending the burning torch spinning from his grasp. Elinor had a brief terrible glimpse of Grendel's face with the stark glare of blood lust and then Grendel sank his teeth into Kaspar's face and Kaspar began to scream, the sound echoing and bouncing through the narrow space.

The deep underground thunder came again and the walls of the tunnels began to crack. For a moment none of them moved, and then Raffael shouted, 'They're caving in! The whole place is collapsing! Run for it! Get out while there's time!'

The angry underground thunder pursued them as they fled deeper into the ancient buried city.

Raffael and Elinor had both grabbed Lewis, handling him roughly but driven by desperation. He had shouted to them to leave him and get clear, but none of them paid him any heed. Ginevra snatched up the nearest haversack and Grendel's discarded torch, and moving by instinct they went forward.

Huge pieces of rock were falling so that they kept their hands over their heads as the only protection they could manage, and the centuries-old dust was billowing upwards in choking red clouds. Elinor flung a frightened glance over her shoulder. Kaspar and the Tashkarans were screaming and fighting to get free, but the ancient walls were falling in everywhere, and they were already half buried by falling debris. Little trickles of flame had started up in a dozen places where the burning torches had been helplessly flung down and the entire underground city was becoming buried in fire and falling rock.

'The roof's coming down!' cried Elinor, coughing through the dust and trying to dodge the bouncing skittering boulders. 'Go *on*, go forward, we can still get through!'

'Where!' yelled Ginevra, her eyes streaming, but tumbling forward, trying to direct the torch as she went. 'Jesus God, Nell, where are we going?'

'I don't know but there must be a way. We can't have got this far and not get free.'

And then Lewis said, 'The old city gates!' And heard, like a sweet soft echo, Touaris's voice across the decades: 'I wanted to see the original city entrance, which our chronicles say was one of the most beautiful things ever built by man . . .'

Hope surged up within him, and he cried, 'Go forward! There's a way out – the original entrance! The gates that the first Bubasti built to enter Tashkara!' And thought: and if you bequeathed me nothing else, my poor lost love, and if I lost your son at the end, still you gave me the means to escape from your city!

Raffael said suddenly, 'You're right, Sir Lewis! There's a light up ahead.'

Thin dawn light, pure and cool and spangled with glistening dew-soaked cobwebs, streamed into the tunnels, and Elinor, her eyes gritty and her throat almost closed up with the dust, saw that the tunnel was widening. Over their heads, was a glint of something that might once have been pure sawn ivory, and that might have been burnished bronze or gold, veined with fiery threads of gold and of turquoise . . . The Gates of Paradise, made from chalcedony and turquoise and jasper and fire . . .

As they went forward to where the sacred peaks reared up against the impossibly beautiful dawn sky, behind them was a dull roar, and then a louder one. Thick clouds of dust belched out of the cave and there was the ominous crackle of fire.

Raffael paused, and looking back, said softly, '"And the cities of the plain were totally destroyed by fire and brimstone"...'

Chapter Thirty-nine

'We discovered afterwards,' said Raffael, facing Cardinal Fleury in the Bloomsbury house, 'that Lewis had been right: we really had found the original city entrance. It had long since fallen into ruins, of course; the city walls had crumbled and they were almost completely buried, and the entrance was barely more than a tunnel going into the ground. But thank God it was still there.'

'And it was lama monks who picked you up?'

'Yes. They were amazingly kind. A couple of them had a few words of English and a couple more had a little Italian and we communicated surprisingly well. They smothered Lewis's wounds in something – I never found out what – and fed the rest of us rice wine and made up beds as if it were part of an ordinary day's work. It's an astonishing religion, Buddhism.'

Fleury regarded Raffael for a moment, and then said, in an expressionless voice, 'And I believe that the Tibetan monasteries do not list celibacy among their requirements.'

Raffael grinned. 'I'm not about to renounce the world a second time, Eminence,' he said. 'There are too many sins I still haven't committed.'

'Ah. Miss Craven? I should say,' said His Eminence, a stickler for accuracy, 'the younger Miss Craven.'

'Returned to university,' said Raffael shortly, and Fleury said, 'I see.'

It was still possible to feel the pang of loss for Ginevra. She had cursed at returning to Durham, but she had gone philosophically enough. It was only when they were standing on King's Cross Station that she said, 'Do I come back, Raffael?'

'You mean, do you come back to me?'

'Yes.'

He stared at her, and after a moment, said, 'I don't know. There are so many years between us.' And stopped, and thought: and even if those years could be bridged, there are other gulfs which are uncrossable, my love. Too many wrong decisions; too much cynicism . . .

And then he remembered that Ginevra was not uncynical herself under all the romantic idealism. She was an enthusiast and a bit rebellious, but she was nobody's fool. The realisation that the romantic idealist might one day turn into a cool-headed pragmatist brought an abrupt clear-cut pleasure.

He bent to help her lift her case into the carriage, and as he hauled it up on to the rack, Ginevra said abruptly, 'I'm going back to get a double first.' She eyed him. 'And when I've got it, will you celebrate it with me?'

'Yes,' said Raffael, after a moment, and had the satisfaction of seeing the mischievous grin light her face. 'Yes, I'll celebrate it with you.'

There was another pause. All around them commuters scrambled on and off trains, and British Rail blared its tannoy announcements.

Then Ginevra said, softly, 'It's all right, isn't it? I mean – we don't need to say any more because we both know it's all right.'

'It's all right.' He held her against him for a brief minute. 'And now get you gone, wench. The train's about to start and if I'm not careful I shall end up travelling all the way to Durham.'

'Or you'll have to jump off while it's moving, which is dangerous because you might land anywhere.'

'But,' said Raffael, 'not knowing where you might land is the best part.'

* * *

426

It was not possible to say any of this to Fleury and probably none of it needed to be said anyway.

His Eminence merely remarked, 'An unusual girl, Ginevra Craven,' and Raffael replied, 'Extremely,' and Fleury, with his customary good manners, switched subjects, asking courteously after Lewis Chance.

'He's recovering, but it's a long process. And he'll almost certainly be disabled for life.'

'At least he still has his life. I shall pray for him, of course.'

'Of course.'

Fleury fixed Raffael with a hard, shrewd look, and Raffael thought: here it comes.

'And now,' said His Eminence, 'what about the Decalogue, Raffael?'

Raffael sat back and spread his hands. 'I truly don't know,' he said. 'None of us knows. But the destruction of the tunnels was so complete – they simply crumbled and folded in.'

'Burying Grendel and the Tashkarans?'

'Yes. And parts would certainly have burned,' said Raffael, remembering how the torchflames had licked greedily at the ancient stones. 'We couldn't possibly have gone back in. Even if we had been strong enough it would have been beyond us.' He frowned. 'I truly think we can regard the Tashkara Decalogue as buried beyond recall, Eminence. I don't think the Church needs to be concerned any more.'

There was a brief silence; then Fleury said thoughtfully, 'I have often wondered how much credence Patrick Chance gave the prophecy. He was scrupulous about reporting it, but I do wonder if he believed it.'

Raffael said, 'In that monastery there were several *geshes* – that's a very high level of knowledge and deep contemplation – but there were also two monks regarded as reincarnates – the Buddhist word is *tulkus*. These *tulkus* seemed to have some knowledge – inherited or acquired, I wouldn't know which – not just of the original Bubasti tribe, but also of Patrick.' He paused and then said, 'It was probably nothing more than a snippet of their sparse history being handed down, but nevertheless—'

'Nevertheless, memories are long in that part of the world, and one must accept the existence of Great Mysteries in all religions,' said Fleury.

'Yes. In the monastery they had tales of how Patrick and a travelling companion – a young man – had spent a few nights at their monastery on their way into Tashkara and then again on the return journey,' said Raffael. 'But they said that if they had not recognised the features, they would not have taken it for the same man. They believed that something had happened to the two of them inside Tashkara, but they didn't know what and Patrick never told them.'

'Something connected with the Decalogue?' hazarded Fleury. 'Even something to do with the prophecy?'

'No,' said Raffael. 'I don't think it was the prophecy at all. I don't know what it was, and I don't think anyone ever will know.'

'Does Sir Lewis know?'

'Lewis Chance doesn't know any more than we do,' said Raffael. 'I'm sure of it.'

'And so Patrick's secret died with him,' said Fleury softly.

'Yes.' Raffael frowned. 'It's odd, isn't it, that even with that brief notoriety, no one ever knew where or when Patrick Chance died.'

Patrick Chance's Diary: Closing Entries

Cheyne Walk, August 1891

It feels odd to be back in London. It feels very odd indeed to be in Cheyne Walk again with absolutely nothing changed. Not even Father. Especially not Father.

It's not going to work, of course, this idea of falling back into ordinary family life. Father's started off by saying things like, Good to have you back, my boy. (I give *that* sentiment two weeks at the outside.)

There's also been, Glad to see you've settled down at last, not before time, of course ... Expect you'll come into the Bank now, and marry and continue the name ...

No, it assuredly won't work.

I wonder what house prices are like in London these days?

September 1891

I think I've managed to put up a fair smokescreen to conceal what happened to me in that accursed palace, and I'm absolutely determined that no one, save Theodore and Fenris and Sridevi, will ever know the truth. Cardinal Gregory may have suspected, of course, and those lynx-eyed monks on Tashkara's outskirts probably came close as well. Shrewd creatures, men of God – any god.

But I'm hanging on to Sridevi's words about sliding the nightmares back across the silent black waters, and ushering in the light. And I'm spinning an illusion, although I have to say it's excruciatingly difficult to take matters to seduction point with a female and find a reason to stop short of actual penetration. Sorry, my dear, I feel faint/sick/over-come by scruples/undermined by drink ... I've taken a vow of celibacy ... I'm suffering from pox ... You're going to exhaust the possibilities very quickly, Patrick, you might as well face it.

Later. A letter arrived by the afternoon post from Theodore. I fell on it avidly; it's astonishingly good to hear from the old chap. He writes rather entertainingly as well – what an irony if he took to writing in earnest – articles or short stories, or even novels – as a result of what happened to him in Tashkara. It wouldn't hurt to just nudge him in that direction, because he'd never think of it for himself.

It occurs to me that if I did move out of the family mausoleum I could do worse than share a place with Theo.

But wherever I live, will I ever grow accustomed to this half-life? Sridevi, I'm still waiting for the light to filter across the black waters of despair . . .

September 1891 continued

Am finding London oddly enervating, and am suffering vague aches and occasional feverish fits. I grazed my hand last week and it won't heal. Father says it is a lingering debility from travelling and why don't I come along to the House of Chance, because it is a long time since I set foot in the place. I will see to it that it is longer still, because if I am to find a way of getting through life, I don't think I shall do it in the prim ambience of a banking house.

I read an article in the *Morning Post* yesterday about the number of music halls that are falling into disuse and ruin all over London. The piece was written in a rather florid style, but the burden of the song was clear: how sad to see so many fragments of theatrical history vanishing. Among others, St Stephen's Road was listed, and there was a coy hint of a scandal involving Certain Illustrious Personages a couple of years back.

It's a rather uncomfortable notion that I might have had something to do with the place being abandoned. I might take a look at it one day, for old times' sake and curiosity.

Theodore writes that the St Stephen's Road property is indeed available for purchase, but adds, caustically, that if I continue to employ cloak-and-dagger tactics to obtain information he will wash his hands of the entire affair, and if I must needs buy a house at all, why can't I go about it openly and honestly instead of skulking behind ridiculous incognito.

It's good to know that he still reads the same kind of bravura literature, that Theo.

Hand still not healing which is a nuisance, in fact original small graze seems to be spreading. Have consulted doctor who plastered it with evil-smelling salve and charged 3 gns.

Have made up my mind to buy St Stephen's Road property. This has received mixed reactions, ranging from Father, who stormed cholerically about Cheyne Walk demanding to know if family home not good enough – all right for my father and his father before him, dammit! – to Theodore, who disapproves on various grounds and also on principle. This last no more than I expected, however.

Father adds that St Stephen's Road is disgraceful address for gentlemen, no better than a slum, and: I suppose you'll be getting up to mischief out there, bringing shame and disgrace on the name all over again – if only I could! – to say nothing of: Well, I'm just glad your poor dear mother didn't live to see this day.

'Don't expect me to tow you out of the River Tick when that place gobbles up all your money!' he shouted, before storming off to the bank, there to strike terror into the hearts of most of his employees.

'And don't come crawling to me to rescue you from social ruin, either!'

I shan't.

Theo now adopting attitude of determined practicality, and listing all reasons against buying St Stephen's Road – or any property at all, come to that. He argues that (a) it's been empty for nearly two years and will therefore be squalid ruin, (b) it will take several fortunes to adapt it from former risqué use to gentleman's private residence, (c) area is a slum and I can't possibly live in a slum, and (d) he doesn't believe I can afford it.

Will worry about (a) and (b) later, and will use Mamma's legacy and godmother's for (d) which will have the two-fold result of getting me what I want and infuriating Father, who never forgave either of these ladies (both far from impoverished) for cutting him out of their wills. He still regards the Married Women's Property Act as a piece of monstrous mismanagement and insufferable impertinence, and considers Government going downhill. Mark his words, they'll be giving women the vote next and then where shall we be?

As for (c), I don't give a damn whether I live in a slum or a mansion.

January 1892

So the thing is done and I am the owner of St Stephen's House.

It's a peculiar feeling. When I walk through the rooms, my footsteps echo in the emptiness, and I have the feeling that other footsteps walk with me, just out of sight and just beyond hearing.

(Echoing across the surface of that eternal black silent ocean . . .?)

I watch the fog rolling in from the Thames and there are ghosts there as well, only I'm not sure if they're ghosts from the past or from the present.

On rereading this last sentence, think I may have caught the habit of contemplation from the lama monks.

Hand still troublesome.

Battles royal with Theodore over his coming to live here.

He scribbled impatiently about 'charity' and 'patronage', and I tore the paper up, and went off to get drunk, and he stormed out and so we went on. But I will wear him down, because I know that under it all he is strongly attracted by the idea.

And I *cannot* let him endure any kind of hardship because of what happened to him in Tashkara!

Composed rather good piece for diary today (the public version, that is), set in one of the private upstairs rooms of the Café Royal (they have several of these, as a number of surprisingly august people could testify), and where the touch of a button on a velvet-covered sofa caused the panelling to part and reveal an immense silk-draped double bed.

Had great fun describing an outrageously lascivious supper at which I and my imaginary companion fed one another portions of duckling à la Montmorency, and how afterwards I poured tiny portions of champagne into her navel and licked it up. On consideration, however, think I will change this to claret, since champagne apt to turn acid if brought up to body temperature and does not really go with duck anyway.

Nota bene: would it be amusing to give these mythical bed-partners provocative initials, ostensibly to preserve discretion but in reality to titillate people's interest? Or would anyone actually believe I slept with Lillie Langtry and Daisy Brooke ... Or those blazingly beautiful creatures who sit for the Pre-Raphaelites ... or Mrs Patrick Campbell, or the Duchess of Manchester ...?

I defy anyone to prove I didn't, though!

Elinor had rationed herself to two visits a week to the nursing home just off Cavendish Street where Lewis was, and had been scrupulous about discussing business and nothing else. It was not very likely that Lewis, enduring grisly operations to repair torn flesh and leg muscles, would want a female dripping with sentimental reminiscences and it was even less likely that he would want any embarrassing reminders of that moment when he had held her against him.

And so Elinor, after muttering an awkward sentence about Grendel's death and a careful enquiry about medical progress, plunged into the affairs of Chance House, and tried not to wish she could be plunging into a very different kind of affair.

The Lifeline Service had been granted three more phone lines, which was good news. And there had been an encouraging letter from one of the Duchess of Kent's private secretaries, tentatively indicating that Her Grace might not be averse to her name being used as patron of the CCT. The boiler for the midday dinner had blown up and everyone had been spattered with oxtail soup ... It was good to see Lewis give the thin painful smile at this last.

'But best of all, the National Lottery Charities Board have confirmed that we can bid for a share of the loot,' said Elinor. 'That's good, isn't it? I saved that bit of news until last.'

'Very good indeed. Elinor, you're doing well.'

Elinor coloured, and said, 'Yes, but I don't think it'll be much of a share because we're competing with a lot of bigger organisations.' And thought: damn! Why do I have to always belittle what I've done?

Lewis said, 'Anything would be a bonus.'

'Well, yes. The bids have to be in by the end of December, so I've drafted an initial proposal using their guidelines. It reads a bit dry, I think. It needs your touch.' There you go again, denigrating yourself!

And all the time, beneath the ordinary businesslike exchanges that anyone might have listened to, she was aching to reach out and touch him, and to smooth away the lines of pain.

'Ginevra's gone back to Durham,' she said. 'In a tearing temper, because she wanted to stay and discuss the adventure *exhaustively* with everyone for at least a month.'

Lewis grinned. 'I can hear her saying it. And Raffael?'

'He did leave an address,' said Elinor. 'It's somewhere in Hampstead. But I don't know what he's doing.'

'He's a maverick,' said Lewis, lying back on the pillows, his eyes shadowy with pain. 'A *rara avis*.'

'A loner.'

'Yes, but also a survivor. He'll come back, Elinor. He'll come back for Ginevra. Just as I shall come back to Chance House.'

He smiled again, but his face was so thin that the bone structure showed too sharply and Elinor wanted to wrap him in her arms, and keep out every scrap of pain, and feed him rich good meals that would drive away the haunted thinness. If he was going to smile like this and tear her heart out by the roots every ten minutes it was going to be difficult to remain at Chance House at all.

She said, 'This is the architect's layout for the lift at Chance House.'

435

'For the cripples and the wheelchair-bound?'

'You won't be wheelchair-bound.'

'No, but I'll be crippled. Two sticks – one after a time if I'm lucky.'

'You don't have to hate it quite so strongly,' Elinor said with sudden vehemence.

'I hate it very much.'

She sat waiting for the thin whirr of the lift on the day of his return, hearing it a hundred times in her mind. But when finally it came it still caught her off balance.

It was not, of course, possible to go racing across the small landing to his flat immediately, but it was probably all right to knock lightly on the door after about an hour, and ask if there was anything she could do. Elinor rehearsed it several times.

'Just to see if you're all right, and in case you're short of milk, or bread—'

It was the ridiculous over-romantic scenario she had visualised all those months ago, only then it had been Lewis coming into her flat for the time-honoured half-pint of milk or cup of sugar, and staying. Now she was going to him. It was odd how your daydreams worked out in an inverted fashion, except that it was not going to be anything like any of the daydreams.

He called to her to come in as if he recognised her tap at the door – as if he had been waiting for it? No, of course not! – and he was seated in the deep armchair before the window, the portrait of Patrick behind him. The hated walking sticks were propped on each side and he had left the curtains undrawn so that the room was bathed in the fading light of the November afternoon.

Elinor said, 'I came to see if you needed anything.' And stopped because it could only be her imagination that he was looking at her as he had done that astonishing night in Tashkara. It was a trick of the light, or a reflection from

436

the portrait. Or wishful thinking, even.

Lewis said, 'I can stand up, Elinor, but I'm afraid I can't walk across to you – at least I can, but it would be an awkward slow sort of half-trudge.' He paused, and Elinor's heart did one of its painful somersaults. 'But I can't talk to someone who stands scowling from the door. Come and sit down.'

He indicated the low padded stool, and Elinor said, 'At your feet?' It was possible to say it lightly. I'm doing quite well, thought Elinor, sitting down. I'm not showing any emotion at all.

Lewis said, 'If I said, "To lie in my bed," I suppose you'd run a mile.'

'Well, I—' It was ridiculous to be thrown so off balance. Elinor twisted round to look at him. He didn't mean it, of course; it was a joke, although it was not the kind of joke he had ever made before. But wouldn't a man crippled and maimed have to throw it out flippantly in case he was rejected? The idea of anyone rejecting him was unthinkable, of course.

Elinor said carefully, 'No one's ever asked me that before – even as a joke.'

'How undiscerning of them. But I'm not joking. I meant it in the tunnels before we got out – before I passed out – and I mean it now.'

Elinor stared at him. I don't believe. I can't believe. Yes, but he's looking at me as he did that other time, and I'm beginning to think it was worth waiting for, it was worth the danger and the fear— If he keeps looking at me like that I'll die. 'You mean it, don't you?' she said at last.

'Yes. But I should warn you that you'll have to help me to the bedroom.'

Elinor stood up and held out her hands.

It was probably coincidence or imagination, but as they crossed under the portrait, the last sliver of light from the dying afternoon caught the painted eyes and lit Patrick Chance's enigmatic stare to luminous and amused life.

Epilogue

November 1913

Just as a sense of tidiness prompted me to take up these very private diaries again, so now a sense of completeness forces me to set down the ending.

It's many years now since I went outside during the daylight hours. Occasionally, when the brooding silence of this house becomes oppressive, or when I crave the sounds of other human voices, I venture out after dark. But at such times I wait for the creeper fog to steal in from the Thames – we are old friends now, the fog and I – and I don the long dark overcoat and the deep-brimmed hat that so effectively hides my face, and I walk slowly along St Stephen's Road down to the wharf, occasionally pausing between the gas lamps to watch a party of revellers pass by on the other side of the street.

St Stephen's Road is becoming more of a haunt for street women; last night I was even accosted by one. What an irony.

Provisions are delivered to the house three times a week: bread and milk and fish and vegetables. And I hear news of the world, still. After Theodore moved out – after I virtually threw him out – he insisted on

439

visiting me every day and has never been turned from it. I sit on the farthest side of the room from him, always with the light behind me, and I never touch him, of course, or offer him a glass of wine or a cup of tea.

He brings me the newspapers each day, and I think only a fool or a blind man would fail to see that there is war ahead. The foreign news seems to me a powder keg: I can't believe this business in Serbia won't break out again. Soon these squabbles are going to erupt into a full-blown conflict, and England will certainly become involved.

I don't think I can bear that. I don't think I can bear the turmoil and the disruption and above all, the possibility of being forced into the world so that the world will know the truth. There are no longer mirrors in this house – I smashed them all a long time ago: five years to be exact – but even without mirrors I have a very good idea of how I must look now. The disease of Fenris and Sridevi is progressing slowly, but there is no mistaking it. I have made a bolt hole for myself in one of the small cellar rooms and furnished it. Just in case I ever need to really hide from the world.

But I don't think I shall ever use it, because I have made my decision now. I am going back. I am going back to where it all began: to the stone palace on the outskirts of Tashkara. To Fenris and his people.

And to Sridevi. She may be dead, but somehow I think she will still be there, and I think when I go through those immense gates in the heart of that remote tranquil valley she will hold out her hands and I shall take them.

It's a thought to cling to in the morass of despair and fear.

Theodore has fought me every inch of the way, but he has today given in and agreed to make the necessary arrangements. I shall travel in absolute seclusion – a private railcar, a cabin on the ship from which I shall not emerge.

I have given Theo a power of attorney and he will deal with selling the house, so that even my name need not appear in the transactions. I wonder what the house's fate will be?

But I can't really think of anything except that I'm going back – and it's a thought that's buoying me up. As I move slowly and awkwardly about the house, deciding what to pack, discarding what's unnecessary, the words of Sridevi's philosopher are with me. Like a soft thrumming on the air, filled with life and hope and the joyous expectancy of something marvellous and light-filled beckoning to me:

'Throw me your nightmares, beloved, and watch me spin them like a juggler and one by one exorcise them of their devils, and return them to you with their fangs drawn and their red poison sucked out ... And then you will see how the nightmares will depart; they will slide back across the silent black waters of the oceans, and usher in the light.'

I can't see the light yet, but I know now that it's there. It's waiting for me in Tashkara. I think Sridevi is waiting as well. I think she knew, even all those years ago, that I should return. And these last few days I've had the astonishing feeling that at last I'm going home ...

People in London will scarcely notice I've gone and if I have an epitaph at all, it will probably be 'Death of a Recluse'.

But it would be nice to think it might equally be 'Death of a Philanderer'.

Extract from The Times, *20 March 199–*

Excavations began this week in a remote part of Tibet, after a small group of workers from Amnesty

International spotted what they believed could be the entrance to a ruined city on the western edge of the little-known Tashkara valley.

Professor Leon Undershaw of Oxford flew out to Tibet last month with a team of archeologists, and says there are already indications that an ancient Egyptian tribe from around 1500 BC may have found their way to Tashkara and built a city there.

'Several *steles* in some of the tomb-chambers near to the Valley of the Kings refer to the banishing of a renegade group around that time,' he said. 'And although it's too early to draw any conclusions this is certainly a site of immense antiquity and great archeological importance. Several of the sandstone and granite columns already uncovered bear striking similarities to the form and construction used by the Egyptians in the Twelfth Dynasty.'

A *stele* is an upright slab or pillar, frequently found in Egyptian tombs, often bearing inscriptions.

'We are expecting that the excavations will reveal a number of interesting artefacts,' said Professor Undershaw.